Dreamfever

also by kit alloway

Dreamfire

Dreamfever

kit alloway

st. martin's griffin ✿ new york

DREAMFEVER. Copyright © 2016 by Kit Alloway. All rights reserved. Printed in the United States of America. For information, address St. Martin's Press, 175 Fifth Avenue, New York, N.Y. 10010.

www.stmartins.com

Designed by Anna Gorovoy

The Library of Congress Cataloging-in-Publication Data is available upon request.

ISBN 978-1-250-07811-7 (hardcover)
ISBN 978-1-4668-9316-0 (e-book)

Our books may be purchased in bulk for promotional, educational, or business use. Please contact your local bookseller or the Macmillan Corporate and Premium Sales Department at 1-800-221-7945, extension 5442, or by e-mail at MacmillanSpecialMarkets @macmillan.com.

First Edition: February 2016

10 9 8 7 6 5 4 3 2 1

For Gosha,

my favorite

List of Characters

Family

Josh Weaver (Joshlyn Dustine Hazel Weavaros)
Will Kansas: Josh's apprentice
Deloise Weaver: Josh's younger sister
Lauren (Laurentius Weavaros): Josh and Deloise's father
Kerstel Weaver: Lauren's wife, Josh and Deloise's stepmother
Peregrine Borgenicht: Josh and Deloise's grandfather, Dustine's estranged husband
Dustine Borgenicht: Josh and Deloise's grandmother, Peregrine's estranged wife (deceased)

Friends

Winsor Avish: Josh's best friend
Whim Avish: Winsor's older brother
Saidy and Alex Avish: Whim and Winsor's parents
Haley McKarr (Micharainosa): Ian's twin brother
Ian McKarr (Hianselian Micharainosa): Haley's twin brother (deceased)
Bayla Sakrov: Whim's ex-girlfriend
Bash Mirrettsio: a dream theorist, Bayla's boyfriend
Mirren Rousellario: heir to the deposed Rousellario monarchy
Katia: Mirren's cousin
Fel and Collena: Mirren's aunt and uncle
Young Ben Sounclouse: the local seer

The Junta

Peregrine Borgenicht: a member of the junta, and leader of the Lodestone Party

Anivay la Grue: a member of the junta and leader of the Troth Party

Davita Bach: the local government representative

Ithay Innay: a member of the junta

Gor Speggra: a member of the junta

Dreamfever

First Prologue

This is my last entry: I'm going into the Dream tonight.

I didn't know I was going to do it until this morning. I woke up to the usual pitiful celebration—coffee and pastries on the good china and everyone dressed as if we were going to visit a restaurant. Aunt Collena gave me yet another robe, mostly, I think, out of the subverted hope that I'll give her my silk one with the peacocks on it. Uncle Fel gave me a computer mapping program, which now holds top honor as the single most ironic gift I've ever received; how long does he think it will take me to map our little universe? Katia was the only one who actually took my preferences into consideration and gifted me with *Vampire Nazi Hunter 4: Mars.*

A pity I won't live to play it.

At the end of the meal, Uncle Fel said to me, "So, how does it feel to be nineteen?"

At that moment, I knew I was going through the archway, because being nineteen felt like nothing. It *meant* nothing, just like my life has thus far and may forever if I don't do something to give it meaning. I will live and die here, in my perfectly mapped cell, having wasted my mind and extensive education playing video games and drawing comic books no one will ever read, a girl who never had cause to wear anything besides luxurious robes and will likely demand to be buried in the silk one with the peacocks on it just to spite her aunt.

Aunt Collena may be right that the dream walkers don't need me and that the people of the World—overcrowded as it is—don't need another rich white girl, but I know for certain that *I* need them.

I must go now, before I lose my nerve.

<del>Amiryschka Heloysia Solei Rousellario</del>
Mirren

Second Prologue

Josh gazed out the windows at Warsaw. Far below ran a wide, tree-lined boulevard set with ornate five- and six-story buildings. Streetcars rushed up and down the boulevard, but on either side, horses drew carriages loaded with crates and burlap sacks. Hundreds of people moved below, swarming and seething, climbing up and down from trams, dodging carriages, migrating in and out of buildings, the men in trench coats and fedoras, the women in calf-length skirts. From four stories up, Josh watched them, astonished at their multitude and how all of them seemed to have a destination to which they could not be late.

A sound—laughter?—made her turn, and she took in the sunny apartment. Here in the parlor, art predominated. Lamp shades boasted stained glass in shades of green and yellow; on the fireplace screen, three young women in Empire ball gowns dined on a green lawn; and above the mantel, an ornately carved wooden clock ticked away the time with generous lassitude. Someone had left a cloth-bound book open on the striped sofa, and a half-full teacup cooled on the marble-topped coffee table.

Feeling happy and at peace, Josh sat down at the spinet piano, opened the keyboard cover, and began to play. She couldn't have named the tune, but she liked how the slow notes resonated in the air above the din from the street below.

A girl with long blond sausage curls dashed through the room wearing a green velvet dress and white tights. Her skirt's pleats were in disarray, and the white satin sash meant to tie around the dress's drop-waist had come undone. A pure white puppy followed on the girl's heels, barking, and the girl laughed in the breathless, drunken way of children as she ran into the hallway.

"Bryga, stop!" a young man called, but he had more or less given up by the time he reached the parlor. Seeing Josh, he smiled. He was a handsome youth, perhaps fifteen years old, not tall but nicely proportioned, and very neat in his gray pants and white shirt. With his gray eyes and blond hair, he could have been a charcoal sketch come to life.

Josh's fingers missed a note when she saw him, and she fumbled the next few measures. She recognized the young man, she even remembered that his name was Feodor, but she felt uncertain about him. Despite his trim appearance, she sensed that he was dangerous.

Someday, his eyes would be shadowed by painful memories, hardened by horror like steel thrust into an ice bath, his glance turned strange and clever, his lips thinned by an ironic, grimacelike smile. Josh knew this. Someday, he would be unable to speak a single sentence without disgust or mockery or manic glee clipping his words.

But not yet. Now he was still a young man, a bit overconfident but full of wit and exuberance and, yes, even goodness.

"We'll never get her trained, will we?" he said.

"The dog, or the girl?" Josh asked.

Feodor sat down beside Josh on the piano bench. "Preferably the girl—she'll live longer."

He began to play a gentle counterpoint. Bach himself could not have written a sweeter harmony, and for a time, they sat companionably and drew song from the instrument before them.

But Josh's eyes lingered on Feodor's hands. A scrape marred the skin on his left index finger, and she couldn't help thinking that soon there would be more scrapes, and cuts, and burns, and blood dried beneath the nails, and someday his scarred hands would build things, terrible things. . . .

"Josh?" Feodor said, so softly that her name blended with the notes of the piano.

"Yes?"

Without warning, he wrenched his hands from the keyboard and slammed the cover shut.

Josh jumped, and she would have run except that Feodor's eyes clenched her. He no longer smiled, no longer joked, and she had been wrong—he was not innocent—they had not gone back far enough—perhaps they never could—

"What are you doing here?" he asked in a low hiss. "And why did you bring those?"

He cut his head to the left, and when Josh looked behind them, she saw two devices sitting on the marble coffee table. Their curved metal panels and wire-wrapped crystals stood in contrast with the soft elegance of the room. Josh turned and moved from the piano bench to kneel beside the coffee table, and she reached out to touch one of the devices.

She explored the wire-wrapped circlet first. She knew it was meant to be worn on the head like a crown, even though it bore little resemblance to one. A bundle of wires and metal bands formed nearly a complete circle, with a jagged crystal on each side situated to rest above her temples and another cluster meant to press against the base of her skull.

The metal felt oddly warm, and she detected a faint vibration running through it. "What did you do to these crystals?" she asked Feodor.

She no longer felt afraid of him. In fact, seeing the two devices, she felt excitement stir inside her. She didn't know what these things were, but she knew they were powerful.

Feodor reluctantly knelt beside her. All his bravado had abandoned him. When a siren began to wail beyond the open windows, he sat up very straight and looked toward the street with alarm.

"Feodor," Josh said. The siren held no interest for her; she knew what it meant. She touched his arm. "What did you do to these crystals?"

Frowning, he returned his attention to the circlet. "I reversed their polarity."

Outside, an explosion. The apartment building shook and the

windows rattled. On the coffee table, cold tea sloshed over the rim of its teacup. Feodor clapped his hand to Josh's back as if he meant to force her to the floor, but Josh didn't feel concerned.

"It's just the war starting up," she said.

The second device was meant to be worn on the forearm like a vambrace. Inside a metal sheath, more crystals—some of them flecked with ash—were connected by a network of fused wires made of a variety of metals: copper, selenium, chromium, molybdenum.

Above the street, air fire filled the sky like a cosmic snare drum. The collapse of a nearby building began as the shattering of stone and evolved into deafening white noise.

"Feodor!" the little girl called from the other room. Her voice was high with fear.

"I'm coming, Bryga! Stay where you are!"

The apartment building shook again. A painted landscape behind the couch crashed to the floor, and in the other room, the puppy barked.

Feodor tried to leave the parlor, but Josh grabbed his arm. "Show me how to put these on," she ordered.

"Bryga—" he began.

"Can wait. Show me."

He obeyed, but with angry speed.

"The wires have to run along the cephalic, basilic, and median veins." When he lifted her right arm, Josh saw all of her veins pulsating just beneath the surface of her skin, as if they were fighting to escape her flesh and join with the device.

The firing of cannons continued outside. Human and mechanical screams wove together in a single wail. The apartment darkened as smoke blocked out the sun.

"Feodor!" Bryga called again.

Feodor snapped the vambrace closed around Josh's forearm. The ends of the wires dug into her skin, and she sensed that she had just hurt herself but couldn't feel it yet. Then she forgot her concern as warmth flowed down her arm and into her hand. Feodor placed the headband around her skull, and when he used a leather cord to close the open ends, he tightened the headband so that the crystals cut into Josh's scalp. For a moment, she had a dire headache; then the same warmth began to fill her head.

Yes, she thought. Yes. She felt as though she were expanding, extending outside her body, into the devices, past them, into the world around her, spreading, unstoppable.

A bomb exploded in the street outside, shattering not just the windows but the stained glass lamp shades as well. Feodor dropped to the floor, covering his eyes, but Josh stood up while the building still shook, shaking her head and flinging glass from her hair.

"Feodor!" Bryga screamed.

"I'm coming!" Feodor called to her, and he crawled toward the hallway.

"Stop!" Josh commanded, and he did stop, though his expression was furious. "Watch."

She held out her equipped arm. Spreading her fingers wide, she extended her hand toward the window and reached.

She didn't imagine what she wanted to happen—that would have been degrading. She didn't have to justify herself by explaining. All she had to do was reach. The warmth crawled down her forearm into her hand and then flooded her fingers. When heat burst out of her fingertips, the world outside the empty windows froze, then repaired itself in fast motion. Shards of glass pieced back into the window frames, the fires sucked up their smoke, the fallen buildings righted like people rising and brushing themselves off after an earthquake. The painting slid up the wall and resettled on its nail. The screams and sirens fell silent and were replaced by the idyllic ding ding of the tram and the hollow knocking of horseshoes on cobblestone streets.

Calm, steady sunshine again filled the parlor. Josh, stunned by her own strength, slowly retreated to the piano bench and—after a moment of staring at her hands and thinking, They aren't even shaking—resumed playing. After a few measures she recognized Poland's national anthem rising around her. She played it with a decisive, valiant hand, and though she did not know the lyrics, she remembered the first line.

Poland has not yet perished!

This time, when Feodor sat down beside her, he didn't try to play along. He only turned her face with gentle fingers on her chin and kissed her.

Josh hummed as she kissed him back.

She woke, shuddering and aroused, and went into the bathroom to splash cold water on her face. When her blood had stopped pounding, she tiptoed to Will's bedroom and crawled into bed with him. Lying beside him helped her remember who she was with.

And who she was.

One

Josh Weaver shaded her eyes as she mounted a low dune, her heels digging deep into the hot sand with each step. Above her, an oversize sun the color of goldenrods roasted the landscape, and around her the desert stretched endlessly in all directions, like a dusty orange carpet that just kept unrolling.

"I'm getting sand in my shoes," Will Kansas, walking beside her, complained.

Josh glanced at his torn-up sneakers, one with a ripped heel and the other burdened with black tar, and smiled. Will could destroy a pair of shoes faster than anyone she knew.

Along with the shoes, he wore jeans—also in bad shape—and a navy-blue T-shirt with a Serena's Pizzeria logo on it. Unruly clumps of auburn hair stuck to his damp forehead, his blue eyes were screwed up against the light, and a pink streak was swelling across his cheek where he'd been hit by a shutter in an earlier nightmare, but he looked good to Josh. He always looked good to Josh.

Out of the corner of her eye, she saw him glance at his watch.

"You too tired for this?" she asked. Since they'd gotten the crap kicked out of them by a zombie and a deranged scientist four months earlier, they both wore out faster.

Will shrugged. "Nah, I'm okay."

"I could help with this one," she offered.

"No," he said firmly. "Stay here. Practice your merging."

Josh heard the anxiety in his voice but didn't know how to soothe him. His skin graft had healed, his stitches had come out, and he had the feeling back in his fingers, but emotionally he was far from recovered.

She put a hand on his arm. "If you need me, just give a shout."

"Don't worry," he said, checking his shoulder holster. "I won't."

Josh sighed.

The structure atop the dune didn't look quite like anything else Josh had ever seen. Long adobe walls stretched toward the open sky, reminding her of the Southwest, but the lack of roof meant the building offered little protection from the sun.

Closing her eyes, she carefully broke Stellanor's First Rule of dream walking: *Never let the dreamer's fear become your own.* She'd been breaking it for so many years that she didn't even pause to consider the wisdom of her action.

She allowed the dreamer's fear to touch her, just one fingertip, then two, and the taste of panic she felt wasn't the connection with the Dream that she wanted, but it told her what she needed to know.

"It's not a building," she said, her eyes flying open. "It's a labyrinth."

She and Will reached an opening into the structure and stopped walking.

"I was pretty sure this is a monster dream," Will told her. He had been the one who had chosen the nightmare back in the arch-room. "And you know what monster lives in a labyrinth, right?"

"The Minotaur. Half bull, half man."

Will's blue eyes widened in surprise. "Yeah."

Josh frequently napped during world lit, which Will knew. Six months ago she might not have known the word "labyrinth," let alone been able to identify the Minotaur. But that had been before a madman with an extensive classical education had downloaded his memories into her brain. Now she not only knew the Minotaur, she could quote lines about him from both Ovid and Dante.

But Will didn't know that, and Josh had been biting her tongue pretty hard the last four months to make sure he didn't find out.

From inside the labyrinth came a deafening bellow. The ground shook so hard, Josh had to grab Will's shoulder to keep from falling over. She wasn't certain, but she thought she heard a word in the cry.

"Did it say 'spheres'?" she asked Will in a whisper.

"I thought it said 'deers.' Are you sure you want to try this *now*?"

Josh nodded. "Just keep it distracted."

Will unbuckled his shoulder holster and removed a .22 semiautomatic. "I should have brought a bigger gun."

Today was the first time Josh had let him bring any sort of gun into the Dream. He was not actually much good with them, despite having practiced more than most Olympic shooters. She tried to figure out a polite way of taking the .22 away from him and couldn't come up with one.

"Love you," was all she said.

He grinned, kissed her quickly, and headed into the labyrinth. "Love you back!" he called over his shoulder.

Josh sank to the ground until she could sit against the labyrinth wall. The heat captured in the adobe felt good against her back and shoulder blades, and she took a few long, deep breaths to settle her heart rate.

She was already losing interest in the nightmare—what she wanted was to merge with the Dream itself. She felt hungry for its ease and expansive freedom. She had felt it once, felt her mind blown open to contain all the World's dreams and nightmares at once, and she had been trying to recapture that sense of unity and connection ever since.

So far, she had been unsuccessful.

Inhale, exhale. Inhale, exhale.

She closed her eyes and focused on the air moving in and out of her lungs.

Inhale, exhale. Inhale . . .

She stopped thinking, as much as she could. Instead she felt her body's weight on the sand, the relentless heat of the sun tightening her skin, and the dull ache in her right elbow that never fully went away. She focused completely on her physical self.

An image flashed in her mind. With a phantom's eyes, she saw the labyrinth as if from above. The walls were moving on tracks hidden beneath the sand, sliding from side to side, blocking off and opening up routes at random. Staying lost forever in such a maze would be easy.

Then the flash was over, and she was back in her body.

The night she and Will and Haley had almost died, she had felt the entirety of the Dream inside her, the whole universe filling her skin. This comparatively meager merger felt like being teased, but it was as close as Josh had been able to come.

More deep breaths, more focus . . .

The next flash showed her Will, jumping out of the way just in time to avoid being crushed between the ends of two walls, and the dreamer, a little old Middle Eastern man in jean cutoffs and a red tank top that hardly covered his pot belly.

Finally she saw the Minotaur, and she understood for the first time why the Greeks had considered it a terrible monster. It stood taller and overall larger than she had ever expected, so large that its bull's head looked proportional, and its swarthy body rippled with muscle. It didn't even have a neck—its jaw just expanded into its shoulders, and its whole upper body twisted when it turned to look at something. Its horns were chiseled to needle points, each pointing forward and slightly out to the side.

But none of that made the Minotaur anything more than intimidating. What scared Josh was what the monster had done to itself: it was trying to become human, one body part at a time. Swaths of human skin in varying shades of pink and brown had been sewn over its fur. Its cow's eyes had been torn out and replaced with human eyes, one blue and one green, and they were too small to fully fill the Minotaur's cavernous eye sockets. Strangest of all, it had pulled out all its teeth and was wearing a pair of human dentures that filled only the front third of its bull's snout.

It released a roar, half bull's bellow and half human shout, and the word it shouted was neither "spheres" nor "deers" but *"EARS!"*

Gross, Josh thought.

Just before the flash ended, she caught a glimpse of someone else: a young woman, her face hidden by a curtain of dark red hair, collapsed at the end of one corridor. She appeared to be fast asleep.

Who is that? Josh wondered, the surprise jerking her back into her body. *And how can she be sleeping?*

From somewhere nearby came the sound of adobe being crushed. It sounded like the Minotaur had gotten tired of searching the maze and started tearing walls down instead.

Josh tried to settle back into her breathing, but she was distracted by the flash of the young woman sleeping in the sand. She didn't seem to fit in this nightmare, which meant she was probably a second dreamer.

More than one dreamer could participate in the same nightmare; sometimes people really *did* meet in their dreams. But multi-dreamer nightmares were usually more chaotic than this one thanks to the manifestations of multiple subconsciousnesses appearing simultaneously.

But a dreamer was what the redhead had to be, and since Will hadn't found her, that made her Josh's responsibility.

For the hundredth time since she'd woken up from her coma in February, she felt overcome by frustration. The power of the True Dream Walker that she had used to save Will, Haley, and herself had abandoned her. She had retained only one ability, and it was a small one.

It wouldn't help her now. She was going to have to do this the hard way.

As she jumped to her feet, gunshots echoed through the labyrinth. Josh counted three, and then she heard the Minotaur's inhuman roar: *"SKIN!"*

Sounds like a hit, she thought.

As Josh ran into the labyrinth, Will fired again, and the bullet must have hit home, because the Minotaur released a bellow more terrible than any he'd emitted before.

"EST!"

She ran toward the Minotaur, whose location was easy to identify because it stood taller than any of the walls around it.

Sooner than she'd expected, she saw the redhead collapsed at the far end of a corridor. She loped down the corridor while calling, "Come on! Let's get you out of here!"

The redhead didn't stir until Josh shook her. Then she opened bleary gray eyes, examined Josh briefly, and went back to sleep.

"You've got to come with me," Josh said.

"Go away please," the girl said.

For an instant, Josh considered opening an archway and waking the girl up. But two-dreamer nightmares didn't always play by the rules; if Josh woke the girl up, the nightmare might end, causing the Dream to shift and tossing Josh and Will into different nightmares. He'd never been in-Dream alone before.

"You can either run or I can drag you," Josh told the redhead, and when she got no immediate response, she grabbed the young woman's ankles.

"No, no!" the redhead protested. "I can walk. Just help me up."

Moments later, Josh began questioning whether or not she should have carried the redhead after all. The young woman could hardly stumble along at a fast walk, never mind run.

They made it to a clearing where the rubble of shattered walls covered the desert floor. "Stay here," Josh told the redhead, and helped her sit down behind a partially demolished wall. Two more shots went off.

From deeper within the labyrinth, the Minotaur bellowed, "*UUUMMMS!*"

Gums? Josh wondered, beginning to run again.

She headed for the bellow, into the passage of fallen walls it had created. She hadn't gone far when she caught sight of the Minotaur. It crashed through walls, head-butting one and punching through another, and the skin on its hands had been peeled back to reveal raw bone and muscle. Its thumbs were missing.

Oh, Josh thought, pulling the .32 from the holster at the small of her back. *Not "Gums!" It meant "Thumbs!"*

How Will had managed to shoot off both its thumbs was a mystery to her.

"Will!" she shouted, taking aim, and then she shot the Minotuar twice in the back of the head.

One bullet stuck in his flesh, but the other actually bounced off his scalp and fell onto the sand. Even before the creature turned and fixed a look of gross hatred on her, Josh was pretty sure that neither shot had penetrated the creature's skull.

"Josh?" Will called out incredulously. He peeked around a corner and—seeing that the Minotaur's back was turned—ducked into the corridor. His expression startled Josh: he looked almost as mad as the Minotaur. "What are you *doing*?"

"Come this way!" Josh called. "I'll cover you!"

He protested, and she fired three shots, this time into the beast's chest. Its breastbone was covered in a patchwork quilt of pieces of skin, each a different hue, but they all bled the same dark blood where the bullets pierced them.

"Go back!" Will called. Behind him, the little Middle Eastern dreamer peeked out at the Minotaur, which had dipped a finger in one of its wounds and was now sniffing its own blood.

"No, come this way. There's another dreamer."

"*CHESSST!*" it roared, throwing its head back.

Josh fired again. Will's expression grew even darker, but he grabbed the dreamer's hand and dragged him down the corridor toward Josh.

Clearly, the bullets were doing little to slow the Minotaur down. *I should have brought an ax,* Josh thought. *Axes are always more useful than guns.*

Suddenly she flashed back on the nightmare she'd had the night before. Feodor, and the war, and the strange devices. What would she have given at this moment to have the circlet and vambrace, to be able to reach out and change the Dream, to have whatever she needed to protect Will?

She would have given almost anything.

But she didn't have the circlet and vambrace, or even an ax, so she tried something new. Instead of aiming for vital organs, Josh shot at the Minotaur's knees. One shot went between its legs, but the other two hit their mark and blew the creature's kneecaps off like corks exploding from wine bottles full of blood and bone fragments.

Unfortunately, the shot that had gone wild had hit the dreamer's foot as he and Will tried to scramble past the Minotaur. "I'm hit! I'm hit!" the little old man cried out. Then, rather comically, he added, "Good-bye, cruel world!"

Josh and Will both rolled their eyes. Will dragged the dreamer toward Josh, who shot the Minotaur a few more times to distract it as they passed by. Then she slung one of the dreamer's arms around her neck, and she and Will carried him at a run back to the clearing.

Behind the partially demolished wall, she found the redhead asleep on the sand. Stunned, Josh stood with her mouth hanging open for a moment. Dreamers could dream that they were sleeping, but when they did, they inevitably began dreaming that they were having another dream.

"Wake up," Josh said, kneeling down. She shook the girl's shoulder through her windbreaker. "Come on, you have to wake up."

"Just leave me," the redhead murmured without opening her eyes.

"Nope, you're coming with me."

As Josh helped/forced her to her feet, the Minotaur emerged from the labyrinth. It appeared to have torn its lower legs off completely and was now walking on the ends of its thighbones. The method proved surprisingly speedy.

Josh didn't have time to open an archway to the World in the traditional fashion, by reflecting light into a doorway, so she closed her eyes and imagined an archway right in front of them, standing in the open air with no need for a doorframe to hold it up. With that image in mind, she opened her eyes and thrust her left arm out. A burst of dense air flew from her palm, shot ten feet forward, and then expanded with a ripple into a freestanding archway. Its surface glittered like a gossamer fabric, but when Josh and Will shoved the redhead through, no material held her back. Josh cast one more glance at the Minotaur—now only a dozen paces away—and she grabbed the other dreamer's hand and jumped.

Creating archways was the only True Dream Walker power Josh had retained. If not for that, she would have questioned her destiny entirely.

The burst of air conditioning that greeted her in the sterile white archroom was both soothing and refreshing. She inhaled, feeling satisfied, until she saw Will glaring at her.

"What the hell were you thinking back there?" he demanded.

His anger caught her off guard. "What?" she asked, more out of surprise than defiance.

"I could have dealt with that by myself. But what did you do? You—*you*, who was perfectly safe—decided to jump into the middle of danger for no reason at all!"

"I had to get the girl out," Josh protested, finding her voice again.

"No, you didn't! Who cares about the girl? She was just one dreamer!" And he must have known what Josh was thinking, because he added, "She sure as hell wasn't *your* responsibility!"

"And I'm not *your* responsibility!"

Josh didn't like the tone she was using. She knew it meant she had already lost her temper and all she could hope for now was that she wouldn't kick anybody or say anything she couldn't take back.

Will must have recognized her tone, too. He got that condescending look in his eye that meant he was retreating into psychoanalyst mode. Josh hated that look.

Both her tone and his look had become all too familiar recently.

"I told you that I don't want you to be reckless anymore, remember?" he said hotly. "I told you after that *Titanic* nightmare that it freaks me out when you take stupid risks."

"And you get to decide which risks are stupid? I'm supposed to check in with you before I do anything? *You're* the apprentice, Will, remem—"

A whimper interrupted Josh's rant. She and Will looked in the direction from which the sound had come.

The redheaded girl was huddled against the far wall of the arch-room, her blue-green windbreaker sparkling with fairy dust.

Josh saw movement out of the corner of her eye and realized Will was pointing his gun at the girl's head.

"Will!" she cried, and at the same moment, the girl fainted.

Two

Shoot her.

That was the only thought in Will's mind. The girl had come out of the Dream, just like two others once had, and if somebody had been around to shoot them the moment they arrived, a lot of people wouldn't have gotten hurt.

Shoot her in the head.

His finger twitched against the trigger. Only the sound of Josh shouting his name stopped him from firing.

Josh rushed forward in a valiant effort to catch the young woman as she fainted. She failed, but the stranger collapsed in a rather neat pile, with her head resting on one forearm. Will kept his sights on her as she fell, like a hunter following the flight of a bird.

"Crap," Josh said. She got down on her knees next to the girl's inert form, then glanced at Will. "Could you *not* point the gun at me?" she demanded.

Her words broke through the dark tunnel in which Will's mind was caught; still, he lowered the gun with reluctance. "I'm out of bullets," he said, realizing the truth of the statement as he spoke.

"Do I care?" Josh asked. "What was the first thing I taught you about guns?"

It had been *Never point a gun at a person unless you're going to kill them.*

But I was going to kill her, Will protested silently. *I think that maybe I still should.*

He aimed the gun at the floor with one hand and rubbed the back of his neck with the other. He had to stop thinking that way.

Feodor was dead. He hadn't sent the girl.

"Go get me some smelling salts, would you?" Josh asked.

"Yeah, sure." Will heard how hollow his voice sounded.

"And Will? Don't bring the gun when you come back."

"Sure," he said again.

He exited the archroom into the basement, a long, concrete room with small windows near the ceiling. In the center of the room sat the training mats and equipment: heavy bag, kettlebells, cardio machines, a rack of weights. At the far end of the room, where storage bins of holiday décor were piled to the ceiling and out-of-style furniture kept house for ghosts, Will had set up a research center with his files organized in the drawers of a gray metal desk and a timeline of Feodor Kajażkołski's life strung across mismatched corkboards.

Will's friend Whim Avish called the timeline Will's "stalker wall."

Ostensibly, Will was investigating Feodor in hopes of learning something that would help Whim's sister, Winsor, who had remained comatose since one of Feodor's goons had attacked her. But Will was self-aware enough to know that his real motivation was more personal and less reasonable: Will was afraid of the man. And he was irrationally afraid that Feodor was coming back.

Pulling his eyes away from the stalker wall, he locked the .22 back in the gun safe. Then he opened the giant emergency first-aid kit and found a few packages of smelling salts. Plastic tubes in hand, he typed in the code to open the vault door to the archroom.

The arch to which the room's name referred stood in the center of curved white walls. Two pillars of gray stone rose out of the ground beneath and up through the floor to create an archway overhead. Nearby, a slab of frosted red glass the size of a textbook stood suspended at waist height on top of a metal pole. At the moment, the archway appeared empty, but Will knew that if he pressed his hand to the red stone—the looking stone—the archway would become a portal leading to the Dream universe.

Josh was sitting on the floor with the redhead's feet in her lap.

"I'm sorry about that," Will said. "With the gun."

"It's all right," Josh replied. "Her coming out of the Dream like that was . . . well, unexpected."

Josh didn't say, *Freakishly similar to last time, when my grandmother got killed and my best friend got her soul sucked out and my stepmother got beaten into the ICU and almost lost a baby she didn't even know she was carrying.*

Josh didn't say that, because she didn't talk about Feodor. Not ever.

As Will broke open a plastic tube of salts and held them close to the girl's nose, he got his first good look at her face. He had never seen a beauty quite like hers. Delicate, feminine features were laid over a heavy—almost masculine—bone structure, and the combination made her appear both winsome and strong. Her dark red hair hung all the way to her waist, even tangled into early-stage dreadlocks as it was.

She was beautiful in spite of her current state, which included shadows beneath her eyes so dark and deep that they looked like Halloween makeup, a scratched and swollen chin, dirt lines discoloring her broken nails, and chapped white lips.

Almost immediately, the girl woke with a grimace and began trying to rise.

"Wait a sec," Josh said. "Take it easy. You fainted."

The girl looked around the room with large gray eyes and an expression of distress that suggested she thought she might not have woken up at all.

"What's your name?" Josh asked.

The girl stared at her, panic-stricken. "Am I dead?"

"Definitely not," Josh said.

The answer relieved some of the anxiety in the redhead's face. "Are we still in the Dream?"

"No," Josh repeated.

"It's a miracle," the girl murmured.

She closed her eyes, slowly this time, and released a long sigh. Josh and Will waited for her to open her eyes again, but she didn't, and when her breath began to deepen, Josh said, "Did she pass out again?"

"I think she just went to sleep." Will touched the young woman's shoulder. "Miss? Can you wake up?"

He gave her a little shake, then a less little shake, and finally her eyes opened again.

"You need to stay awake," Josh said. "You might have a head injury."

Will assumed Josh was making this suggestion based on the fact that the redhead had visible injuries to her hands, neck, and face, and blood stained her ripped turquoise jacket.

The young woman's eyes fluttered shut and then dragged open again. "May I sit up?"

"Slowly."

Once sitting, she insisted on climbing to her feet, and she took a few slow steps toward the archway. Josh stayed close by, as if worried the redhead would try to leap back into the Dream.

"I didn't catch your name," Josh said.

The redhead made no reply. She touched the stone archway with one hand, then passed her fingers through the empty space between the pillars. Will noticed that her right pant leg was torn vertically and something dark had seeped through the back of her jacket. A patch of hair had been torn out of her scalp.

"I'm sorry," she said, turning back to them. "You'll have to forgive me. I can't recall my name. It's on the tip of my tongue, but I can't quite catch it."

"You don't remember your name?" Josh asked. "What about where you're from, or how you ended up in the Dream?"

The redhead shook her head. "Nothing."

"You don't remember *anything*?" Josh asked. Her tone had gone from skeptical to incredulous. "You have . . ." She hesitated before using the word, as if embarrassed to put forth such a silly idea. "*Amnesia?*"

"Yes. Yes, I think I do."

Josh looked at Will, and that was all she needed to say, *Do you believe this?!*

Will held a hand up for her to be patient. Not that he believed the redhead—her downcast eyes and the speed with which she'd spoken had broadcast her lie. He was just hoping to figure out *why* she had lied.

"Does your head hurt?" he asked.

The redhead looked at him beneath eyelids that kept threatening to close. "Yes," she said. "It hurts. I need to sleep."

"Take off your windbreaker," Josh said, "so I can check you for injuries."

She fumbled with the zipper on her jacket and finally tugged it open.

"Damn," Will said when he saw her.

Bruises, cuts, scrapes, a serious bite, puncture wounds, and even what appeared to be burns covered her skin.

Josh's animosity vanished. "What hurts?" she asked briskly.

The redhead gave a long list of pains, and Will believed her about every one. Joints were swollen, scrapes ran in every direction, bruises spread far and wide. She had a three-inch gash on her back that was clearly infected and another bite on her leg beneath the tear in her pants.

While Josh inspected the visible injuries, Will did a quick and dirty evaluation of her mental state. She knew who was president, how many continents were on the Earth, and that Schwarzenegger had played the Terminator, but she was two days off the date and claimed not to remember anything about herself except the name Nan.

"Is that *your* name?" Will asked.

"I don't know."

When they were finished, Josh and Will conferred on the other side of the room.

"She needs stitches, antibiotics, and probably a rabies shot," Josh whispered. "Obviously she's been in the Dream. How else did she get burned *and* bitten by an animal *and* hit in the head *and* shot with an arrow? But the weird thing is some of those bruises are fresh, but some of them are a few days old."

"What does that mean?"

"Maybe she's just been dream walking nonstop for the last week—and doing a terrible job—or maybe she's been lost in the Dream for *days*."

If she had been in the Dream for days, fighting off monsters and running from disasters and enduring the fear of so many dreamers, that would explain why she was so exhausted and possibly even her bizarre lie. People could easily become delirious after several days without sleep.

"There's no way to be sure without a CT, but I don't think she has a concussion," he told Josh. "Or at least, if she did have one, she's recovered enough that she's able to go to sleep without falling into a coma. The best treatment might be to just let her sleep, at least until Saidy's off work."

Saidy was Whim and Winsor's mother, and she lived on the second floor. She was also a paramedic, and over the years she had cleaned a lot of wounds, stitched a lot of cuts, and driven a lot of people to the ER.

Josh nodded. "She can take Grandma Dustine's old room. She probably needs food, too. Let's get her upstairs."

Watching Josh gather the redhead's discarded jacket, Will felt the muscles around his rib cage contract and press painfully on his lungs. *It's so easy for you to feel responsible for people,* he thought. *If they're in the Dream and in danger, their well-being is instantly more important than yours.*

She'd told Will once that she felt ashamed of the fact that she sometimes had difficulty caring about other people's problems, that she worried she wasn't as compassionate as she should be. But Will thought that this sense of absolute responsibility was its own kind of compassion and astonishing in its own right.

He just hoped it didn't get her killed someday.

Josh explained about Saidy and that they'd get the girl medical attention as soon as possible. "You said you remembered a name? Nan? Is that what we should call you?"

"I suppose . . . Nan will do as well as any other name."

"All right. Are you a dream walker, Nan?"

Oddly uncertain, Nan said, "I believe I am, Josh."

"Well then, you can stay here until we figure all this out," Josh said. "Salt among oceans, right?"

Will didn't know what that meant, but it made Nan smile for the first time. She had a beautiful smile; it conferred a sense of wise benevolence and, at the same time, vigor. She didn't look tired when she smiled. "Salt among oceans," she repeated, as if in agreement. "I am very grateful for your hospitality." She added ruefully, "Although I doubt I'll be able to sleep in someone else's bed."

"Why not?" Will asked, opening the archroom's heavy door. "You don't remember your own, right?"

Nan almost tripped over her feet as she followed. "Right," she agreed.

As they crossed the basement, Will noticed Nan's eyes fall on his stalker wall. "Is that . . ." she muttered, and then shook herself, as if she had started to fall asleep again. Will put a hand on her elbow to nudge her up the stairs.

Josh and Will lived in a large Greek Revival–style mansion that had been converted into a triplex. Josh's family lived on the third floor, and Saidy and Alex Avish lived in one of the second-floor apartments. Will had recently been booted from his third-floor bedroom to make room for his adoptive parents' new baby, but he didn't mind. He and Haley and Whim were living in the other second-floor apartment, where they had created a teenage dude paradise.

As they crossed the first-floor landing, Will caught a glimpse of a hideous lime-green-and-butter-yellow-striped cardigan walking into the library farther down the hallway. "Haley!" Josh called. "Come here for a minute!"

Will hoped Josh wasn't about to do what he thought she was about to do.

Haelipto McKarr, most often addressed as Haley, was best known for not saying very much. When Will had first met him, Haley was being haunted by his brother Ian's disembodied soul, which had occasionally possessed Haley's body. It had taken a while for Will to suss out who Haley was apart from his brother, but when he finally had, he'd discovered an observant, infinitely kind guy whose subtle sense of humor was easy to miss. Will liked him tremendously.

Hell, by the time they freed Ian's soul—no easy task—Will had come to like Ian, too.

Will understood immediately what Josh intended. Haley's psychic powers operated partly through touch; a handshake or kiss on the cheek could tell him all kinds of things. Will didn't like the idea of Josh using Haley's abilities to get information from people against their will, but he didn't argue, because as long as Nan kept up the amnesia act, he still considered her an unknown. And unknowns had a way of becoming dangers in his experience.

"Nan, this is Haley," Josh said, careful to set the introduction up properly. "Haley, Nan."

Nan pushed herself upright from the wall she had been leaning against and held out her hand. "How do you do?" she asked.

Haley took her hand slowly, hardly touching her with more than his fingertips.

Then, just when Will thought he would let go, Haley grabbed Nan's hand like a drowning man clutching at the side of a boat. Nan released a cry and pulled away.

Haley sucked in a wet, sick-sounding breath and ran for the stairs.

"Oh, my," Nan said in a dreamy, drowsy voice. "I should have washed my hands first."

Her eyes closed and she fell against the wall. Josh, grabbing Nan to keep her upright, gave Will a look.

"I'll go," Will said. As Josh revived Nan, Will jogged up the stairs to the second floor.

The guys' apartment looked exactly as one would expect an apartment occupied by three teenage boys to look. Nothing on the walls except a flat-screen TV and a poster for *Alien,* carpet that hadn't been vacuumed in months, a bag of chips spilled on the grubby old couch, and a trash-rescued bookcase packed with movies and video games.

Haley had taken the master bedroom when he moved back in— this was, in fact, *his* apartment—but his bedroom looked just as bad as the living room did.

"Hey," Will said when Haley let him in. He brushed some clothes off the desk chair and sat down. "What happened back there?"

Haley didn't look good. He looked like he'd just realized he had food poisoning and would inevitably begin vomiting soon. He'd even opened the window, in spite of the June heat.

At Will's question, he started to pull a steno pad and pen out of the pocket of his awful green-and-yellow cardigan, then stopped himself. He and Will had begun their friendship on the premise that Haley could tell Will things—even crazy things—and Will would believe him, but sometimes Haley still fought the urge to censor himself, and sometimes Will still found the things Haley told him hard to swallow.

"I saw . . . a lot," Haley managed to say. "She's in danger."

"Okay. What kind of danger?"

Haley cracked his knuckles. "I can't . . ."

Will hadn't seen him reduced to sentence fragments in a long time, and that worried him. "You can tell me, Haley. You know I only want to help her."

He realized he sounded patronizing at the same moment Haley sent him a sharp glance. The days when he had to talk to Haley like he was a five-year-old were over. Will shrugged apologetically, and Haley shrugged back in forgiveness.

"I can't tell you," he said, as if forcing the words out. "The more people who know who she is, the more danger she's in."

Well, that explains why she's lying about having amnesia, Will thought, but otherwise, he hated this news. He needed to know who Nan really was, what sort of trouble she was in, and whether or not her troubles could expand to encompass those around her.

But he saw a rare determination in Haley's eyes. *I can trust Haley's judgment,* he told himself, even as he remembered how Haley had eaten that cheddar with the mold growing on it two weeks before.

Cheese and people are not the same.

Will sighed. "What do we do?"

"Hide her. Call Davita."

"Davita?"

Davita Bach was the local representative of the dream-walker government. Although she had stuck her neck out to protect Josh and Will on more than one occasion, Will had never felt entirely confident that he could trust the woman. Anyone who worked for one government while wearing the symbol of another hidden beneath her blouse made him doubt her capacity for loyalty.

"Call her," Haley repeated. "Tell her to come here. Don't tell her why until she's here."

"You're worried about the phone?" Will asked, half-disbelieving.

Haley looked him square in the eyes then. "No one can know she's here. She can hide in my room. I'll sleep on the couch."

"*Your* room? *Where?*" Will cast his hand about the room.

"I can clean up," Haley protested. "Please, Will."

Will felt too frustrated to smile back. Six months ago he would have respectfully let the subject drop, but today he wanted to make demands. He wasn't just curious—he *needed* to know what was going on. If they were in danger—if Josh was in danger—and he didn't see it coming, something terrible could happen and he'd be helpless to stop it.

He knew that Gloves—Feodor's zombie henchman—trying to kill them had changed Will. These days, he wanted to know everything going on: who was where, and with whom, and when they would be back. He wanted to do everything himself to make sure it got done properly, so he could know with certainty that things were taken care of.

He knew he wasn't okay. But he also knew that he should trust Haley in this, that he had no reason not to. Besides, letting Nan stay in their apartment would allow Will to keep a close eye on her.

"Can you promise she isn't a danger to us?" he asked.

Haley looked perplexed. "She just needs a place to hide."

"Okay," Will said. "I'll call Davita."

Haley sank back against the bedroom wall, relieved. "Tell her . . ." He thought. "Tell her that the tragedy isn't a tragedy yet."

"Will she know what that means?" Will couldn't help asking.

Haley frowned again, uncertain. "I hope so," he said.

Will went downstairs to tell Josh the new plan, and by the time they got Nan up to the second floor—she swayed on each step— Haley had cleaned 90 percent of the mess in his room. He'd accomplished this by dragging the mess into the living room, rendering it a minefield of dirty clothes, sci-fi novels, steno pads, and Sharpies.

While Haley put clean sheets on his bed, Will tried to coax Nan into eating a peanut-butter-and-blueberry-preserves sandwich. She made it through about half, but Will could tell she was out of energy—she couldn't even remember how to open a soda can and just kept spinning the tab like the hand on a clock. Finally, Josh took her into the bedroom and helped her out of her filthy clothes and into a T-shirt and pajama pants. Nan was asleep before Josh closed the bedroom door.

Hours later, Saidy confirmed Josh's earlier suspicions: Nan had a sprained wrist, two broken fingers, one twisted ankle, a ruptured eardrum, three infected wounds, and a toenail that had to come off immediately. Since Nan was able to remain awake long enough for Saidy to evaluate and treat her, they decided it was safe to let her go back to sleep afterward.

The story they had agreed on and told Saidy was that Nan was a dream walker who had gotten lost in the Dream for a number of days and that they wanted to let her rest before putting her on a plane home. The only part of the story Nan got wrong was that instead of saying she was from Chicago, she named Geneva as her hometown. Frantic glances were exchanged until they discovered that Nan knew an inordinate amount about Switzerland and was able to converse easily in French.

"Maybe she's really Swiss," Josh whispered to Will.

Saidy left, and Nan slumped over on the bed, mumbling, *"Au revoir,"* as she fell back to sleep.

Late that night, Will woke to the sound of his bedroom door opening. No light came from the living room, but he knew that the figure darting into his room was Josh. He rolled to the far side of his twin bed and held up the blanket for her to climb under.

He didn't have to ask what was wrong; he knew from the way she trembled that she'd woken up from a nightmare. Ever since Feodor had tried to kill her with his memories—and Feodor had lived through the worst parts of World War II—she'd been having nightmares. He suspected that some of those memories had simply stayed in her subconscious.

"Sorry," Josh whispered.

"For what?" Will whispered back, tucking her in beside him. "Letting me sleep next to my girl?"

He kept his words light to hide his rage. He had never hated anyone the way he hated Feodor Kajażkołski. Feeling Josh hide her face in his shoulder and hold him with her fists clenched against his back made Will want to go buy a bigger gun. It made him regret the peaceful death he had allowed Feodor. The man should have suffered the way Josh was suffering now.

But Will knew that anger was only ever a shield against hurt or fear, and he didn't want to burden Josh with either of those, so he just tightened his arms around her. Her neck was sweaty, but he kissed it anyway. "You're safe. Go to sleep, Josh. You're safe here."

He didn't know what she'd dreamed of, and he didn't ask because he didn't think he could bear to know.

He was right.

 # Three

Waking was difficult. Mirren struggled up into her mind, which was as gray as early morning, but her body kept calling out to her like a foghorn: *Sleeeeep. Sleeeeep. Sleeeeep.*

She opened her eyes, despite the pain, and saw that the foreign bedroom was dark and empty. She didn't understand why she had woken up until she realized how full her bladder was. Since entering the Dream, she had peed in a lot of weird places, and she wondered what new dreamscape she would mark as her territory this time.

Then she remembered: She had left the Dream. She was in the World.

Her heart thumped, causing an echoing throb in her bladder. The *World*. She had finally escaped and reached the World.

She recognized the bedroom she'd fallen asleep in. Someone had closed the window, and the room had grown cool. Mirren wished she had asked where the bathroom was before she'd fallen asleep, but perhaps this way was better. She'd have an excuse to walk around without an escort.

Suddenly the stranger's bed felt safe and familiar, the house beyond it a vast and dangerous vista.

You're in a house, she told herself. *No doubt it's similar to the houses on TV. There will be a kitchen, and a bathroom, and bedrooms.*

She hoped there weren't any dogs.

Summoning strength against the numerous pains and stiff muscles that protested her movement, she climbed out of the bed and approached the window. The anticipation she felt at looking through the glass was so intense, it felt almost like fear. After a minute spent wrestling with the lock, she knelt in front of the open window to press her face against the screen.

She closed her eyes and breathed deep.

The warm air that entered her lungs smelled faintly sweet, but also ruddy. She didn't have names for the scents—one note was grainy and rich like velvet, another carried a sour smell like spinach. Ripe, gaudy florals; a faint chemical odor she imagined to be smog; even the metallic burn of the window screen. The air felt damp in her throat, and every time she inhaled she tasted something new. Crickets chirped charmingly—she recognized them from films—and tree leaves rustled one another as a slow breeze blew. Mirren opened her eyes and stared out at the branches and the moon passing behind them.

She felt dizzy from the wonder of it all.

But her bladder ached. She made herself stand up and go to the door; the window would still be open when she returned.

Although she didn't remember changing her clothes, she now wore a T-shirt and too-short flannel pants. She hesitated at the door, unsure if this was an appropriate outfit to wear outside of the bedroom or if she should attempt to locate a robe.

The thought made her laugh. All those beautiful robes she had left behind, only to find herself in need of one here.

Her hand closed around the cold metal doorknob. *Just a house,* she reminded herself, but she had never been in any house besides her own.

Her mind was waking up, and it was full of warnings. It reminded her that she was trapped in the World with no way to get home, that her family likely thought she was dead, and that if anyone here found out who she was, they might very well have her executed. She had done a terrible job of blending in so far—she knew she had. She should have figured out how to open the Coke on her own, and her amnesia story was ludicrous, not to mention whatever had gone wrong with the handshake.

But she was pinching her thighs together as though trying to carry a dime between her knees, and she realized she couldn't put off finding a bathroom any longer. With a resolute motion, she turned the knob and opened the door.

She'd thought everyone would be asleep, but someone was sitting on the living room couch watching television. When he heard the door open, he turned his head, and she recognized him as the guy who had squeezed her hand and then run. *Haley,* she remembered. Mirren hadn't realized it was a unisex name.

The people on television were dancing in a club, and the colored lights wavered over the living room walls like aquarium lights. Mirren had always wanted to visit an aquarium. So many romantic scenes in films took place in them.

But Haley stood up and turned on a lamp missing its shade. Then he picked up a remote control and shut off the television, and after that they were just two people standing in a brightly lit room amid piles of dirty laundry.

Haley appeared younger than the teenage boys on television, less muscular, still a little gangly. His hairstyle looked less like sculpted bedhead than just bedhead, and she couldn't tell if his green-and-yellow cardigan was fashionable or some sort of security blanket he wore at night. As she watched him, wishing she had something witty to say, he reached into his pocket and pulled out a small pad of paper and a Sharpie.

Should she walk away? Was their earlier mishap his way of tell-

ing her that he didn't care to know her? He flipped pages on the
pad as if looking for notes, but after reaching a blank page and staring at it for several seconds, he put the pad and pen down on the
couch.

"Hey," he said to Mirren. The word seemed to require a great
deal of effort to pronounce.

Mirren smiled, because she knew the socially appropriate response to his greeting. "Hey," she replied.

He thought some more. Then he said, "I know who you are."

Her breath caught in her throat.

*I must have given myself away the moment I opened my mouth. I
have to get out of here.*

"Is there a ladies' room nearby?" she asked.

Haley wet his lips, looking confused. He pointed at a door next
to an open laundry closet.

The bathroom was small and not very clean. It smelled of something both sour and musky that Mirren couldn't identify. Throwing back the soap-streaked shower curtain, she saw what she was
hoping for: a window.

A very small window.

I won't fit through that, she admitted to herself. Her rapid breath
grew frantic as she sat on the closed toilet lid. She was so scared,
she couldn't imagine removing a single article of clothing, let alone
urinating.

*I just got here; this can't be my end already. What sort of destiny
is that? They told me so many times that I wasn't ready—why didn't
I listen? What was I thinking when I left home?*

She had been thinking that she had been a prisoner all her life
and that she didn't intend to die a prisoner. She had been thinking
that she was nineteen, the age of royal majority, and she needed to
prove—to herself and her family—that she was worthy of being
her parents' daughter. She had been thinking that she couldn't
stand one more day in the Hidden Kingdom.

In retrospect, her behavior appeared very foolish and very
immature.

Haley knocked softly on the bathroom door. "Mir—Nan? I—I don't know what to call you. Are you okay?"

He didn't sound like he was going to kill her. That was some comfort.

"Just a moment, please," she called back.

Still shaking, she rose and faced herself in the mirror. Her red hair hadn't been washed in days and hung in strands of rat's nest. Her gray eyes were bloodshot, her lips nearly colorless, high spots of color dominated both cheeks, and various bruises, braces, and bandages covered her appendages.

What would Aunt Collena say if she could see me now?

The thought made her smile, and the sight of her own smile made her realize that she had not lost all of her dignity.

"Heed these words," she whispered to her reflection. "You are the last member of a deposed monarchy, and you may never become queen of so much as a prom, and you have no idea how to act or speak or even shake hands. But you were raised to be a dream-walker queen and you are going to conduct yourself like one, even in the face of appalling circumstance. Now empty your bladder before you piss yourself with fear."

Then she washed her face, combed her hair, brushed her teeth with someone else's toothbrush, and forced herself to use the toilet.

Haley was sitting on the couch, knees pulled up to his chest, when she exited the bathroom. Mirren squared her shoulders beneath her borrowed T-shirt and sat at the other end of the couch.

"I apologize for making you wait," she said. "I had to attend to a personal matter. But my attention is entirely yours now."

Haley stared at her with hazel eyes as helpless and uncertain as a child's. Despite his rumpled and—what was the word, "grungy"?—apparel, he had an attractive face with well-balanced features and fair skin that his sisters or girlfriends must have envied.

"If I may ask, how did you recognize me?"

He wet his lips again, said nothing.

Either I am terrible at making conversation, Mirren thought, *or else he's even worse.*

"You said you didn't know what to call me. Mirren will be fine, when we're alone. Naturally, I'd rather you didn't disclose my identity to anyone else, but that's your decision. In the meantime, I'd like to hear your demands."

Haley blinked in alarm, then picked up his pad of paper and his Sharpie and began to write. As she waited, she recalled having once heard something about the odor of Sharpies. She wondered if it would be inappropriate to ask to smell his pen.

He tore the page out of the pad and held it out to her.

I just want to help you get home.

"Oh," Mirren said. "Oh." She closed her eyes briefly because there wasn't a wall nearby for her to bang her head against.

"I'm so sorry," she said, the words tumbling out. She felt trapped and stupid and rude. "I assumed that because you're a dream walker—well, I shouldn't have assumed that . . . I'm sorry. I assumed incorrectly." She felt breathless. "May I open that window?"

Before he could reply, she stood up and pushed a floor-length curtain aside, only to discover that the glint of glass she had seen had come from a door and not a window.

A *sliding glass door,* she recalled. She pushed the handle sideways and one layer of glass slid alongside another, making a soft *swish.*

What an aptly named architectural element, she thought.

Then she inhaled, and all the scents she had tasted through the bedroom window returned—stronger, richer. She tilted her head back to lift her nose and stepped onto a porch that ran the length of the house. Until the warm air hit her bare arms, she hadn't realized how cold she was.

Tilting her head back farther, she could see the stars. Real stars—living, burning stars that had reached across the galaxy to show themselves to her. They looked the same as the fake stars at home, and yet something made them indefinably beautiful and filled her with wonder.

"Dear God," she whispered.

The door made its *swoosh* sound, and she turned to see Haley closing it behind him. For an instant she felt fearful again, but he gave her a very small, very meek smile, and she remembered his note.

She wanted so much to trust him, to have an ally in this huge World, to have a friend to . . . just to have a *friend*.

"I've never been outside before," she admitted. "It's . . ."

She wanted to say *magical,* but she was afraid of sounding stupid and childish. Instead, she turned her face back up to the brilliant sky. She almost thought she could feel the moonlight on her skin, light and lively and cool.

"There's no sky where you live?" Haley asked.

"There is. I mean, there's an imagined sky. An excellent likeness, I'll admit. But when I look up at it, I don't feel anything except that I'm looking at a very high ceiling. This feels . . . vast. Open." Touching the wooden railing, she added, "Like I might even fall off the planet if I don't hold on."

Haley smiled, but when she caught him, he ducked his head.

"I've always been a little obsessed with gravity," she admitted. "I used to spend hours dropping stones off a bridge where I live. When I was little, I thought that the reason the stones fell so fast was that the creek was where they belonged, that things meant to be together would draw each other. Birds got drawn up into the sky, plants reached for the sun, bodies fell to the ground when they died. It was all part of my distorted childhood theory of physics." She laughed. "Actually, I sort of feel like that's how I ended up here, that I was so meant to be here that I . . . attracted a path."

Haley leaned against one of the columns that lined the porch. "The place you live . . ." His mouth twisted in a little frown. "It's not in the World, is it?"

Mirren stared at him, confused as much by what he didn't know as by what he did. "Should I know who you are?"

He smiled more easily this time. "No. I'm nobody. I just—sometimes when I touch someone, I see things. About them. I guess it's . . . like a, a psychic thing."

A *psychic* thing?

"Oh," she said. She had no idea what an appropriate response to such a declaration might be. Nor was she entirely certain whether or not to think him crazy.

"S'okay," Haley told her in a tiny voice, his smile fled. "You don't have to believe me."

"No, no, I don't mean to—I mean, I—I'm sure you're telling the truth."

According to your own distorted version of reality.

She felt guilty as soon as the thought crossed her mind. How was Haley's belief that he was psychic any less reasonable than her own belief that she had somehow manifested a way to join the World because it was where she belonged?

Bewildered, she fought the urge to tug on her right earlobe, a gesture her aunt Collena had often said made her look ten years old. "I'm so sorry—apparently I'm awful at conversation."

Haley chuckled. "I'm the one who writes notes."

"Is that what you do when you're nervous? I should try it."

"Here." He extracted his steno pad and Sharpie and held them out to her.

Mirren laughed. "I'll let you know when I need them." She looked up at the moon again, taking another deep breath. "So, what did you see when you shook my hand?" she asked.

"I saw . . . You were holding a jewelry box. It had a fancy star on the lid, and inside was all this jewelry, with like red-orange stones. You and a younger girl put them on, and then you danced around in long nightgowns. Like you were at a party, or a . . ."

"A ball," Mirren finished, her voice flat. "Dear God, you *are* psychic."

Haley shrugged.

"I remember that night. Katia and I—Katia, she's my cousin, but we were raised like sisters—we got all the royal jewels out and put them on, and we listened to the waltz from *Eugene Onegin* over and over and acted out the ball scene from *Anna Karenina*." Mirren peered at Haley as if she might find the explanation of his ability somewhere on his face. "My aunt and uncle told exactly one person besides me about Katia. No one else knows she was ever born."

Haley shrugged again.

"You're right, too, that we've never lived in the World. We call the place the Hidden Kingdom, but it's really just a pocket universe, which is sort of like—"

"I know what they are."

A pocket universe was a section of the Dream cut off from the rest and formed into its own miniature universe.

"Really?"

He nodded but didn't explain, so Mirren continued. "After my parents were killed, my aunt and uncle took me to the Hidden Kingdom to keep me safe. I've lived there my whole life." She tried not to sound bitter. "They thought they were protecting me by keeping me there. They wouldn't even tell me *how* to leave; I had to find my own way. Truthfully, I'm not sure if they ever would have let me go."

Despite the heat, chill bumps rose on her arms.

"So," Haley said carefully, "you don't need my help getting home?"

They looked at each other and smiled. "No, I don't need help getting home. I've been dreaming of the World for so many years; now that I'm here, nobody's sending me back. I can just be me here—nobody's niece, no queen-in-training. I can go to college and swim in the ocean and eat fast food. And I can dance at a real ball. This is where I'm meant to be."

"Gravity," Haley agreed.

"Exactly! And . . ." She swallowed. "I could have real friends."

She didn't know if she was being presumptuous or not. To her relief, Haley turned so that he stood beside her, facing the lawn, and said in a timid voice, "You can have all the friends you want."

Filled with impetuous delight, she said, "My name is Amyrischka Heloysia Solei Rousellario. But please call me Mirren."

He ducked his head, but this time Mirren knew that meant he was smiling. "Haelipto Krismon Mozeiush Micharainosa. But everyone just calls me Haley."

Mirren wondered if the gravity that had drawn her to the World had drawn her to Haley as well. If so, she was grateful to gravity. She was so happy, in fact, that she turned and hugged Haley.

The hug seemed to catch him off guard, and Mirren immediately realized her mistake.

"Oh, I shouldn't have done that," Mirren said. "Did I make you see things again?"

"No," Haley said softly. He managed to raise his face long enough to emphasize the point. "No."

"I'm just so excited," she said by way of apology.

Haley nodded. With his hand, he gestured to the World beyond the balcony. "You should be."

Four

Josh loved waking up next to Will, but less so when the thing that woke her up was Haley letting himself into Will's bedroom unannounced.

"Um, hi," Josh said. She rubbed her eyes and poked at Will, who was sprawled out in bed beside her. "Will, wake up. Haley brought us doughnuts."

"Huh?" Will's eyes flipped open, then scanned the room. "Wait—there are no doughnuts! You little liar!"

Josh laughed and inserted herself between his arm and side. She supposed she should be more polite or demure or whatever—dream-walker culture was painfully prudish—but instead she nestled her head against Will's chest and closed her eyes again.

"What time is it?" he asked.

"Quarter of still-too-early," Josh told him. "Haley, what's up?"

"I need to tell you something," Haley said. "It's bad."

Skippy, Josh thought. "It's too early to hear bad news."

"No, it's not," Will said. He propped a pillow against the head-board and sat up, causing Josh to slump awkwardly against his side. "Go ahead, Haley."

Josh grumbled to no avail. She knew that in the future, Will would be one of those psychiatrists who was available to his patients no matter the hour.

"It's about the girl," Haley said. "Her name isn't Nan. It's Amyrischka Rousellario." To Will, he added, "She's the lost dream-walker princess."

"What?!" Josh nearly shouted. "Are you serious?"

Haley nodded.

"Wait, the princess from the old monarchy?" Will asked.

"Yeah," Josh said. "The one my grandfather overthrew. The king and queen had a baby daughter who either died or went into hiding after the revolution, and no one's seen her since. Until now, apparently."

Josh—who had never cared about princesses—knew this only because Deloise had several books on the monarchy. As the years had passed, a certain romantic nostalgia for the old regime had developed, as is wont to happen with royals who die tragically—and leave behind princesses who may or may not have died.

"What was the princess doing wandering around in the Dream?" Will asked.

Haley explained the situation—that Mirren lived in a pocket dimension for her own "safety" but had eventually found an archway leading to the Dream and jumped through it, only to get lost in the Dream.

"You're telling us she ran away from home?" Josh summarized.

Haley considered. "Yes."

"Great. So her aunt and uncle are probably going to be pissed at us. Please tell me she's not here because of the Accordance Conclave."

After twenty years in power, the dream-walker junta was finally going to hand over power to a permanent government. At the Accordance Conclave, the dream-walker population of North America would be allowed to vote for the form of government they wanted.

Josh was a conservative, a member of the Troth Party. Her grandfather, on the other hand, was the head of the Lodestone Party and was running on a platform of dream-walking reform. *Radical* reform.

"I don't think she knows about the Conclave," Haley said, answering Josh's question. "I think . . . she was very sheltered."

"So you didn't want to tell us who she was because you think she'll be in danger if people find out she's a member of the old monarchy?" Will asked. "Does anyone still care?"

"Yes," Haley and Josh said in unison.

"There's still a party trying to have the monarchy restored," Josh explained. "It's led by some distant cousin. My grandfather tolerates them because they don't have much real power, but technically what they're advocating is illegal under the junta. Part of why they have so little power is that the cousin was twenty-sixth from the throne or something, but if they actually had the legitimate Rousellario heir, they might come up in the ranks real quickly, and I'm pretty sure Peregrine would have them all arrested. But you said Mirren's not here about the Conclave, right, Haley?"

"Right."

"So, she just has the worst timing in the world. And apparently the worst luck, too, since she's now her worst enemy's granddaughter's houseguest." Josh ran a hand through her hair, feeling how tangled and dirty it was. She wanted a shower. "If she's not here for the Conclave, then what's her plan?"

Haley shrugged. "She said she wants to go to college, swim in the ocean, and eat fast food."

None of those things sounded very princessy to Josh. "There wasn't a McDonald's in her pocket dimension?"

"No. Her aunt is a health nut."

"That would explain why she didn't know how to open a can of Coke," Will remarked.

"Wait a sec," Josh said. "Couldn't she have just imagined a McDonald's and her pocket universe would have created it?"

"Feodor could only do that because he was lucid dreaming," Will reminded Josh. "His physical body was asleep, remember?"

"Oh, yeah. I had forgotten that."

But as soon as Will brought it up, her mind filled with the image of Feodor's time-ravaged body, each limb and digit wrapped in a cobweblike sheath. Only his toenails and fingernails, grown hideously long and curved, had protruded from the shroud. Even worse, she remembered what it had been like to be *inside* the sheath, an uncomfortably hot, stiff cocoon.

"If nobody in Mirren's pocket universe could lucid dream, then the place where they lived probably never changed from what Feodor created it to be," Will said.

"What?" Josh asked, looking at Will and wondering if she had heard Feodor's name only because she'd been thinking of him.

"Come on," Will said, "who else would have built a pocket universe where the royal family could hide out? Who else *could*? In the 1950s, everybody knew that Feodor was secretly working for the king and queen. Half the stuff he invented ended up in the royal family's hands before his bosses at Willis-Audretch could even get a patent on it."

"Oh," Josh said hollowly. She'd known all of that before, of course, she just hadn't realized that Will knew.

Will's eyes were alight with an anger that had become all too familiar recently. Josh always saw it when he talked about Feodor, which was part of why she avoided the topic. She was afraid of his anger, especially afraid of what would happen if he turned his rage on her.

Will didn't know it, but he had so many reasons to be angry at her.

Josh knew that things between her and Will weren't right, but she didn't know how to fix them. Since Feodor and Gloves had tried to kill them, a tension had grown inside Will, and it never really went away. He always seemed to be on high alert, and the smallest things startled him. He'd begun trying to train again so soon after he got released from the hospital that he'd torn the stitches out of his hand. And there was his obsession with guns, too.

Not that Josh felt she was in a position to judge him. On a good week, she slept through the night twice. But the problem with the nightmares wasn't just that they terrified her; far worse was how she had become Feodor's unconscious conspirator.

She had a theory that when Feodor had tried to kill her with his memories, the bad memories weren't all that got through. Somehow, everything that Feodor had ever known or experienced had been planted deep in her subconscious. At night, all sorts of memories played themselves out in her head, twisted and warped, yes, but she believed they were based on true events. How else had she known what his sister, Bryga, looked like long before Will pinned a photo of her on his stalker wall? How had she aced a chemistry quiz even after she daydreamed through all her classes? How had she understood two women in a sporting goods store when they were speaking Russian?

She couldn't have. But Feodor had spoken Russian almost as well as he had Polish, he'd mastered chemistry before puberty, and his sister's face had haunted him until the day he died.

Josh certainly wouldn't have minded a free education obtained without studying, or even memories of Bryga, who had been a beautiful, brilliant child, if she hadn't felt like a part of Feodor was living on inside her. He had died, but not before he'd downloaded himself into Josh. Almost every night, she found herself in his world, often standing beside him in the lab as he broke new ground in quantum physics and dream theory.

Upon waking, she'd scramble for a pencil and write so quickly that she didn't know what she was recording until she examined it later. Formulas, algorithms, diagrams, explanatory notes in Polish or French that she might or might not remember how to translate the next morning, exquisite three-dimensional sketches—and she wrote everything down while switching the pencil from her right hand to her left and back again, as Feodor would have.

And that was why she hadn't told anyone about the nightmares. Deloise might have understood, and sometimes Haley looked at Josh in a way that made her think he recognized the demon inside her, but Will would have shot her on sight.

One morning in late March, she'd realized that among her growing collection of sketchbooks were the complete plans for a wristwatch that Feodor had built when he was nine. The wristwatch performed one delightful function: it kept accurate time within the Dream.

Such an innocuous invention. Feodor had built it when he was a mere child, before the war, before he went mad. Surely it was harmless.

That was what Josh told herself when she started building the watch—that she wasn't crossing any line, wasn't falling prey to Feodor's strange charisma, that just because she had to hide her actions from everyone she cared about didn't mean she was doing anything wrong.

The wristwatch worked as perfectly as the plans had promised it would. Just told the time, and it was always right. Josh felt reassured after she took it into the Dream for the first time. *See,* she thought. *It's no big deal. Just because Feodor went crazy later doesn't mean that every single thing he invented was dangerous.*

The successful completion of the wristwatch had been thrilling. In some ways, it had actually reassured Josh that she was in control, and for a few days, she had contemplated telling Will. *We can turn what he created into something good,* she would have said. *We don't have to be afraid of him anymore.*

But the fear that Will would reject her, be horrified and sickened by what she had become, and the unsettling romantic developments in the nightmares held her back. The first time Feodor had kissed her, she'd woken up choking on her own vomit. Her waking self didn't want that, but her sleeping self grew more and more infatuated, and eventually even her conscious mind grew sympathetic. She was reminded of something Winsor had once theorized: that no one could know another person fully and not fall in love with them, at least a little bit.

Maybe so much of Feodor's mind lived on inside her that she couldn't help seeing the best in him.

But she'd be damned before she fell in love with him.

That evening, when Will was out with Whim, Josh put on the wristwatch and went into the Dream alone.

The nightmare she chose belonged to a man in his forties, corporate type: clean-cut, boring hair, the kind of body that came from doing lots of cardio but no weight lifting. She stood on an elevated platform beside him. Before them stretched a mechanical gauntlet. The path over nine more platforms was obstructed by swinging axes, bursts of boiling steam, wooden logs that closed together from either side, and huge metal teeth that shut so hard, sparks flew from the incisors.

No way was Josh going in there. But she could try to help the dreamer.

"I'm going in," he said. "I'm just going to go as fast as I can."

"Wait a sec," Josh told him. "We can figure out a pattern to get you through safely."

"No, I don't think that will work. I just have to be fast."

Josh put her hand on his shoulder to keep him from leaping to the next platform, and he was lucky she did, because a flamethrower overhead filled the space between platforms with fire just the instant he would have been jumping through.

He cursed.

"It's all right," Josh told him. "There's a pattern. We can count it out. The next time the flames appear, we'll start counting."

They spent the next five minutes working out the pattern. Josh had chosen this nightmare because it presented an opportunity for her to try out the wristwatch, which allowed her to accurately time the sequences. The pattern wasn't nearly as complex as it first appeared, and Josh was almost tempted to try the gauntlet herself. If only the course had been slightly less fatal and any attempt to leave it wouldn't have resulted in an endless plunge into darkness.

"You ready?" she asked the dreamer.

He was jogging in place. "Put me in, coach!"

"We go on four. Wait for the fire burst . . . One, two, three, four!"

The dreamer jumped to the second platform. Josh kept calling out numbers as the seconds passed. He waited for the ax to pass overhead twice before leaping to the third platform. From there he had less than a second to get to the fourth platform before a burst of hot steam scoured his skin. . . .

He made it, but just barely. Josh knew his timing was already off, and she shouted the numbers as loudly as she could, but he missed his cue.

The fifth platform broke in half every nine seconds, dumping anyone standing on it into the abyss below. The sequence shouldn't have been a problem, but the dreamer was still standing there, looking confused.

"Above you!" Josh shouted. "Jump!"

The dreamer leapt straight up just as the platform broke apart beneath him. He grabbed the metal bar overhead and hung there, squirming, as the platform came back together.

"Drop!" Josh yelled, but she'd lost the count. Between the fifth and sixth platforms were the chompers—a five-foot-wide metal jaw that snapped shut every two or three seconds. Josh knew the sequence, and she told the dreamer to wait while she sorted out what part of it the chompers were currently in, but he either couldn't hear her or was too panicked to listen. He saw the chompers close, then reopen, and he dove headfirst through them.

The metal jaw closed.

"No!" Josh screamed as the teeth bit into the dreamer's chest. Over the bursts of fire and steam, she heard his ribs crack. The jaw opened, but not far enough for him to escape, and then a tongue appeared, and a hollow metal throat, and the teeth were chewing the dreamer up and swallowing him.

Josh stood alone on the platform, cursing wildly. She knew that she could jump through the chompers and follow the dreamer into whatever horror his subconscious had in store for him next, but instead she furiously thrust her hand out and opened an archway back to her basement.

Back in the archroom, she grabbed a white towel off the table and wiped the Veil dust from her face. "Stupid, stupid, stupid," she muttered. If she'd been able to access her power, she could have saved the dreamer. He would be sleeping peacefully right now; instead he was probably being digested.

She pulled off the wristwatch and hurled it across the room. "What use were you?" she yelled at it.

No use, she thought. *It was no use. I was no use.*

Her nightmare came back to her—the war, the devices, the comfort of being able to put everything to rights.

She wanted that power.

Five

Whim drove a monstrous 1981 baby-blue Lincoln Town Car with matching leather interior that he called Liberace. It was the only car Will had ever felt embarrassed to be seen in. He didn't care much for Whim's driving, either. Josh drove too fast and with too much confidence; Whim just drove *badly*—he'd once clipped a city bus.

The Grey Circle—or Feodor Fan Club, as Josh called it—met once a month, and members rotated hosting duties. Tonight the front door of the Fosperaida mansion had been propped open with a geode the size of a basketball, so Will and Whim let themselves inside. They crossed the foyer's parquet floor into a living room so large that it contained three different seating areas.

Will was still getting his bearings when a feminine voice as smooth and slick as hot oil said, "Well, if it isn't the Pied Piper of conspiracy rats. Hello, Whimarian."

The young woman stood taller than Will, almost as tall as Whim, but she walked with the stealthy sway of a panther, gouging the carpet with her stiletto heels. Although Will couldn't say why, he thought her short blue-and-white kimono looked expensive, and she wore a silver bracelet with diamonds running all the way around it, too.

Will noticed her beauty at the same moment he noticed her expression, which was somehow both seductive and mocking. She looked up at Whim from beneath long brown lashes, like she was peeking at him through a hedge, but the corners of her painted lips pulled back in the faintest of smiles, as though someone had gently pricked her there with the end of a dagger. "Here for the free food?" she asked.

Whim's eyes were so large, his eyelids had vanished into his brow. His voice shook as he hissed, "What the *hell* are *you* doing here?"

The girl shrugged, holding her shoulders at the top of their range of motion as if she were posing briefly. "I could ask you the same thing," she said. She sounded unfazed by Whim's anger. "I've been coming here for two years. Then I go away to college for a couple of months and when I come back they're letting anyone in."

"I was invited," Whim said sharply, which wasn't technically true. Will and Josh had been invited, and Will had brought Whim.

The girl released a puff of air with a *pffff* sound. "Whatever you say, Whim."

Whim gritted his teeth, but when he spoke this time, his voice carried a determined casualness. "Will, this is Ozbeilia Sokkravotaine."

She held out a cool, fine-boned hand and Will shook it. "Call me Bayla."

"This is Will Kansas," Whim said. "Josh's apprentice."

"Oh," Bayla said, and she laughed. "You've cleaned up very nicely, I'm sure."

Will didn't know how to respond to that. "So have you," was all he could think to say.

Bayla laughed again. She lifted two glasses from a nearby table and held them out. "The wine is superb. Have a glass."

"No, thank you," Will said, but Whim accepted one of the glasses she held out.

According to dream-walker tradition, seventeen years of age made one an adult, and it was more or less the dream-walker drinking age as well. But Will had a genetic predisposition for alcoholism that ran back at least three generations.

"Oh, come on," Bayla said, nudging him with a sharp elbow. "We're all dream walkers here. No one's going to yell at you for having a glass of wine."

"Seriously, no," Will said. "Stop asking." The words came out more firmly than he'd meant them to, and a little too loudly as well.

Bayla laughed and looked to Whim, as if she thought he would join her in her bemusement. Instead, he set his own glass of wine pointedly back down.

Bayla rolled her eyes. "Have a nice evening, children."

Just as she turned to walk away, a young man joined them. He slipped an arm around Bayla's waist and smiled. Straight-nosed and bespectacled, he carried an air of aristocratic intelligence at odds with his friendly smile and wrinkled clothing.

"Friends of yours?" he asked.

Bayla leaned against him and said dryly, "I suppose. Bash, this is Whim Avishara and Will . . ."

"Kansas," Will supplied.

"Kansas," Bayla repeated, as if the name tasted sour.

Bash enthusiastically shook Whim's hand, but he dropped it when he heard Will's name. "Will Kansas! Well, this is quite a thrill!"

He shook Will's hand like he wanted to take it home as a souvenir. "I'm Bashuriel Mirrettsio. Call me Bash. You're a nominee for the Nicastro Prize this year, aren't you? I won six years ago. My own experiment never went anywhere, I'm afraid."

"Oh," Will said, relaxing. "Congratulations. Yeah, Josh and I are nominated."

"You're a shoo-in," Bash said. "I read your paper. I read all the Nicastro finalist papers. I'm hoping that one day they'll put me on the selection committee." He was so excited that he was completely ignoring the glares Whim and Bayla were exchanging. "I think your experiment could have terrific applications for making archway creation safer. I'd love to talk to you about your paper. Both of you, I mean."

That was the first time a dream walker had ever remembered Will in an invitation while forgetting Josh, instead of the other way around. Will felt vaguely charmed in spite of himself.

"Sure," he said. "That would be fun."

"Darling," Bayla said, "I think we should go find seats before the presentation starts."

"Oh." Bash looked at her as if he'd forgotten she was there and wasn't thrilled to have been reminded. "Yes, of course." He pulled a business card out of his pocket. "Please, feel free to give me a call anytime. And give my compliments to Josh."

Will accepted the card and said, "I will."

Bayla was practically dragging Bash away by then. Will glanced at the business card.

Bash Mirrettsio
Associate in Applied Physics
Willis-Audretch

Willis-Audretch, Will thought, recognizing the name of the shady dream-walker think tank and invention corporation. *I should have known.*

"What a loser," Whim said. "I can't believe she's with such a dork."

Will gave him a withering look until he said, "What?"

Will sighed.

He tried to pay attention to the presentation, but he had too much on his mind. Partly Whim and Bayla, but mostly the way he'd responded to Bayla's offer of wine. He knew he'd overreacted, and although he could justify himself by saying that no one should ever have to turn a drink down twice, he knew exactly why he'd gotten upset: he'd been scared he would accept the glass Bayla had held out to him.

Before he'd become Josh's apprentice, he'd gotten drunk a few times. The anxiety he'd felt had outweighed the fun, though; he'd found himself constantly evaluating his behavior for signs of addiction. Finally he'd decided that drinking wasn't worth the stress or the risk that it would get out of control.

But since that night spent in Feodor's nightmare Warsaw, he'd found himself thinking about alcohol. About how it made everything lighter, how it made pleasure easy and trust easier. He never drank it, just thought about it.

But he thought about it a lot.

Finally, the lecture caught Will's attention. He'd found that the content of the presentations fell into two categories—romantic re-hashes of Feodor's troubled life and hard-core scientific lectures. Tonight's presentation was the latter, with a hint of the former thrown in: Feodor's last book.

Sometime after Feodor had vanished from public life, he had apparently mailed to his editor a partial copy of a manuscript for a new book. The editor, although well versed in dream theory, had been unable to make sense of the manuscript, and he wrote back to Feodor saying that his work was the incomprehensible excrement of a troubled mind and that he should consider check-ing himself into a hospital. Shortly afterward, Feodor had been arrested for dream staging, and the editor had burned the man-uscript.

Or, at least, he had claimed to. But for half a century, supposed fragments of the manuscript had floated around the dream-walker underground.

The presenter that night had gathered the pieces of the manu-script available and was attempting to put them together into some sort of cohesive idea.

The word that had grabbed Will's attention was "magnets."

"Magnets are a vital part of Kajażkołski's theory of light har-monics," the presenter was saying when Will turned his attention completely to the lecture. "He understood the relationship be-tween energy and magnets and that there is more than one energy field surrounding the human body. According to him, the first energy field is esoteric, the so-called spiritual body. The second energy field is the body itself, and its energy is made up of the subatomic particles from which matter is formed.

"Some attempts have been made to manipulate the physical

I would come out of it and know things I hadn't known before. Crazy stuff people would never have told me. But it was like I could see inside them."

Will pondered this. Veil dust was a drug, but it wasn't a drug. It made a person hallucinate, but it also showed them the truth, or it showed them what they were afraid of.

"Why would the Grey Circle be using it?"

"I don't know. But one thing I do know: we can *not* tell Josh and Del that they're doing Veil dust here, or they're never going to let us come back."

Will glanced at him across the front seat. "I don't want to keep secrets from Josh."

"You don't have to keep it a secret, but don't bring it up."

"That's the same thing, Whim."

"Not in my book. I'm telling you, Josh will flip out. She *hated* it when Ian did Veil dust. She considered it a violation of the Dream's sacredness or something."

Will groaned. That did sound like Josh. And he did want to keep coming to these meetings, even if "the real meeting" was upstairs. He'd just started making progress figuring out what was wrong with Winsor.

"I won't bring it up," he agreed.

"Thanks," Whim said. "One other thing. Could we maybe not mention that we bumped into Bayla?"

"Okay, who *is* Bayla?" Will demanded. "What is the story with you two?"

Whim, pulling off the interstate, grimaced. "So, this is embarrassing, but when I was fifteen, Bayla and I tried to elope. We bought a car for four hundred dollars and we tried to drive it to Mexico because we thought we could get married there without our parents' consent—which is not true, by the way—but the car broke down in Louisiana. I wanted to hop a bus, but . . . Bayla bailed. She'd pretty much been losing patience since the A/C went on the fritz outside Mobile. She called her parents and told them to come get her."

A shade of sadness tinted Whim's voice, which surprised Will. Whim wasn't much for regrets, but four years had passed and he was still hurt that Bayla had given up on him. "Wow," Will said. "That sucks, man."

"Yeah, well, I don't know what I was thinking in the first place. Bayla's a treacherous bitch. I should have seen that from the start."

Apparently he's still angry, too, Will thought.

"She did look good, though," Whim added. He smiled at the memory. "She looked amazing, actually."

Uh-oh.

"I won't mention that part to Deloise, either," Will said.

Six

The French toast tasted like happiness.

After every bite Mirren took, she closed her eyes to savor the sweet, eggy goodness. The flavors made her want to write an overblown ode stuffed with words like "sultry" and "delirious" and "profane."

Now I understand why people get fat, she thought.

Whim had woken her that morning with the announcement that they were going to brunch at Fat Mac's Flapjacks. "They" turned out to be Whim, Deloise, Josh, Will, Haley—and Mirren. She couldn't tell him that she'd never been to a restaurant before, but she was relieved when he and Josh ordered the breakfast bonanza for the entire table. Shortly afterward, platters of pancakes, waffles, biscuits, eggs, sausage and bacon, and six different types of syrup had arrived. Mirren was determined to try every single thing.

Katia would love this, she thought, and for the first time since she'd left the Hidden Kingdom, she felt a little homesick. But the emotion was largely drowned out by her excitement at being out in the World. She'd ridden to the restaurant in Josh's car, which had been utterly terrifying, but during the parts when she hadn't been screaming, she had stared out the window in awe at the buildings, the people, just the size of the World, and the space of the sky. Now she couldn't help gazing around the restaurant's dining room at the people assembled with their different hairstyles and clothing and constant cell phone use.

The people at her own table fascinated her as well. Haley sat to her right and had rolled up sausages in a pancake, which Mirren recognized as the classic pioneer dish "pigs in a blanket." Josh had drenched her waffles in syrup and powdered sugar, while Will preferred bacon and eggs. Deloise was neglecting her own plate so she could hand-feed Whim strawberries with whipped cream and chocolate sauce. Mirren found that endearing, although everyone else seemed to find it nauseating.

"Whim," Josh said, "if you don't get my little sister's finger out of your mouth, I'm going to break your legs with a hammer."

Whim rolled his eyes, but he did quit sucking the whipped cream off Deloise's finger. She remained sitting in his lap, however.

"Nan," Whim said. "What's that short for?"

"Gertrananette," Mirren improvised.

"Wow," Whim said. His eyebrows shot up, but he looked down at his plate as if trying to hide his reaction. "Is that, uh . . . German?"

"German and French. We speak both in Switzerland."

"I think it's pretty," Deloise offered.

"Thank you." Mirren personally thought it was hideous, but she liked Deloise.

She wasn't finding it hard to lie about being from Switzerland. Her ridiculously thorough education was finally paying off.

Whim, while carefully angling a forkful of blueberry pancake into Deloise's mouth, asked, "What do they think about staging over in Switzerland?"

Staging? Mirren wondered, and felt uneasy.

Staging was the practice of creating dreams in order to manipulate dreamers. It was banned in North America because—all too easily—it could be used to control people's minds. The example Mirren always remembered was a first mate on a naval ship who staged dreams for the other crew members until they joined him in a mutiny.

"Much of Europe is divided into hectorates," Mirren said. When she got blank stares, she explained, "Small, self-governing regions that are loosely affiliated. Most have agreed not to stage in hectorates other than their own, and most hectorates are either too small or too oddly shaped to allow for well-targeted staging, so it's largely a nonissue."

Thank heaven, she added silently.

"Staging is a big issue here," Whim said, "what with the Accordance Conclave coming up. Looks like it will finally pass."

Halfway through his sentence, Mirren bit into something hard in her sausage. She took care to be polite as she spit it into her napkin, but she couldn't resist glancing down; a fragment of bone stared back at her.

Staging is a big issue here, Mirren repeated silently, and she tasted blood and realized she must have cut her gum. *No wonder Collena worked so hard to keep me in the Hidden Kingdom,* she thought. *Out here, there are bones hidden in food and staging is about to become policy.*

Haley leaned close to Mirren, his shoulder brushing hers, and whispered, "Are you okay?"

"What is the Accordance Conclave?" she asked him. Then, seeing that they had the table's attention, she repeated the question to no one in particular, "What is the Accordance Conclave?"

"Nobody in Switzerland has heard of the AC?" Whim asked Mirren. "That's bizarre."

"Don't be so American," Deloise told him. "None of us know

anything about the European hectorates. Why should they know anything about us?"

Will and Haley exchanged a glance Mirren couldn't read.

"The Accordance Conclave is a continent-wide vote on what type of government to replace the junta with," Will explained. "The group with the most support is the Lodestone Party, which is—"

"I know the Lodestone Party," Mirren interjected. "They—"

They killed my parents.

She folded the napkin so she wouldn't have to look at the bone any longer.

"You probably should know them," Whim said with a laugh. "You're eating breakfast with the party leader's granddaughters."

The happy bubble Mirren had spent the last hour inside of popped and left her feeling very full and very sick.

"Please excuse me," she said, rising. Her napkin unfolded as it floated to the floor; the bit of bloodied bone mocked her.

You think this hurt? Just wait for what comes next.

She knew what was coming next. She could see the thought on the horizon like approaching storm clouds, and she knew she had to get out of the restaurant before the rain fell. She headed for the front door. Behind her, exclamations of Whim's confusion and Deloise's concern filled the air.

"Do you want me to come?" Will asked.

"No," Haley said. "I've got it."

Mirren hit the door with both hands, causing a harness of bells to ring, and ran straight into the parking lot. Tires squealed, a horn blared, and Mirren shrieked as a hulking red vehicle stopped less than two feet from her. The driver screamed obscenities at her.

"I'm sorry, I'm sorry," Mirren cried, and dashed toward the only thing she saw that looked comforting: a large grassy area with a small creek running through it.

She didn't slow down until she reached a place where the creek ran through a channel beneath the road. A concrete slab buried next to the water protruded enough to create a little bench where she could sit without ruining her borrowed clothes.

Although she had closed her eyes, she felt Haley sit down beside her. Maybe her skin picked up his body warmth, or maybe she just sensed his presence, but she knew he was there even when he didn't speak.

Some people don't speak with words, she thought, and she felt grateful not to be alone at that moment.

Wasn't it silly of me to think I could come here and not confront Peregrine? she wondered bitterly. *We have been circling each other from afar, drawing slowly closer, since the day he killed my parents. We've swung around our orbits, but gravity has always been moving us toward the moment our paths would cross.*

When she opened her eyes, she saw that Haley had picked a few long blades of grass and was twisting them together. "My family didn't tell me about the Accordance Conclave," she said.

Haley nodded as if he'd already known. Maybe he had.

"Now that I look back on it, they must have been hiding things from me for years. Newspapers kept getting lost on their way to us, or a page or two would be missing. Our liaison to the World started having"—she made air quotes with her fingers—"'computer problems' and couldn't print the blogs I was reading. There's no Internet in the Hidden Kingdom, of course." She rubbed her eyes. "They must not have wanted me to know that support for staging was gaining so much traction."

"Why not?" Haley asked.

"Because they knew I'd be obligated to try to stop it."

Haley ran a blade of grass between his thumb and forefinger. "It's . . . Staging is very dangerous, isn't it? More dangerous than people know."

Mirren realized then how much Haley might have seen. She'd brushed his hand while reaching for the butter in the restaurant—or perhaps before that, the time she'd hugged him, the handshake . . . any contact could have revealed her secrets.

"Mirren," he said, and he touched her again then, so hesitantly, just his hand on her back. He struggled for a moment before saying, "Everyone has secrets. I don't . . . I don't share what isn't mine. It's like . . . a responsibility." He blushed prettily and added, "It's a duty."

Mirren knew then that gravity had brought her to Haley just as it had brought her to Peregrine. She had arrived alone in a strange land, and she could not believe that by mere chance, she could have met someone who so perfectly understood her responsibilities.

"Thank you," she said.

Haley shrugged as if to say, *Of course.*

"No," she said. "For being my friend."

And he smiled.

"There's something about you," he said, his voice even quieter than usual but his words more certain. "I can't look away."

Her heart beat hard, twice. She wanted him to keep looking, yet she felt obligated to say, "You should get as far away from me as you can. It's entirely possible that Peregrine Borgenicht will have me assassinated as soon as he finds out I'm alive."

Haley shook his head. He took a deep breath and straightened his back, and Mirren saw that it was hard for him to sit up straight, to take up so much room in the World. "I'll keep you alive—I mean, I'll help. If you want, I mean."

Then he ducked down a little, as if afraid of being such a tall target, and Mirren felt inspired by his tiny act of courage.

"I feel so betrayed," she admitted. Her voice cracked with tears, but she didn't care. "Now I have to forget about living my normal, peaceful life, because I have to stop the Lodestone Party from taking power." She glanced around the park, which was spotted with dandelions she'd never had the chance to smell. "It would be such a shame to die now."

"We won't let you die," Haley promised. "The others will help. They all hate him."

"I just want . . ." She reached out to touch Haley's face and then stopped herself. "I want everything, I suppose."

She *did* want everything. She wanted to kill Peregrine and take over the government and go to college and eat sugar and kiss Haley.

But somehow her life in the World was already becoming as pre-
determined as her life in the Hidden Kingdom had been. *Gravity,*
she thought again, with less gratitude this time.

"Come inside," Haley said. "We'll find a way."

"All right." Mirren climbed to her feet. "But we should come
back to this park sometime."

"Park?" he asked.

"Yeah. This is a park, right?"

He smiled like he was trying not to laugh at her. "It's an unde-
veloped lot with a storm drain."

Mirren burst out laughing. "It *is*? But it's so pretty!"

Haley held out his hand, and she took it. As they walked back
toward the restaurant, he said, "I'll take you to a real park."

"Can we have a picnic?"

"Yes."

Mirren squeezed his hand, even as she thought, *We'd better
go soon.*

Seven

Feodor's laboratory—all scorched ashes of
*roses wallpaper and metal autopsy tables covered with dirty crystals
and shattered beakers. Josh sat in the window seat and looked out at
the ruins of Warsaw, admiring how the different columns of smoke
wove together like strands of silk thread, each its own subtle shade
of gray.*

*"You can see so much more of the sky now that the buildings have
been knocked down," she told Feodor. "They should never have been
put up in the first place."*

He laughed, a sharp sound that cut her ears. Josh winced and looked back out the window just in time to see the worsening rain bring down one of the few remaining chimneys. It made a sound like the rush of a creek as it fell.

Josh loved the city. She could sit in the window seat and stare out all day, or wander through the wreckage, admiring the poetry of shattered pottery, the tenderness of one-eyed dollies, the poignancy of discolored photographs. Sometimes she liked to try on stained clothing or broken jewelry that she found, modeling ripped silk stockings and blackened wedding dresses for Feodor.

But the city just as often infuriated her. Each time she tripped on rubble, coughed on the filthy air, felt a wall she was leaning against collapse, she thought, Something must be done about all this.

Leaving the window seat, she went to stand beside Feodor at one of the long tables where he had laid out his experiments. She recognized the circlet and vambrace immediately.

"Show me how these work," she said, thinking of what their power could do to rebuild the city.

"I already showed you."

"You showed me, but I want to understand. To know them the way I know you."

He smiled at her, and when he spoke again, his tone was intimate, so soft that she had to lean forward to hear. "And how do you know me?"

She pressed the side of her leg against his, winding her foot around his shin like a snake. "Completely."

"Is that so?"

"Yes." He continued to fiddle with the devices, and Josh insinuated herself between him and the table until she stood in the circle of his arms. "I know you better than I know myself."

"Benefit of hindsight, I suppose," he murmured, before kissing her lightly. His eyes were so many shades of gray, but each of them glowed with their own light, as if they still carried a bit of the fire that had turned them to smoke.

"Very well," Feodor said, and he cupped her face in his hands. "I'll help you understand. . . ."

He squeezed her head between his palms and began to lift. Josh scrambled to catch hold of his wrists, but her heels were already leaving the floor. A terrible pain spread from the base of her skull down into her neck as Feodor continued to lift her up. She clutched at his wrists, his arms, scratching, digging, then reached for his face, but her arms were too short. When her toes lost contact with the ground, the pain in her neck grew fearsome, the pain of a body's weight hanging on sinews that simply could not support it.

Feodor's eyes glowed white. "Now you know," he said, and he shook her once, up and down, hard.

Her body fell to the floor.

Her head did not.

Josh actually screamed as she woke up. She had never done that before, but she did it now, and her hands came up around her neck to make sure it was still connected to her head. She tried to run from the nightmare but succeeded only in cracking her cheek on the bedroom wall, because for some reason she had woken standing on her bed.

I'm going to die, she thought. *I'm dying. No, I'm awake. It's a trick. Where's my head?*

Strangely, it was her head she felt she had lost, not her body. She choked on her own breath, ran into the bathroom to retch, and ending up only coughing into the toilet. The invasive scent of the toilet bowl cleaner nauseated her even more.

She couldn't calm down. She couldn't stop touching her throat, her neck, digging with her fingers to make out each tiny vertebra.

Damn you, Feodor. Damn you, damn you, damn you. I should have killed you myself. I should have kept you alive and made you reverse what you did to me. I should bring you back to life and make you fix this.

The door at the other end of the bathroom opened, and

Deloise—wearing a matching floral tank top and lace-edged shorts—rushed to Josh's side.

"What's wrong? Are you sick? I heard you scream." She hugged her sister close. "It's okay, Josh. It's okay. You just had a bad dream."

Josh hugged Deloise back, letting some of the hysteria work itself out in the embrace. Slowly, though, her breath did calm, and finally she was able to release her sister and sit back against the vanity.

Deloise poured her a glass of water and sat beside her as Josh drank it. "Want to tell me about it?"

Josh shook her head. She was aware that Deloise was worried about her, that she knew enough about Josh's nightmares to be rightly concerned, but telling Deloise the details would have felt like deliberately exposing her to a deadly virus.

"Maybe you should go talk to a therapist," Deloise ventured hesitantly. "I mean, it seems like the nightmares are getting worse instead of better."

Josh stared into her water glass. She didn't need a therapist—she needed an exorcist.

"I thought I was dating a therapist," she joked. Deloise didn't laugh.

"He's not a therapist yet, and he's in even worse shape than you."

"I know, I know," Josh said. She would have had a hard time not noticing. "I'll be all right, Del.".

She spent a few minutes reassuring her sister, then Deloise hugged her again and went back to bed. Josh washed her face and returned to her own room.

She stopped dead in the doorway.

In her blind panic, she had not noticed the walls. Josh, who had never cared much for interior decorating, hadn't painted or papered or hung posters, so until tonight the walls had been quite blank. But her subconscious—or perhaps Feodor's subconscious—had thought them too blank, blank canvases, even, and she must have climbed on the mattress in her sleep, and that was why she'd woken standing, because the walls that formed a corner around her bed were covered in writing.

Mostly the writing appeared to be mathematical formulas. Some chemical. A large number of annotated diagrams showing how wires should be arranged, where magnets and crystals should be placed. An astonishingly detailed anatomical diagram of the circulatory system in the right arm.

He did this, she thought.

Six months before, she might have been able to grudgingly recognize $E=mc^2$ as something Einstein had discovered. Tonight she knew it meant that an object's mass multiplied by the square of the speed of light described how much energy the object could emit.

No, she didn't *know*. She *remembered*.

Because Feodor had known.

She climbed onto the bed on her knees and traced the diagrams with a fingertip. There was the circlet, there was the vambrace. The drawings on the wall showed her how to treat the crystals, how to connect them to the wires, which wires to use, where the magnets should go, the direction of polarization.

Show me how these work. I want to understand.

Well, he had showed her all right.

She glanced at the clock—3:27. There was still time.

Sitting down with a large sketch pad, she transferred the writing on the wall onto paper. She did this almost entirely from memory, only occasionally checking the walls.

Exactly how much of Feodor's memory she had was unclear to her. She suspected that all of it was in her mind somewhere, but information recall often had to be triggered by a dream or situational necessity. She hadn't remembered that a Minotaur lived in a labyrinth until she'd needed to know.

Except that . . . As she copied, she realized that the plans were incomplete. The vambrace and circlet worked by using a signaling network built across the Dream, like cell phones communicating via cell phone towers, but the walls contained no instructions on how to build this network. Without it, the equipment was useless.

Josh felt disappointed and, at the same time, relieved. The vambrace and circlet were incredibly powerful. If she put them on, she'd be able to forget about connecting with the Dream mentally, forget her breathing exercises, forget struggling and fighting. The Dream would open to her like a flower blossoming. The vambrace and circlet would give her exactly the power she had been trying so hard to attain.

But since she didn't have the complete plans, that was one moral argument she wouldn't have to have with herself.

She worked until almost seven and then went down to the basement. A search of the numerous half-empty paint cans turned up no white paint, but she did find half a gallon of white primer, which was even better.

As Feodor's diagrams and formulas vanished beneath the primer like rubble hidden beneath snow, Josh wondered if she should have copied the plans at all. Maybe they were somehow as morally corrupt as Feodor had been, as fundamentally dangerous. . . .

But she remembered the nightmare from a few nights before, how he had tried to save his little sister and her puppy, how angry he had been when Josh stopped him, and Josh thought of her own sister. If he had loved Bryga the way Josh loved Deloise, there had to have been something good in him, right? He had to have had a good heart beneath all the madness.

Was that even possible?

When the walls were again innocence white, Josh opened the window and turned on a fan, then tiptoed down to Will's room to sleep. She managed not to wake him up this time as she slipped into bed. His back was turned to her, but she put her arm over his side and tucked her hand inside his. He was endearingly responsive when he slept: If she snuggled up against him, he would hug her close; if she put her hand in his, he would hold it.

But that morning, for some reason, he didn't. His fingers fell heavy and lax against the back of her hand, and a sense of loneliness washed over her. Lately they were always off doing their own thing—he was in the basement with his laptop and his stalker wall, she was in the attic with her secret projects. She had begun to miss the days after their encounter with Feodor, when the medications kept the nightmares away and they were both too banged up and loopy on painkillers to do anything besides sit on the apartment couch together, watching movies, occasionally either making out or ordering pizza. For a few nights they'd even slept on the pull-out couch together, their proximity sanctioned by the celibacy of their injuries and the public nature of the living room, and during the days they'd found time for what they'd never done previously: hanging out. They'd told each other crazy stories and jokes and made fun of television. Will had taught her card games. Josh had taught him knife tricks. She'd thought then that she was so lucky to have him, lucky to be with someone so genuine, who believed she was good enough just as she was, who always looked in her eyes when he said that he loved her.

She'd felt like she could tell him anything then, but the memories had come between them—his *and* Feodor's. Now she had a whole new world of secrets she hadn't shared with him and *couldn't* share. He hated Feodor, and if he found out that the man's memories were living in Josh's subconscious, she was afraid he might start to hate her.

Or at least break up with her.

Someday we'll both get over it, she told herself, watching dawn break over Will's sleeping form. *We'll figure out how to live with it. Someday I'll be able to tell him about the nightmares without him freaking out.*

Yeah, and he'd take down his stalker wall then, too.

Sure.

# Eight

"So," Will said, "maybe we should talk about what happened yesterday."

Josh, who was sitting at the kitchen table and sharpening a knife with a whetstone, looked at Will with confusion.

"I mean at the restaurant," Will clarified.

They were getting ready to meet with Davita, each in his or her own way. Mirren was arranging the tea set and trying to keep Josh from getting metal shavings all over the lace tablecloth. Haley was writing on his steno pad. Will was trying to prepare everyone emotionally. Out of all of them, Will felt he had the hardest job.

"The restaurant?" Josh asked.

"Yes. When Mirren went running out of it."

Mirren's face was as composed and distant as it had been the day before, her eyes politely cast toward the floor. After she'd returned from the parking lot with Haley, she'd claimed to have vomited into the bushes outside, blaming all the sugar and refined flour she'd eaten. Will hadn't believed her for a moment.

Apparently Josh had. "She needed to puke."

Will sighed. "Right. She needed to puke because Whim had just dropped it on her that your grandfather is the one responsible for killing her parents."

"Oh, that." Josh began sharpening her knife again, the blade grating loudly against the stone. "Whim didn't know that would freak her out."

"Josh." Will felt himself quicken with anger, the way he did so often and so easily these days, and he briefly made his hands into fists in an attempt to release the energy. He couldn't blame Josh for being Josh. "I think Mirren would feel more comfortable if she understood a little more about your relationship with Peregrine. Specifically the part where you aren't fond of each other."

"Oh," Josh said again. "All right." She spoke to Mirren but didn't stop sharpening her knife. "I hate my grandfather. Like, a lot. He's a terrible person, he treated my grandmother like crap, and he tried to get me, Haley, and Will tortured to death last February. I figure that makes you and me allies." She used a towel to wipe the grit from her blade. "So we're good?"

Will would have given a very different explanation, but Mirren was smiling with her lips pressed tight together, as if trying not to laugh. "We're good," she said. "And I would be happy to have you as an ally."

She put the kettle on for tea, and shortly afterward, the doorbell rang. Will got up to answer it, but Kerstel beat him to the door.

Will loved his adoptive mother like he'd loved his alcoholic birth mother, who had given him up to the state when he was twelve. Sometimes he thought he loved Kerstel more. She hadn't just gone out of her way to make him part of their family, she'd taken the time to build a real friendship with him, even reading his favorite self-help books and teaching him about her own passions, philosophy and posthumanism. But every time he looked at her since the attack, a blind black hatred for the man who had hurt her filled him like black smoke, working its way from his gut to his limbs, his fingers and toes, his eyelashes.

He immediately felt bad for having made her get up and answer the door. In addition to the terrible injuries she had sustained when Feodor's zombies had come out of the archway and attacked the household, Kerstel had learned in the ICU that she was six weeks pregnant, and the combined toll had worn her thin and weak. She still had nerve damage in her right arm, and she couldn't stand for more than ten minutes.

"You should have let someone else get it," Will told her.

"I need the practice," Kerstel said as she held the door open so Davita could enter. "You think Lauren's going to get up with the baby in the middle of the night?"

"No," Will said sincerely. "I think Deloise will."

They all laughed, even Davita. Deloise was so excited about a baby joining the family that she had learned to knit baby booties.

Davita Bach stood five feet ten, knew fifteen different ways to French-twist her titian-red hair, and wore a power suit like she'd been born in one. That afternoon she had on a cream-colored suit with dark brown pinstripes. Usually the small gold Rousellario family crest she wore on a chain around her neck was hidden beneath her clothes, but today it hung in full view against a light brown silk blouse.

"Have you picked out a name?" Davita asked.

"Lauren and I are at war over the name," Kerstel admitted. "He wants Bramko, I want Popolomus."

Will secretly thought both names were hideous, but Davita expressed admiration for the choices. Finally, they left Kerstel to her protein shake and a book called *A Child's Understanding of the World* and headed for the kitchen.

Although Josh and Will believed Davita would feel the same loyalty to Mirren that she had to Mirren's parents, they'd agreed not to take chances. When they entered the kitchen, Josh was sitting beside Mirren with her knife hidden in her lap. She remained sitting when Mirren stood.

Davita looked to Will in the silence that followed, and he realized she was waiting for him to make introductions. Dream walkers loved formal introductions. "Davita, this is Mirren Rousellario. Mirren, Davita Bakareilionne."

Mirren extended a hand across the kitchen table, but Davita laughed uncomfortably at the sight of it and instead dropped to one knee. The unexpected motion caused Josh to spring out of her chair, knife in hand. Dismayed, Mirren touched her lips with two fingers.

"Please get up," she said to Davita, pushing Josh's knife arm down. "There's no need for that."

Davita straightened, but she said, "I want you to know that I'm here only to serve you, Your Majesty."

The title made Mirren wince. "Please, just call me Mirren."

"You are the daughter of my king and queen," Davita insisted.

"The king and queen are dead and the kingdom destroyed," Mirren said flatly. "Please call me Mirren or nothing at all. Let's sit down."

The kettle whistled, and Haley got up to fill the teapot.

"I'm relieved to see that you're well," Davita said, taking a seat. "Your family has been very worried."

Mirren smiled, but her anxiety was evident in the lines around her mouth. "My new friends have taken excellent care of me."

We're her friends? Will wondered, and snuck a glance at Josh out of the corner of his eye. He could see her trying to hide how taken aback she was.

But Will noticed that when Haley returned to the table with the teapot, he scooted his chair very close to Mirren's, and he remembered how he had offered to go after Mirren with Haley the day before and how quick Haley had been to say no.

Five months ago he was in love with Josh on Ian's behalf, Will thought. *Now he's putting the moves on a princess.*

He wondered how Haley had come out of their encounter with Feodor so much stronger when Josh and Will had come out so damaged.

The sudden intensity in Mirren's voice drew him out of his thoughts.

"I am sorry that Katia has been worried," she was saying. "I'm truly sorry for frightening her." Her voice hardened. "But as for my aunt and uncle, it serves them right—for what they've hidden from me, for how they've lied to me, and especially for keeping me trapped in that universe for nineteen years."

Whoa, Will said. The tone of the conversation had changed abruptly, and he saw Josh's right arm tense, no doubt tightening her grip on the knife beneath the table.

"Who's Katia?" Will asked as Haley poured him a cup of tea.

"Katia is my cousin," Mirren explained. "She was born in the Hidden Kingdom fifteen years ago and she's never once been allowed to leave it."

"Miss Mirren," Davita said, her tone distressed, "even I didn't know you have a cousin, and I'm sure your aunt and uncle would be very upset if you let the word get out. They're trying to—"

"Protect her?" Mirren finished as though she'd heard it a hundred times before. "Like they protected me by imprisoning me? By lying to me?"

"I'm sure they did what they thought was best for you."

Haley said, "Mirren is an adult. She has the right to make her own decisions now."

Davita stared at him as if he were a talking toaster, but Mirren smiled her beautiful, wise smile and softened.

"My family and I have very different priorities," she said. "Their priority is to see me live out my life trapped in a medieval castle, married to a man of their choice, and breeding like a rabbit, and my priority is to stop staging from becoming government policy."

Josh and Will exchanged glances. This was the first Will had heard of Mirren's intentions, but it put her panic in the restaurant the day before in perspective.

"I see," Davita said, her painted mouth slack with surprise.

"I have to make sure that the Lodestone Party does not win the vote at the Accordance Conclave and make staging permanent policy," Mirren said. "I know unequivocally that this is what my parents would want me to do. But I don't know how best to do it. And that's why I need you, if you're willing to help me."

Davita smiled faintly. "I've been waiting eighteen years to help you, Miss Mirren. But I'm concerned that you don't know how dangerous Peregrine Borgenicht is."

Mirren laughed. "I don't know how dangerous the man who killed my parents is?"

"I'm sorry." Davita blanched, her blush standing out against her pale cheeks. "That's not what I meant to say."

"I know it wasn't. And it doesn't matter. What I need, and what I would ask you to do, is to assess the political situation and figure out the best way for me to get involved. Should I run against Peregrine or try to sabotage him? Who else has a chance of winning and how can I support them? Do I need to come out publicly as the former princess, and will I get arrested and executed if I do?" Mirren tugged her earlobe. "And, if there's any way to convince Aunt Collena to let Katia join me in the World, I would like that. I hate thinking of her stuck back in the Hidden Kingdom. And I miss her."

Davita gazed down into her teacup, tapping one red fingernail against the gold rim. When she lifted her face, its color had returned, and she nodded resolutely. "If this is what my sovereign intends, it will be my honor to help her achieve it."

Mirren gritted her teeth, but they spoke a while longer, Davita taking notes on her tablet before departing. When she left, she took the tension in the kitchen with her, and everyone else began breathing easier.

Josh set her knife on the table and put four sugar cubes in her cold tea. "So, that went about as well as it could have."

"Yes." Mirren's shoulders slumped, and she pretended to sag with relief against Haley's side, which made him smile shyly.

Okay, Will admitted to himself. *They're kind of cute together.*

"Thank you all again for your help. I had no idea how nervous I was." Mirren threw back the rest of her tea like it was a much stronger drink, and Haley refilled her cup. "I realized, as I was making demands, that I've taken your support for granted, and I shouldn't have. I can't fully predict how much trouble my actions could stir up for you, and I don't want to make your relationship with your grandfather any worse, Josh."

Josh released a sharp laugh. "I thought I explained this earlier. My relationship with Peregrine is *over*. We aren't going to end up on *Dr. Phil* crying and hugging each other. I think he's a power-hungry monster who wants to control me—and," she added, catching herself, "everyone else. So if you need support with keeping him from grabbing even more power, I'm on board."

Mirren's reply was, as usual, diplomatic. "Regardless, I'm grateful."

Since Haley was obviously now on Team Mirren, Will supposed that meant it was his turn to decide where he would throw his hat. "Let me ask you a question," he said. "Josh told me that the monarchy shot down staging proposals for hundreds of years before the issue came to a head with Peregrine and your parents. She also told me that your family refused to give an explanation for why they wouldn't allow staging."

Mirren nodded, giving away nothing.

"I guess . . ." He wet his lips. "I guess my question is, are you sure you're doing what's in the best interest of the World and not just following in your parents' footsteps?"

Instead of taking offense, Mirren chuckled. "Allow me to explain as much as I can. Something most people don't know is that the earliest dream-walker kings and queens weren't heads of government, but of religion. They oversaw the seers, and since religion and science were tightly tied together back then, they controlled the knowledge of both dream mysteries—the spiritual elements—and what we call dream theory.

"One of their functions was the keeping of dangerous knowledge—because there *is* dangerous knowledge in the World, and in the Dream. Some knowledge must be protected."

Will remembered the terrible discoveries Feodor had made, the soul-destroying inventions, and he understood what Mirren was saying.

"With staging, the situation is such that if I explain to you *why* staging is so dangerous, I will be giving you the knowledge to make it far, far more dangerous. So I can't tell you why I have to keep staging from becoming standard practice. But I can tell you that—based on what I know—staging is one of the most serious threats to the balance of the three universes ever discovered. And that's more than I've ever told anyone, even my family, so I would appreciate it if you wouldn't repeat it."

Will believed her. She hadn't lived long enough in the World to be a great liar.

"Okay," he said. "I can live with that. But since I'm sticking my neck out for you, I need a favor."

Mirren tilted her head as if intrigued. Josh just looked confused.

"Four months ago, Josh and Haley and I had an encounter with Feodor Kajażkołski. It ended with him dead and a lot of people hurt."

Her gray eyes widened. "Yes, of course, I read about it. That was you three?"

"Yeah," Josh said. "And in case you're wondering, it sucked."

Mirren's lips parted with something like awe. "I had no idea I had recruited such powerful allies." She gazed at Haley, and it was apparent that she was as drawn to him as he was to her.

"What we need," Will said, trying to regain her attention, "is your help to save a friend of ours. One of Feodor's minions sucked her soul into a canister, and we need to put it back in her body."

That got Mirren's attention. "How did he suck out her soul?"

"Violently," Josh put in.

Haley, who had kept his eyes on Mirren throughout most of their discussion, stared at the floor then. Will wondered if courting a girl was harder when one's ex was wasting away in a coma.

"We don't know how Feodor did it," Will said. "From what I've discovered, he began developing the technique he used before he was exiled. The Gendarmerie probably confiscated his notes as evidence, then turned them over to your grandparents. Is there any chance his papers might have survived the fire at the palace?"

Mirren tugged her earlobe. "Feodor's house burned to the ground with his papers inside it the night before his arrest. However . . . he was the one who built the pocket universe where I grew up. It was meant to be a safe haven my grandparents could retreat to—I think they sensed that the tides were turning against them. Please don't spread this around, but they filed thousands of documents in an underground vault in the Hidden Kingdom for safekeeping."

"That must be a lot of paper," Josh said.

"It's massive," Mirren agreed. "I can't guarantee that any of Feodor's things from Maplefax are down there, and I don't know how we'd convince my aunt to let me leave once I set foot inside the Hidden Kingdom, but I would be glad to see if there's anything filed away that might be of use to you."

Josh crossed her arms over her chest.

"Then I'll do what I can for you," Will told Mirren. He raised his teacup. "Long live Queen Mirren."

"I've gotta go work out," Josh said, and stood up. "Let me know what you need when you need it, Mirren."

"Thank you," Mirren said, but Josh was already striding away. Mirren looked at Haley with a raised eyebrow.

"Not you," he said, shaking his head.

"No, it was definitely me," Will agreed, and he got up to go after her.

By the time Will caught up to Josh, she was already in the basement throwing punches at a rubber boxing dummy.

"Josh," he said. "I'm sorry."

She ignored him; sometimes she tried to avoid confrontation by literally refusing to acknowledge what was happening.

"Come on, talk to me."

"I'm busy," she said, and landed a spin kick so hard that the dummy rocked on its stand.

Before she could throw another punch, Will stepped between her and the dummy. "This will go easier on both of us if you just tell me how you feel."

Reluctantly, she dropped her arms and released her fists. "I just wish you would stop obsessing over him," she said. "It's . . . it's creepy! I mean, you have all these pictures of him and news articles about him and you spend hours every day thinking about him and you go to those meetings. And now you want to dig through Mirren's archives for *more* stuff about him? I think you need to . . . try to let go or something."

I can't, Will thought. *I have to . . .*

"We have to help Winsor," he said. "We have to undo what he did."

"Yeah, I know. And I'm completely on board for that. I just wonder if, once she's better, you'll stop."

"Of course I will."

But he was already imagining the future differently, and he knew he wouldn't stop until he had collected every known piece of information about Feodor and built them up around himself like armor, so that when Feodor came back—

"I just want things to go back to normal," Josh said.

Did she still think of the first six weeks of his apprenticeship as "normal" time? To him, the four months that had passed since their encounter with Feodor had redefined "normal," shaped the time before it into something naïve and full of unseen dangers. Sometimes he felt like he'd been living in the Dream since February.

"It doesn't work like that," he told Josh. "Things don't get undone. All we can do is try to learn from what happened so that we'll be better prepared the next time."

Josh hugged him tightly. "Will," she whispered. "Don't you get it? Feodor is *dead.* There isn't going to *be* a next time."

Nine

The next day, Mirren met Winsor.

Josh could count the number of times she had visited Winsor on one hand. She hated going. She hated the perfume of piss that permeated the nursing home, the false cheer of the nurses' scrubs, and, most of all, the silence of the patients.

Winsor's room was a little less depressing than the rest of the place. There, the scent of urine was somewhat mitigated by a vase of lilies and irises, and silver-framed photographs lined the windowsill. A rocking chair sat on a rag rug, and a patchwork quilt in blue and white covered the bed . . . and the patient within it.

Not only had Winsor lost a great deal of weight in the last four months, but her very skeleton seemed to have shrunk, giving her the appearance of a twelve-year-old. She lay on her left side, propped in place with foam bolsters, but her right arm hung awkwardly behind her, the fingers on her hand curled into a half fist. Her hair—cut short for ease of maintenance—was dull and lank, and her pale skin sagged. Although her eyes were open, they didn't register her guests, only gazed at the wall in front of her.

The sight of her made Josh sick. It made Will angry. But strangely, it brought out the best in Haley.

"Hi, Winsor," he said, and he walked into her line of sight. Gently, he rearranged her arm and straightened the sleeve of her flannel pajama top. "I'm happy to see you."

Winsor said nothing and gave no indication that she had heard Haley. Mirren glanced at Will and Josh, as if she expected them to follow Haley's lead, but Josh couldn't imagine talking to Winsor any more than she could imagine striking up a conversation with a department store mannequin. She went to sit in the rocking chair, as far from her friend as she could get. Will just stood at the foot of the bed, frowning.

"Josh and Will are here," Haley said, "and we brought someone new. Her name is Mirren."

"Hello," Mirren said, only a little awkwardly. "It's a pleasure to meet you."

Haley crouched down to look Winsor in the face. He knelt there for several seconds before rummaging around in the nightstand drawer and removing a tube of lip balm.

"Winsor is Whim's sister," Will said. "She's in a stage three coma; she goes through cycles of waking and sleeping, but she's never fully conscious."

"That's so sad," Mirren said.

"Her brain can hear us, though," Haley said as he carefully applied balm to Winsor's lips.

Will shrugged. "There's no proof of that, but if Haley says it, I believe it."

All Josh could think was how Haley had said "her brain" instead of "she." Because Winsor's soul didn't occupy her body; *that* was trapped in a canister at Willis-Audretch.

"She's been like this for four months?" Mirren asked. "I read about the attacks in the papers, but the reports were vague. They didn't say anything about what happened to the victims later on."

"They're all like this, or worse," Will said. "Except the three who died."

"Four," Josh muttered from her seat at the window.

"What?" Will asked.

"The little girl died last week," she said, casting a guilty glance at Will.

Will ground his teeth.

"What is their diagnosis?" Mirren asked.

Still angry, Will said, "Persistent vegetative states due to frontal lobe damage. The CDC called it catatonic sinoatrial dysfunction, but they've stopped investigating since new cases stopped appearing. But most vegetative patients make sounds, some even scream or cry. Some of them will follow objects with their eyes. CSAD patients never do. They never move on their own, either, not even in response to pain."

"Do we know why not?"

Will shrugged. "Ask Haley."

Josh shut her eyes. She didn't know if she was upset because they were talking about Winsor like she was an interesting species of fish or because Josh didn't want to talk about her at all.

"She's not really here," Haley explained. "Her soul is still in the canister. Without her soul, her body . . . it doesn't care."

"We have the canister," Will said. "It's at Willis-Audretch being studied, but they haven't raised any hope that they can free Winsor's soul from it."

"It's wired to explode if they mess with it," Josh added, staring out the window again.

"Even if they could open it," Will continued, "we don't know if her soul could just fly back into her body or if we'd need to do something to help it. But Winsor is lucky in some ways—the majority of the other victims' souls were in Feodor's universe when it collapsed."

"What happened to them?" Mirren asked.

"They're lost in the Dream," Haley said.

Josh twisted her fingers together, bending her joints in uncomfortable ways. If all those souls really were lost in the Dream—probably sixty or more—then Josh and Will and Haley were to blame. They were the ones who had killed Feodor, collapsing his universe and forcing the souls into the Dream.

"You want to see something really creepy, though?" Will asked. "Look at Winsor's eyes."

The tone of Will's voice disturbed Josh. He sounded bitter, but a sort of pleasure underlined his rage, as if it felt good to him to be angry.

He turned on the bedside lamp. "Look," he repeated to Mirren, but Josh couldn't stop herself from obeying as well. Will turned Winsor's face—gently, but not as gently as Haley would have. Haley himself stood pressed up against the bedside table, as if unwilling to leave Winsor's side.

"What am I looking at?" Mirren asked.

"Her eyes used to be blue," Will said.

A bold, bright blue, Josh remembered. Like lapis lazuli.

Now they were a charcoal color, a single shade away from black. A fine black web, as thin and sharp as iron shavings, stretched across the surface of Winsor's eyes. The whites were tinted gray, as though a fine layer of ash had settled over them.

"Feodor's zombies had eyes that were completely black," Will said. "It seems to be slowly happening to all their victims. The doctors don't know what it is."

Her eyes were so beautiful, Josh thought. Now they were damaged, just like the rest of her—the frail, thin limbs; the skeletal face; the shiny luster gone from her black hair.

"I'm very sorry for your friend," Mirren said. "I understand now why knowing as much as you can about Kajażkolski is important."

Josh stopped herself from laughing. No matter how much they learned about Feodor, they would never be able to fix Winsor. Josh had half his memories, and even she couldn't figure out what he'd done.

"There are seventeen—sixteen, I mean, other people just like her," Will said.

"Sixteen," Mirren repeated. She shook her head. "Kajażkolski was working at the cutting edge of dream theory, and scientists are still trying to analyze his theories. My understanding of dream theory is good, but if no one at Willis-Audretch can help you, then what you're fighting against may be something only Feodor could comprehend."

"All I'm asking is that you help however you can," Will said in a way that made Josh think he had just ignored every word Mirren had spoken.

"I will," she promised. She placed a comforting hand on one of Winsor's fists. "How old is she?"

"She just turned eighteen," Haley said. He'd insisted that the whole household go to the hospital and sing to her and eat cake.

Mirren marveled. "I never would have guessed."

They left a few minutes later. Haley kissed Winsor's forehead and promised he'd be back in a day or two; Mirren said a polite good-bye; Will ignored the girl in the bed and started down the hallway. As she followed them out, Josh heard Haley admit to Mirren, "Winsor and I used to date."

"Oh," Mirren said.

Josh had no idea why Haley had told Mirren that. Now that she thought about it, she had no idea why they'd brought Mirren here in the first place. Will had said it was to show her how much Winsor needed her help, but Mirren hadn't met Winsor before this happened. She couldn't know that the small, shrunken body in the bed had once been vibrant and beautiful, that the mind that barely registered on an EKG had been clever and sharp-witted, that those eyes clouded by the veil of Death had been capable of seeing through everyone around her.

All Mirren saw was a sick child in a bed. She couldn't know the friend Winsor had been to Josh or understand all that Winsor had lost.

The guilt Josh felt after seeing Winsor led her to begin work constructing the vambrace and circlet. Not because the devices could help Winsor, but because Josh kept recalling how the devices had filled her with complete confidence and power in her dreams. She wanted to feel like that. She *needed* to feel like that. She needed to save the next Winsor.

Sitting in the first-floor office a few days later, she was clicking through the online database of dream-walking-related articles for anything that might help her build the network the devices required, when her eyes caught upon "Possibilities for Continual Dream Monitoring" by Bashuriel Mirrettsio.

The name looked familiar, but it took her a minute to connect it to the man Will had told her about from the Grey Circle meeting.

Will said he won the Nicastro Prize, she recalled. *Let's just see what he won it for.*

She printed the paper out.

Although today the trimidion is considered the gold standard in Dream monitoring, at the time of its invention, many considered it a mere first step toward observation of turbulence within the Dream, the paper began. *Inventors of the trimidion lamented its inability to pinpoint specific areas of turbulence and its vulnerability to cosmological events. It is the author's purpose to propose a next step in the evolution of turbulence monitoring through the creation of an in-Dream trimidion broadcaster.*

Josh read on with interest. The trimidion was a very old dreamwalker tool—so old that she was surprised a record of its invention existed. A scale with three corners, it measured the amount of emotional turmoil with the Dream, the World, and Death at any given moment. Dream walkers used it as an early alert system that would inform them before the negativity in the Dream reached the point where it could rip the Veil between universes and cause nightmares to come pouring into the World.

Bash's paper proposed that trimidions be placed *within* the Dream. Each one would be monitored by a small computer that would broadcast—via radio waves—the degrees of balance or imbalance to a central computer near an archway. All a dream walker had to do was consult the central computer to determine which areas of the Dream contained the most emotional turbulence, then follow the radio signal toward the trimidion in the area where the most dream walking was needed.

The idea contained the hallmark of a Nicastro paper: innovation. Instead of expecting young dream walkers to be on the cutting edge of dream theory, the prize committee looked for ideas using available technology—often even technology considered out-of-date. Josh had never read anything that suggested using radio waves; she wasn't even certain they would act normally within the Dream.

The problem with the idea was that Bash lacked a method for anchoring the trimidion stations within with Dream. In fact, it was the same problem Josh had run into—

"Holy shit," Josh whispered.

Bash's trimidion station problem and Josh's cell network problem were nearly the same. She wondered if, in the years since he'd written this paper, he had come up with a solution.

She needed to talk to Bash.

 Ten

Ten days after Mirren's arrival in the World, Davita called her and said to plan for a dinner meeting that night. Davita discouraged her from letting Haley join them, but since Davita was bringing a mystery guest, Mirren felt justified in bringing a familiar one.

Besides, she was all awash in adoration for Haley. She supposed she should have felt threatened by seeing how tender he was with his ex-girlfriend—and she did plan to ask him his feelings about Winsor at some point—but mostly what she felt was admiration. When Winsor's own friends had treated her like a plague victim, Haley hadn't hesitated to touch her or talk to her, which Mirren found endearing.

The restaurant was cozy, everything covered in green velvet and gold trim, and the maître d' led them to a private horseshoe booth near the back, hidden from the view of other patrons by two curtains.

Davita and another woman were already seated when Haley and Mirren arrived. They couldn't easily get out of the booth to say hello, but the stranger offered her hand for Mirren to shake.

"I'm Anivay la Grue," she said. Mirren realized she should have recognized Minister La Grue as the leader of the Troth Party and a member of the junta, but the woman no longer looked like she had in the photographs Mirren had seen. She appeared frail and desperately thin, yet at the same time her face was puffy. Her copper skin had darkened, and when Mirren shook her hand, that also felt swollen.

"How do you do?" Mirren asked as she sat down, careful not to show her surprise at the minister's condition.

They made small talk for a while. Minister la Grue—who insisted that Mirren and Haley call her Anivay—asked Mirren a bit about her life, which made her realize that Davita hadn't revealed her other-universe origins. Then they discussed the Accordance Conclave and staging and Peregrine Borgenicht. Anivay was still a sharp mind, and she had a warm, easy laugh. She criticized Peregrine's politics but not him personally, which Mirren liked.

The third time Anivay had to stop speaking to catch her breath, though, Mirren felt she needed to say something. "Are you unwell?" she asked gently, putting her hand over Anivay's.

While the older woman struggled to breathe, Davita said, "Anivay suffers from polycystic kidney disease. In the last several years, it has rapidly worsened into end-stage renal failure. She has difficulty breathing due to the buildup of fluid around her lungs."

"I'm so sorry," Mirren said, genuinely saddened.

Anivay held up a hand, as if to block Mirren's pity. "I'm seventy-two," she said. "I've lived longer than expected already."

"Anivay asked for this meeting," Davita said, "because she feels that her declining health has reduced support for the Troth Party. No one wants to elect a president who might—" Davita stopped short.

"*Die*," Anivay said firmly, finishing Davita's thought. "That's why I want you, Mirren, to take over for me."

"Me?" Mirren asked, astonished.

Anivay took a few shallow breaths before explaining. "You're young and beautiful. Davita says you're well-spoken, well-educated. And you're against staging."

"But I've never been involved in the Troth Party."

"We believe you can win them over," Davita said. "And we believe that we'll lose fewer people than we'll gain when the Monarchist Party joins us."

"The Monarchist Party wants a monarchy," Mirren pointed out, "not a republic."

"We'll change our proposal to a constitutional monarchy," Anivay said. "That way, the Troth Party will still get its republic and the monarchists will still get their queen."

Mirren glanced at Haley, but he appeared to be thinking.

"So I'd be a figurehead," Mirren said. "Would I have any real power?"

"Enough. You would have the right to propose legislation and to veto any legislation that you didn't feel was in the best interest of the North American dream walkers," Davita said. "Granted, the latter power is one I would recommend you use sparingly, but it would allow you to keep staging from becoming policy no matter what anyone else wanted."

Anivay took a long drink of water and then said, "Miss Mirren, I don't know you. But I knew your parents, briefly, and your grandparents before them. They were good people, the best sort of people. They never forgot that, whatever their titles, they were servants. They did what was best for their people, not themselves. Even dream walkers who disagreed with them never would have risen up and killed them without Peregrine Borgenicht. The spin he put on their assassinations afterward made it sound like the monarchy's downfall was inevitable, but remember: It was a coup, not a revolution. It only took one man to set fire to the palace. I'm telling you this because I want you to know that Peregrine is your enemy, not the dream walkers."

Mirren had to look away because of the tears in her eyes. She wanted so much to be accepted, to have a people. . . . She wanted to believe that Anivay was right and that the dream walkers had never lost faith in her parents. She wanted to believe even more that her inevitable confrontation with Peregrine could be as easy and civilized as running a campaign against him. But an uneasy feeling inside warned her even as it urged her forward.

"What are her other options?" Haley asked.

"The issue is time," Davita said. "She can join the dream-walker community and go into politics from the ground up, but that will take years. She can join the Monarchist Party, but they don't have enough votes to win the Accordance Conclave. This is the only way I could find of putting her into power immediately."

"What if I fail?" Mirren asked.

"Then Peregrine wins," Anivay said, "and we're no worse off

than we were before. Mark my words, if nothing changes, the Troth Party will lose this election."

"Do you think he'll try to kill me?"

"Depending on how well you're received, quite possibly," Anivay admitted.

Mirren liked Anivay, and liked her even more for not mincing words. But she didn't want to die.

"We each have our own reasons for wanting staging stopped," Anivay added. "You don't know mine, and I don't know yours. But we want the same thing. Let's work together to get it."

She had beautiful brown eyes, dark as just-tilled earth. When Mirren looked only at her eyes, she never would have guessed the woman was ill.

This is her last chance, Mirren thought. *And maybe my only chance.*

"Yes," she said.

When they left the restaurant, the clouds that had caught the sunlight earlier had turned dark blue, not with night but with rain. Mirren's breath caught in her throat, and she walked slowly toward Haley's truck with her palms turned up to the sky. She jumped when the first drops hit her skin, giggling at the same time, and only when the lightning cracked above her head and lit up the parking lot as if gilding it with silver did she run for the truck.

"It's amazing!" she cried, jumping into the front seat. "It rains where I live, but there's no lightning, no—*ahh*!" The rumbling, grinding thunder hit her body with the pressure of a shock wave. "No thunder!"

Haley grinned at her from across the bench.

She fumbled with the controls on the car door but quickly discovered how to roll her window down. She laughed, giddy with the excitement of the air pressure, the sight of tree branches being lashed by wind, the abandon with which the raindrops dashed themselves against the windshield.

She stuck her arms out the window the whole ride home, letting the cold rain pour down on her and the wind whip her arms until her skin burned. Only then did she realize how much the conversation with Davita and Anivay had frightened her.

They know Peregrine will kill me, she admitted to herself. *They don't care if I'm a queen or a martyr.*

The rain was still pouring when Haley pulled into the driveway. Instead of going into the house, Mirren took off into the yard and the shelter of a large willow tree, and Haley ran after her.

Beneath the tree's spreading branches, the world was as beautiful as she had imagined. Darkness and water had turned the tree leaves a rich olive green, and she flung off her shoes so she could feel the rainwater squishing between her toes in the grass. Rain far colder than the kind that fell at home drenched her purple dress, and she threw her arms around the tree trunk like she'd seen hippies do in movies. The willow didn't speak to her, but she did find comfort in its unyielding steadiness, especially when the lightning and thunder shook her.

"Isn't this beautiful?" she asked Haley as he ducked under the shelter of the branches. "I love nature. I love being outside. And . . . I'll do what they ask, because it's my duty. But I don't know how long I have—to live, or maybe just to do things like this and not have any consequences. And there are so many things I want to do. . . ."

He smiled like he knew. He was shivering, too, arms wrapped around himself, even in today's pink-and-brown cardigan, so she felt justified in inserting herself between the sweater and his chest. To her relief, he wrapped his arms and the wet fabric around her.

"I want to help you," he told her. "Tell me how to help."

She hugged him tight. He felt steady, almost as steady as the tree trunk had. "Don't let me lose myself."

Somehow, she knew he smiled. "I can do that," he said.

She looked up at him. He trembled harder against her, but his fingers moved in small circles against her back, so timid and yet so bold.

This is a perfect moment for a first kiss, she thought, but instead of kissing Haley, she said, "Are you still in love with Winsor?"

He tilted his head. "No."

"If we put her soul back in her body, is she going to wake up and feel like I stole her boyfriend while she was in a coma?"

"No," he said. "We broke up almost a year ago."

"You broke up with her?"

He swallowed. "She slept with my twin brother."

"Oh," Mirren said. "Is that why he doesn't live with you?"

"He's dead."

"I should stop asking questions." She felt like she had tried to kill one hornet and instead woken an entire nest. "I think I should have just kissed you when the moment presented itself."

Haley actually laughed aloud. "We can wait until it comes around again."

"Thanks."

So they stood there, nestled in Haley's cardigan, his face turned so that he could rest his cheek on the top of her head, and slowly, they both stopped shivering. Mirren didn't know how long they stood that way or how long they might have gone on, but eventually the rain stopped and the sun reemerged, turning the dampness around them to glowing orange mist.

The next day, Mirren announced that Davita had given her the go-ahead to admit her real identity to the household. She asked Josh to break the news because she felt that Josh had the highest status of the three people who knew her secret, but almost as soon as she began speaking, Mirren realized she should have asked Will instead.

"So," Josh said without preamble, "Nan's really the lost dream-walker princess. Her name's Mirren Rousellario, and she's going to try to beat the Lodestones at the Accordance Conclave." Josh stopped to think before adding, "Deal with it."

Laurentius and Kerstel exchanged glances. Deloise's jaw dropped, then her mouth slowly formed an O. Whim gave Mirren a skeptical look and squinted, as if trying to recognize her. His father, Alex, slid off the couch so he could fall to his knees.

"No, no, please," Mirren said. "Not this again."

"The Avisharas have always been loyal to the monarchy," Alex proclaimed. "The safety and protection of our home is yours, my queen."

"Thank you," Mirren said, because she honestly didn't know what else to say.

"Get off the floor," Alex's wife told him. "You look like an idiot."

"I should have figured it out," Deloise said. "You look so much like your parents! I have all these books about them, I used to read them all the time."

"Wait, we're taking her word on this?" Whim asked. "Remember that chick who spent her whole life claiming she was a Russian grand duchess, and after she died it turned out the real grand duchess was rotting in a mine shaft?"

"No, no." Josh waved at the words in the air. "Davita's doing a DNA test, but we've already pretty much confirmed it."

"Wasn't she convicted of treason?" asked Saidy, Whim's mother.

"Um," Josh said.

"Yes," Mirren admitted. "And even though the conviction was largely symbolic, helping me could be considered treason. I don't want to mislead you on that point."

"Oh my," Kerstel said.

Whim reached for the phone with exaggerated slowness, and Deloise shoved him.

"You're not calling anyone," Deloise said. "She was a baby!"

"So? It sounds like she's going to try to bring your grandfather down."

"Do *you* want to see him stay in power?" Deloise demanded. "Because if you're rooting for the guy who tried to kill my sister to lead our government, I need to seriously rethink this relationship."

Whim released an aggravated "*Aarrggg.* You know I don't like your grandfather. You know I don't want anybody snuffing Josh out. But he's not the only person in the Lodestone Party, and I *do* support staging."

"So go vote for him," Will told him irritably. "Mirren running isn't going to change the fact that you'll still have a ballot. Just remember not to check her name."

"How about a deal?" Deloise suggested. "You keep Mirren's secret, and in return, she gives you a scoop here and there for your website?"

"Website?" Mirren asked. She hadn't had a chance yet to explore the Internet, but it was near the top of her list of things to experience in the World.

"Hell, yes!" Whim exclaimed, and then he explained about his blog, *Through a Veil Darkly*. "If I break the story that the lost dream-walker princess is alive, I'll be a legend in the underground blog movement."

"Oh, for God's sake," Saidy said.

"So you want me to . . ." Mirren said.

"Just give me a call before you go public. Give me a good twelve hours' notice so I can post an announcement. I'll run it all past you before it goes live."

Mirren shrugged, but she'd have to check with Davita. "All right."

And that was the end of Whim's issues with Mirren.

Whim's mother was less interested in the political implications of Mirren's joining the race than she was concerned about bringing Peregrine's wrath down upon them, which was Lauren and Kerstel's major fear as well.

"Personally," Lauren said, holding his pregnant wife's shaky right hand, "my only concern is for the safety of my family. You're welcome to stay here, Mirren, until such time as your presence endangers my family, and at that time I'll have to ask you to leave. And, as long as I'm making speeches, I might as well add that I'm sorry for what happened to your family and for my former father-in-law's part in it."

"The same goes for me," Kerstel added.

"Thank you," Mirren said. "I would never want to endanger your family, and I'll do everything in my power to avoid doing so."

The household agreed on a code of silence regarding Mirren's presence there, but Mirren didn't know how long it would last. Davita was anticipating bringing her before the junta in just a day or two. With the Accordance Conclave so soon, they didn't have any time to lose.

Somehow they still made it to Young Ben's barbecue that evening, though.

Eleven

Young Ben lived in a crazy cabin on stilts at the edge of a swamp. He'd built onto the cabin several times, with the result that each addition had made the building more ramshackle and sprawling, like an aboveground bunker.

When the Weaver-Avish caravan pulled up the mud-and-gravel drive, Young Ben was standing on the porch beneath the light of orange bulbs—the better to keep the West Nile mosquitoes away. "Welcome, friends!" he called.

Everyone tumbled out of the car, grabbing packs of soda and sacks of groceries. Will took a bag of buns away from Kerstel, who protested that they weighed less than her purse, and told her to be careful on the steps. Josh hiked a microwave-sized watermelon up on her shoulder, and they followed everyone else up the rickety staircase to the porch.

"Will, good to see you," Young Ben said as Will passed him, and clapped him on the back.

Young Ben, who was somewhere between ninety and a hundred

years old, had only recently begun to stoop. Always plump, he'd put on a significant amount of weight in the past few months, and now a line of hairy, pale stomach protruded from what Will was pretty sure was an original *Ghostbusters* T-shirt.

"Get the groceries into the kitchen," Saidy called. "You can say hello afterward."

Everyone ignored her and clustered on the porch.

"Abendirk Sounclouse," Deloise said, her voice excited and a little formal, "allow me to present Mirren Rousellario."

Mirren held out her hand. "How do you do?"

Ben clasped her hand between his instead of shaking. "Ah, Princess Mirren. What a genuine joy it is to meet you."

Mirren smiled, but stiffly. Will knew she was about to tell Ben not to call her princess when he went on.

"I had the honor of knowing both your parents and your grandparents. In fact, when I was born, your great-grandparents were on the throne."

Ben kept hold of Mirren's hand and beamed reverently at her. Will felt an unexpected pang of jealousy; over the last week he'd realized that, in many ways, Mirren was as much an outsider as he was. But here Ben was fawning over her, having only met her two minutes before, when after six months he still told people that it was "Josh's paper" up for the Nicastro Prize.

Will slipped past Deloise and into the house.

They ate an hour later, sitting around a grill built into the back deck so that it doubled as a fire pit. The food was abundant: hamburgers and hot dogs, potato and pasta salads, BBQ beans, ambrosia, chess pie, and Kerstel's own carrot soufflé, which Will thought he could probably live off of for six months or more.

"You can count on my vote," Young Ben promised Mirren. "Staging is an amoral plague upon the earth."

"What? That's a wild exaggeration," Whim told him, "and I say that as someone who's accused of wild exaggeration on a near daily basis. Ninety-nine percent of people who are in favor of staging want it because it could do a lot of good for a lot of people."

"And the one percent who don't?" Ben asked. "What about that fellow in France last year, the one who staged nightmares for his wife until she killed herself so he could collect the insurance money?"

"Obviously, that guy was just an asshole," Whim said.

"How did he find his wife in the Dream?" Will asked, curious in spite of himself.

"He built an archway in their bedroom closet," Josh explained. "After his wife went to bed, he'd sit there with the looking stone and wait until one of her nightmares came up. Then he'd jump in, dressed up like Death with the cloak and a sickle, and tell her she was getting sick, that she was going to die soon. Her doctors couldn't find anything wrong with her, but eventually the nightmares wore her down until she killed herself."

"That's awful," Deloise said. "How could he do that to his own wife?"

People are capable of terrible things, Will thought, thinking of Feodor, and suddenly he wanted to be away from this conversation. *Ben's right—staging is a plague upon the earth.*

Will went for a second serving of the soufflé and came back from the kitchen with that and a glass of punch. He didn't usually drink punch, but the liquid smelled unusually appealing tonight. As he sat down beside Josh on the cooler they were sharing, Kerstel said with surprising urgency, *"Will.* Which pitcher did that come out of?"

Will realized she was asking about his drink. "Ah, the pink plastic one. The glass one was empty."

"The plastic one has sangria in it," Kerstel told him.

"Oh," Will said. Sangria—fruit punch and wine. His brain flatlined; he didn't know what to do, so he just held the glass away from him as if it were an angry cat trying to scratch him. "Ah . . ."

The conversations around the fire died down for a moment.

"I've got it," Josh said, and took the glass from Will's hand. She jumped up and headed inside, and everyone started talking again.

Will didn't embarrass too easily, but he was glad his face was hard to see in the firelight. "I'm sorry," he said to Kerstel.

She reached out from her chair and touched his shoulder. "I wasn't criticizing. I just wanted to make sure you knew what you were drinking."

"I didn't," he said firmly.

But of course he had, hadn't he? He'd smelled the contents of the pitcher, but instead of telling him, *Booze,* his brain had just said, *Good. Drink that.*

He didn't doubt for a second that, subconsciously, he'd known what he was doing. And that scared the hell out of him.

His first instinct was to pretend nothing had happened, to go off by himself and find a distraction, to go home and work on his stalker wall. Yes, that's exactly what he wanted: to open his files and dig through the articles Feodor had written until he understood what the madman had been doing, how he could be outwitted, outsmarted, outfoxed.

Instead, he left his plate of soufflé on the cooler and went into the house to find Josh.

This is what girlfriends are for, he reminded himself. *Isolating myself right now is the worst thing I can do.*

In the kitchen, Josh was pouring the sugar water from a bottle of maraschino cherries into a glass of soda. "Hey," she said. "I'm making you a special drink."

"That's okay," Will told her.

"It'll be like sangria without the wine," she insisted, and he watched her mix cream of coconut into the glass. He was pretty sure she didn't know what was in sangria.

"It's fine. I'm not even thirsty. I . . . I'm kind of freaking out."

"It's no big deal. You just mixed up the pitchers."

"No, Josh, Saidy made sure to tell me which one had the sangria in it. I think I . . . I didn't realize it, but I poured the sangria on purpose."

Josh opened the refrigerator and hunted around, finally surfacing with a plastic lime full of juice. "You wouldn't do that. Besides, so what if you did drink it? You can have a sip of sangria. You *aren't* an alcoholic."

The room began to tilt, and Will grabbed on to the countertop. No, technically he wasn't an alcoholic. *Yet.* But hearing Josh brush off his fears frightened him more than pouring the sangria had. She didn't understand—he had to stay ahead of himself. One wrong step—one wrong *sip*—and it could all fall apart. *He* could fall apart.

Josh finished peeling a banana and stuck it in the glass. "Here. Drink this." She gave him a kiss on the cheek. "It's all good," she said. "Come on, let's go make s'mores."

She didn't notice when Will failed to follow her back outside. In the glass she'd shoved into his hand, one end of the banana rested surrounded by clots of unmixed coconut. Feeling at once panicked and numb, he carried the drink to the sink and poured it down the drain.

Josh had left the glass of sangria sitting on the counter.

Will poured that out, too.

He didn't want to go back outside afterward. He'd reached out for support and hadn't found it; now he wanted to be alone.

One reason Young Ben kept building onto the house, Will reflected as he wandered into the living room, might have had to do with his tendency toward hoarding. He had two complete sets of *Encyclopaedia Britannica*, a laundry basket full of wire hangers, a book called *Social Media for Grandparents*—although he had no computer—a cardboard box labeled "Blankets," and a display stand for pipes with only one pipe in it.

Will sat down on the couch. The clutter itself was sort of comforting, in a weird way, and he browsed through the mess on the coffee table. Beneath several stained pairs of pants, he found a photo album that must have been fifty years old. The black-and-white photos were glued to black pages, each picture smaller than Will's palm. The book was open to a photo of a beautiful young woman with a man who was a few years older than her, posed together on the porch of a house. She wore a plaid shirt and close-cut shorts, and the man wore high-waisted pants that showed off an infant beer belly. They were both grinning, and the woman had her face turned toward her lifted shoulder.

The pose struck Will. It seemed familiar, as did the woman's figure—

"Oh, my God!" he said aloud. "It's Dustine!"

The woman reminded him of Deloise because she was Deloise's grandmother. Will had known her for only a few months before her death, but now that he had identified her, he couldn't see anyone else. She even had Josh's chin.

If the woman was Dustine, that meant the man with her was probably Young Ben. This was, after all, his photo album. Will recognized him now, too—the height, the square face, the emerging gut.

I didn't realize they had known each other for so long, Will thought.

He peered more closely at the photo. Behind Ben and Dustine, a blurred figure moved inside the house, crossing the doorway at the moment the photo was snapped. The blurring was bad and the figure's face was turned away so that only part of his profile appeared, but if Will hadn't known better, he would have sworn the man was Feodor.

Ridiculous, of course. But he felt as if Feodor had somehow inserted himself in the photo just for Will's benefit, as though his ghost were infiltrating the edges of everything.

Will shivered, then chastened himself. As he forced his hand to turn the page, Whim, cell phone pressed to his ear, walked hurriedly from the kitchen to the hallway, cutting through one corner of the living room without noticing Will.

Whim loved that phone. He used it so much, he had to charge it twice a day. But something about the speed in his step aroused Will's suspicion that this was not a normal call from one of Whim's legion of friends.

It's none of my business, Will told himself, but he was already rising from the couch. *I'll just make sure nothing's wrong. . . .*

He followed Whim down the hall and stopped outside the door to Ben's office.

"I have fifteen people waiting on me," Whim was saying inside, "so this had better be pressing. . . . Maybe. . . . Is that what you think of me? . . . Charming. . . . Maybe. . . . If you want to see me, just come out and say it. . . . See, was that so hard? . . . Maybe."

The conversation went on in the same vein for several minutes. Whim seemed to be setting up a meeting, but he did a lot of arguing—the sort of arguing that's flirting at the same time—in the process. By the time he finally hung up, Will had a pretty good idea who had been on the other end of the line.

He was waiting in the hall when Whim emerged.

"Jesus," Whim said, stopping just short of walking into Will. "Where did you come from?"

"Was that Bayla?" Will demanded.

Whim continued to act startled. "Were you standing here eavesdropping?"

"Yes, I was," Will said. "And it's a good thing, because you seem to have lost your mind."

Whim stepped carefully around him, looking less amused. "She just wants to catch up."

"I thought that's what you two did at the Grey Circle meeting."

"I have a girlfriend. Bayla has a boyfriend. Remember any of this?"

"I remember that your girlfriend is more than capable of kicking your ass."

Whim waved the idea away. "Del couldn't kick my ass."

"You live on salami and Chex Mix," Will told him. "You're a paper doll."

Whim laughed and started back down the hall. "Well, this paper doll can dress himself. Worry about your own outfit, Will."

There was nowhere else for the conversation to go, Will realized. Whim was going to do what he was going to do, and there was nothing Will could do to stop him short of telling Deloise, and he really didn't want to do that.

So he went back outside and sat next to Josh, who held his hand. He watched Deloise and Haley teach Mirren how to make s'mores; Deloise's technique was refined, while Haley preferred to just immolate his marshmallows. He took Kerstel's side in the Kerstel-versus-Lauren baby-name debate.

He hadn't felt so alone since he'd left the county home.

Twelve

 the morning of her presentation to the junta. She'd called the day before as well, twice in the afternoon, once after brunch and once before, and several times the day before that. So when the clock in Mirren's hotel suite in the Dashiel Winters Building struck 12:30—the presentation began at one o'clock—and Davita had not yet appeared, Mirren's concern became grave.

"She's probably dead," Josh said.

"Josh!" Will, Deloise, and Haley all cried.

Josh, pacing the floor-to-ceiling windows, said, "It's a logical conclusion."

"Even I wouldn't go that far," Whim said. He was sprawled out on the ultramodern couch, eating peanuts from the minibar.

"She's not dead," Haley told Mirren.

"She hasn't called," Josh reasoned. "If Davita can't operate her cell phone, she's either unconscious or dead."

"Or she's stuck on the side of the highway with a flat tire and no bars," Will said. "There's no reason to assume she's *dead*."

"Peregrine knows he'll be blamed if anything happened to Mirren, so he's taking out a key element of her support."

"I can't listen to this," Mirren muttered, fleeing to the adjoining bedroom. She dropped onto the end of the giant bed and flattened her palms against the skirt of her blue taffeta gown to keep herself from tearing the fabric to shreds.

She loathed the gown, but Davita had insisted that she dress both traditionally and conservatively, and for dream-walker ladies, that meant floor-length dresses with long sleeves. Worse still, Deloise had fluffed and pinned Mirren's hair into a style that made her look like Anne of Green Gables.

Haley appeared in the doorway and leaned against it.

"What do I do if she doesn't show up?" Mirren asked.

Haley didn't hesitate. "Go anyway. You'll do great."

Mirren didn't know if she wanted to hug him or slug him.

A hard knock on the suite door made them both turn their heads. As Mirren rushed, skirts rustling, into the living room, Josh opened the door and said, "Oh. I guess you aren't dead."

"Where have you been?" Mirren demanded, and she heard in her voice that she wasn't just anxious but angry.

Davita ignored them both. "I need everyone to leave except Mirren."

"Why?" Josh asked.

"Leave," Davita repeated.

"Where are we supposed to go?" Whim complained, but he followed Deloise into the hallway. The hotel suite was located on one of the upper levels of the Dashiel Winters skyscraper in downtown Braxton. A dozen floors below was the junta's amphitheater.

Haley hung back, and Mirren told Davita, "It's fine, he can stay," but Davita was firm.

"Everyone leaves."

When they were alone in the suite, Davita threw the dead bolt and fastened the chain on the door. "What's going on?" Mirren asked. "Where have you been?"

Davita sat down on the couch and motioned Mirren to sit beside her.

"I'm sorry I didn't call this morning to tell you I'd be late. I couldn't, because I went to see your aunt and uncle."

Mirren straightened with surprise, then leaned close again. "You went *into* the Hidden Kingdom?"

"Yes. I received a package from your aunt with a summons and instructions for getting there. As you anticipated, your aunt and uncle are vehemently opposed to your plan. They gave me this, to give to you, in the hope that it will convince you to abandon your ambitions."

From inside the jacket of her suit, Davita withdrew a bulky linen envelope. She handed it to Mirren, who couldn't prevent a heartbeat of homesickness when she saw the royal seal stamped in orange wax on the back.

"They told me what it is, but not what it says," Davita explained. "They said there's also something inside to prove that it came from them."

Mirren began to open the envelope, but Davita grabbed her hands to still them. "No! Wait until I'm gone. If you still want to go through with this after you read the—what's inside, call my cell phone. If not . . ." Davita paused, and she squeezed Mirren's hands again, not in a forceful way, but as if out of sympathy or even pity. "I'll understand."

Then she flew out of the room.

Careless of the linen paper, Mirren tore open the envelope. Her family's seal cracked, ruining the imprint of a star tetrahedron.

A flashing piece of sparkle and a torn piece of parchment, folded once in half, fell into her lap.

The sparkle came from a brooch the size of a silver dollar, with a platinum star tetrahedron set against a gold field. The edges were encrusted with her family's gem, the fire opal, deep blood-orange stones outlining the circle. Except near the bottom, where one opal had fallen out.

Someone could have faked the piece, but they couldn't have known that—over the course of years of being treated as a plaything by two little girls—one of the stones had fallen out. Mirren knew for certain now that this envelope had come from her family.

She clutched the pin in one hand, glad for this small relic of home, and used the other hand to unfold the parchment.

If a queen she would become,
one of two things have begun:
a martyr's death to seal her ruse,
or lead to Death Dream Walker True.

Mirren read the parchment three times before balling it up in her fist and hurling it across the room. Then she stormed into the bathroom and yanked the pins out of her hair.

If a queen she would become . . .

"Absurd," she muttered.

The pins fell into the sink. *Plink, plink, plink.*

. . . one of two things have begun . . .

"An absurd, appalling scare tactic dreamed up by *pathetic* control freaks."

The last of the pins fell into the sink, and she briefly tried to brush her snarled hair before slamming down the brush so hard that the handle snapped off.

. . . a martyr's death to seal her ruse . . .

"Who has ever heard of a clause in a scroll?" she shouted, stomping into the bedroom and kicking off her shoes. "*If* I try to become queen, then I'll either die a martyr—"

She grabbed at the zipper of her dress, catching it on the second try and yanking it to her shoulder blades, where it stuck.

. . . or lead to Death Dream Walker True.

"Or what? Magically summon the True Dream Walker, and then kill him? It's *absurd!* It's a forgery! It's Aunt Collena trying to ensnare me again. If she can't control me physically, she'll control me mentally!"

Mirren jumped up and down, grabbing at the dress's zipper,

which had stuck in the most awkward, unreachable spot. After cursing aloud at it, she gave up, ran back into the living room, and retrieved the ball of parchment from under the desk.

She knew it wasn't a forgery. She recognized the handwriting of the seer who had written it; his name was Freigh Vescomballetti, and she had studied a number of other scrolls he'd composed. Her aunt might have torn it from a scroll other than hers, but how many other people had tried to become queen *and* had scrolls written by Freigh? The odds were too high to seriously consider.

At the sound of a knock on the door, Mirren folded the parchment and hid it in her sleeve. Through the peephole, she saw Haley standing alone in the hallway.

"Something feels wrong," he said when she opened the door. "I got worried."

Mirren stepped back to let him inside.

"Will you unzip this?" she asked, turning her back to Haley.

"Um . . ." he said, and only then did she realize she was asking him to undress her.

"Please. I would rather be immodest than spend another minute in this taffeta tar pit." She gained a small measure of relief when she felt the dress come loose around her. "I'm going to change."

She went into the bedroom and closed the door partially. After removing the dress, she changed into the outfit *she'd* wanted to wear to the presentation: straight gray slacks and a white silk blouse with sheer sleeves. Feeling calmer, she fished the scrap of parchment out of the dress and stuck it in her pocket.

When she returned to the living room, Haley was examining the brooch. "The *Anna Karenina* jewels," he said.

"Yes." Mirren smiled faintly as she took the brooch from him. It was one of the jewelry pieces she and Katia had worn while acting out scenes from *Anna Karenina*.

She ran her thumb over the brooch's face. How many times had she pinned this brooch to a nightgown and had "afternoon tea" with Katia, both of them sticking their pinkies out as they raised their cups, discussing princes who didn't exist and—inexplicably—

speaking in English accents? They had pretended to be princesses then. How cruel that the same brooch that had inspired so many royal fantasies was now being used to crush Mirren's royal ambitions.

Mirren held out her arms and Haley wrapped her up in his. She closed her eyes and just felt how alive and real he was—his body warm and moving, a field like energy rising off him to surround her. None of those tea party princes had ever been so real.

If she died, he would hurt. Maybe his heart wouldn't break to pieces, but it would at least ache. Mirren wondered if she had the right to risk his emotions that way. And Davita—Davita would be devastated. Mirren *knew* she didn't have the right to take chances with someone's feelings like that. And her cousin Katia—her heart's sister—would lose her only friend.

"What do you want to do?" Haley asked.

Truthfully, she wanted to spend the afternoon letting him hold her. But that wasn't the direction her life was pushing her.

"I want to tell the junta I'm here," she said.

"Do you need to change?" Haley asked.

"No." Mirren picked up the brooch from the coffee table and affixed it to her blouse. "This is what I'm wearing."

Realizing that her bid for queen was likely a kamikaze mission filled Mirren with a strange fearlessness. She had to slow her stride as she entered the amphitheater in order to keep from barreling into Josh, who was walking in front of her. Will and Haley flanked her sides, with Whim and Deloise behind them, and Davita brought up the rear, all of them wearing hastily donned robes in various colors.

Sound rose in a flutter of whispers and then stopped short, silent as Mirren passed by. Whim's blog had posted the news of her return the day before, but even he hadn't expected it to be taken seriously. Mirren allowed herself to meet people's eyes as she passed, giving them a serene smile no matter how hostile their looks. Most of them, though, appeared curious rather than angry.

Except for one man who spit on the floor near Mirren's feet, causing those nearby to admonish him and Will to unsheathe his machete. Mirren just laughed as she sidestepped the wet spot and continued toward the stage.

I'm going to get killed doing this, she told the man silently. *Your spittle does not frighten me.*

The amphitheater stretched endlessly upward like a dovecote, with rows upon rows of balconies and mezzanines. At the bottom, the ocean of audience broke around a raised circular platform. Josh stepped to the side of the stairs leading to the platform, allowing Mirren to ascend alone.

The platform's polished wooden boards shimmered like gold. Mirren kept her chin up as she took a seat on a single ottoman placed before the junta's seven thrones, and she folded her hands loosely in her lap.

She recognized all seven members of the junta from her studies. Of course, identifying Peregrine Borgenicht was easy, even before he leapt out of his throne in a sparkling green robe. Mirren had looked at hundreds of photos of him, starting the day her uncle pointed Peregrine out as the man who had set fire to her parents' palace. She had memorized the jumble of oversize features that made up his face: the giant, rheumy eyes; the red ears with lobes like hanging fruit; the thick, perpetually wet lips—all of them mounted on an undersized, bald head.

He looks like he's going to do magic, Mirren thought, taking in his sequined robe, and she had to stop herself from laughing. He was, after all, a dangerous man.

"Before we begin," Peregrine said, giddy with excitement, "I want to clarify what you want us to call you. Should I call you Lady, or Princess, or Your Royal Highness?"

Mirren didn't flinch. "Miss will be fine."

"Miss? That's odd. It is the understanding of this court," Peregrine said, striding toward her, "that you are claiming to be Amyrischka Rousellario."

"The court is misinformed." Mirren locked her eyes on Peregrine's and ignored the surprised murmurs of the onlookers.

"Is it?" Peregrine asked.

"Yes. To say that I am claiming to be Amyrischka Rousellario implies that I am asserting something that may or may not be true. Since I am, in fact, Amyrischka Rousellario, and have already proven such with DNA, my claim has already been verified. Furthermore, since I am not a princess of any existing monarchy, the most appropriate form of address is *miss*."

Be calm. Be polite. Be brief.

Davita's advice rang in Mirren's ears, but she couldn't follow it—not with the rage and the carelessness that were running through her veins.

"Well then, *Miss* Amyrischka, would you like to tell us why you're here?"

"To submit a proposal for a constitutional monarchy to the Accordance Conclave."

Shocked rumbling came from the crowd. Even Peregrine's eyebrows darted up—for an instant.

"A noble intention. But why would you think the dream walkers would elect someone who has been convicted of abdication of duties, betrayal of moral duty, and treason?"

Peregrine moved continuously. Mirren would have thought he was pacing except his expression was one of exhilaration and not anxiety. He looked more like he was an actor making use of every inch of the stage.

"Because I was convicted," Mirren said as amiably as she could, "in absentia, of crimes I supposedly committed as an infant."

"You're still a criminal," Peregrine replied curtly. "As of this moment, I am taking you back into custody in order to fulfill your original sentence."

The crowd filled with voices, but Mirren—who had anticipated something similar—said, "Beheading, wasn't it?"

"Yes." Peregrine's mouth twitched, and then he shuddered as if with repressed pleasure.

"Wait a moment," one of the other junta ministers interjected. Mirren was pleased, but not surprised, to see that the speaker was a middle-aged, dark-skinned man with glasses. His name was Ithay Innay, and he was one of Mirren's favorite ministers of all time. Although his deep thoughtfulness sometimes led to indecision, the stands he took were well reasoned and rooted in compassion.

Minister Innay stood up from his throne and motioned the audience to quiet down. "We aren't going to impose a death sentence on someone whose convictions were clearly symbolic. At the very least, she should be retried."

Peregrine smiled smugly. "I have no issue with that," he said. "Let's put it on the books."

Dammit, Mirren thought.

He'd danced her right into a corner.

Having pending criminal charges would make Mirren ineligible to submit a proposal to the Accordance Conclave.

"No," said Minister Speggra, a giant bearded man who looked like a cross between a biker and a Viking. Mirren held her breath despite her desire to appear calm; Speggra was one of the ministers Davita had anticipated would be against Mirren.

"We aren't going to waste time retrying her," Minister Speggra declared. "She was an infant, for God's sake! If she weren't a Rousellario, we'd laugh at the idea of charging a baby with treason."

As little as Mirren had been expecting Speggra to come to her aid, she got the feeling Peregrine had anticipated it even less. "But," he began with an actual sputter, "we brought those charges to ensure that no one could reestablish the monarchy—"

"*You* brought those charges against her," Speggra replied, "back when this council really was a fascist junta. I want a vote. All in favor of vacating the previous conviction against Amyrischka Rousellario, rise."

Five judges rose from their seats while Peregrine scampered to sit back down in his.

I can't believe this, Mirren thought.

"Then that's that," Speggra said. He settled back into his throne;

despite its size, the wood still creaked beneath him. "Ithay, tell them what we decided yesterday, when Peregrine conveniently failed to mention he was going to pull this stunt."

Mirren had forgotten how much Speggra hated "malarkey."

Minister Ithay rose.

"To clarify," he said, "no one is doubting Miss Rousellario's identity. However, because she has no experience in our current form of government and has been raised in hiding, outside the bosom of the dream-walker community, she will be required to pass Agastoff's Trials before her proposal will be accepted."

Agastoff's Trials, Mirren repeated in her mind. *I should have thought of that.*

Agastoff's Trials had been created to prove the worthiness of rulers who were either not of royal blood or only distantly related to royalty.

"For those of you who haven't read your dream-walker history, there are three trials. The first is the Learning, an exhaustive interview intended to test the knowledge of the applicant regarding our history, laws, culture, and traditions. The second is the Tempering. However, because no one has ever seen Miss Rousellario dream walking, we will instead ask her to prove her ability to dream walk by resolving three nightmares that the junta will select for her. The third is the Proving, a terrible task that will test the applicant's cleverness and loyalty. Miss Rousellario, do you accept Agastoff's Trials as a means for determining your worthiness?"

What could she say? Historically, she had little room for argument. Agastoff's Trials had been the accepted course for more than a thousand years. She could have argued over the modifications, but she wasn't certain she'd win.

Davita met her eyes from the crowd and shook her head.

Mirren knew that Davita would tell her to go on the defensive and demand to know what evidence they had that she wasn't loyal, well trained, and well educated. But Davita's main goal was to protect Mirren, even more than to see her succeed. She'd proven that an hour ago when she'd given Mirren the envelope from home. And what Mirren realized was that enough of this audience was against her that she needed to win their affection. If they needed to see her triumph over impossible odds, she'd show them that.

Or die a martyr trying.

"I agree," Mirren said.

Through a Veil Darkly

Interview with Princess Mirren

Princess Mirren was presented to the junta yesterday, amid gasps of surprise and the awed faces of those in attendance. She demonstrated phenomenal poise as Peregrine Borgenicht hammered at her and tried to reinstate her original sentence of beheading. (Good for Minister Speggra for calling Borgenicht out on attempting to use the legal systems to enact personal vendettas.) When the junta demanded that she pass Agastoff's Trials, not only did she know what those are, she agreed without complaint. No one else running in the AC is being forced to pass weird trials. When is the last time Peregrine Borgenicht even went into the Dream?

Today, she took a break from preparing for her trials to chat with me. Click **here** to listen to the audio of this interview, or read the transcript below.

Me: So, Princess Mirren, how are your preparations going?

Mirren: Really well. I'm excited.

Me: You have the Learning in just a couple of days. Are you ready for it?

Mirren: Absolutely. The Learning is the trial I feel most confident in, actually. My aunt and uncle were a little obsessive about my education, so I've spent a lot of time studying.

Me: How do you feel about the other two trials?

Mirren: I have to admit I'm nervous about those, because I don't know what to expect.

Me: The dream-walking trial seems pretty straightforward, but what about this Proving? What sort of terrible task do you think the junta is likely to assign you?

Mirren: I haven't the slightest idea. Historically, it could be anything. A lot of people think that Agastoff included the Proving in his trials as a way to veto truly unsuitable candidates. The basic idea is to test the candidate in whatever arena he—or she—is weakest.

Me: What are some previous Provings?

Mirren: Well, they've run the gamut from riddles to feats of strength. One man was asked to bring the head of his newborn daughter in a box.

Me: Ew!

Mirren: Luckily, he was a very clever man. He cut a hole in the bottom of the box and stuck his daughter's head through it. He actually ruled for some years.

Me: Is it true that legendary dream-walker wunderkind Josh Weaver has agreed to help you prepare for your dream-walking trial?

Mirren: Yes, and I'm deeply grateful. She's an amazing teacher. I'm learning a lot from Will Kansas, too.

Me: Has Josh made you do that Romanian circuit-training video?

Mirren: No. . . .

Me: Good. Don't let her, or you might never walk again. Well, that's all I have right now, Princess. We'll be rooting for you. Good luck at the Learning.

Mirren: Thanks, Whim.

Comments:

jlouston says: She forgot to tell him not to call her princess.

> BParKw2 says: That's because she secretly loves it.

>> Mari_Onette says: She told everyone not to call her princess when she was presented to the junta. She shouldn't have to remind each individual person.

sWord says: Rock on, Princess!

Byzantine_m993 says: In 1492, Agastoff's Proving for Paijenno Barikna was to sentence his own father to life in prison for selling DW secrets. I hope she gets something like that.

> Trewbador says: Make her admit to everything her parents did.

> Mari_Onette says: She's not her parents. Why can't people figure that out? She didn't even know them.

amynewhousen2415 says: She's so beautiful!

knight_of_darkness says: Shame on Borgenicht and the rest of the junta for laying the sins of her parents on her. She didn't even know them.

pratto391 says: Let's not go royal-crazy. This isn't Britain. Sure, she's hot, Borgenicht's not, but she hasn't proven herself in any way yet. Hold off on the unadulterated worship.

Thirteen

It was a beehive.

At least, Will thought it was a beehive. Wax hexagons formed the walls, floor, and ceiling, and they were thin enough to diffuse the light passing through them. In the center of the six-sided chamber, in an even larger wax cell in the floor, the light outlined a body curled into the fetal position.

"Assessment," Josh said to Mirren.

"Ah . . ." Mirren glanced around. "We're in a beehive, obviously."

"What are common associations with beehives? What do they represent?"

"Honey?"

"What's the source of danger?" Josh asked.

Mirren winced. "Unclear?"

"Where's the dreamer?"

"In the big wax cell in the floor? I don't know." Mirren tugged on her earlobe. "She's the only person here. Shouldn't we be *doing* something?"

"No," Josh said. Will—who had been her pupil for much longer than Mirren had—knew that unless Josh saw something requiring immediate action, she was more than capable of standing around dissecting the situation with no more anxiety than an audience member lingering in a theater complex hallway discussing a film. Will also knew how infuriating her calm could be.

Will was fairly certain that Mirren was dealing with some post-traumatic stress from having spent four days in the Dream. Josh had been training her for a week already, but every time they brought her into the Dream, her usual poise gave way to stuttering and shaky hands. Will was hoping that enough trips back into the Dream would act as a sort of exposure therapy to help her work through her anxiety.

Assuming none of the nightmares retraumatized her, of course.

As Mirren struggled to answer Josh's questions, Will noticed that within the cells that made up the walls, black shapes were moving against the light.

"What's that?" he asked.

"Bees!" Mirren cried. "We should go."

"They don't look like bees," Josh said, and that was when the first finger burst through the wax and toward them.

A field of fingers followed, popping through the walls like dandelions. They shot out of the wax in ones and twos, not just pointing fingers but digging fingers, fingers eager to escape their enclosures.

"What's happening?" Mirren cried.

Before another word could be uttered, the fingers freed themselves, and they were not only fingers but *hands,* hands that ended before they could become wrists. Some of the hands sprang from the walls to the floor, but many launched themselves directly at the three dream walkers in their midst, an avalanche of appendages.

Even Josh screamed.

The first hand that landed on Will grabbed his elbow and crawled toward his shoulder. He shouted and swatted it, but it held tight to his arm.

Then a dozen hands were clinging to him, climbing up his pants like spiders, grabbing hold of his hair, weighing down his shirt, digging nails into his skin. With his own hands, he tore at the vermin, but for each one he pulled off, another half dozen jumped onto him. Somehow one got a thumb inside his mouth at the same moment a pinky slithered into his ear canal.

He bit frantically at the thumb, but its fingers were joining it, forcing Will's mouth open and climbing inside. Another hand jammed two fingers into his nose.

They're suffocating me! They're going to choke me to death!

Josh shouted something unintelligible. Will stomped his feet and felt small bones crunch beneath his sneakers. Fingernails scraped the back of his throat, and he stuffed his own fingers into his mouth, forcing his jaw open to an unnatural degree, as he tried to get a grip on the spit-slick intruder.

Josh shouted again, and this time Will heard her: *"Lighters!"*

Only when he heard her voice so clearly did he realize that Mirren had stopped screaming.

He yanked his lighter out of his pocket and lit it on the first spin of the wheel. He held the flame so close to his face that he smelled his hair burning. One hand and then another dropped to the floor, skin singed pink, and Will stomped the life out of each one. He paused only to hook his finger around the thumb in his mouth and yank the hand out of his throat. He stomped that one really, really hard.

"Cough, Mirren!" Josh was shouting. "You have to cough!"

The hands—*They must have some kind of group consciousness,* Will thought—realized he was winning the battle thanks to his lighter, and they fled his body in an exodus of extremities. Together, they began digging open the cell in the middle of the floor where the dreamer lay trapped.

"Will!" Josh said. "Mirren needs the Heimlich! I'm too short!"

Mirren was in serious trouble, Will realized. A hand had managed to get all the way into her throat, and it was now too far down and too wet for either Josh or Will to extract. Mirren was swaying on her feet, her lips a dusky violet shade getting bluer by the second.

"I've got her," Will told Josh, wrapping his arms around Mirren from behind. Josh had taught him the Heimlich maneuver months ago, and it wasn't very complicated, but he'd never performed it on someone actually choking.

He made a fist and wrapped his other hand around it. Then he jammed his fists into Mirren's diaphragm and forced them upward—hard. So hard that he felt bad.

But Mirren coughed.

"Bend over!" Josh ordered, and Will released Mirren so that she could bend at the waist while Josh dug around in her mouth and finally tore out a squirming hand.

A buzzing sound made Will look away from Mirren, and he finally got a glimpse of the person in the floor. Mirren had been right that she was the dreamer. She was also a giant bee.

Her woman's body had sprouted thick black-and-yellow fur from head to hip, and instead of legs, she had a stinger with multiple razor-sharp barbs. Her eight-foot wings beat so hard that not only did they fill the room with a buzzing as loud as an airplane engine, they kicked up a gale.

She had domelike bee's eyes, too. And barbed antennae. And for some reason, a mouth full of dagger-shaped fangs. Will pulled the plastic compact out of his pocket and ran to the only doorway—a six-sided opening that led to an identical chamber.

"Josh, we need to go," he said, watching the dreamer rise through the air to hover near the ceiling. He used the mirror to reflect his lighter's flame into the doorway, and a rainbow shimmer filled the opening.

Mirren was still coughing.

"She just needs a minute—" Josh said.

The bee-woman turned toward them, and her buzzing intensified. Her stinger dripped a substance that looked like honey but sizzled where it hit the wax floor.

"Josh!" Will shouted. *"Now!"*

He'd never told her what to do in-Dream, let alone shouted at her, but it got her to look up.

"Holy shit!" she yelled, and she grabbed Mirren's arm and yanked her through the glittering Veil.

Will followed, and an instant later he tumbled onto the archroom floor. Beside him, Mirren coughed and cried simultaneously.

"Well," Will said, "I think we've succeeded in retraumatizing her."

They took Mirren to the kitchen to calm down. Josh made her hot chocolate, and then Deloise wandered through, and when she heard what had happened, she insisted on making Mirren a batch of her famous gingerdoodle cookies.

As Deloise was beating the butter and sugar together—and swatting at Josh's hand to keep it out of the bowl—the back door opened and Whim walked in. He looked at Mirren's white face and hunched posture and asked, "Do I even want to know?"

"Where have you been?" Deloise asked, turning off the hand mixer. "I couldn't find you."

Whim balked just long enough that Will knew the answer.

"I went down to the minimart for a KitKat," Whim said.

Sure you did, Will thought.

While the girls argued over the safety of eating raw eggs, Will said, "Hey, Whim, did you notice that scratch on the Lincoln's bumper?"

"Scratch?!" Whim cried.

"It's not long, but it looks deep. Come outside and I'll show it to you."

Will led him out the back door and down the steps to the Lincoln.

"I don't see it," Whim said.

"Forget the scratch. I made it up."

"What? Why would you do that to me?"

Will opened the driver's-side door and stuck his head inside the car.

"Do you know what that smell is?" he asked.

"Vintage luxury?" Whim suggested.

"Perfume. Which Deloise doesn't wear, because she has allergies." Will opened the backseat door and examined it. "Right here, we have dirt on the inside of the door."

"I'll get some leather cleaner," Whim said, but Will went around the car to the other side and opened that rear door. After a few seconds of looking . . .

"Hah!" He raised his arm triumphantly. "And here we have the smoking gun."

"I can't even see what you're holding," Whim said. His expression was decidedly unamused, and he'd put the uneaten half of his candy bar in his pocket.

"It's a hair. It's a very long, very dark brown hair. I found it on the seat on this side, which is where Bayla was lying while you two made out in the backseat, your shoes rubbing against the inside of the door and leaving that dirt because you're too tall to fool around in the backseat of a car, but you had to do it in a car so that no one would see because you're *cheating on Deloise!*

"And then you stopped at the mini-mart to buy a KitKat on your way home so you'd have evidence to back your story up, right?" Will slammed the car door shut.

Whim rubbed his mouth and chin with his hand. "Okay, all right, just . . . hold your horses for a minute. Stop freaking out."

"I'm not freaking out," Will said indignantly. "And if you think I am, then that tells me exactly how little you care about Deloise, because you ought to be freaking out over what you've done to her."

"Oh, my God, Will, calm down. Can you hold off your next nervous breakdown for five minutes so we can talk about this like reasonable people?"

"What the hell does that mean?" Will shouted, even as his mind said, *It means you're shouting.*

Whim threw his hands up in the air. "It means you've been so high-strung and judgmental lately that there's no point in trying to have a rational conversation with you!"

Whim turned and strode away across the back lawn, which stretched for several acres. Will was too stunned and hurt to even think of following him.

I haven't been judgmental, he told himself.

Yes, I have. But I've had to be, because everyone else is being so careless!

No, that's a ridiculous thought. Whim's right—I'm becoming really high-strung. I can't even think clearly.

He rubbed the back of his neck, suddenly aware of how tight and painful it was.

Everything needs to stop, if it would just stop for a couple of minutes, if I could just catch up . . .

The thoughts were coming too fast for him to keep up, and he realized he was actually holding his head in both hands, digging his fingertips into his scalp the way the disembodied hands in the nightmare had. He let go, cursing himself.

I can't think, I can't think.

"Will."

Will opened his eyes and saw Whim was standing in front of him, and the concern in Whim's expression far outweighed the anger.

"Will, man, what is going on with you?" Whim shook his head. "Let's talk for a minute."

Will silently followed him across the lawn to the run-down gazebo, where they sat on wooden benches with peeling white paint.

"Spill," Whim said.

Will shrugged. "I don't know."

"You can do better than that, psychology boy."

Will knew he'd meant it as a joke, that his friend was trying to lighten the mood, so he forced a tiny smile.

"I just . . . I used to feel like people needed to make their own mistakes and learn from them. And now I feel like I have to stop them, at least from making terrible mistakes, because they don't understand that— I don't know. There are repercussions for things, right? I'm just trying to keep it all together."

Whim listened to this shoddy explanation and then said, "But it isn't all falling apart."

"I don't know how you can say that. You're cheating on Deloise. Mirren's probably going to be assassinated. Josh can't even sleep through the night without waking up screaming. I mean, *somebody's* got to step in and fix things."

"No, they don't," Whim told him. "You're blowing all this out of proportion. Peregrine won't kill Mirren because everyone would know it was him. Josh needs to go see a doctor and get some sleeping pills or a massage or something. And I'm not cheating on Deloise."

Will gave him a look that he hoped conveyed a skeptical-bordering-on-scornful question. "Really?"

"I'm *not*," Whim insisted. "Bayla and I are just working through some emotional stuff from the past."

"With your hands?" Will asked.

"Don't talk about it that way," Whim said sharply, surprising Will. "Bayla and I went through a lot. We're still going through a lot. So, no, we shouldn't have fooled around today. But if I don't get her out of my system, I'm never really going to be able to *be* with Deloise. She'll never have all of me, you know? I want her to have all of me."

That's not how love works, Will thought, but he managed not to say it.

"Besides, even if I was cheating on Del with a dozen girls, it still wouldn't be *your* problem, Will. You aren't responsible for me."

"I know that."

"Are you sure? Because during that little demonstration back at the car, you looked a lot like my mom."

Will laughed ruefully. Saidy was known for her temper.

Whim grinned. "You feel a little better?"

"Yeah. I'm sorry I went off on you."

"It's okay."

"Really?"

"Yeah. I grew up with my mom *and* Winsor *and* Ian. I'm not afraid of the strap."

"You're so nuts, Whim."

"I know it. Look, about Bayla . . . If you feel like you have to tell Del, I can't stop you. And I'll try not to get pissed off at you. But all I'm asking for is time. You don't have to cover for me, you don't have to lie for me, I'm just asking you not to say anything, and I promise, a month from now I'll have Bayla out of my system for good."

I'm going to regret this, Will thought.

But Whim was such a good friend to him, and it wasn't like he was trying to make a fool out of Deloise.

"Okay," Will said.

Whim clapped him on the shoulder. "You're a good man, Will Kansas."

Will sighed. "I hope so."

ourteen

Mirren's kamikaze attitude vanished after she nearly choked to death on the hand. Somewhere in the back of her mind she had assumed that hers would be a swift death carried by an unseen bullet. One second she'd be talking, or eating, or laughing, and the next . . . nothing.

Her near murder by the hand had been the opposite: visceral, messy, agonizing. She didn't want to die like that.

The next day, instead of going into the Dream again, Mirren let Haley take her to the pool to teach her to swim.

Josh had been appalled when she'd learned that Mirren couldn't swim, even after Mirren explained that the only body of water in the Hidden Kingdom was a foot-deep creek. Mirren thought that the swimming lessons were a waste of time—what were the chances she'd need to swim in one of the nightmares the junta chose for her trial?—but she was glad to be with Haley and away from the Dream.

Tanith's outdoor swimming pool was packed with vacationing children, but the indoor pool was nearly deserted except for lap swimmers. Haley led Mirren to the shallow end, where she forced herself into the cold water. "I'm freezing," she said.

She was also very nervous about being in a swimsuit, although the one-piece she had picked out had come from what Deloise referred to as "the old-lady bathing dress" section. So far, though, Haley had politely refused to look at anything except her face.

Despite her attraction to Haley, he was not a good teacher. His patience seemed to be infinite, but he couldn't explain worth a damn. While teaching her to float, he kept telling her to "just lie back," but every time she did she went under. They'd been in the water less than fifteen minutes when she began to miss Josh's ordering her around.

Finally, Haley put his hands under her back while she stretched out, and she managed to rest comfortably on the water's surface—although she was fairly certain Haley was holding her up.

"Relax," he told her.

She tried, but it caused her to sink down, and only Haley's hands kept her from going under. "S'okay," he assured her. "You're okay."

After that, Mirren tried to keep her body rigid. The effort threatened to exhaust her.

All of this is exhausting, she thought. *Why am I putting myself through this when I'm going to die anyway?*

"Haley, have you seen my scroll?" she asked. She assumed that, at some point, he might have seen it when he touched her.

He hesitated, then nodded.

"So you know I'm going to die."

He looked away, and Mirren felt herself sink into both despair and the water. So he *had* seen it.

Then Haley turned back to her, and his face had changed. He looked older, more awake, and he straightened his perpetually slumped shoulders. "No future is certain," he told Mirren. "I know that better than anyone. And I'm tired of being afraid of what will come."

"Have you been afraid?" Mirren asked. "I never knew."

"I have been afraid every day of my life," he admitted, still moving her gently through the water. "I've been afraid of what I know, what I don't know, of trying to change things."

"How do you live like that?" She didn't mean to challenge him, but she had gotten her first real taste of fear these last few weeks, and she couldn't imagine living a whole life that way.

"I haven't. I mean, I've done nothing. I've been so passive. I've hidden. And people have gotten hurt."

She'd never heard him say so much or express himself so intimately. With a little thrill, she whispered, "Tell me about it."

His hazel eyes turned distant with memory. "I sat back and watched my brother fall apart. Maybe I could have saved him from himself, but I was so afraid he'd turn on me. And instead he hurt Josh, and he hurt Winsor, and then he got himself . . . Maybe I could have done something. I never felt like I had the right."

"And now?" Mirren asked, in awe of the ease with which he spoke and the strength that had come over him.

"And now there's you." He smiled, without ducking his head. "You're so strong. My friends—my family—it's easier for them if I'm weak, if I'm just backup. But you make it okay for me to be strong, too."

"Oh, Haley," Mirren said. She didn't try to hold back her tears; she wanted him to see how much she admired and adored him, and she was about to hug him when he held up his hands for her to see.

She was floating all on her own.

"I'm doing it!" she cried, and Haley laughed, and then she did hug him, hard.

Thank you, gravity, she thought, *for drawing me to someone who can both help me and be helped by me.*

Gravity had known what it was doing.

Three weeks after she left it, Mirren returned to the Hidden Kingdom.

Returning involved none of the difficulty or trauma that leaving had required. Mirren's family had two faithful servants who functioned on their behalf in the World; their primary duty was to procure supplies—food, medicine, complete DVD sets— and deliver them to the Hidden Kingdom, which they accessed through a special archway secreted in a furnace room. Mirren had never been allowed to know to where in the Hidden Kingdom the archway opened, and she was surprised to pass through and find herself in the stables. She had checked for archways there a dozen times.

"So, if you came through this archway," Josh said, "why didn't you come out in the furnace room? Why did you end up in the Dream?"

"Because," Mirren explained, brushing hay off her skirt, "this isn't the archway I found. There's a second one under a bridge in the woods, and it leads to the Dream. That's the only one I could find, so that's the one I went through."

"Wait," Will said. "Your family didn't tell you where either of the archways were? What if something terrible happened to your aunt and uncle?"

Mirren shrugged and petted the nose of her horse, Natasha. The animal sniffed suspiciously at Haley's hand but finally decided to lick it.

"Then Katia and I would have been stuck here forever," Mirren said.

She rubbed her nose against Natasha's so she didn't have to see the looks being exchanged behind her back. "I missed you," she whispered, and Natasha licked her hand.

"That was insanely brave of you," Josh told her as they left the barn. "I mean, to jump into the Dream for the first time by yourself?"

Mirren smiled and accepted the compliment. She decided not to bother adding that she'd had no way out of the Dream, since her aunt and uncle had never allowed mirrors or fire-starters in the Hidden Kingdom.

Walking with Haley behind Mirren and Josh, Will said, "I have to admit, I wasn't expecting a universe Feodor designed to look quite so much like Disney World."

Mirren followed his line of sight to the castle, and her time away allowed her to see it with new eyes, all peaked red roofs and white stone walls, guarded on all sides by evergreen trees and the steep face of the hill it had decapitated. They'd arrived just before dawn, hoping to slip in and out before Mirren's family woke. Beyond the castle, orange light encroached on the horizon like dust kicked up by the horses of an approaching army.

"It's huge," Josh said. "I didn't know it would be so huge."

"According to Aunt Collena, Feodor based it on Moszna Castle in Poland," Mirren said. With a grin, she added, "Except this castle has one hundred turrets, and Moszna Castle only has ninety-nine."

She had been the one to suggest they visit the Hidden Kingdom and look for Feodor's papers. She knew Will had been biting his tongue to keep from bugging her about it, and besides, if she was really going to die, she wanted to go home one last time.

She'd forgotten how steep and long the steps to the castle door were. Her legs were used to the discipline, and Josh seemed unfazed, but Will and Haley were panting by the time they got to the top.

"From here," Mirren warned, "we need to be very quiet." She wondered if she should make them take their shoes off—Aunt Collena was very strict about shoes in the house—and decided not to bother.

As she led them through the dark castle, noting how the gold and silver in each room caught the early light, she found herself wanting to stop and tell stories—the year they'd celebrated Christmas in the library, how Katia had once gotten stuck under a claw-foot tub while playing hide-and-seek, Uncle Fel's obsession with Post-it notes. How could she have had such a wonderful childhood and been a prisoner at the same time?

Too soon, they had to descend to the basement.

"This place is massive," Will said in a low voice when they were deep enough underground that Mirren felt comfortable turning on a light.

"It starts to seem small if you spend enough years here," Mirren assured him.

She led them into a vast carpeted room filled with row after row of red filing cabinets that matched the red-and-gold carpet and the pale gold wallpaper.

"Whoa," Will said. "How much do you have down here?"

"This isn't everything," Mirren said. "There are other rooms like this. But the files on Feodor will be in here." She took a basketball-sized ring of keys off a brass hook on the wall. "Remind me what we're looking for precisely?"

"Feodor's last manuscript."

Josh and Haley went to examine some of the gilt-framed portraits hanging on the wall, but Will followed Mirren into the stacks and stayed glued to her side.

"Do you mind stepping back?" she asked. "There might be things in this drawer that—that I shouldn't share."

Will frowned as he took two small steps back. "I need to know—"

"I brought you here, didn't I?" Mirren asked. "I think I've earned a little trust."

Will looked abashed. He took two much larger steps back. "You're right."

Mirren spent the next ten minutes digging through files, looking for anything relevant to Winsor's condition. "This is just Feodor's history," she told Will, feeling guilty for making him wait. "Do you want a transcript of his trial?"

"I already have one," Will said.

They moved on to other drawers and other disappointments, but finally Mirren saw a note tucked in a file on Feodor's translations: *For light harmonics, see file #8938007.*

Rising through the file numbers, Will and Mirren ventured deeper into the maze of cabinets and to the far end of the room.

One of the chandeliers had burned out above them, giving that row a darkened, ominous feel. Mirren hesitated before unlocking the drawer.

"Step back, Will."

When he had backed up a full yard, she turned the third key.

Compared with the other files in the drawer, the one labeled "Kajażkołski—Theory of Greater Evolution" seemed out of place. As she flipped through the first ten pages, she saw nothing on the same scale as in the other files. She was noticing mathematical errors while just leafing through.

"I think this is a manuscript, or at least part of it."

Will took the file as if she were handing him a premature infant and immediately carried it to an area with enough light to read.

Alone with the drawer, Mirren glanced through the files again. At the back was a thick collection of papers labeled "Staging."

She knew what the pages inside said. She knew that she was risking her life to keep those pages' secrets.

With a sigh, she began to close the drawer. Then her eyes caught on another file.

"Death," was all the label said.

Death? Mirren thought. *I don't remember a file on— Oh, wait.*

The key ring slipped from her hand.

Inside the file was the oldest known copy of a ritual, held safe in protective plastic. Beside it was an Italian translation from the sixteenth century, also enclosed, and beside that, a slightly fragile English translation from the early 1900s.

Would I? she wondered.

After reading the page through, she glanced at Haley. He and Josh were examining a jeweled trimidion in a display case, and he was wearing his little Haley smile.

What wouldn't I do? she asked herself. *If it means staying in the World, living my life, being with Haley, what wouldn't I do?*

Mirren removed the English translation, folded it into eighths, and tucked it in her bra.

Through a Veil Darkly

Princess Passes the Learning with Flying Colors

Princess Mirren appeared before the junta today and gave a phenomenal performance. Over four hours of questioning, she answered questions regarding dream-walker history, government, culture, and mission and proved that she knows everything there is to know about being a dream walker. Even Emfyte Kresskadonna couldn't stump her.

The princess again demonstrated remarkable poise, despite her voice becoming more and more hoarse as the interview went on. She even sang a few bars from *Opan Omgritte,* the only dream-walker opera ever written. (Who listens to that? I never have.) And who isn't impressed by a young woman who can actually understand dream theory? She even speaks fluent Hilathic! The junta didn't even bother taking a vote before declaring that she had passed the trial.

Comments:

Byzantine_m993 says: No one speaks "fluent" Hilathic. We only know the meaning of a thousand words in Hilathic, so anyone can memorize them and then call themselves fluent, when in reality they probably don't know enough words to have a conversation.

> 2400jokes says: She sounds stuck up. Just like Byzantine_m993.

>> amynewhousen says: She's not stuck up. She's just a nerd.

tetracycline says: I had this dream last night that I was a priest and she came to confession and told me she helped Webishinu fake his own death and she knew all along that he didn't die in the Dream.

babykim says: She probably DID know. Didn't Webishinu work in dream theory? Maybe she wanted to keep him quiet.

tetracycline says: I'm pretty sure she was in preschool when that happened.

Worchester_RWatson says: The Learning is the easiest trial, hands down. We'll see how much all her book-smarts do for her when she has to go into the Dream.

pouter40242 says: She wouldn't shut up! Shut up! SHUT UP!!!!!!!!

lochtess says: You all shouldn't be laughing. The Dream is a dangerous place, and the smallest mistake can be fatal.

jshg_hammer says: Go back to your loch, Tess.

Fifteen

Against the black-and-gray ruins of Warsaw, the brightly lit house stood out like a blazing beacon of hope. Both the exterior and interior walls were made of glass, so Josh and Feodor could stand outside and see straight into the cozy yellow kitchen, where a plump woman in a ruffled apron was trying to force her son's hands into a cauldron of acid.

"No!" the boy was screaming. "You can't make me do this!"

"Stop fighting!" his mother admonished.

At the kitchen table sat on older man, smoking a pipe and perusing a newspaper. "Listen to your mother, Caleb," he said.

Outside the glass house, Feodor chuckled. "The unquestionable wisdom of parents," he mused.

The acid in the cauldron bubbled and spit, and its droplets burned tiny wormholes into the white granite countertop.

Caleb's mother had bound his wrists with cooking string and was pushing him closer to the cauldron. "Afterward you can have a big bowl of ice cream," she promised.

Caleb's fear hit Josh like a chaotic crash of musical notes played all at once—too loud, too fast, too urgent.

"I have to save him," she said. She attacked the exterior wall of the house with a sharp side kick, but the glass barely reverberated.

"Do you?" Feodor asked.

His placid, amused expression confused her. "Of course I do."

"You're certain?"

She couldn't figure out what he was asking. How could she not save this boy from having his hands burned off? How was that even an option?

"But how will I play the piano with no hands?" Caleb wailed.

"You won't," his mother replied. "Won't that be a relief? No more arpeggios."

"No more paying for lessons," Caleb's father added. "No more paying to get the damn thing tuned every six weeks. No more Bach."

"Amen to that," Caleb's mother agreed.

Feodor continued to look at Josh as if waiting for an answer. Holding her eyes, he gestured silently to a wooden table sitting outside the house. A black velvet cloth had been spread over the tabletop, showcasing the harsh metal forms of the circlet and vambrace.

"I thought you said I shouldn't use them," Josh told him.

"Did I?" Feodor pondered.

Caleb's mother had succeeded in forcing him close enough to the cauldron that splashes of acid were nipping at his skin. "It burns!" he wailed.

Josh stroked the circlet. The metal felt unnaturally cold to her, and the idea of pressing such frigidity against her skin made her hesitate to put on the devices.

But Caleb screamed as the acid burned his fingertips, and the terror in his voice gave Josh the courage she needed to clamp the vambrace around her forearm. Immediately, the metal warmed against her skin. When she slipped the circlet around her head, a sensation of relief ran down her scalp. She aimed her arm at the glass house, and the power streamed into her hand like molten pleasure. Her mind expanded, beyond her skull, beyond the Dream, beyond space and time. From there, from God's point of view, she knew everything.

"It feels good, no?" Feodor asked, tracing the metal hinges with his fingertips. "So very, very good."

Josh couldn't deny that it did. With a thought, she slammed a lid over the cauldron, sealing it tight against the acid.

"No!" cried Caleb's mother, staring at Josh through the glass wall. "You don't understand!"

But Josh knew everything. She felt everything. Her wisdom swept through her, unimpeachable. She would sit in judgment of the whole world.

With dancing fingers, she manifested a long strip of duct tape over the mother's mouth.

Caleb tore away from the woman with a gleeful shout and ran to the piano in the living room as the strings that bound his wrists fell away.

"You know what is best for them," Feodor assured Josh. "Your field of vision is so much wider than theirs."

"Yes," Josh whispered as her thoughts bound Caleb's parents in splendid, weblike shrouds.

Caleb flung open the piano cover and began playing even before he sat down. "Poland has not yet perished!" he sang.

Josh barely recognized the tune. Caleb had rearranged it, changed its pace and key so that instead of the strident, honorable anthem Josh knew so well, what emerged from the piano was a mocking two-step fit only for a honky-tonk bar.

Feodor hissed through his teeth, and the piano lid slammed down on Caleb's wrists. Josh heard bones break beneath Caleb's rending scream, and she shook her vambraced arm at the house, but nothing happened. She thrust again, slamming her hand against the glass wall, directing her thoughts . . . nothing.

The devices had abandoned her.

The piano lid flew back up and sucked in Caleb's arms up to the elbows, the black and white keys chomping at his flesh.

With a desperate cry, Josh resorted to beating on the glass exterior of the house. Caleb screamed as the piano pulled him in, rivulets of blood running down the keyboard, and from the kitchen, his bound and helpless parents watched as the instrument devoured their child.

And Feodor laughed and laughed.

Josh turned on him, but before she could summon the power of her thoughts, he kissed the tip of her nose.

"Your wisdom," he said. "All yours."

In the morning, Josh called Bash Mirrettsio. She was anxious—anxious and hiding in the garage, where no one was likely to overhear her—but Bash sounded delighted to hear from her and not at all surprised. When she said she was hoping to discuss his Nicastro paper, he was even more delighted and invited her to his office the next day.

Josh had only been planning a phone call, but his office at Willis-Audretch was in downtown Braxton, and coincidentally, Mirren would be in Braxton at the same time, meeting with Anivay la Grue. The only difficulty lay in finding an excuse to go without taking Will. Finally, she told him that the elbow she had broken in February had been bothering her recently, and she was going to Braxton to see her orthopedist. Will offered to come along anyway—him being a good boyfriend—but she assured him that the trip would be boring and not worth his time.

It was easily the biggest lie she had ever told him.

When Josh walked into the lobby of Willis-Audretch, the World's only dream-walker think tank and research center, her knees weakened.

Feodor's memories bloomed in her mind, like a gray tint coloring everything she saw. Yes, the décor had changed, the reception desk was in a different place, and a metal detector had been installed, but she *recognized* this place and the bones of the building.

Not me, Josh thought. *Feodor.*

"Ma'am?" the man at the receptionist's desk asked. "May I help you?"

She gave her name at the desk, then paced the waiting area, and only a few minutes later, Bash appeared. He was both nerdier and better-looking than Josh had expected. His blue pants clashed with his red-and-brown shirt, and they all clashed with his orange tie, which he'd obviously yanked on a few times, but none of that distracted from his crow-black hair or the bright smile that revealed tidy square teeth. Despite his classic good looks, Josh couldn't get past his white Velcro sneakers.

As they headed up to his office, Bash made small talk without Josh's help, which worked well since she was too overwhelmed to carry on a conversation. Everywhere she looked, she saw not only the modern reality, but the past superimposed over it: doors painted two colors, floors with two different carpets, even two different series of creaks in the elevator.

Josh began to feel a sort of dread as they passed through the door labeled "Applied Physics Department." Her shoulders sagged when they entered Bash's office without disturbing the door to room 327, which Feodor had unlocked every morning when he came into work. Josh didn't know if she felt relieved or disappointed.

"Help yourself," Bash said. "I'm sure there's a pot in the break room."

Josh blinked at him. "What?"

"You said you wanted coffee, right?"

No, she had turned over her shoulder and barked, "Cree, where's my coffee?" just like Feodor had done every single time he'd come in to work.

This confusion resulted in Josh ending up sitting in front of Bash's desk with a large mug of coffee, which she didn't drink and had doctored into a warm milkshake.

"So, as I mentioned, I loved your paper," Bash told her. "Particularly the part where you performed your experiment without any sort of supervision or permission. Sometimes I think that the Nicastro encourages young people to get into trouble."

Bash laughed. Josh made herself smile again.

"I'll be frank," he said. "You look anxious. What did you want to talk about?"

Josh swallowed; the drink did nothing to relieve the bitter taste in her mouth. Reluctantly, she opened the manila envelope she'd brought along and drew out a handful of pages. "I was reading your paper, and you talked about using trimidions to monitor the state of the Dream at various points, then sending radio signals back to a central location."

Bash nodded, apparently unsurprised that she had followed the paper.

"I've—" She struggled with the first word, since it wasn't quite a truthful one. "I've been working on sort of the opposite idea, that a central device could broadcast signals to various points within the Dream."

His aristocratic brow furrowed. "To what purpose?"

"Well," Josh stumbled again. Somehow she had been hoping to avoid telling him *why* she wanted to do this. "I've been . . . I mean, it might be possible to . . . The central problem is how to create fixed broadcasting points on the surface of the Dream, since it's constantly expanding and contracting."

Bash didn't protest the leap in topics. "Which is exactly why nothing in my original paper has proven applicable. We'd need to place trimidions throughout the Dream at fixed locations, so that we'd be able to know exactly where the signals were coming from. But the Dream is always changing shape, like . . ."

"The sea," Josh suggested.

"A sea without a bottom. How can you fix something to the surface of the sea?"

Josh fiddled with the papers, not sure which ones to show him.

"What if . . . we could change the polarization of Dream particles to prevent them from shifting?"

For the first time, Bash seemed surprised.

"That would be quite an accomplishment. That isn't actually what you're working on, is it?"

Josh pushed forward one of the pages she'd torn from her sketchbook. Bash immediately drew it toward himself.

"What is this?" he asked, but then he began reading and stopped asking questions. Josh anxiously checked over the calculations again, once grabbing a pen to scratch out a couple of words in Polish, hopefully before Bash noticed them.

"Where's the rest of this?" Bash asked, the lighthearted tone in his voice gone.

Josh showed him the next page.

For the next forty minutes, he read, sometimes tapping the equations with a capped pen as he worked through them in his mind. Finally, he sat back in his chair and blew out a long, marathon-runner breath.

"This is mind-blowing," he said. His voice was very serious. "You wrote this?"

Josh hesitated before nodding.

"How? I mean no offense, but your Nicastro paper wasn't anywhere near this. Who have you been studying with?"

Josh squirmed in her chair. "I haven't been studying with anyone. I've just been reading a lot."

Bash wasn't buying it. "I find that impossible to believe."

She was going to have to tell him *something*. "You probably heard that I had a run-in with Feodor Kajażkołski a few months ago."

"Yes, I did hear that. You're telling me that this is his work?"

That would make more sense, wouldn't it? Josh thought.

She'd considered telling Bash at least part of the truth. The problem was, if she admitted she had gotten her ideas from Feodor, how would she explain when she kept coming up with new ones?

"No, the work is mine. But I hit my head while I was in his

universe. I fractured my skull really badly, and since then . . . I've been thinking differently. Dream theory just sort of makes sense to me now." She tried to give Bash a light smile, like it was no big deal. "My dad's really confused about why my grades have improved so much."

That part, at least, was true. She'd been accused of cheating twice in the last months of her junior year, and she'd resorted to taking proctored Saturday exams to prove herself.

"I bet," Bash said. He flipped through the sketchbook again. "I would have been surprised if you had said this was Feodor's work. It's too orderly, too much hard science."

She smiled for real then, even as she wondered what Bash's comment might imply. Were Feodor's ideas being filtered in some way as they passed through her brain, altered and made more orderly, possibly even less dangerous?

"I didn't get the impression he was a super orderly person," she said.

"What *was* your impression of him?" Bash asked, looking up at her.

No one had asked Josh the question that way, but the answer poured out of her mouth before she could give it a thought. "I think he was a luminary whose light was distorted by the shadow of evil."

Where had *that* come from? Was that how Feodor saw himself? Josh had never said anything so poetic. She added, to break the strange tension she'd created, "What did the monarchy say before they exiled him? That his genius was matched only by his madness?"

"I hadn't heard that one." Bash gave himself a little shake. "Unfortunately, if we come back to this brilliant work you've written, we're faced with a problem that perhaps only Feodor could have solved. How are you going to stabilize the Dream particles in their new polarity?"

"I was hoping that was where you could come in."

"Flattering." He tapped the pages with his capped pen and thought. "Give me a while to work on it."

"I would be grateful if you would."

"I'm excited, honestly. I haven't seen anything like this since— I don't think I've ever seen anything like this. May I keep these pages?"

Josh nodded after a pause. "I'd appreciate it if you wouldn't show them to anyone else, though."

Reluctantly, he said, "It's a temptation, but I'll respect your wishes. I wouldn't want anyone showing my work around before it was ready."

"Thanks."

As she stood up, though, he added, "Josh. You must realize the implications of what you've created."

Suddenly she felt his excitement, not just at the ideas she had given him, but at the thrill of this secret.

"If you could build this machine and find a way to anchor transmitters in the Dream, you could transform Dream particles in any way you wanted. You could alter the Dream."

Josh swallowed. She knew only too well.

"Let's not get ahead of ourselves," she said. "One step at a time."

By the time she reached the elevator, she was trembling.

Sixteen

Long after everyone else had gone to bed, Will remained sitting at the desk in front of his stalker wall, trying to put together the pieces of Feodor's last manuscript.

Combining the copies from Mirren's archive with the four copies of the manuscript the presenter at the Grey Circle meeting had given Will, he had seven total copies. None of them were complete individually, but put together they appeared to make a whole manuscript.

Except . . . When Will went to check a page number on the last page of one manuscript to see how much it overlaped with another, he noticed that the last words were different on what should have been identical pages.

Maybe one is a revised copy, he thought, but he lacked the knowledge of dream theory to make heads or tails of either version. Instead, he reexamined all the copies he had, page by page, to make a list of places where they diverged.

The longer the list became, the more certain Will felt that the discrepancies had nothing to do with revision. He was still poring over the pages, trying to make sense of the words, when Mirren came downstairs in a green silk pajama set.

"Oh, hello," she said. "I thought everyone had gone to bed."

"So did I. Trouble sleeping?"

"I'm nervous about tomorrow."

The next day was her dream-walking trial.

She perched on the corner of Will's desk. "I'd never been nervous before I came to the World. I had nothing to be nervous about. Now I'm finding that I don't like it very much."

"No one does," Will agreed.

"I keep wondering what nightmares the junta will pick, and if I'll have any idea what to do when I face them. I know that if I can just get over the hump of figuring out an approach . . ."

Will decided not to tell her that after six months of training with Josh, he was still learning the same thing. Instead, he said, "Why don't we go pull up some nightmares in the archway, and we can toss ideas around about how to approach them? We can't go into the Dream, of course, but—"

"I would be extremely grateful," Mirren said. "Would you mind?"

"Not at all. Playing the teacher instead of the apprentice is sort of fun." He started to rise and then realized the opportunity he was passing up. "Oh, wait, before we do that, could you take a look at these copies of Feodor's last manuscript?"

He explained to her about the numerous versions of the text, and she pulled up a chair beside his so that she could examine the pages more closely.

"How much dream theory do you know?" Will asked.

"Quite a bit. Of course, that in no way means I'll be able to read this. I've read some of Kajażkołski's earlier work, and it always took me hours to parse it out." She read over a page of which they had four copies. "This doesn't even sound like his other work. And the first paragraphs on these two versions are the same, but the equation that follows them is radically different."

"Are either of them right?" Will asked.

Mirren required a calculator and scrap paper to figure it out. "I don't think so. This one is pure nonsense. But . . ." She tapped some more. "The second equation is much better, but it only fits with the explanation given on this Xeroxed copy over here."

"So you're saying that none of these pages make sense by themselves, but if you take parts of each one and fit them together, they start to make sense?"

"They might," Mirren said. She copied out the explanation and the equation it referenced onto a new sheet of paper, then two more paragraphs—from different copies—and another equation from yet another source. "Now *this* makes sense. This I could believe Kajażkołski wrote."

"What does it say?"

"It talks about evidence of the subtle body in our DNA. The subtle body is what he called—"

"The soul, I know. The part of us that enters the Dream universe when we sleep."

"Some people prefer to think of it as our consciousness. He says that our consciousness is present in our DNA, and he's written an equation to measure the subtle body's vibration based on DNA content. He compares how our souls function to our ability to see stars. When the sun sets, you can see the stars, but the stars are always there regardless of whether or not they're visible. He thought that when the body dies, part of the soul remains in the DNA."

She frowned. "I shouldn't have said this made sense. 'Reads coherently' would have been a better description."

"You don't believe in souls?"

"I do, but what does he mean by saying that our souls can be found in our DNA? There's a passage here about how if your arm gets cut off, your consciousness is still attached to your arm. This equation at the bottom of the page appears internally consistent, but I have no idea what it does." She shuffled through the pages, seeming to grow more frustrated. "Sorting all this out will take days."

Will felt reluctant to let the subject drop, but he knew Mirren needed to focus on her dream-walking trial.

"Well, we aren't going to manage it tonight," Will said. "Let's go watch some nightmares."

Mirren nodded, the relief plain in her face.

The archroom was cold this late at night. Whim and his father were on nightmare duty, and Will fetched a second chair so that he and Mirren could sit comfortably and watch through the arch as a kitchen tried to eat their friend and his dad. Will attempted to provide some educational commentary, but most of the time he was pretty sure Whim had no sort of plan at all.

When the nightmare ended, Whim and his father left Will and Mirren alone to work the looking stone. "Less than an hour, we promise," Will said, knowing that the middle of the night wasn't a great time for dream walkers to go on break.

"No rush—I'm famished," Whim said as he left.

Will pressed his hand to the looking stone and enjoyed the eerie sensation that the powdered red glass was pushing back against his palm. Touching the looking stone activated the archway and caused a section of the Dream to appear within the archway's confines. The first nightmare to pop up within the archway involved a gunfight on a small fishing boat.

"So I guess the first thing I'd do," Will said, "is make sure I know who the dreamer is. And then I'd try to distract the dreamer away from the guns. I'd say, 'I found it!' or, 'This way!' so they'd think I had something they needed or I'd found an escape route. But Josh says I try to influence dreamers too often."

"That's because you're better at it than she is," Mirren said, making Will glance at her.

"Am I? I guess I am." Even though he knew Mirren was right, the comment unsettled him. "It's not that Josh doesn't want me to be good at things—"

"I didn't mean to imply that."

"It's just, she gets anxious when I use tools she's not sure will work."

Perhaps because he was thinking about Josh while he had a hand on the looking stone, or perhaps just by chance, Josh appeared through the archway.

"Will," Mirren said, her voice somehow different from before.

Josh stood on a battleground, surrounded by half-creature soldiers, and black smoke streaked the poppy-red sky above her. She wore a smoldering, blackened ball gown, something she never would have donned in real life, and she looked on as the goblin-men around her fought one another. They were not so much two armies against each other as just a sea of writhing enemies fighting only for themselves.

Feodor stood beside Josh. He was younger than he had been in his universe, but Will still recognized him. His brown pants and white shirt were the only tidy things in sight. He stood next to Josh with his hands by his side, a smile playing over his lips like sunlight.

"Is that . . ?" Mirren asked.

Feodor stepped up behind Josh, and he slipped those small, clean hands around her waist. As he slid them up her sides, she raised her arms, and Will saw some sort of contraption on her left arm from wrist to elbow, a strange metal brace or piece of armor. It reflected the red sky, and a similar reflection made him notice that she wore a metal crown, hanging down low over the back of her neck.

She raised her arms above her head, and Will stumbled out of his chair, revolted at the sight of Feodor sliding his hands up Josh's body. She opened her mouth; her jaws were full of gnashing fangs, and she released a roar that could have been in either Polish or Demonic.

No, Will thought.

Josh flung out her machined arm, and black fire erupted from her palm. The bolt reached for miles, burning the warring creatures to cinders and charring the earth. She cast her fire as far as Will could see, releasing a triumphant roar, and as she scorched life from the earth, Feodor brushed her hair away so that he could trace the back of her neck with his tongue, his arms clutching her close, his hands cupping—

The Veil popped.

In the silence afterward, Will realized that the dream hadn't ended, he had just broken contact with the looking stone long enough that the archway had let go of that particular nightmare.

"Will," Mirren said, but he couldn't look at her. She touched his shoulder. "I'm sorry," she told him, and then she just stood there, the weight and heat of her hand growing on his shoulder.

Will waited for himself to react. He knew there were any number of psychologically legitimate responses, and he waited to see which one he would experience, but oddly what he thought was that he finally understood why Haley was so enamored with Mirren. She didn't obfuscate or distract, she didn't avoid or pretend, she just told the truth and faced what was ahead of her. And for a guy like Haley, who couldn't help seeing the truth when he touched someone, that must have been a very great relief.

Will nodded to himself, filing the information away, and then noted that the psychological reaction his brain had chosen was avoidance.

"I'm sorry," he told Mirren. "I think that's all we have time for. I'm sure you'll do great tomorrow. Good night."

Then he even managed to smile.

"Remember," she said, ignoring his words. "It was a nightmare, not a fantasy."

He nodded and walked upstairs to the Weavers' apartment. For a moment he paused outside Josh's bedroom door, wondering what he would see if he went and sat in the armchair by her bed. Would she lie trembling, the pillowcase torn by her clenched hands, body rank with sweat? Would she be moaning—

He went back down to the second floor and his own apartment. For the first time, he depressed the lock on his bedroom doorknob.

He climbed into bed, but every time he closed his eyes, he saw Feodor's hands sliding up Josh's small body and her mouth full of teeth and the way the pale green of her eyes had vanished beneath a reflection of the poppy-red sky.

So he didn't close his eyes, and he didn't sleep.

Seventeen

Mirren knew she was squeezing Haley's hand so hard that she must have been hurting him, but she couldn't let go.

I can't do this, she wanted to say. *I'm not ready. Take me home.*

Braxton was a large enough city that the main archways were located in a central hub known as the Arches. Aboveground stood a public park with beautiful Gothic arches decorating the walking paths. Belowground, a nine-archway hub provided an organized area where the local dream walkers could put in their hours.

The archways—all marked by much tidier and more recent stonework than the one in Josh's basement—stood in a wide circle in an underground room. Two archways were in use by dream walkers, but the others stood empty, and one had several rows of chairs set before it. The junta, out of their robes but still imposing in business attire, spoke in a huddle, no doubt arguing some final issue of protocol. Josh had insisted that Will test the archway's looking stone; Mirren didn't know if she was more surprised that Josh thought the looking stone might have been tampered with or that Josh trusted Will more to test it out than she did herself.

Photographers and reporters made up a large percentage of the people in the archroom as well. Mirren counted Whim among them; he hadn't stopped typing on his tablet since they'd arrived. She had been startled by the presence of so much media. How many reporters did one secret society need?

Even though they'd come inside through the janitor's entrance, a crowd had been waiting for Mirren when she'd climbed out of the limo. A lightning storm of camera flashes had blinded her when she'd tried to enter the building. People had shouted questions, and a group of protesters had held up signs and hollered, "Off with her head!" Someone had hurled a tomato at her, and even though Josh had caught it in midair, the animosity had still frightened Mirren.

"Everyone here is rooting for me to fail," she told Haley as they waited for the junta to pick a nightmare.

"Not everyone," he said. She could tell by the way he was ducking his head that being around so many people was making him nervous, but he hadn't hesitated to agree when she'd asked him to come.

The rules of the trial were simple. The junta would pick three nightmares for Mirren to enter, and she had to resolve each one, meaning she had to guide the dreamer to face his fears, or confront her demons, or escape from the nightmare's danger. If Mirren woke the dreamer or exited the Dream without resolving the nightmare, she'd fail.

"Remember Gilcrest's Warning," Josh said. *"An archway reveals no more of a nightmare than a mirror unmasks a soul."*

"Didn't Gilcrest's wife kill him by feeding him bonbons full of arsenic?" Mirren asked, which made Will burst into tremulous laughter and Josh look at him with confusion.

Mirren was worried about Will. He obviously hadn't slept and he'd been wearing a sort of deranged smile all morning.

Mirren promised herself that once this trial was over, she'd reach out to him.

"The point is," Josh said, "the junta will only be able to see so much through the archway. They might send you into a nightmare that's a lot more dangerous or a lot less dangerous than they expect."

"Is that supposed to make me feel better?" Mirren asked.

"No, it's supposed to remind you to stay alert and make no assumptions." Josh ran a hand through her hair. "I could try to think of something encouraging to say, but at this point, either you're ready or you aren't."

Mirren didn't feel ready.

The junta broke their huddle, and Peregrine Borgenicht came over to wish Mirren luck.

Mirren smiled as sweetly as she could and said truthfully, "I wouldn't be here without you."

He laughed and took his seat, but Mirren felt an unexpected fury. She squared her shoulders. "I bet he won't be smiling when I resolve the third nightmare," she muttered.

Josh smiled at her then. "*Now* you're ready."

Mirren soared through the first nightmare. On a cruise ship transporting prison inmates, she avoided being killed by rioting prisoners and coaxed the dreamer—the onboard massage therapist—into saying what she'd always needed to say to her father. The Dream resolved just in time for Mirren to avoid going down with the ship.

The second nightmare was harder. Mirren followed a preteen diver up to the top of a ten-meter platform and tried to talk her out of her performance anxiety. The little girl wasn't afraid of diving as much as she was of letting people watch her dive.

But nothing Mirren said seemed to help. The girl continued to tremble and hyperventilate, and Mirren began to fear that the

Dream would shift before she resolved the nightmare, and finally she just said, "Come on, we're going right now!" She grabbed the girl's hand and yanked it as she ran off the end of the platform.

The fall was two seconds of mindless terror as the air tore at her flailing limbs. The girl fell with her, but they separated halfway down, and while Mirren managed to get her body mostly into the pencil position Josh had taught her, nothing she did could prevent the girl from landing on top of her.

Mirren heard her neck pop against the underwater silence, and her left arm went numb. Time stretched as she struggled to surface. The girl kicked her in the face, knocking Mirren back, and her numb arm was slow to respond, but she finally got her head above water and sucked in a grateful breath.

Beside her, the girl was treading water, a giant grin on her small face. The crowd was on their feet, cheering.

The nightmare dissolved.

"If there was a time limit," Davita told Peregrine, "you should have brought it up when we agreed to terms. But since you didn't, I'm informing you that Miss Mirren is taking a one-hour break to receive medical treatment and recover."

"The fatigue of back-to-back nightmares is part of the trial!" Peregrine argued.

They kept arguing. Minister Speggra got involved, too. Mirren turned the chair she was sitting in away from them, causing Saidy—Whim's mother, who was a paramedic—to admonish her to hold still.

"You need a cervical collar," she added.

"She can't dream walk in a neck brace," Josh said.

"She's sprained her neck badly enough to involve the nerves in her arm. I can tape the hell out of it, but what she really needs is to sit still."

"There aren't too many nightmares we get to fight by sitting still," Josh said.

"She doesn't have to go back in," Haley said, and everyone looked at him, even Saidy.

"Meaning what?" Josh asked finally. Mirren saw Haley flinch a little at her tone, but he pulled himself up and spoke again.

"Mirren," he said, "do *you* want to keep going?"

For a moment, her neck stopped hurting. All she felt was happy. *Out of everybody here, he's the one who thinks to ask me.*

"Of course she wants to keep going," Josh said. "This was all her idea. None of us would be here if she didn't want to do this."

On the one hand, Josh was right. Everything had been put into motion by Mirren herself. On the other hand, such endeavors had a way of taking on a life of their own, and Mirren knew that if she gave up, a small chorus of people would try to convince her to keep going.

Haley wouldn't be one of them. He didn't care if she was a princess or a queen or a nobody. And he didn't care if she got something started and realized halfway through that it wasn't what she thought it would be and needed to back out. She didn't have to prove anything to him.

Strangely, that made her want to be brave.

"Mirren?" Davita was asking.

Mirren made herself look away from Haley. "I just need an Advil and a cup of coffee, and I'm good to go."

The sound of the rain beating on the car's roof startled Mirren with its volume. She'd been in a car during the rain only once, and she couldn't remember if it had been this loud. She didn't think so.

She sat in the passenger's seat, and hot air from the defroster bounced off the windshield and onto her, carrying a dry, staticky scent. In the driver's seat was a teenage boy, black, maybe three or four years younger than her. He hardly looked old enough to drive, but he was scrawny to begin with—thin wrists, knobby elbows, a hairless chin he needed to lift to see over the dashboard.

He didn't react to Mirren's presence in the car, prompting her to ask, "Where are we going?"

He glanced over then, smiled. His smile turned down at the corners, sad or maybe wistful. "Green Lake."

"This is poor weather for a day at the shore."

The boy nodded, giving another empty smile.

They drove past a wooden sign announcing the entrance to the marina. The road wove between stands of maple and birch, passing turns toward various campsites. Mirren didn't know if she should try to pump the dreamer for information or let the nightmare unfold, but when they entered the marina she felt safe saying, "So, we're getting on a boat?"

The boy didn't answer, and Mirren realized the marina was empty at the same moment he slammed down on the gas pedal and sent the car flying toward the water.

"No!" Mirren shouted, grabbing for the wheel.

The dreamer pushed her away, grimacing. The sound of the rain on the car roof was drowned out by the rhythmic *thwack* of the car tires bouncing over wooden boards.

The dreamer had managed to drive the car right up onto the pier, which was barely wide enough for the car. They were still a third of the way from the end when the vehicle's left tires slipped off the edge, and their inertia sent them careening straight into the lake.

What Mirren felt was not fear but fury.

"What the *hell* is the matter with you?" she shouted at the boy.

The car began to sink, and the sound of the rain hitting the roof grew fainter as more and more of the vehicle sank underwater. Mirren frantically pushed the button to roll down her window, but it must have shorted out.

"I want to die," the boy said with surprising calm and dignity. He tightened his seat belt.

Mirren didn't know what to say to that.

Josh had briefly covered how to escape from a sinking car. Very briefly. In fact, the only thing Mirren could remember was that unless they got out before the car was submerged, their chances of surviving were, as Josh had put it, "complete shit."

The car was nearly completely underwater already, sinking fast, and the weight of the water against the car door was enough that Mirren couldn't open it. Water lapped at her ankles.

She realized she was breathing too rapidly. She would need to hold her breath if they were going to reach the surface. But the way the light inside the car faded as they sank deeper, and the knowledge that they were going to have to wait until the car was completely full of water before escaping, was freaking her out.

She closed her eyes for a moment. She'd been to the pool half a dozen times, three times with Josh and three with Haley. She knew how to kick, to stroke, to float. . . .

We must be fifteen feet under by now.

The water reached her waist, so she unhooked her seat belt. "Get ready to swim," she told the dreamer, but he'd closed his eyes and was holding out his arms like he was inviting the water to take him.

"Stop that!" she said, and when he didn't react, she slapped him.

He started, lips parting with surprise.

"I'm getting out of here, and I'm taking you with me."

"No, I want to die." He held out his arms again. "I'm at peace."

How can he be sitting there like Buddha under the tree while he's drowning? Mirren wondered furiously. *This is a nightmare—*

A nightmare.

She slapped him again. "Hey!"

"Ow!"

"If you're at peace, why are you so scared?"

The boy's lips parted, and then his fear rose to the surface, even as they sank deeper into the water.

"I just don't know what to do!" he told Mirren, blurting out his problems like she was his best friend. "Mom is always mad at me, but she'll never forgive me if I go live with Dad, and I *hate* Leann and the way she nags me about my grades."

He went on and on while the water level inside the car rose.

Mirren kept hoping that the emotional disclosure would be enough to resolve the nightmare, but when the water reached her chest, she felt she had to interrupt him.

"That's a lot to deal with," she said as calmly as she could. "Why don't we talk more once we're back on dry land?"

The dreamer surveyed the car's dim interior. "I think what's done is done."

"No, it isn't!" she cried, panic overwhelming her. "I'm going to the surface, and I'm taking you with me!" She grabbed his shoulders. "The water pressure against the car doors is too strong for us to open them yet. We have to wait until the car fills. Then the water pressure will equalize, and we can open the doors and swim to the surface. You have to take a deep breath and hold it right before the water fills the car, okay?"

The water was already lapping at their chins.

"This is never gonna work," the dreamer said. For the first time, he looked upset.

Mirren wished she could slap him again, but her arms were underwater. "Yes, it is! It *is*! Ready? Now!"

She took in a deep breath, but she had waited too long, and a gulp of water entered her lungs along with the air. Immediately, she coughed, and she'd lost half of her air before she was able to overpower the spasms in her chest. Still, she felt her lungs seizing up, trying to expel the water, and beneath that, despair.

I can't make it.

The car was nearly pitch-dark. She groped along the door, feeling for the handle. Every second she didn't find it was a second wasted, and by the time she wrapped her hand around it, she didn't know if she was seeing black spots because light no longer reached the car or because she was already passing out.

The door opened grudgingly, but the meager breath in her chest wasn't enough to draw her toward the surface. She kicked, meaning to kick off the side of the car but instead just smacking the door with her foot.

The surface was a misty green light far above, and her legs were heavy. The terrific shoes Deloise had helped her find weighed so much. She paused to take them off, but afterward, her legs felt no lighter. Was the surface getting dimmer instead of brighter? Mirren realized she was forgetting to use her arms.

I'm going to die, she thought very calmly. *I'm just . . . going to die.*

She began to understand how the dreamer had faced his death so peacefully. Or at least pretended to. Like him, deep inside she was terrified. But the water was so cold, and each time she moved she lost what little heat she had accumulated, and finally she could no longer hold off the need to cough and watched those bubbles of air she had fought so hard for drift away.

Like tiny moons, she thought, and closed her eyes.

And then something jerked her, hard, and she was cold again, very cold, and she struggled against a tight, warm noose around her neck, pulling her, pulling her, and then her head burst above water and she heard herself gasping and the dreamer laughing.

She opened her eyes. He *was* laughing.

She tried to speak and ended up coughing, and the dreamer caught her when she threatened to slip under again.

"I thought you were a goner," he said. His eyes were bright, elated. "When I got up here and realized you weren't with me, I was sure you were dead."

He looped an arm around her waist and helped her to the pier, where she clung to a wooden piling slick with moss.

"You went back down for me?" she asked between coughs.

"Yeah." Somehow he managed to shrug sheepishly while still treading water. "I'm actually captain of the swim team."

They both began laughing, and Mirren was coughing again when she splashed onto the archroom floor in a puddle of green water.

"How can you say she resolved the nightmare when the dreamer had to save *her?*" Peregrine demanded.

Mirren wasn't even on her feet before the politicians began arguing.

"Haley, Haley," she said between coughs, turning her head from side to side. "Get me out of here. Haley, get me out of here."

She caught sight of Will, and Haley was beside him, and the two of them lifted her bodily off the floor. They didn't even discuss a plan, just linked their arms behind her back and under her knees, and they had her out of the archroom before anyone could protest.

"I'm freezing," she said, clinging to Haley. She just wanted everything quiet, to sit down, to get warm.

They guided Mirren into the empty men's room. "Set me down, set me down," she begged.

They set her on unsteady feet, and her knees dipped dangerously before steadying. Haley drew Mirren into the communal shower and turned warm water on over her, not bothering to fuss with their clothes before wrapping his arms around her and stepping into the spray.

Standing between the hot water and Haley's warmth, she realized she was going to live.

At least, one more day.

Eighteen

Will and Whim stood guard at the men's locker-room door while Mirren changed. Deloise, who was not biologically related to Kerstel but had nonetheless inherited her practicality, had packed not only dry clothes for Mirren, but also dry shoes, a few toiletries, a protein bar, and vitaminwater.

Whim wasn't helping much with the guarding; he only had eyes for his tablet. "Which is better? 'Mirren inspired the dreamer to heroism' or 'By playing the damsel in distress, Mirren tricked the dreamer into affirming the importance of life'?"

"Which one means she drowned?" Will asked.

Will needed to be done for the day. He hadn't slept the night before, and he'd spent most of Mirren's trial watching Josh instead of the archway. She seemed no different today from any other day in the last four months, and she hadn't knocked on his door the night before.

"Maybe I can combine them," Whim mused.

When they reentered the large archroom behind a mostly dry Mirren, a few people began clapping. A few others booed—one woman started hissing like a cat. Mostly, though, people were silent.

Minister Innay made the announcement. "By a vote of four to three, the junta has determined that Amyrischka Rousellario has passed the second trial." Afterward both the clapping and the booing were louder.

"Because she has successfully passed the first two of Agastoff's Trials," Minister Innay continued, "we now charge Miss Rousellario with her third and final trial, a terrible task, known as the Proving. The junta charges you to locate the Karawar, also known as the gathering whistle, and present it to the junta. You have nine days to complete this task."

Immediately, reporters showered Mirren with questions. Davita rushed her out of the room before she could answer, Haley on their heels, and Will and Whim followed, with Josh and Deloise bringing up the tail.

They left through the front entrance this time and exited the building into the park above. Among the park's decorated arches, the protesters had doubled in number, and whatever semblance of order had existed before Mirren's trial was gone. Before she got halfway to the curb and the waiting limo, one of the protesters hurled an egg at her. The shell fragmented into a hundred pieces when it smashed against the side of her face, and yolk dripped onto her dry T-shirt.

Will was still frozen with surprise when the protesters let loose, eggs flying from all directions. Josh twisted one fist up in a protester's shirt collar and pulled the other back for a punch, but she stumbled after the woman ground an egg into her eye.

Despite Will's confused feelings toward Josh, a sense of protectiveness spurred him to hit the protester as hard as he could. He'd never hit a woman outside of the Dream, but he didn't hesitate to do so then, or to raise a threatening fist when she straightened up with a sneer.

"You want anoth—" Will began, and then half a dozen eggs riddled his body. Some of them, he discovered, were frozen solid and felt like paperweights. He fell to his knees.

"Run!" Josh shouted, covering her dripping eye with one hand.

Davita hustled Mirren into the limo parked at the curb, but Haley was on the ground wrestling with a guy twice his size. As Will tried to rise from the pavement to help his friend, the woman he'd hit earlier slugged him in the gut. Josh reached his side in an instant, her eye squished up against further attack, spinning like a whirling dervish of pain as she cleared away the protesters who had gathered around Will. She even head-butted a man.

When the protesters had backed off enough, Josh grabbed Will's hand and dragged him toward the limo. Will saw Deloise break a man's nose with the heel of her palm while Whim pulled Haley up from the ground, and then they were all diving through the car doorway.

Someone grabbed Deloise's ankle as she tried to pull it inside the vehicle, and she used her other foot to kick him in the face.

"Go!" Josh yelled at the driver, and he tore away from the curb with the back door still hanging open. Whim wrapped his arms around Deloise's waist to anchor her. More eggs pelted the vehicle, each shell bursting like a firecracker.

"He took my shoe!" Deloise protested.

"You're lucky that's all he got," Whim told her, and he dragged her deeper into the limo.

After hours of ice packs, ultrasounds, and waiting for an ophthalmologist to come pick the eggshell out of Josh's eye, they were released from the ER into Davita's care. Mirren was wearing a neck brace and had her arm strapped to her side, Josh looked like a very short pirate in her eye patch, Haley's ear was bandaged beside his black eye, and Deloise was wearing a paper surgical shoe over her bare foot.

All in all, Will suspected they'd gotten off easy.

Despite attempting to land anywhere else, he ended up sitting next to Josh on the ride home. He felt awkward, but he doubted she could tell because he was sitting by the eye she couldn't see out of. The doctor had said she had to wear the patch for a couple of days, but he didn't expect any damage to her vision.

Will's relief confused him. He'd been up all night, obsessing over her betrayal, yet he couldn't stomach the thought of anyone hurting her. Neither of them had hesitated to defend the other, but he still didn't want to be anywhere near her.

"I don't mean to be indelicate," Davita said as they got on the highway headed back toward Tanith, "but I'd like to talk about the Karawar for a moment. Only if you feel up to it, Mirren."

Mirren had been unable to stop crying in the ER, and the doctor had given her a sedative—a strong sedative. Will suspected that if she hadn't been wearing a cervical collar, she wouldn't have been able to sit up.

"I don't care," she whispered.

"I care," Josh said. "Forget the next trial—why did we get attacked back there?"

"Apparently the crowd didn't agree with the junta's decision to pass Mirren," Davita said.

"Most of the protesters were there before we arrived," Whim

pointed out. "And some of those eggs were frozen, which means they planned this at least a day ago."

"How did they know we were going to use the janitor's entrance?" Josh asked. "Davita, did you tip them off?"

"Of course not," Davita said, but Will could tell Josh didn't trust the answer. He didn't either.

"I thought I'd win them over," Mirren whispered. "If I did well."

"There weren't any protesters when Mirren came into Braxton for the Learning last week," Josh said. "What happened between now and then?"

None of them knew. Like Mirren, Will would have expected her success to bring people over to her side, not alienate them.

"I've been monitoring DWTV and *The Daily Walker*," Davita said, "and they haven't posted anything overly critical. A few editorials that were, perhaps . . . unkind."

"What about online?" Josh asked. "What about *Through a Veil Darkly*, Whim?"

"I'm practically running a Mirren fan club," Whim told her. "Which you'd know if you bothered reading it."

Josh opened her mouth to retort, but Deloise said quickly, "What about the comments you said were weird?"

"What comments?" Mirren asked.

Whim shrugged uneasily. "Just, you know, a few conspiracy nuts have basically blamed her for every single political screwup and scandal since the beginning of time. Including the St. Edward's Island Massacre."

"That was more than a hundred years ago," Deloise pointed out. "Accusing Mirren of being involved doesn't make any sense."

"Yeah, I tried to explain that, but nobody really wants to hear it. I think some people are getting a kick out of being over-the-top. I mean, who would actually believe that Mirren's going to lead the Gendarmerie in a coup? It's the Internet, you know? It's all just hyperbole."

"Hyperbole?" Davita asked, her voice rising within the limousine. "Two gendarmes were beaten by a crowd in Braxton last night."

"Oh," Whim said with a wince. "I did not know that."

"I can't have someone Mirren is associated with fomenting rebellion," Davita told him.

"I'm not fomenting anything!" Whim replied. "I wasn't even part of that conversation!"

"Why not?" Will asked. "You're the moderator, aren't you?"

Even Deloise was angry at Whim. She smacked the back of his head and said, "Did you at least ban those people from the site?"

"Yeah, of course," he said. "I mean, I will."

"Oh, my God," Josh said. "What else are they saying?"

"Everybody loves her," Whim protested. "Everybody except the people who don't want a queen and the people who . . . think she's Adolf Hitler. But it's really a very small group of people who have flipped out. I assume they're the ones who showed up with eggs today."

Will remembered the twisted expression of the woman who'd smashed the egg in Josh's eye. Her rage had billowed around her.

Isn't all of this somehow disproportionate? Will wondered. *What is it about Mirren that makes people act like idiots? Is there really that much animosity toward her parents, all these years later?*

Or is it something else?

Mirren was crying again. "Can we talk about this later?" Haley asked pointedly.

"Yeah, of course," Whim said, straightening up. He put a hand on Mirren's shoulder, which made her jump. "Don't worry, friend. We won't let anything happen to you. That pretty head's gonna stay right where it is."

Mirren cried harder.

"Whim!" Deloise cried, and smacked the back of his head again.

"This is all very disturbing," Davita said. "I think we should arrange professional security for you, Mirren."

"The Accordance Conclave is less than two weeks away,"

Deloise said, pulling a package of tissues from her purse. "You just have to hang on a little longer."

Mirren dried her face slowly, taking deep breaths as she did so. "I'm sorry," she said. "I'm being childish."

"No, you aren't," Haley told her.

"You really aren't," Josh said.

Mirren wiped her nose. Somehow she managed to look elegant even when crying. "Maybe I should quit. Maybe the dream-walker community is trying to tell me that they don't want me to lead them. Maybe we don't need to wait until the AC to hear them."

Everyone protested—except for Haley, Will noted. He kissed her hair and said nothing.

"But you're so close," Josh said. "All you have to do is give the junta that thing, that—what's it called?"

"The Karawar," Mirren said.

"Yeah," Josh said. Then she added, "What is that?"

"It's an ancient horn," Mirren said tiredly. "When blown, it emits a sound that only dream walkers can hear. The archaeological evidence suggests it called dream walkers to an annual meeting, before the advent of quick communication."

"Why would Peregrine want it?" Josh asked.

Mirren and Davita looked at each other with identical expressions of bewilderment. "I don't know," Mirren admitted. "Everyone stopped using the Karawar after the Industrial Revolution. My family only held on to it so it wouldn't be lost."

"So you have it?" Deloise said. "What would happen if you gave it to Peregrine and he used it?"

"My understanding is that all the dream walkers in the area—up to three or four hundred square miles—would hear a whistling sound and feel a strong urge to walk toward Peregrine. But the urge wouldn't be undeniable, and since almost no one knows what the sound means, most of them would probably fight off the urge and stay home."

"Like a dog whistle for dream walkers," Whim said. "That's awesome."

"My only thought," Mirren said, "is that Peregrine's trying to prove I'm as secretive as the monarchy used to be. Admittedly, they never would have turned the Karawar over to anyone. Maybe Peregrine thinks I won't, either, and that he'll be able to point at me and say I'm nothing new. But I have no issue with giving the Karawar to the junta, or to whatever government the dream walkers elect. If that's the trap Peregrine is trying to set for me, why would he have chosen the Karawar? He must guess I have access to far more powerful instruments, ones I *would* resist giving up."

"Maybe the other ministers chose the task," Davita suggested.

"Or maybe," Josh said, "Peregrine is planning to use the Karawar in a way we haven't thought of."

Mirren sank down into her neck brace, like a turtle withdrawing. "Let's hope not."

Exhausted, they lapsed into silence during the second half of the trip. Josh let her head fall back and took Will's hand in hers, but her touch made his skin crawl. *Does she let Feodor hold her hand in her dreams?* he wondered, pulling away.

Josh lifted her head. She turned halfway in her seat so she could see him and whispered, "Is everything okay?"

If he'd caught her dreaming about Ian, her ex-boyfriend, he wouldn't have been nearly as upset. He didn't expect her never to think about anyone else or to control the content of her dreams. What bothered him wasn't that she'd dreamed of someone besides him; it was that she'd dreamed of *Feodor*.

Feodor had hurt Will. He'd hurt Josh, too, and Haley, and Ian, and Winsor, and dozens of other people whose souls he had trapped. That Josh dreamed of him touching her, kissing her, was perverse. It suggested that something was deeply wrong in Josh's mind, and as much as anything, Will felt like a fool for not having seen that in her sooner. She'd tricked him, just as Feodor had.

"Did you have a nightmare last night?" he asked her.

Did she hesitate before shaking her head? In the dim light, he couldn't tell.

We had one of our most important talks in a limo, he thought, recalling how a thunderstorm had darkened the car's interior that day; today the summer sun had set and left them in a purple gloaming. That day she had told him the truth, and today she'd lied.

"Will?" she asked.

He couldn't deal with it all just yet.

"Tomorrow," he whispered. "Let's talk tomorrow."

Through a Veil Darkly

A Royal Romance?

We here at *TaVD* have obtained the first confirmation of a romance blossoming between Princess Mirren and Haelipto McKarr. Some of you will remember Haelipto as one of the three teens who confronted and defeated Feodor Kajażkołski back in February, although he is the lowest-profile member of the trio. Humble, thoughtful, and good-natured, he's also able to turn heroic at a moment's notice, as he demonstrated when he and Will Kansas rushed the freezing and half-drowned princess into a hot shower (photo below).

Princess Mirren seems to have fallen hard for young Mr. McKarr, whom she calls Haley, as do his close friends. Although they met only a few short weeks ago, rumor has it they not only spend every waking moment together, but the princess even sleeps in his room! Will he prove to be the steady support she needs as she works her way through the trials, or will their royal romance crumble under the stresses of life in a world that long ago gave up on a dream-walker monarchy?

Comments:

scorpio_666 says: What a slut.

> JMallShopper says: Seriously. Three weeks and she's already living with him!

> FemmeFatal says: I'm shocked to hear you slut-shaming someone you don't even know. Young women need to support each other in building self-esteem. Maybe if Mirren had friends who helped her do that, she wouldn't need to throw herself at a guy to feel confident and beautiful.

pouter40242 says: I thought that guy was a deaf-mute.

MCampbell_TarkenElectric says: I had this dream that she told me she was secretly behind the Silty incident.

> fgh243l says: Of course she was!

> MCampbell_TarkenElectric says: She said she faked Silty's death, that he's really been living with her in Switzerland.

>> FemmeFatal: What? That's crazy. I knew Silty. He never would have abandoned his wife and kids to live in Switzerland.

Nineteen

When Josh entered the living room, the first thing she noticed was that someone had spray-painted the word "tulz" across the windows at the front of the house.

"What is that?" she asked Deloise.

"Oh, my gosh!" Deloise cried. "That's awful! Who did that?"

Deloise had already returned to the kitchen to warn Mirren by the time Josh figured out that she was looking at the word "slut" reversed. Someone had graffitied the living room windows.

Haley didn't let Mirren see the slur and instead took her straight upstairs to rest. Whim and Will followed them, leaving Josh and Deloise in the kitchen with Lauren, Kerstel, and Whim's father, Alex.

"I'll clean the windows tomorrow," Josh promised, disturbed by this further sign of acrimony toward Mirren. "Do I need to find her somewhere else to stay?"

"I don't know," Lauren said. "But I'd be lying if I said I wasn't concerned about her being here."

"Where would she go?" Alex asked. "We're the closest thing she has to family."

Everyone except Josh, Will, Haley, and Davita believed that Mirren's family was back in Switzerland and didn't approve of her political ambitions. Even Deloise didn't know about the Hidden Kingdom.

"Davita said the security team should be here before midnight," Kerstel said.

"I don't know that two men will be able to hold off a mob," Lauren told his wife. "But I have to admit that I can't imagine turning her out now."

"And she and Haley are so fond of each other," Kerstel said.

"As my son has so carelessly informed the world," Alex added.

"What does that mean?" Josh asked.

"I think I'm the only person in this house who actually reads Whim's blog," Alex reflected. "A few hours ago he posted a picture of Haley and Mirren in the shower together after the trial."

Can't people just lay off Mirren for a day or two? Josh thought, even as she got up from the table. "I better go warn Haley. Maybe he can make sure she doesn't see it."

She went upstairs to the guys' apartment. Haley was watching TV in his raggedy old flannel bathrobe, looking tired and like he didn't want to interact anymore that day. But when Josh relayed the news, he grabbed his tablet and pulled up *Through a Veil Darkly*. Josh stood near him so they could read the latest entry together.

Haley finished before she did, but not before she'd read the brunt of the post and caught a glimpse of the photograph of Haley and Mirren in the shower. "Whim!" Haley shouted, and Josh jumped at the volume of his voice.

Haley banged on Whim's door, then let himself in. His eyebrows were drawn together in anger, making his features sharper and his face older. "What is *this*?" he demanded.

Josh followed him into Whim's room, which was outfitted with a minifridge, a hot plate, and a microwave stationed among the mess. Whim was lounging on his bed—just a twin mattress on the floor—and typing on his laptop.

He sat up when Haley stormed into the room. "Okay, dude, don't freak out. I'm trying to do Mirren a favor."

Haley waved the tablet at him. "You said she's sleeping in my room!"

"Technically, that's true," Whim said, but under the heat of Haley's glare, he admitted, "Okay, so I juiced it up a little. Everybody loves a royal romance."

"They're calling her a slut," Haley said.

"I was trying to bring in some of the good press you got after the Feodor thing. You know, unpopular girl dates a popular boy, and then she's popular, too?"

Through his teeth, Haley said, *"I'm not popular."* He held up the tablet. *"Pouter40242* thinks I'm a deaf-mute!"

Josh struggled not to crack up. She felt terrible for Haley and Mirren, and she was proud of Haley for laying into Whim, but that deaf-mute rumor had been going around since they were in middle school.

"Well, now he knows you're not," Whim said. "Look, somebody was going to write this article eventually. People have noticed that you're glued to Mirren's side. Better that I choose the tone for the story."

Haley's lips were pursed so tightly, they were almost white. "You didn't do this for Mirren. You did it for yourself."

"Haley," Whim said, clutching the hilt of an imaginary knife in his chest, "you wound me."

"Stop writing about her!" Haley demanded.

"I can't do that," Whim said. He turned faintly green. "Do you know how much traffic I'm getting these days? The website is finally paying for itself."

Haley turned and stormed out of the room.

"At least close the comments section," Josh told Whim before following Haley.

She found him on the balcony off the living room, leaning against the railing and glaring at the lawn. "I'm sorry about Whim," she said. "He's—"

"I know who Whim is," Haley said curtly. "He's a fundamentally selfish person."

Josh gawked at him, and he ducked his head, his momentary confidence fled.

"Sorry," he muttered.

"No apology necessary. I mean, you aren't wrong. Just . . . you reminded me of Ian for a second. In a good way."

For a moment, Josh wondered what Ian would have thought of Haley and Mirren together, then decided she didn't want to know. But Haley's thoughts must have taken a similar course, because he said, "Next week is the Fourth of July."

The holiday would mark one year since Ian's death. Or rather, one year since they'd thought he had died. One year since Feodor had turned Ian's body into his puppet. Josh had been trying not to think about the approaching anniversary, but the flags and holiday sales had made it impossible.

"We could go put flowers on his grave or something," Josh said.

"I'm not—" Haley stuttered, and then in a familiar half whisper finished, "I might not be around."

Before Josh could ask what he meant, he retreated into the house, his shoulders drawn up to his ears.

That was weird, she thought. She hadn't seen Haley panic like that in a long time. And his phrasing had been so ominous. . . .

She set aside the urge to question him further—he'd tell her when he was ready—and went upstairs, unsure what else to do.

Will had said they'd talk the next day; did that mean he didn't want to see her tonight? It wasn't even eight yet.

She sat on her bed, digging her big toe into the carpet and trying to figure out what she could have done to upset him. Had he found her notes or her workshop in the attic? He couldn't have been too angry, or he wouldn't have punched that lady who crushed the egg in Josh's eye.

The apartment phone rang, and since no one else was around, Josh answered it.

"Hello?"

"Hello. Is this Josh, please?"

"It is."

"Hi, Josh, this is Bash Mirrettsio calling."

Suddenly she was glad she had been the one to answer.

"I hope it's all right, me calling you at home like this," he said. "I realized after you left that I'd forgotten to get your phone number."

"I don't have one. But it's all right." She closed her bedroom door firmly.

"Good. Well, I won't beat around the bush. I was inspired by our meeting the other day, and I've done nothing since except try to figure out how we could make your inventions work. Honestly, Bayla is going to kill me if I don't pay her some attention; but I simply can't focus on anything else. And I think—I *think*—I may have found a way to attach our cell phone towers to the sea."

Josh sat quietly for the next ten minutes and listened to Bash describe what he had done. He'd taken her idea of reversing the polarity of the particles and run with it, and he talked so fast that Josh had a hard time following the science behind his explanation.

"Wait a sec," Josh burst out. "How did you do this without a particle accelerator?"

"Willis-Audretch has a particle accelerator."

He went on, but Josh couldn't keep up with all his jargon and his peculiar use of analogies. She'd have to ask Bash to explain everything again when they had a pad and pen in front of them.

"I suppose there is one other question," Bash continued, "which is simply this: Do we want to keep moving forward? Up until now, this conversation has been purely theoretical. But if we place these towers in the Dream, we'll have taken a very large step into the actual."

Did I spend all these months writing on sketch pads and walls and my own body parts just to stop now? Josh wondered. She recalled last night's dream again, not the red sky, but the feeling of quiet peace that had filled her when all the monsters were dead and the fighting was over. She wanted that peace.

She wanted that power.

"Let's do it," she said.

"I was hoping you'd say that. Excellent. Do you want to come see the particle accelerator?"

Of *course* she wanted to see the particle accelerator. But how would she explain another trip to Braxton without Will?

"I'd love to, but things are kind of a mess around here at the moment. I might not be able to get away."

"Oh, yes, I saw the news reports. They said your princess made a poor mermaid, despite the long red hair."

Josh laughed, even though the joke was a little lighthearted for a near-death experience.

"I'm just glad they passed her."

"Any chance she'll turn over the Karawar?"

"A pretty good one, I think," Josh admitted, and she knew she probably shouldn't be telling Bash any such thing, but it felt nice to talk lightheartedly with someone, and he was sort of a friend. "Listen, can you come by tomorrow night around eight? I'm scheduled to dream walk. We could try attaching the towers then."

Bash's voice brightened. "Splendid!"

"Come to the back door, all right? Don't ring the bell out front."

"Are we playing cloak-and-dagger?"

More than I'd like, Josh thought, but she told Bash, "Just a bit. I'll see you tomorrow—have fun with your particle accelerator."

By the time she woke up the next day—well after noon—Will had already left the house. He'd taken off to the mall with Whim and Deloise, which left Josh confused because he hated the mall.

Is he just trying to get away from me? she wondered. For the first time ever, she wished he had a cell phone she could call.

Since he didn't, she spent a couple of hours scrubbing the spray paint off the house and the rest of the afternoon training. The doctor had told her to leave the eye patch on until the next day, but she thought she'd be safer training with it off. Her eye didn't hurt unless she rubbed it.

When Will, Deloise, and Whim didn't return for dinner, she helped Kerstel cook and then put herself through three rounds of a Romanian circuit-training video that left her gasping for air.

Afterward, she sat on the back porch and waited for Bash, watching the security guards wander around the yard. One of them was texting. While Josh glared at him, Haley and Mirren walked out the back door. They were holding hands.

"You guys going out?" Josh asked, concerned about their safety.

"We're going back to the Hidden Kingdom," Mirren said. "I've decided to give the Karawar to the junta."

"Oh," Josh said, and then realized how unsupportive she sounded.

"I just want all this to be over," Mirren admitted.

"Do you want me to come? We could wait until early morning, like last time."

"Thank you, but I think we'll be fine. My aunt and uncle are usually in bed by ten, and if we bump into my cousin, she'll likely just ask to come back with us."

"Be safe," Josh told them as they climbed into Haley's truck.

Alone, listening to the security guard argue with his son's mother on his phone, Josh wondered if Haley's cryptic comment the night before might have meant he would be in the Hidden Kingdom on the Fourth of July. That was a less frightening thought than others she'd had.

The security guard was threatening to sue for custody by the time Bash drove up the driveway and around the back. He parked and exited his car, at which point the security guard called from twenty yards away, "Is he okay?"

"Who's that?" Bash asked, squinting into the darkness.

Josh raised her hand and gave the okay. "He's the world's worst security guard. He might be tied, though, with the guard in the front yard, who I'm guessing didn't stop you."

"No one stopped me. I did notice a man taking a smoke on your porch swing, though."

Josh swore to call the security company and give them hell. *After* she and Bash tried out his invention.

"Are you wearing an eye patch?" Bash asked.

"Yeah. It's a long story."

"I heard you were in a fight."

"All right, it's not that long a story. Do you need help with these boxes?"

"Sure," Bash said, smiling, and they each grabbed a large cardboard box from the backseat of his car.

Luckily, Saidy was at work, Alex had retired to his apartment for the evening, and Haley and Mirren were out, so no one saw Bash as Josh led him down to the basement.

"Nice setup," Bash said, watching Josh type her code into the bank-vault door that protected the archway.

"It works," Josh agreed. Only then did she realize that he had likely memorized her code, and she made a mental note to change it after he left. Not that she didn't trust Bash, she just . . . Well, it seemed prudent.

"What's in the boxes?"

Bash grinned and opened one up. "Your towers."

Josh picked up one of the metal devices. Once they'd started calling them "towers," she had begun mentally picturing a tiny cell phone tower, but what Bash had created looked more like an aerosol can with a glass button on top.

The idea was to plant towers at intervals within the Dream. The circlet and vambrace would relay Josh's thought to the towers, and the towers would broadcast a signal to the Dream, telling it what Josh wanted it to do.

"I still don't completely understand how you stabilized the polarity of the Dream particles," she told Bash as she examined one of the towers.

"Like I said on the phone, I took them down to nearly absolute zero . . ."

His explanation made even less sense to Josh than it had on the phone the day before, partly because he kept using unfamiliar acronyms like "ARN" and "UH" and then throwing in abbreviations like "Z-tat" and "fro." For the first time, Josh became aware of how much progress dream theory had made after Feodor's exile. Except for his own research, he'd been out of touch with the field for fifty years, and Josh felt like an idiot when she had to stop Bash over and over to ask him to explain.

When she asked him to explain why the type of radiation he'd used wouldn't fry her brain as soon as she put the circlet on, a fleeting expression crossed Bash's face, so quickly that Josh wasn't able to fully grasp it. Anger? Irritation?

But the expression was gone when he said, "No one has to worry about that since the invention of simo pulsation."

"Simo pulsation?" Josh repeated.

"Yes, but that led to a larger issue with the polarity of Z-tat in relation to the ARN . . ."

And he was off again.

Bash does this for a living, she told herself. *And he isn't half a century behind. I'm sure all of this makes sense if you know the lingo.*

"Let's give it a try," she said.

Bash grinned again. "Excellent."

Josh had hidden the circlet and vambrace under a pile of towels in the archroom. When she produced them, Bash admired the construction.

"This is a hell of a job," Bash said, running his fingers over the wires in the vambrace. "Show me how it goes on."

"These three wire bundles have to align precisely with the veins in my arm, especially the tips here." Josh winced as she clamped the vambrace shut around her left forearm. This was the first time she'd had the nerve to do so. "They actually cut into my skin at the wrist."

The pain was curiously momentary. After the initial bite of the wire tips, Josh's arm began to feel warm and relaxed—just as it had in her nightmares. She experienced the same thing when she put on the circlet, only the pain occurred at the base of her skull.

"How do they feel?" Bash asked. This time she recognized his expression—envy. He wanted to be the one wearing the devices. Josh didn't blame him.

"They feel good. I think I'm ready."

She placed her free hand on the looking stone and watched the Veil come to life inside the archway. After several minutes of flipping through nightmares, she found one with kids playing basketball. "This one might work."

Bash pushed his glasses up his nose and peered at the archway. "Yes, that's good."

He picked up one of the boxes and jumped through the archway, and Josh grabbed the other and followed him. To her surprise, the box felt much less heavy than it had earlier, and she wondered if the vambrace provided increased strength in her left arm.

The nightmare they jumped into featured a nighttime basketball court lit by streetlamps so bright that they turned the sky beyond them pitch-black. A number of races were represented on the team, but there was only one Korean kid, and Josh touched his fear just long enough to know that he considered this chance to impress his friends a matter of life and death.

Josh was carrying the box with one arm by then—no question that the vambrace increased her strength.

Standing near the corner of the court, Bash pulled a tower from one of the boxes. "Attaching them is straightforward. Decide where you want to put it. Set it down, and then push the button on the top as firmly as you can. It takes a little force. You'll hear a snap when it attaches." He demonstrated, pressing the button down until Josh heard a sound like a pencil snapping, and the glass button glowed white.

"If the button is glowing, it's attached," Bash said, sounding pleased with himself. "But we can double-check by trying to pull it up."

He grabbed the tower and tugged, and although Josh couldn't see anything that would be holding it in place, the object refused to move. She even tried digging away some of the earth around the can's base, but the tower seemed to be attached to space itself.

A *cell phone tower on the sea,* she thought.

Bash grinned at her, and she smiled back.

"How many towers do we need to attach before the circlet and vambrace will work?" she asked.

"Just one, I assume. But they probably only have a range of about fifty feet. Maybe we should try putting one at each corner of the court?"

Josh nodded and took two towers from the box. She walked to the nearest corner of the court, where the teenagers were attempting a Globetrotters-style ball-passing display. The demonstration wasn't going well; the dreamer, especially, seemed to be letting his nerves get the best of him.

She knelt at the corner where the court ended and the lawn began and set the tower on the ground. With her unencumbered hand, she pressed down on the button, hard, then harder, then so hard that she thought the can would collapse, and finally it made a snapping sound. The button on top lit up.

"My eye!" one of the players screamed, and the guy's teammates all turned slowly to stare at the dreamer.

"You popped his eye!" a player accused.

"I'm sorry! I was just throwing him the ball. I didn't mean to—"

"I'm blind!" the bloodied guy cried.

A strange sensation filled Josh then, as if something had shifted subtly inside her head. In her mind, she felt a growing awareness of the towers she and Bash had just placed, and as she walked toward the kids on the court, her awareness changed based on her proximity to each tower. They had become her spatial reference points, her cardinal directions, and the warmth in her arm and head grew hotter.

The basketball players had gathered in a circle around the dreamer. They were badgering him, calling him names, and darting forward to shove him. Josh felt the impending violence fill the air like a low-pressure front before a thunderstorm, and her heartbeat sped up to match her step as she broke into a run.

No, wait, you don't have to run.

She stopped running and raised her left arm instead. Just like in her nightmares, she spread her fingers and *reached,* past the air, past the substance of reality, and heat shot down her arm and out her fingertips like matterless beams.

The dreamer rose into the air and out of the reach of the bullies. He started screaming—he didn't know what was happening, even his *subconscious* didn't know what was happening—but Josh smiled as she watched the kids below jump up and down, futilely attempting to grab his feet. She caught hold of the fabric of the Dream as though it were a bedsheet, and she gave it a hard shake. The bullies fell like bowling pins.

As Josh reveled in her power, she caught a glimpse of her own outstretched hand, with the fingers spread unnaturally far apart and the sinews beneath her skin rising, and saw how much they resembled the hands of Feodor's zombies. At the same instant, she felt the dreamer's fear evolve into true dreamfire, the deepest and most primordial of fears. He believed then that he was going to die.

Unease filled Josh. Didn't he understand that she was protecting him?

Maybe not. Maybe he couldn't see the situation from her point of view, from such a wide field of vision, but she was doing this for him. She knew what was best. . . .

No, Josh thought. Memories of the nightmare in which the piano had eaten Caleb flooded back to her. *I don't have the right to do this,* she thought. *I don't have the wisdom.*

Josh let her arm drop, let the power retreat into her arm, and released her hold on the Dream. The dreamer, dangling in the air, fell and landed on two players, who began cursing him.

I thought I wanted this. Even as the words formed in her mind, a dozen arguments against the admission were rising. She just didn't know how to use the power yet—the dreamer didn't appreciate her help—next time she'd make sure the dreamer knew she was on his side—

What we're all afraid of is having no control, she realized, in a voice louder and calmer than the others. *And I can't help someone by taking even more control away from them.*

"Josh?" Bash asked, coming to stand beside her.

Josh tried to rub her temple, but the circlet was in the way. "Let's get out of here."

"Wait, are you done?"

"Yeah."

With a thrust of her hand, she opened an archway in the middle of the court.

"How did you do that?" Bash asked, his eyes wide, and only then did Josh remember the exact balance of how much and how little he knew. The circlet—she wasn't thinking clearly.

"The vambrace did it," she lied, and walked through the archway.

The moment she landed in the archroom, she began unlatching the vambrace. Bash landed behind her as she pulled the device from her arm, and she gasped at the sight of the damage the vambrace had done. Not only had the wires that bit into her skin created bloody marks like leech bites, but the magnets had left quarter-sized burns.

"Shit," she said, and let the vambrace fall to the floor. Her arm looked shriveled, too, like a salted snail, and her veins pulsed bright blue beneath her skin. Quickly, she pulled the circlet off, taking more than a few strands of hair with it.

She touched her temple and her fingers came away bloody. "I need—" she began, and then the back of her head exploded.

She was on the floor before she realized what had happened—that Bash had hit her with the folding chair. Even then, her primary concern wasn't to fight back but to avoid passing out. Because she'd fractured her skull and had a serious concussion four months before, she had to be especially careful about not hitting her head again, and she felt somehow that if she could remain conscious, that would lessen the damage done to her brain.

The archroom door opened and closed. She heard it; she couldn't open her eyes.

I'm awake, she thought. *I'm awake. As long as I'm thinking, I'm awake.*

The door opened and closed again. She felt Bash roll her onto her stomach, and she tried to ask him not to hit her head again, but the words just came out, "Ddddaaaaa."

He didn't hit her head. Instead he tied her up with a rope, ankles and wrists together so that she was unable to stand.

Josh heard him gather up the vambrace and circlet and realized for the first time what he had been after. *That's probably not good,* she thought.

"Nice working with you," Bash said.

The archway door opened and closed one last time.

Through a Veil Darkly

Message board: Princess Mirren: She's just like all the other Roussellarios

Trashprotractor says: Didn't her mom start out the same way? Everyone thought she was so lovely and elegant, and she told us all that she would be open in a way the Rousellarios had never been, and then she turned out to be just as elitist as the rest of them.

> scorpio_666 says: Uh, her mom was not lovely and elegant. Have you forgotten those satin dresses she always wore? I don't think the woman even owned pants.
>> JillKramer says: Oh my God! I DID forget those dresses! They were so hideous.

wingnut24the says: I had a nightmare about her where she was wearing one of those dresses, and she had a crown on. She told me that the Gendarmerie is planning to overthrow the junta.

> jshg_hammer says: Dude, I had the same dream! Sort of. I mean, she was wearing the dress and the crown, but she was showing me around her secret hiding place. It was like the Bat Cave, and it was full of weapons and armored tanks and stuff.

Worchester_RWatson says: I had a dream she was my French teacher, and she wouldn't stop giving us more homework.

copenite says: Trashprotractor is right. Maybe she wasn't raised by her parents, but she still has their money and their priorities. For every single thing she said at the Learning, I bet there are five secrets she knows but won't tell.

> markamBCGI says: That would be a ridiculous number of secrets.

pashtofrank says: Being educated and being elitist are not the same thing.

gilandsons says: I hope she dies in the next trial. I want to see blood in that red hair.

> JillKramer says: That's so sick!
> prancingpony says: HAIR BLOOD! HAIR BLOOD! HAIR BLOOD!

Twenty

When Will had woken up that morning, he'd known one thing: he couldn't face Josh.

So he went to the mall.

He usually relished emotional disclosure; Josh was the one who was afraid of expressing her feelings. But today the thought of telling Josh what he'd seen made him want to cut out his tongue. As he followed Whim and Deloise from store to store, he wondered if he wasn't less afraid of asking Josh about her nightmare than he was of hearing her answer. Maybe he just didn't want to know.

So he stayed at the mall. He bought Deloise a pair of shoes to replace the ones she'd lost the day before. He choked down a plateful of greasy bourbon chicken in the food court. He helped Whim pick out a new cell phone case.

When his friends were done shopping, he convinced them to go to the movies. He swore that a new action flick was awesome, when in fact he had heard the exact opposite. Then he sat in the theater, hands clenched around the armrests, revolted by the scent of popcorn butter.

Unbelievably, the movie contained a scene in which the hero's girlfriend tried to seduce the villain.

I can't stay here, Will thought. *I can't watch this. I'm going to lose my mind.*

"Can I borrow your phone?" he whispered to Whim.

Whim looked surprised but offered up the phone.

Will carried the phone into the mall. He figured out Whim's contact list but didn't find the name he was looking for. Then he opened up the call log and saw a lot of recent calls to and from someone named Mike. He dialed the number.

"Hello, sexy," a female voice said.

"This is Will Kansas."

After an instant of silence, Bayla gushed, "Will! What a nice surprise!"

"Remember what you and I talked about after the last Grey Circle meeting?"

"Mmm, of course. Have you changed your mind?"

"Yeah. Yeah, I guess so. How soon do you think we could do that?"

"Whenever you want, love."

"How about tonight? You, me, and Whim?"

"Sounds heavenly. I'll come by around nine?"

"Fine. And, ah, thanks."

"See you in a few."

Whim was startled but not displeased by Will's arrangements. "Haley and Mirren are going to go get the Karawar, so we don't even have to get them out of the apartment," he mused. Then he set about manically cleaning up the living room. He even changed the sheets on his mattress, which Will tried not to think about.

At eight thirty, Bayla texted that she was on her way, but the news seemed to worry Whim. He began rubbing his mouth and chin like a contemplative villain, and maybe the reference was subconsciously intentional because Will had noticed he did it only when feeling guilty.

"Suddenly I'm worried this isn't a good idea," Whim said.

"Why not?"

"Don't you have trouble with drugs?"

"Not exactly, and according to Bayla, Veil dust isn't a drug; it's a mystical substance."

"True. But it can still be misused." He clapped Will's shoulder. "What the hell, right? If you say you're cool, that's enough for me."

Will felt strangely disappointed that Whim hadn't pushed him harder to find a different solution to his anxiety problems. Maybe with a little help, he could have found one; instead, he was using Veil dust as a stopgap to keep himself from drinking. Even if he wasn't technically an alcoholic and wasn't technically working at staying sober, he felt like he would still be giving something up by using Veil dust.

Just pride and the future opportunity to feel self-righteous, he told himself. *What do I need pride for, anyway?*

What made the decision for him was the fact that he had no idea how else to go on. Something had to change, and quickly, some pressure had to be relieved, and if this was what it took to unclench his stomach and calm his mind, so be it.

Bayla arrived half an hour later dressed in very tight gray jeans and a wispy purple top. She'd painted her eyes a smoky purple, but she must not have been wearing any lipstick, because Will was pretty sure that if she had been, it would have been all over Whim's face after their ardent kiss hello.

Oh, man, Will thought. *I don't know if I can watch this all evening.*

He closed the apartment door behind her, even though the house was basically deserted—only Whim's dad and Josh were around; Alex was watching his game shows, Josh had taken a double shift in the archroom, and Deloise had gone to her school friend Nate's birthday party. Still, Will couldn't shake the feeling that they could get caught at any moment.

"So," Bayla said, plopping onto the couch. "Whim, what have you got to crush this up with?"

"Give me a minute."

Bayla pulled a ring box from her purse. Inside was a tiny plastic bag.

Will held out his hand. "Do you mind?"

She passed him the bag and he held it up to the light. Inside sat about a tablespoon of sparkling, iridescent dust. When he shook it, he caught glimpses of rainbows.

Josh is right, he thought. *There's something magical about this.*

Despite the feeling that he was violating something sacred, he handed the bag over without comment when Whim returned with a mortar and pestle. "How much Veil dust have you been doing?" Bayla asked at the sight of the tools.

"They were Ian's," Whim said.

"Oh, Ian." She sighed. "I miss that guy." She poured the Veil dust into the mortar and began crushing it up. To Will, she said, "How's his widow?"

She meant Josh. "Bayla," Whim said sternly.

"She's not his widow," Will told her.

Bayla smiled, both bashful and coy. "Sorry, I forgot she's yours now." She took a bottle of water out of her purse and poured a few drops into the mortar. "This is just sugar water, to bind it. Also, some people don't like the taste." She kept grinding away until the dust and water had been mashed into an elementary school–style superthick white paste. "All systems are go."

"What do I do?" Will asked.

"Just scoop some up on your fingertip and rub it inside your lower lip."

"Then what?"

She pulled a battered pack of tarot cards out of her purse. "Then I'll tell your fortune while we wait to get deep."

They each scooped up a bit of paste about the size of a die— Will took less than the others—and rubbed it inside their lower lips. Aside from sugary, the Veil dust tasted of something Will couldn't identify—smoke? maple syrup? He rubbed his tongue against his lip, trying to catch enough of the flavor to identify it, but it kept getting away from him.

Bayla pushed aside the mortar and pestle and the bag of Fritos Whim was working on to make room on the coffee table for her cards. "How long does this take to kick in?" Will asked as she shuffled.

"Not long."

Whim stretched out on the couch with a smile and closed his eyes. Will couldn't stop sucking on his lip, the way he'd always chewed on his cheeks when the dentist numbed them to fill a cavity.

Bayla let him cut the deck and then she dealt. As she laid out the first card, Will realized that she was using not a tarot deck but some sort of dream-walker oracle system. "Two of Spirals, reversed," she said, naming the card as she turned it over. "The Two of Spirals is a relationship card, but when reversed it suggests a relationship based more on fantasy than reality. It suggests that you care about Josh more in your head than your heart."

"What?" Will asked. "I think you're reading that wrong."

"Well," she admitted, "the card might mean that Josh cares more about *you* in her head than her heart."

"I'm not the one in her head, either," Will said, thinking of Josh's nightmares, but he found himself picking up the card to look more closely at it. Two black spirals were set against a fuchsia background, connected by their tails. Will grew dizzy as he looked at them and tried to follow the lines with his eyes. The spirals appeared to be turning, not in a steady motion but in a pulsating one.

Will put the card down, but the room looked wrong. Or else the room looked fine, but Will felt that he remembered it differently. He expected to see a green sofa on the wall where the TV sat, though he couldn't imagine why.

"Who's in her head, then?" Bayla asked.

"What?" Will asked.

"Who's in Josh's head if not you?" Her eyebrows twitched suggestively.

Feodor, Will thought, looking back at the card. He had an idea for a painting then—a painting of Josh, Feodor's face visible within a spiral drawn over her head, Will's own face cast in the spiral above her heart.

She's not in love with him, Will thought, afraid to hope the idea might be true. *He's just in her head.*

"The Archway," Bayla said, turning over another card on the coffee table, "means an arrival or departure."

"That's not at all vague," Whim cracked. He leaned over to sniff Will's shirt, which was weird. "Why do you smell like vodka?"

"Because you're high. I haven't had any vodka." To Bayla, he said, "What kind of arrival or departure?"

"Well, it came right after the Two of Spirals, so it could mean you and Josh splitting up."

"Are you at all serious," Will asked; "or just trying to make me feel bad?"

Bayla giggled. Her pupils were the size of shirt buttons. "Sorry, that's what the cards say."

Her response only made Will more confident that she was screwing with his head. "Let me see the cards. Don't you have a book with explanations for these?"

"Let's turn on some music," Bayla said, ignoring his question even as she handed him the deck.

Whim turned on the television and fiddled with the remote. "Everybody fond of George G?" he asked. Apparently he was referring to Gershwin, since "Let's Call the Whole Thing Off" began playing.

Will examined the Archway card. It depicted a stone archway, not unlike the one downstairs, built in a grassy meadow. The archway appeared empty, but when Will looked closely at a pond in the background, he realized the water's surface didn't reflect the archway. The longer he looked, the less certain he was which universe the card depicted.

Deception, he thought. *Trickery. That's what the card really means.*

He glanced up at Bayla and Whim, who were dancing in imitation of Ginger Rogers and Fred Astaire. *The card's about them, about the people they're lying to.*

Or maybe not. He didn't believe in this sort of thing, not usually. But his thoughts had started to move in strange directions, making connections he might not have seen otherwise: how Josh had deceived him about her nightmares, how he had deceived her by hiding how much he knew, how Whim deceived Deloise and Bayla deceived Bash, even how Mirren deceived everyone by hiding why she wanted to stop staging.

How Feodor had deceived them all by pretending to die.

No, no, Will thought. *He really did die. I saw it.*

His gaze had fallen on the green couch, only there was no green couch in the room. If there had been, it would have been sharing the same space as the TV.

Children's nightmares, he thought. *The most unstable of dreams.*

He couldn't exactly see the green couch in front of him, but he could picture it so strongly that it might as well have been in the room. In fact, as he stared at the place where it should have been, two figures appeared, lying with their limbs entwined, their mouths sealed together.

It's Haley, Will thought, but as the boy's polo shirt and slacks grew more solid, he realized his mistake. *No, it's Ian. And the girl is Josh.*

Her hair was longer—Will had never seen it long, and that, along with a certain softness in her features, made her look younger.

"When's your mom coming home?" Josh asked.

"Hopefully never," Ian said, and they laughed between kisses.

Will sat mèsmerized by the two ghosts.

"What about Haley?" Josh asked.

"Who cares if he walks in? Let him. He might learn a thing or two to show Winsor."

Josh frowned in admonishment and Ian grinned.

"I think this really happened," Will said, not to them but to himself. "The room remembers."

"You're starting to get deep," Bayla told him as Whim dipped her. "Let the dreamfever take you."

Will brushed his hand through the air, expecting the images to ripple, but his fingers touched the back of Josh's head, ruffling her silky hair. She and Ian both looked at Will.

"Excuse me, this is a private party," Ian said, but Josh tried to straighten her clothing.

Will didn't think she recognized him. Why would she? Until he'd become her apprentice, they had barely spoken two words to each other at school.

He held out the deck of cards, and Josh drew one.

"I can't protect you from this," Josh whispered as she stared at the card, and her features aged. The playful smile disappeared and her green eyes appeared paler than ever.

"The thing about Josh," Ian said, reaching up to wrap his arms around her waist, "is that she doesn't need a friend, or a therapist, or an apprentice. She needs a *man*."

He yanked her down on top of him and the card floated from her hand.

Will picked it up. The label at the bottom of the card read, "Walker of Stones." It depicted a man with his pockets turned out, holding a brass scale in one hand. The card had landed upside down, so that the tiny people standing on the scales seemed about to plunge into open air. When Will turned it right-side up, he couldn't shake the idea that the people were going to be thrown from the scales and that the man holding the beam above them was a puppet master.

Peregrine, Will thought. *The Walker of Stones is Peregrine.*

He didn't know if that made sense. Organizing his thoughts was growing more difficult. *Feodor is in Josh's head. Deception. Peregrine.*

He tried to sit down, but the chair he lowered himself onto turned out not to exist, and he tumbled onto the carpet. Bayla laughed at him. *The chair is from the past,* he thought. *There used to be a chair here. Or there will be. It's a future chair.*

Instead, he got up and sat on the couch—not the green one, which had disappeared along with its occupants—the regular grayish-brown one he sat on every day. He watched Bayla and Whim dance to "The Man I Love."

Feodor. Josh's head. Deception. Peregrine. They all go together somehow.

Whim was a good dancer, and Bayla knew how to let him lead. A cloud of violet smoke enveloped them, like a fairy-charmed cloud, and the tender expression in Whim's eyes when he looked at Bayla made Will feel like he shouldn't be watching them.

In her head. Deception. Peregrine.

Bayla smiled, and Whim kissed her briefly, gently, before she turned her face to rest her cheek against his shoulder. As they turned, the light shone on her silver bracelet, creating the illusion that she was holding a silver blade against his neck.

Will sat up. They kept turning, and Whim's eyes closed, a peaceful expression on his usually animated face.

Bayla drew the Two of Spirals, Will thought. *It's about her and Whim—not me and Josh.*

He scrambled to lay the three cards out in order on the coffee table.

Bayla is in Whim's head. Deception. Peregrine.

He didn't know if he was hallucinating or not when Bayla lifted a finger to her lips as she rotated past him.

Aretha Franklin came on, singing "It Ain't Necessarily So."

Bayla is a spy for Peregrine. All this with Whim has been an act. I can't protect you from this, Josh had said.

Bayla grinned at him as she and Whim twirled around the room. Her lips pulled back to reveal bloodstained teeth. .

"Will!"

Ian was standing in the doorway to Whim's room—no, it had been Ian's room once. He beckoned Will with a finger.

Uncertainly, Will gathered up the cards and followed Ian into Whim's bedroom. Everything inside it was different. All Whim's crap was gone, replaced by a queen-sized bed that was much too big for the room, a pile of sports equipment, and a shoe rack full of expensive sneakers.

"Check it out," Ian said, crouching at the foot of the bed. With a fingernail, he pried the metal heat duct cover away from the wall. "Reach inside."

I'm going to regret this, Will thought, but he couldn't resist sticking his hand into the wall. A few inches past his wrist, he felt something cold and smooth.

He pulled out a pint of vodka.

"That's for you," Ian told him. "I saved it all this time for you."

Will gazed at the bottle, at an incomprehensible label written

along the way. He reached the archroom door and frantically punched in his code, only to see the light turn red instead of green.

"And you wonder why she comes to me at night!" Feodor taunted. "I can give her the World, the Dream, the Death—all of it!"

Will punched his code again, and the light turned green as internal gears unlocked the door. Before it had finished opening fully, Will was through and yanking the door shut again.

"You are a child—"

Will could still hear Feodor screaming on the other side of the door. As he backed away, he heard a different voice: Josh's.

"Will?" she asked.

He turned around and saw her tied up on the archroom floor.

"You're not real," he said.

"What? Of course I am."

"No," Will told her, sinking to the floor. "You're just inside my head."

He curled up in a ball and ground his face against his knees until his brow bones hurt. "Will," Josh kept saying. "It's really me. Are you all right? Can you untie me? I promise I'm real."

His head hurt. His eyes ached deep within every time he tried to open them. He needed to sleep, but Josh kept talking to him.

"Will, look at me. Please."

He forced his eyes open against the daggers of light. "What?"

Her face was only a few feet away, a black patch over one eye, but he thought he saw something foreign in her expression, and he wondered if she had come from the future or the past.

"What's wrong?"

Will closed his eyes again. "I'm deep on Veil dust," he told her.

Then he took a long swig of vodka from the bottle in his hand and went to sleep.

Twenty-one

Haley found Josh sometime after midnight. By then she had been bound for hours, watching Will sleep and wondering if he'd been serious about the Veil dust. She hoped not.

While she slowly coaxed her stiffened muscles out of the positions to which they had become accustomed, Haley sat on the floor beside Will's unconscious form and explained how he and Mirren had come home to find Deloise standing on the second-floor balcony and emptying Bayla's purse onto the lawn below.

"I guess Bayla brought over some Veil dust," Haley concluded. "And then Deloise got home and found her with Whim. . . ."

He winced.

"How bad was it?" Josh asked, remembering how she and Haley had once caught their respective loves naked in the forest. Together.

"Bad," Haley said.

"That's just skippy," Josh said, thinking about which punch she'd use on Whim.

They woke Will, but he was too disoriented to make any sense. "The seeker of blood," he mumbled as Josh helped him to his feet. "The two of blood. The nine of—"

"Blood," Josh finished in unison with him. "Yeah, we get it."

Haley was examining the bottle of vodka curiously. "This is the brand Ian used to drink."

Josh hated the idea that Ian had been a heavy enough drinker to have a favorite brand.

"Ex-boyfriend," Will slurred, "of blood."

"Should we take him to the hospital?" Josh asked.

"The bottle's nearly full. He's probably still just coming down from the Veil dust."

As they prodded Will up the stairs, Josh asked Haley, "Have you done Veil dust?"

"No. I'm— It would be bad for me."

"It's bad for everyone," Josh said. "It never did Ian any good."

Haley frowned. To her surprise, he said, "It has its uses. But not for Will."

As they crossed the first-floor landing, Josh said, "You never asked why I was tied up on the archroom floor."

Haley pursed his lips. "I . . . try not to see other people's business. But sometimes I can't help it."

"So you already know?" Josh was still getting used to having this side of Haley out in the open, and the idea that he could spy on her—whether or not he did so deliberately—freaked her out. She'd had a lot to hide lately.

"I know that you're going to explain it to all of us in the morning," Haley said. "I can wait."

He gave her a smile then and guided Will into their apartment. Josh forced her throbbing muscles to carry her up to the third floor, and she found Deloise in her bedroom, sitting on her bed amid a sea of tissues.

"What happened?" Deloise asked at the sight of her sister's burned and bloody arms.

Josh gave her a very short version of the evening's events and promised to tell the whole story in the morning, but Deloise heard that Josh had gotten hit on the head and insisted they go to the ER that moment.

"I'm all right," Josh insisted. "I just had a CT yesterday."

"Either you can come with me to the ER," Deloise said flatly, "or I can wake Dad up."

They went to the ER.

"Haley told me what happened earlier to night," Josh said as they sat in a curtained room waiting for the scan. "Do you want to talk about it?"

Deloise removed a packet of tissues from her purse. "I got home from Nate's party, I went upstairs to say hi to Whim, and the living room was empty but music was playing. Then I saw light coming through the slats in the door to a laundry closet, so I opened the door, and there they were making out on top of the washer and dryer. They were even doing laundry at the same time, and Bayla had dryer lint in her hair."

For a fleeting moment, Josh was tempted to laugh. Nobody was better at making a complete fool of himself than Whim.

"Were they naked?" she asked instead.

"No, but they had every single button undone. Bayla was— Oh, I can't even say it."

Josh took Deloise's hand. "I'm really sorry they did that. And I'm sorry you had to see them doing it. I know how that feels."

"Yeah." Deloise picked at an imaginary pill on her skirt. "Is there something wrong with us Weaver girls, something genetic, that makes guys cheat on us?"

"No!" Josh said. "There's nothing wrong with you, Del. This wasn't your fault."

"I don't know. I've never done what Bayla was doing to him in the closet."

"Deloise!" Josh cried. "Don't even think that! If Whim has been putting pressure on you to do things . . ."

Deloise gave her a look Josh couldn't read. "You're too young!" Josh said.

"I'm sixteen. You were sixteen."

"That was completely different. Ian and I had been together for years. We were committed to each other."

"Well," Deloise said angrily, "obviously Whim isn't committed to me." She folded her arms across her chest. "Oh, stop looking at me like that, Josh. I haven't had sex with Whim. And after tonight, there's a pretty good chance I never will!"

Then she burst into tears. Josh had never felt that she was the world's greatest big sister, but she at least felt confident that the right thing to do was coax Deloise to sit beside her on the bed so Josh could hold her while she cried.

"Sorry, Del," she said, smoothing her sister's blond hair.

"I just can't believe he screwed this up!"

I can, Josh thought.

The sun was rising by the time they left the hospital, Josh with a clean bill of health. Haley was already up—or maybe he'd never gone to sleep—and made them cheesy eggs with bacon for breakfast.

"I think we should have a meeting," he said afterward. "All of us."

Josh reluctantly agreed. She went upstairs to pull on clean clothes, but as she brushed her hair in the mirror, she wondered if Haley had been right that she was going to confess her secrets at this meeting. The thought filled her with panic, and she rubbed the plumeria charm she wore on a chain around her neck as she walked down to the guys' apartment.

In addition to the bright red burns where the magnets had touched her skin, the points where the wires had cut her flesh were inflamed, both on her arm and on her forehead and neck. She'd managed to hide the burns from the ER doctor using her bangs and a sweatshirt, but when she entered the guys' apartment, Mirren looked up from Haley's tablet and immediately said, "Josh, what happened to your arm?"

"Um, I'll explain in a few minutes," Josh said. "Let me wait until everyone's here."

Will appeared in his bedroom doorway; maybe he had heard her voice. He had changed clothes, but he still looked haggard, his cheeks shadowed with stubble, his eyes blinking often as if they wouldn't clear. Anger and defeat warred in his expression.

He fell onto the couch next to Deloise, so Josh sat beside Haley on the floor, glad for his silent support. "Who are we missing?" she asked.

"Whim," Will said. "He's in his room."

All eyes turned to Deloise, who said, "Somebody else call him."

After a moment of silence, during which no one made any move toward Whim's room, Will hollered, *"Whim! Get in here!"*

Whim emerged, looking like he'd slept well and awoken refreshed, and except for an underlying sheepishness in his expression, he appeared no different from the way he had the day before. "Did I hear someone ever so sweetly call my name?"

He dropped onto an oversize beanbag chair that—because of his height—looked proportionally normal in size. "What's up, friends? Why the official summons?"

"Why do you think, Whim?" Deloise asked.

Whim made an exaggerated wince while shrugging his shoulders. "I guess it might *possibly* be because Will and I got a little carried away last night."

"A little carried away?" Deloise repeated at the same time Haley said: "We're here to talk about a lot of things."

But Deloise was going to have her say. "You used a sacred substance to get high and then got your freak on with Bayla in the laundry closet!"

Genuine alarm flashed on Whim's face. "I don't actually remember that last part. Although it would explain why I woke up reeking of fabric softener."

"This is not a joke!" Deloise snapped. "I'm angry at you, and I have every right to be!"

Mirren was looking everywhere except at Whim and Deloise. Haley was staring at the floor. Josh wondered if she should suggest her sister take her conversation somewhere private, but she couldn't get a word in edgewise.

"I'm not saying that you don't," Whim told Deloise. "Obviously, I screwed up last night. I don't know what Bayla was doing here or why I didn't shut the front door in her face—"

"Stop," Will said suddenly. "Just stop it." He took a deep breath, and the weariness of the movement almost made Josh get up and go to him.

"He's been seeing her for weeks, Del," Will said. "Ever since the last Grey Circle meeting. I've known almost the whole time, and I should have told you, but he kept saying he was going to break it off, but I didn't want to hurt you. I'm sorry. It was my fault she was here last night, though. I called her and asked her to bring over some Veil dust."

"Weeks?" Deloise cried. *"Weeks?"*

Whim cast a pleading glance Josh's way, but she had no intention of helping him, not after seeing Deloise break down in the ER earlier. The only reason she wasn't breaking his nose right now was that she didn't want to take the opportunity away from her sister.

Or maybe not the only reason. She also felt stunned that Will had known and not told her, and that he had initiated the Veil dust party the night before.

I thought I was the one keeping secrets.

"Thanks, bro," Whim told Will, his usual lightheartedness gone. To Deloise, he said, "Okay, so, I've been seeing her for a few weeks. At first we were just sorting through some emotional stuff from the past, and then I guess we got sort of caught up in memories—"

"Oh, shove it," Deloise said. "Unless some part of this story involves you taking a blow to the head and forgetting I exist for the past month, I don't want to hear it." She crossed her arms. "Next topic, please."

"We aren't done with this one," Will said grimly. "Bayla is a spy for Peregrine."

"What?" Josh cried, and she wasn't the only one.

"That's ridiculous," Whim said, though the defensiveness in his voice had been replaced with surprise.

"Think about it," Will said. "How did the junta know that a dream-walking trial would be harder for Mirren than a Tempering? Someone told them she'd already passed an informal Tempering, but didn't have much dream-walking experience. Is it coincidence that the junta picked *three* water nightmares for her to resolve, or did someone clue them in that she just learned to swim? Who told the protesters we were going in through the side entrance? Whim called them, or else he called Bayla, who called Peregrine."

"Whim," Deloise said, "how could you?"

"I didn't!" Whim told her. "Will's making all of this up!"

Josh wanted to believe that Will was making it up, that he was seeing things that weren't there, but . . . *If Whim's been cheating on Deloise,* she thought, *who knows what else he might have been up to?*

"Why?" Mirren asked Whim, her voice trembling. "Why would you do that? What have I done to you?"

"Nothing, you're awesome," Whim told her. "I'd never screw you over like that."

"Not on purpose," Will said, his tone sour. "That much is true. Our Whim doesn't have a malicious bone in his body. But he does have lots and lots of vain bones; I'm sure he told Bayla those things to impress her. He didn't know she was a spy."

"She's not a spy," Whim said, but he sounded less sure than he had before. "That's crazy talk. Why would she be a spy for Peregrine?"

Because Peregrine has always suspected I'm the True Dream Walker, Josh realized. *That's why he tricked me into entering Feodor's universe, so Feodor could test me. And that's why he sent Bayla to spy on Whim—because he thought Whim knew about me.*

"Maybe I'm wrong," Will conceded, and he shrugged. "I've only met Bayla twice. And I'll be the first to admit that I came up with this theory while on Veil dust. So I'll put it to those of you who've known Bayla for years. Do you think she's capable of something like this?"

There was a long silence, and then Josh said, "Shit."

"I second that," Haley said.

"You told me you hadn't heard from her in years!" Deloise raved at Whim. "She's a—a bad person! I remember what she was like!"

"Del, you were twelve years old the last time you hung out with her," Whim protested.

"That's right, and she laughed at me when I wouldn't smoke with her."

"That doesn't make her a spy for Peregrine!" Whim argued. "That just means she's a terrible babysitter!"

"She wasn't *baby*sitting me!"

"Stop!" Josh ordered. She sighed. "Whim, get out of here."

"What?" Whim said, nonplussed. "What does that mean?"

"It means we need to talk about some sensitive things and we can't risk you relating them to Bayla."

Whim threw his hands up in the air. "Okay, so I bragged a little to Bayla. I didn't know she was working for Peregrine!"

"Nobody's accusing you of being a traitor," Josh said, to which Will added, "Just a patsy."

Whim glared at him. "You have been a lousy friend to me today."

"So? I've been a lousier friend to Del," Will snapped.

As Whim reluctantly made his way toward the hall, Deloise added, "Oh, and in case you weren't sure, we are officially broken up."

He gave her one look—angry and desperate and frightened all at once—and then left. He didn't quite slam the apartment door, but he shut it hard.

Josh ran a hand through her hair and tried to think of what to say next. She wasn't ready to admit her own misdoings yet, so she said to Will, "Can I ask you about the Veil dust?"

He shrugged again. "Yeah."

"It was your idea?"

"Yeah," he said flatly.

"Was last night the first time you'd done it?"

"Yeah. And last."

"And the vodka? Did Bayla bring that, too?"

"No." He frowned and rubbed the back of his neck. "This is going to sound crazy, but . . . what I remember is Ian giving it to me."

Josh and Haley looked at each other, and Josh knew they were both recalling what he had said about the vodka being Ian's brand.

"I thought he pulled it out of a heat vent in Whim's room," Will added. He dared a glance at Josh. "How much did I drink?"

"A little more than two shots," Josh told him. She'd actually measured out how much was missing from the bottle before deciding whether or not to take him with her to the ER.

"That's something, I guess," he said.

Josh tugged on strands of carpet. "Why did you do it?" she asked.

Will released a deep breath, but it wasn't so much a sigh as the beginning of anxious breathing. "Ironically, I thought the Veil dust would keep me from drinking."

Will, Josh thought, taken aback. Had he been struggling not to drink? When had that started?

Then she remembered how upset he'd gotten at Young Ben's barbecue and realized that Will had tried to tell her how much he was struggling. She'd been too caught up in her own secrets to hear him.

"Why did you want to drink?" Deloise asked, her voice gentle and sympathetic.

Will's lower lip trembled for half a second; Josh had never seen it do so before.

"Because," he said, "Mirren and I saw one of Josh's nightmares through the archway downstairs. She was dreaming she was killing people and . . . kissing Feodor."

Josh didn't mean to move—her body just did. Like a violent, squirming attempt to escape Will's words, she jerked back against the TV stand, uncrossed her legs and pulled them to her chest, and grabbed her forehead with both hands as if she would have torn it off.

"It was a nightmare," she heard Mirren say firmly. "It wasn't a daydream about something she wanted."

Josh had thought she was going to come clean about everything that morning, but now she knew that she never would have admitted to the strange romantic component of her nightmares. She ground the heels of her hands into her eyes.

No wonder Will had been avoiding her.

"Why didn't you tell me you knew?" she asked.

"Why didn't *you* tell *me*?" His voice quivered.

Josh hid her face against her knees again briefly before forcing herself to push forward. "I don't know why the nightmares are like that, and I was afraid you'd think they mean . . . you know."

"That you're in love with the man who tried to kill us both?"

"But I'm *not*. I'm sure I'm not!"

"She wakes up every night crying from those dreams," Deloise said. "Whatever she and Feodor are doing in them, I don't think she's enjoying it."

"Every night?" Mirren asked. "Why haven't you seen a doctor?"

"Because it isn't a medical problem!" Josh burst out. "It's not a psychiatric problem! It's—" She stopped on the precipice of admitting how deeply her encounter with Feodor had changed her. She had known she might never go back to the way she was before, but only then did she realize how afraid she was of letting other people know.

"When he sent all his bad memories into my mind," she admitted, "somehow the bad memories weren't the only ones that I got. I got his happy memories, too, and his ideas, and his education. . . ."

"You remember his whole life?" Deloise asked.

"No, not nearly all of it. But I think that all of it might be in my mind somewhere."

"You said you have his ideas," Will said. "Which ideas?"

This is the last moment he's going to love me, Josh thought, and whatever words she might have said dried up in her throat.

"Yeah," was all that came out.

Haley put his arm around her shoulders.

"Yeah?" Will asked.

She ducked her head beneath Haley's arm and pinched her eyes shut.

"Yes, she remembers his inventions," Haley said. "Yes, she remembers how to build them."

"*Did* you build them?" Will asked.

Josh, eyes still closed, nodded.

Will cursed, and she heard the floor squeak as he got up from the couch. "Josh!" Deloise cried with a gasp.

"What were you thinking?" Will asked.

Josh wanted to hide beneath Haley's arm and behind her closed eyelids forever. Her shame burned like a snakebite.

"Why, Josh? *Why?*" Will shouted.

Haley nudged Josh to face her friends. "S'okay," he told her. "Tell them."

When Josh forced her eyes open, black lines flickered across the room. She blinked a few times, and when her vision cleared all she could see was Will, standing behind the couch and clenching the back edge as if he would hurl the sectional across the room.

"Mostly I just wrote down the things I learned in the nightmares," she admitted. "But I did build three of Feodor's inventions. Partly I did it because I thought that eventually I'd dream of something to help Winsor. And partly, I . . . I just got so frustrated trying to connect with the Dream. I don't know what the point of being the True Dream Walker is if I can't help anyone, and I thought Feodor's inventions could help me. I just want to do my job, I just want to make the Dream safe!"

Will released a bitter half laugh. "Dear God," he said. "You're not in love with Feodor—you're in love with his power!"

And that, Josh realized, was true.

Will shook his head, releasing the couch back to cross his arms over his chest. "You're such a fool, Josh."

"What else was I supposed to do?" she asked. "What would you have done?"

"I would have trusted that whatever fate had decided to make me the True Dream Walker would teach me how to use that power when it was good and ready."

The answer was so stupid that Josh stopped feeling guilty and started feeling angry. "Bullshit!" she told Will. "You don't trust anyone to do anything—you're a complete control freak! You won't even let Kerstel cook by herself! And if you hadn't been panicking over every tiny thing, maybe I could have come to you and told you what was going on months ago!"

"You want to blame *me* for this?" Will said, a hard look coming over his face. "I'm out of here."

"I'm not done!" Josh shouted.

"Yeah? I am!" he shouted back as he headed for the door.

"Last night," she told him, "while you were getting high and helping Whim cheat on my sister, Bash Mirrettsio tied me up and stole two of Feodor's inventions that will allow him to control the Dream."

More gasps from Deloise, a little cry of dismay from Mirren, but Josh looked only at Will. "If Bayla is working for Peregrine," she said, "I guess it's reasonable to assume that her boyfriend is, too."

Will leaned against the apartment door and slid slowly to the floor, his face empty with shock.

"Bash Mirrettsio the dream theorist?" Mirren asked.

"Yeah," Josh said.

"What do you mean by the inventions can control the Dream?"

Josh swallowed. "When you go into the Dream wearing the devices, you think a thought and it happens."

"This isn't . . ." Will murmured. "This can't be . . ."

"And now Peregrine has it?" Deloise asked.

"Possibly. Probably." Josh wanted to hide in Haley's arm again, but he'd gone to sit in the recliner beside Mirren. "I'm sorry, everyone. Will, I'm sorry. I— You were right. I wanted the power that I'm supposed to have."

"How do you even know you're supposed to have it?" Deloise asked. "Maybe Will is right and that part of being the True Dream Walker will come when it's supposed to."

"Maybe he is right," Josh admitted.

"Who's got your blood?" Will whispered.

Josh didn't know if she had heard him wrong or if he was cracking up, but the words made her shiver.

"I'm sorry," Mirren said. "I don't wish to disrupt the conversation, but Josh has mentioned several times that she believes she's the True Dream Walker. Does anyone have evidence of this?"

Josh had been so busy fighting, and had grown so accustomed to Mirren's presence, that she had entirely forgotten to watch what she said. They all had.

"She's definitely the True Dream Walker," Deloise said. "But we don't tell people that usually." She managed a weak smile. "We like you."

"Haley?" Mirren asked. Her eyes swam with tears, which Josh didn't understand.

"It's true," he said, and his smile was much bigger.

Mirren began to cry. She also began to laugh, and one or the other action led her to develop the hiccups. "I'm so—*hiccup*—relieved!"

Deloise smiled again, but she looked as confused as Josh felt.

"Were you afraid it was you?" Josh asked.

"No. But according to my scroll, there's now a—*hiccup*—much greater chance I'll live through all this."

Before Josh could ask what that meant, Will said sharply, "Why are you all celebrating? Don't you see what's going on here?"

He'd gotten up from the floor, but his body was visibly shaking. Josh had never seen his cornflower-blue eyes so large. "What's going on here?" Deloise repeated.

"Peregrine has the devices to control the Dream," Will said. "He's always been obsessed with staging, right? Now instead of going into the Dream and having to bring props and costumes and whatever else, he can just put on these devices and instantly create whatever nightmare he wants."

"So it's a lot easier for him to stage nightmares now," Deloise said.

"And the nightmares can be much more elaborate," Mirren added.

"No, no!" Will said. "That's just the beginning! Now he has the Karawar, too!"

Josh wasn't certain how the Karawar would help her grandfather, but Mirren caught on immediately.

"He can use the Karawar to call the souls of dream walkers to the part of the Dream he controls," she said, "and then stage dreams specifically for them."

"It's not just that!" Will continued. "Feodor tried to tell me last night. *Who's got your blood?* he kept saying. It's Peregrine! He has all our blood, because we all gave blood samples to the junta's DNA database!"

Oh, my God, Josh thought. *He's right.* And at the same time, she couldn't help wondering, *Will saw Feodor when he was high?*

"That means Peregrine has tiny pieces of our souls!" Will ranted. "Evidence of the subtle body is present even in the tiniest fragment of DNA! He's going to use the blood samples and the Karawar together somehow, and then he'll be able to stage nightmares for specific people!"

No, Josh thought. *No, that can't be right. That can't be possible.*

She looked at Mirren, even though Feodor's memories were stirring, each realization flicking on like a ceiling light, and the more memories illuminated her mind, the clearer the picture became.

Yes, Feodor's voice whispered to her.

"I . . . I think it could work," Mirren said, and she touched her fingertips to her forehead, as if she too, couldn't believe her own thoughts.

"Wait," Deloise said. "Are you saying that he could go get the sample of my blood from the junta's database, and use the Karawar to call my soul into the part of the Dream he controls, and then stage terrible nightmares for me?"

"Yes," Will said. "Yes."

"And he's doing all this just to rig the election?" Deloise asked.

"Forget the election!" Will cried. "With this, he can rig anything he wants! He can make you *kill* Mirren!"

"Oh, my God," Josh said again. "What if he's already been staging dreams telling people to kill Mirren? What if that's why everyone's turning on her?"

"But I thought Peregrine needed the Karawar to stage nightmares for dream walkers," Deloise said.

"Yeah, if he wants to target *specific* dream walkers," Josh explained. "But he could have been staging dreams the old-fashioned way, by using the looking stone to find dream walkers' nightmares and then jumping into them."

"Who's got your blood?" Will whispered again.

Josh recalled the day she had taken him to the Dashiel Winters Building to officially become a dream walker. He'd been uncertain about giving a DNA sample, and she'd urged him to do so.

Better safe than sorry, right? she'd said.

Oh, how wrong she had been, just like she'd been wrong about building the devices, and hiding her nightmares from Will, and trusting Bash.

I have to fix this, she thought. *Will's still my responsibility.*

"All right," she said. "What are we going to do?"

Twenty-two

They more or less panicked.

Josh began listing all the awful things Peregrine could induce them to do to one another. Deloise alternated between shushing her and repeating that somehow Whim had to be at fault for all of this. Will just sat on the couch with his bloodless face hidden between his knees.

Mirren didn't know whether to laugh or cry. She had just discovered that she might very well live through this—and that they might very well all die. The only thing she knew for certain was that if she had a chance of surviving, she wanted to fight for it.

She called Davita and impressed upon her the importance of locating and detaining Peregrine immediately.

"Do whatever it takes, even if you have to . . ." She tugged her earlobe. "I don't know—even if you have to personally assault him. Bind him to a heavy chair and then call me. Oh, and do the same thing with Bayla Sakrov and Bash Mirrettsio."

"You want me to assault your main competition in the election?" Davita repeated. "Mirren, do you have any idea what this will do to your reputation? This is career suicide."

"I have bigger concerns than my reputation right now, Davita."

Haley, who had resorted to scribbling notes on a nearby notepad, thrust one into her hand.

protect the cradle he wants our belly button

"Haley, I don't know what this means," Mirren told him. "This doesn't make any sense." To Davita, who was still barking in her ear about explaining herself, she said, "I have to go."

Haley crumpled up the next note and tossed it into a growing pile on the floor, but the note after that he gave to Mirren.

"'Open the Royal Trimidion'?" she read. "They tore down the Royal Trimidion during the overthrow."

After briefly choking on the words, he croaked, "Build another."

"I don't know what to do," Josh said to no one in particular. "Maybe we should break into the Dashiel Winters Building and try to destroy the DNA database."

Mirren had spent enough time at the junta's headquarters to know that the chances they would be able to break in were zero.

"Josh," Will said desperately, lifting his head, "we aren't marines."

"Maybe if we cut the power to the building for long enough, the blood samples will rot. They're probably refrigerated, right?" Josh suggested.

"I'm sure they have a backup generator," Will said, his voice rising with what Mirren suspected was hysteria. "They have a bomb shelter—they must have a generator!"

Although Mirren appreciated that Josh had moved so quickly to problem solving, so far her anxiety seemed to be short-circuiting her brain.

Josh ran her hand through her hair like she meant to rip each strand from her scalp. "We could go to the Gendarmerie and just report the devices stolen. Then we'd have a whole bunch of people looking for them."

The Gendarmerie were the rough equivalent of dream-walker police.

"Now that makes sense," Deloise said. "They can put out an APB for Bash and Bayla, or whatever the Gendarmerie equivalent is."

"Yes," Will said. "Adults. Let adults deal with it."

"What if the gendarmes catch Bash with the devices?" Mirren asked. "Won't they just turn the devices over to the junta? And no one will believe us if we say Peregrine's involved. We have no proof except Will's hallucinations."

"You're probably right," Josh muttered. She sighed with frustration. "At least I can go into the Dream and pull down the towers Bash and I put up."

"How will that help?" Mirren asked.

"If Bash has more of them, he could be putting them in the Dream right now, and making the area he controls bigger and bigger. At least I can dismantle this section."

"But couldn't Peregrine or Bash be in the Dream, using the devices to control that section of the Dream, while you try to take it apart?" Mirren asked. "They'd be able to control you then, too, right?"

"Maybe," Josh admitted, and from her expression, it was clear the possibility hadn't occurred to her previously.

On the couch, Will was so pale and sweaty that Mirren thought he was likely to pass out, which worried her for multiple reasons. Aside from her concern for Will, she knew Josh wouldn't be focused on the issue at hand if she was trying to take care of him.

To Mirren's relief, Deloise was the one who wrapped Will in a blanket and hugged him to her side.

"We'll figure this out," she told him. "It'll be okay."

Will just kept watching Josh pace.

Mirren put her hand over Haley's to make him stop scribbling. "Just let me think for a moment," she said, and he exhaled as if relieved and then capped his pen.

Mirren blocked out the room as much as she could and tried to concentrate on what she knew:

Josh believed she was the True Dream Walker but was unable to access her power for some reason.

Josh had Feodor's memories—if not all, then many of them.

Josh was desperate enough to wield the True Dream Walker's power that she had made a serious lapse in judgment and created dangerously powerful devices, which Bash—and likely Peregrine—now controlled.

Now that Peregrine had the Karawar, he could stage dreams to influence everyone whose DNA was stored in the junta's database. This included everyone Mirren knew in the World, with the exception of herself.

Interestingly, even though Peregrine was now much more powerful, Mirren believed her chances of surviving had increased. The passage torn from her scroll came back to her:

If a queen she would become,
one of two things have begun:
a martyr's death to seal her ruse,
or lead to Death Dream Walker True.

She'd already chosen to try to become queen, which meant she was on her way either to being murdered as a martyr or to killing Josh.

There was one other possibility.

"May I speak to you alone?" she whispered to Haley.

A minute later, they were alone in his bedroom. Mirren went to the drawer Haley had emptied for her and from beneath the linen drawer liner withdrew the sheet of paper she had brought back with her from the Hidden Kingdom. After reading through the secret ritual it described one last time, she held it out to Haley, who took the brittle page from her with light fingers. As he read the handwritten words, he sank onto his bed.

Without looking at Mirren, he gave the page back to her.

"Do you understand what it says?" she asked.

He removed his steno pad from the pocket of his gray cardigan and rubbed his thumb over the glossy cover like it was a talisman. "I can't help you with that," he said.

Mirren glanced at the page, half expecting its contents to have changed since she had last read it. "I don't understand."

"I can't . . . I can't tell you if you should use that."

She had experienced Haley when he was anxious and when he was shy, but she didn't know how to read him now. Gently, she lifted his chin with the edge of her finger.

"Haley?"

His hazel eyes were pained. "I know too much," he whispered. "I see too far. I can't . . . influence what you do."

"Oh." Mirren turned to drop the paper back into her drawer. *The disadvantages of loving a psychic,* she thought, and wondered if she did, in fact, love him.

She had always assumed that love grew from knowing another person deeply, from learning to see all the wonderful things in him or her. She'd expected to have to study her lovers the way she had studied books and physics and languages, to tease out every nuance of personality.

But as she slipped onto the bed beside Haley, she wondered if love couldn't grow from seeing a single profound beauty in someone. If it could, she knew that seeing Haley try so hard to grow was enough for her.

"Don't tell me," she whispered, hugging him. "You don't have to tell me."

"I want to tell you everything," he admitted. He rested his chin on top of her head. "I feel like you're the first person I've met who wouldn't run screaming."

"I wouldn't run," she told him. "Not from you."

He pulled back to look into her eyes, as if he needed to witness the truth in them, and whatever he found there made him smile. Mirren tilted her head and ever so slowly kissed him, not on the mouth, but on the hinge of his jaw. Her own boldness astonished her, and the heady taste of his skin made her open her mouth.

"Mirren," he whispered, but the end of her name turned to a groan that told her he would not always be so quiet or so gentle.

He slid his hand into her hair, and she knew he was going to turn her head and kiss her full on the mouth, and she was going to let him, and at that exact moment Josh opened the bedroom door and said, "All right, the plan goes like this: First, I go into the Dream. If I stand outside the basketball court, I can reach into it and pull out the towers, and that way I won't risk my whole body. Then I start building another vambrace and circlet, although it might take me a few days to build a whole new set since I'm out of beryllium copper."

Only then did she appear to realize what she had interrupted.

"Oh," she said. "Uh, sorry."

She ducked back into the living room, but the reminder of the danger they faced had ruined the moment. "I suppose I should call Davita again," Mirren said, rising reluctantly from the bed.

"I suppose," Haley echoed, smiling.

Mirren caught his hand. "You owe me a kiss," she said.

He stood and placed a soft kiss on the top of her head.

"Now you owe me two," she told him.

Haley and Will accompanied Josh down to the archroom, while Mirren called Davita again. Davita had said that no one could find Peregrine, which was unusual for a Tuesday. He was known for being obsessively punctual and scheduling down to five-minute intervals.

"Where are you?" Davita asked.

"Where am I?" Mirren repeated, surprised by the question.

"Yes. Where are you?"

Something in Davita's voice unsettled Mirren.

"What do you mean—where am I?" she asked, knowing full well that her aunt would have called Mirren rude.

"Are you at Josh and Deloise's house?"

Again, something . . . was Davita's tone too intense? Mirren couldn't shake the feeling that something was off.

"No," she lied. "We're on our way to brunch someplace downtown. Fat Mac's, I think Josh said? And then Deloise is going to take me makeup shopping."

"That's fine, then," Davita said. "Call me when you get back to the house."

"I will," Mirren promised, but she frowned at the phone as she ended the call.

Why does Davita want to know where I am?

What if Peregrine had already gotten to her?

Josh, Haley, and Will returned from the basement much sooner than Mirren had expected, and from their faces, she knew they had brought bad news.

Josh dropped like a stone onto the couch. "Bash lied to me," she said in a voice so quiet and flat that Mirren drew closer to hear. "He told me he had come up with a way to fix the towers to the fabric of the Dream. Something about simo pulsations . . . I thought he knew more than me, that I just wasn't following, and that's why it didn't make sense. But what he really did was burn holes in the Veil and jam the towers in like corks."

"What does that mean?" asked Deloise, who had rejoined them to hear the news.

"It means I can't remove them," Josh told her. "At least, not without tearing the Veil. I can't even disable them, because I'm not sure how they work." She shook her head. "This is all my fault."

Mirren sat down beside Josh. She wanted to say something comforting, but the truth was she agreed that much of their current situation was Josh's fault. So she just patted Josh's shoulder and said, "If we can't remove the towers, then we're going to have to fight Peregrine on the battlefield he's chosen: the Dream. The question is, can you make a new set of devices stronger than the set Bash has?"

"Possibly," Josh said, and she looked at Mirren with a respect that was new. "Although, given what this set did to me, a stronger set might kill me."

We're not so different, Mirren thought, *Josh and I.*

"I'll start working," Josh said, rising.

"No," Will said, speaking for the first time since they had returned, and they all looked at him.

"If Bash can alter the Dream at will," Josh said, "then I'll need something even more powerful to stop him."

"No," Will repeated, and then his voice, which had been so weak and frightened, exploded like a piñata full of gunpowder. "This is an awful, absurd plan," he said. "I don't want to be part of this. The *only* thing we're going to do is go to the Gendarmerie, and we're going to tell them everything, Josh, including what the devices do and that Feodor invented them, because when they hear that, they're going to have a fit and send a small army to find them. They'll have Bash in custody by sundown."

Josh stood frozen, her lips parted, as if Will had never criticized her before or as if she had suddenly realized he was right, and Mirren felt she had to step between them, to break whatever hold Will had over Josh.

"What if the Gendarmerie doesn't catch Bash?" Mirren asked. "What if they do catch him and he's already given the devices to Peregrine? We don't have any evidence that Peregrine is involved. All he has to do is hide the devices and play innocent. What if Josh is detained or even arrested and can't build a new set of devices, and Peregrine starts staging dreams? How are we going to stop him then? The first thing I would do, in Peregrine's position, is stage dreams for the gendarmes themselves to make them unfailingly loyal to me. What if Peregrine builds dozens more devices, and starts handing them out to those loyal guards?"

Will looked at Mirren with something like hate in his eyes.

Whatever is between him and Josh, she thought, *it is very complicated.*

"Fine," he muttered. "Fine. I'm hungry." He barked, "Is anybody else hungry?"

Then he stormed out of the apartment.

"Oh, my God," Josh said—mostly, it seemed, to herself—and went after him.

Mirren felt an emotion she hadn't experienced in a long time and realized it was embarrassment. "I handled that badly," she said.

Deloise gave her a sympathetic smile. "Will is hungover and emotionally exhausted. Don't take him too seriously." She sighed. "But I *am* hungry. Let's go find something to eat."

Mirren let Haley wrap his arm around her waist and lead her toward the stairs. Deloise followed them.

Mirren was still lost in thoughts about the difficulty of navigating other people's issues when she followed Will and Josh into the kitchen. She saw only a flash of movement beside her and heard Deloise cry, "Knife!" before Haley used the arm he had wrapped around her waist to yank her backward into the hallway.

Whim's father, Alex, lunged toward her with a large, serrated knife. As Haley yanked Mirren out of the way, Josh pushed Alex's arm to the side so that the blade missed Mirren's torso and instead pierced the refrigerator door.

Mirren couldn't help screaming as she scrambled across the hallway carpeting. She lost sight of the kitchen, but she heard something big hit the floor, and then Will cried, "Stay down or I'll break your arm!"

Silence filled the hallway. Deloise and Haley stood between Mirren and the kitchen door, both of them in fighting stances as if ready for another attacker.

"What—*the shit*—was that?" Mirren heard Josh demand.

Mirren's heartbeat sounded like a roulette wheel in her ears, but she made herself climb to her feet. She was determined to meet the first attack on her life with dignity.

"She has to die!" Alex cried from the kitchen.

When Mirren entered the kitchen, Will had Alex on the floor and was kneeling on the older man's back, keeping both his arms in a lock.

"Three weeks ago you were professing your family's undying loyalty to the monarchy," Josh was saying. "What happened?"

"I was duped!" Alex cried. "She's lying to you! She's lying to all of us!"

"About what?" Will asked skeptically.

In a hushed, creepy voice, Alex said, "There's sorcery in her eyes."

"Ah, right," Josh said. "Del, we're gonna need some rope in here."

"You're under her spell," Alex warned Will, trying to crane his neck to look behind him. "She'll lead all of you to Death."

"Why do you think that?" Will asked.

"I had a vision. I saw the royal crown upon the skull of Death, I saw the wine she drank spill from her bare ribs, I saw emerald rings slip from her finger bones. Her woman form rotted away and revealed the soul-carcass beneath."

Mirren's family had been accused of many things: greed, secrecy, pride. But this was the first time Mirren could recall "undead" being thrown into the mix.

"*What?*" Josh finally asked.

"Hold on," Will said. "Alex, when did you have this vision?"

"Last night."

"You mean your vision was a dream?"

"A foretelling!"

Mirren took a quick step back as she realized what had happened. Will must have realized it at the same moment, because he said, "Peregrine got to him."

"No," Josh swore, but it sounded more like an emotional denial than a logical one. "But then why not one of us? You or me—or Haley?"

"I slept like the dead last night," Will said. "Maybe the Veil dust knocked me out too deeply to dream. Whim, too."

"And Del and I were at the hospital all night," Josh said, "so we didn't sleep at all. Mirren doesn't have a DNA sample on file."

That left only Haley to account for. "I'm immune," he said, tapping the center of his forehead. "And I never gave the junta my blood."

"Why not?" Josh asked.

He shrugged. "Ian said not to bother."

Will squinted at him like he didn't understand, and Josh rolled her eyes. Mirren still didn't know enough about Ian to understand what either reaction meant, and she was distracted from wondering when the back door opened and Whim walked in, carrying a bouquet of two dozen pale pink calla lilies. He stopped short on the kitchen's threshold and took the scene in with wide eyes.

"Free me, son!" Alex cried.

"So," Whim said slowly, "if this is some sort of payback, I'm gonna say it's already gone too far."

"Where's your mom?" Josh asked.

"Seriously, Josh, do what you want to me, but leave my family out of this." Only then did he stiffen with alarm. "Oh God, what happened to the fridge?"

They secured Alex to a chair, and after a long debate over Whim's trustworthiness, they realized they had little choice but to explain the situation to him.

"So, not only did I cheat on my girlfriend and force Will to lie about it for me and leak some info about Mirren, I actually made Peregrine aware that Josh had built a very dangerous device and more or less helped him steal it and brainwash my father to commit murder?" Whim clarified at the end.

"That's about the square of it," Josh said. "Now, back to my original question: Where's your mom? And where are Dad and Kerstel?"

If Peregrine had gotten to Alex, he could have gotten to Saidy or to Lauren and Kerstel. And convincing them that Mirren was a threat wasn't even the worst he could do; Mirren felt sick at the thought that he might hurt Kerstel's baby.

Lauren was apparently at work, and thankfully, Kerstel was asleep in bed. After a long, tense search, they found Saidy hiding under a tarp in the back of Haley's truck with a syringe containing enough morphine to ensure that Mirren never felt pain again.

"You aren't safe here," Josh told Mirren flatly after wrestling Saidy to the ground.

Mirren's chest hurt at the idea of leaving the house, and only then did she realize how comfortable she had become there. The old Greek Revival had been her home since she'd left the Hidden Kingdom. The world outside it still felt big and scary.

But she knew Josh was right. "Where should I go?" she asked.

At that moment, Whim's cell phone rang. He held it out to Deloise so that she could see the caller's name, but she turned away.

Watching them, Josh said, "I think you should go camping."

Through a Veil Darkly

Message board: Is everybody dreaming about Princess Mirren?

Jacobean says: Maybe all these dreams about her are a sign. Like, the True Dream Walker is trying to let us know what will happen if we vote for her.

dirtybird says: If she is planning an overthrow with the Gendarmerie, why bother with the AC?

    spoooore says: Maybe the overthrow is a backup plan in case she loses.

        dirtybird says: Um, it's kind of obvious she's going to lose. If she has a backup plan, she should have used it already.

    YashaGottleib says: You're all just making this up to make her look bad.

        jshg_hammer says: I'm not making it up! I totally dreamed about her.

    WMRyna47 says: She already looks bad.

JillKramer says: You're all just dreaming about her because she's on DWTV every night. Media influences nightmares. Dream Walking 101, bozos.

    Jacobean says: It's possible. I read this page before I had the first nightmare.

    WMRyna47 says: Nightmares aside, she's still completely corrupt.

prancingpony says: HAIR BLOOD! HAIR BLOOD! HAIR BLOOD!

YashaGottleib says: I agree with Jill. This is all just media influence. She isn't planning a secret overthrow and she doesn't have a secret army.

WMRyna47 says: She turned Josh Weaver against us!

gilandsons says: Yeah! Josh is ours!

JillKramer says: What does that even mean? Turned against who?

brigby9j9j9 says: We gotta save Josh! The princess will use her as a hostage!

WMRyna47 says: Where's she live?

SmokeythePear says: Tanith. Message me for the address.

JillKramer says: Has everybody on this board just gone totally crazy?! I'm calling the Gendarmerie.

gilandsons says: You're aiding the enemy!

prancingpony says: I want in. HAIR BLOOD!!!!!!!!

Jacobean says: I just called Josh's house, Jill. No answer.

JillKramer says: I hope we aren't too late.

Twenty-three

While everyone else frantically packed, Will risked waking Kerstel up and explaining what was happening. Josh had explicitly told him not to because she wasn't certain that Peregrine hadn't brainwashed her stepmother, but after the morning's revelations, Will had decided he didn't have to listen to Josh anymore.

"I was up and down all night peeing," she admitted when he asked how she'd slept. "I think the hormones are giving me insomnia."

"Well, you might thank the baby for that once you've heard what's going on," Will said, and he filled her in on as much as he thought he safely could. He didn't say where they were going, but at least she knew enough to be able to protect herself, Lauren, and her unborn son.

Before he left, she pulled him into a tight hug. "Come back safe."

"I'll try. I mean, we will."

As he headed downstairs to pack, she added, "And Will? Take care of each other."

"I'll try," he said again, but he knew she could tell he was hurting.

Just as the sun began to set over Iph Lake, Josh pulled into a camping space at the campground's far end. Although Iph Lake was overrun with people enjoying the summer fishing and the opportunity to cool off in blue waters, Josh had picked a site so far from a bathroom that they had the block to themselves.

Haley pulled in behind them, and Whim parked in the next spot over. They set up two tents with a speed that surprised Will; he'd never been camping before, but it was a favorite activity of the Weaver-Avish-McKarr household. After raiding the basement for equipment, they'd hardly had to buy anything besides food and soda.

Josh's idea was simple: They had to disconnect. If no one could find Mirren, no one could kill her. Their camping trip would be free from cell phones, computers, and communication with the dream-walker world, and they'd stay off radar until they came up with a better plan.

There had been some debate over who would travel with Mirren. Josh had insisted on going along to protect Mirren, and she'd wanted Will to go with her. Will had been relieved by the idea of getting away—he wanted Josh as far from an archway as possible. Deloise was coming, but she hadn't wanted Whim to come, and when he'd insisted, Deloise had responded by running the calla lilies through the garbage disposal.

Thanks to his psychic powers, Haley was the only one who was entirely safe from Peregrine's influence, but he believed he could protect the others. To that end, he and Mirren had made a detour to buy semiprecious stones, tiny mirrors, five pounds of Himalayan pink salt, and a lot of string. Once Whim got the fire going and Deloise began mixing up a big pot of Velveeta Shells & Cheese, Haley used the string to hang dozens of crystals and quarter-sized mirrors from the tree branches arching over their tents.

"These will help?" Josh asked, peering up at the rocks as they spun slowly in the breeze. "What are they?"

"Moonstone, malachite, black tourmaline, and amethyst. They'll help."

Before bed, Haley gave them each a dose of over-the-counter sleeping pills. "So you'll sleep too deeply to dream," he explained. "And wear these. If the bone breaks in the night, we'll know Peregrine got to you."

He then handed out greasy chicken bones with pieces of string tied to them.

"Are they necklaces?" Deloise asked, putting hers on.

"Are they *lunch*?" Whim asked. They'd stopped at a fast-food chicken place during the drive.

Haley just smiled.

They set up a girls' tent and a boys' tent. Will was happy to turn in early and climbed into his sleeping bag as soon as he began feeling the effects of the sleeping pills.

"Um, Haley?" Whim said, lying down beside Will. "I understand that salt circles are supposed to protect people from evil and all that, but why the hell did you draw one *inside* the tent?"

Haley giggled. "I didn't want to kill the plants outside. This is a forest."

"Dude, there is so much salt in my sleeping bag. Wait . . . chicken bones, salt . . . It's a stew! Run, Will, run!"

Will didn't laugh, but he couldn't hold back a smile. "Why is it so hard to stay mad at you?"

"Because God knew that if he made me any other way, I would have very little chance of survival," Whim quipped.

Will chuckled, but he couldn't resist saying, "For a guy who just got dumped, you're awfully chipper."

"Have no fear, my friend. No woman can resist the charms of the Whimarian. By this time next week, Deloise will be back in my arms and all will be right with the World."

That's a nice thought, Will reflected as he sank into sleep.

But it will never happen.

The next three days were strangely calm for Will. He gave up on the idea that he might be able to help the others sort out their problems and instead began exploring the campground. Leaving Josh and Mirren to pore over a sketchbook full of equations and fret about the devices Josh had built, he pretended he was as carefree as the rest of the campers. He swam with Haley; he kayaked with Deloise; he fished with Whim. If tensions ever arose at the campsite, he just wandered off on his own to hike through the forest and enjoy the quiet. He even bought a cheap digital camera from the camp store and used it to take photographs of the water, the trees, the birds that soared overhead.

He tried to ignore the fact that Josh's and Mirren's stress levels were obviously increasing. The first night, he woke briefly to the sound of Josh thrashing around in the girls' tent, calling out for help, but he was so tired that he fell back to sleep as soon as he heard Deloise calming her. The second night, Josh woke them all up with shrill, animal-like screams that caused Whim to try to leap to his feet. He ended up with his legs mired in his sleeping bag and fell over on top of Haley.

By the third night, Will had grown attuned to the desperate whimpers that preceded Josh's full-blown panic. Deloise must have as well, because Will heard her voice through the walls of the nylon tents as she shook her sister awake.

"You're okay, you're okay, you're awake now. It wasn't real."

Then he heard Josh crying, not just whimpering but full-on crying, and Deloise shushing her.

From the other side of the tent, Whim whispered, "Isn't there something you can do for her, Haley? Different stones or more salt or a tinfoil hat?"

"It isn't coming from outside her," Haley whispered. "It's in her mind. That's Will's arena, not mine."

Will didn't know if Haley meant Will should be the one to comfort Josh because he was her boyfriend or because he'd read a lot of self-help books.

Pick one, he told himself.

Josh was still crying. Will sat up, unzipped the tent door, and brushed the salt off the bottoms of his feet before stepping into his sandals.

"Knock knock," he said outside the girls' tent.

Josh unzipped the door and fell into his arms while trying to climb out. "Sorry," she moaned. "I can stop. I'll figure out how."

The sight of moonlit tears on her face broke him. He'd only seen her cry, really cry with tears—what, twice? She hadn't even cried when Gloves shattered her elbow.

I'm an idiot, he thought, and hugged her.

"Mirren was right—they're nightmares," he said. "They aren't fantasies. I'm not mad at you."

For some reason, that made her cry harder.

They sat down on the cooler together, far enough from the tents that they could whisper to each other in private. Will found such comfort in holding Josh that for a moment he couldn't remember why he'd stopped.

"Why didn't you tell me about the nightmares when they started?" he asked.

"I did," she insisted. "Every time I slept in your room, I was telling you."

She felt so small to him tonight. She always felt small—she *was* small—but usually Will could feel the strength coiled inside her, the power ready to explode the instant she called on it. Tonight she felt small and so fragile, like a hummingbird.

"But why didn't you tell me about the devices and . . . the other stuff?"

"For the same reason you can't say it! Because it's twisted. And it's almost, sort of like cheating on you." She hid her face against his shoulder. "And, honestly, I think I didn't tell you because I knew it was wrong to build the circlet and vambrace and I knew you'd call me out."

"I would have!" he agreed. "I mean, damn, Josh, what were you thinking?" She shrank back, but he kept his grip around her tight. He had no intention of letting either of them pull away tonight. "People need other people, Josh. None of us is complete alone. And one reason you need other people is because sometimes your judgment isn't that great."

She laughed. "Yeah, that's true. Every time I do something stupid and reckless, I do it in spite of somebody telling me not to." He felt her relax against him again. "Do you need me?"

"Of course. I need you to get me out of my head, because when I spend too much time there, I go a little crazy. I'll always need you."

The night was warm, but Will felt her shiver.

"But—but—now you're going to hate me forever."

"What?" he asked. "Why would I hate you?"

But she must have passed him her shiver, because he felt it slide through him like the warning whisper of a ghost. *Don't tell me,* he thought. *Let's just stay at this lake forever. We can be happy here. We can survive.*

"Because," she whispered, "I have to go find Feodor."

"What does that mean? Like, in your dreams?"

"No." Her voice caught in her throat. "I have to break into Death and find him. He's the only one besides Bash who can figure out how to remove the towers."

Will was confused; whatever he had feared or expected, this wasn't it.

"But if you go into Death, you'll die. Besides, even if you went to the afterlife or whatever and found Feodor's . . . soul, and it told you how to remove the towers, you wouldn't be able to tell anyone who was still alive."

Josh gently detached herself from him and stood up so she could pace around the coals of the campfire. "That's not quite how it works. I might be able to—" She turned and called toward the tents, "Mirren? You want to come out here?"

A flashlight came on in the girls' tent, and Mirren emerged a few moments later, pulling a light sweater on over her pajamas.

"Tell him," Josh said.

Mirren sat down in a chair and said, very quietly, "Will, I'm going to tell you something that I never thought I would tell anyone, let alone three people. It's one of the secrets my family keeps, one of the things we know that are the most important to keep secret. You will understand why as soon as I tell you. I need your promise that you will never tell anyone, for any reason."

Will hated every word. More secrets—hadn't he and Josh been trying to get rid of their secrets? Nothing good had ever come of one, and here he was being asked to keep another.

"I'm done keeping secrets," he said. "I'm sorry if that's inconvenient."

He rose from the cooler, but Josh grabbed his arm. "Mirren, tell him."

"If he won't—"

"He doesn't have to promise," Josh insisted. "Will would never tell people things that would hurt them. He's a dream walker; he understands responsibility."

Mirren gave Josh a long, level look and said, "It's on you, then."

"Fine."

Will almost protested that he didn't want to know, but Mirren was already speaking in a low, quick voice that carried only a few feet through the darkness. "My family knows a ritual to break into Death. That is the correct term—'to break in.' It would allow us to enter Death, hopefully to find Feodor and ask him how to remove the towers, and then return to the World, without us dying."

Will waited to see how he would react, but the information was lost on him. What Mirren was suggesting was so unbelievable that he simply didn't believe it.

"And you've done this ritual before?" he asked.

"No," Mirren admitted.

"But you know someone who has."

"No."

"But you have some sort of evidence that this is actually possible."

Mirren glanced at Josh. "The ritual hasn't been performed—or, at least, recorded as performed—in recent memory. But I believe it will work."

"Yeah. That's about what I thought."

Will started toward his tent.

"I don't even know what I got out of bed for," he muttered to himself.

The girls chased after him, but he blocked out their protests and arguments. The plan was crap. The plan wasn't going to work. They were going to have to keep thinking while he went hiking and fishing and photographed ducks.

Finally, Josh jumped in front of him and cut off his path. "All right," she said. "Maybe it won't work. Probably it won't work. But at this point we don't have any other ideas, so I don't see why we shouldn't at least try it."

Will felt boxed in—Josh in front of him, Mirren behind him—and trapped most of all by this terrible thing they were suggesting.

"You don't see why we shouldn't try it?" he repeated slowly. "You don't see why going into the Death universe and calling out one of the craziest people there to ask his advice, which you would apparently then consider following, is a bad idea?"

"He's dead," Josh said. "He can't hurt us anymore."

"You don't know that!" Will felt his pulse speed up. The easy dismissal was wearing off and the realization that Josh was actually talking about going to find Feodor was sinking in. "Do you think being dead made him less crazy? 'Cause I think it probably just pissed him off, and in case you've forgotten, we're the ones who killed him!"

"Mirren says he's a shade, he won't be able to hurt us."

"Mirren doesn't even know if her ritual has ever worked or if it will work for us. For all she knows, Feodor could take over your body as soon as you get there."

"No, I *know* that can't happen," Mirren said.

Haley emerged from their tent, wrapped in his disgusting old robe. "Your girlfriend's insane," Will told him. "You need to— She's trying to find him!"

"Please," Josh pleaded, "listen to us. This is a long shot, but it might work."

"I don't want it to work!" he burst out. "Are you listening to yourself? You're talking about going to find Feodor! The evil sociopath who nearly killed us!"

"We just need to ask him a few questions—"

"What makes you think he'd tell you anything? Why would he help you?"

"Mirren says Death changes people—"

Will began laughing. "Yeah, I'm sure it does." He tilted his head back and the stars above—or Haley's crystals—spun crazily.

He couldn't see Josh clearly, but he heard how helpless she felt when she spoke. "Will . . . we just don't know what else to do at this point."

"Pretty much anything else would be okay with me."

"Will," Josh said, and he saw her turn her head to glance at Mirren before going on.

"Don't look at Mirren!" Will barked, and his control snapped like the chicken bone he wore around his neck. "Mirren doesn't know what happened last time! She didn't see the look on your face when you realized Feodor had Ian, she wasn't the one you called an outsider when she tried to make you think rationally, and she didn't have to watch you vomiting and beating your head against the floor to try to escape Feodor's memories! So don't tell me that *Mirren* is any sort of authority on letting you risk your life!"

He was furious, but for some reason he was laughing, too, a creepy, high-pitched laugh, and he let Haley coax him to sit down at the picnic table.

This isn't happening, he tried to tell Haley with his mind. *This can't happen.*

Josh knelt in front of him and wrapped her small hands around his fists. "Relax," she said. "Relax."

Slowly, he was able to release his clenched fingers, and Josh slipped her hands into his.

"You were right," she said in a soft voice, "about going after Ian. It was lunacy, and I shouldn't have done it. It was exactly what you said—you told me I was being reckless and I didn't listen. I know that every scar you and Haley have is because of me. I know that you're shaking right now because you haven't gotten over what happened in Warsaw, and I know that's my fault, too, because I haven't been here for you since we got back." She swallowed. "I'm sorry, Will, that you're hurting because of me. I'm so sorry."

Will fought tears. He didn't want to break down now, he wanted—he *needed* to stay angry. Seeing Josh wipe her own eyes didn't help.

"I know I've screwed up again. Probably even worse this time than last. And I wish I could go tell my dad what I've done and trust that he and the Gendarmerie would sort it out, but by now Peregrine has probably gotten to all of them. I'm not trying to be a hero this time. But there's no one besides the six of us we can be sure aren't compromised. And there isn't anyone else who can build another set of devices, if it comes to that."

Will slid his hand up her wrist to gently touch the skin near one of the quarter-sized burns on her arm. "But look what they're doing to you."

"I know, I know," she said, choking on tears. "But if you're right about the power my grandfather has now, I don't think these burns will be anything compared to what he'll do to me."

The thought was too much for Will. "Oh, God—" he said, his voice breaking. He leaned forward until his forehead pressed against hers, and he put his hand on the back of her neck, only to find more sores and burns there.

"I don't want to lose you," she said. "Please. I can't go through with this knowing it will mean losing you. I need you now more than ever."

"I can't do this again, Josh. I can't handle it."

"Please, please. Just hang in there while we figure this out. We will, I swear, and then we'll go away. Anywhere you want, for as long as you want. I don't care if we miss senior year. We can go to Tahiti, or Ireland, or Greece."

"Therapy," he said, opening his eyes. "I want to go to therapy with you."

"We can do that," she promised. "We can go to therapy every day if you want."

He was hanging all his hopes on the possibility that they would survive this, and that if they did, whatever new wounds they had acquired would be healable. And he knew those odds were slim, that he should get up and walk away with what he had left of his sanity, but her words kept echoing through his mind: *I need you now more than ever.*

"Okay," he said.

Twenty-four

Gravity, Mirren thought. *It's pulling every-thing together.*

What were the chances that she would read a piece of her scroll that spoke of leading the True Dream Walker into Death, then stumble upon the ritual to do so, and finally discover that she had been walking side by side with the True Dream Walker all along?

These things could not have happened by chance. In all of it, she saw the hand of gravity, drawing her and Peregrine toward their final confrontation, drawing her scroll toward fruition, even drawing Will toward his obsession. She felt herself being pulled along. But she reminded herself, as she followed a weary flashlight beam deep into Iph National Forest, that astronomical odds could only be made more remote by adding one more unlikely scenario to the equation: reason to use the ritual.

This has to be what we're meant to do, Mirren assured herself again. *For all of these circumstances to have come together . . . how could gravity not be leading us to this conclusion?*

Josh had proposed alternatives. They could bomb the Dashiel Winters Building and hope the blast both killed Peregrine and destroyed the DNA database. Of course, they would kill scores of innocents in the process. They could change their names, dye their hair, and begin new lives somewhere else, but that saved only the six of them, leaving the rest of the World in Peregrine's bloody hands. They could, theoretically, wait until Peregrine surfaced, then stalk and kill him. This was the only practical plan they had. But Peregrine might not surface for weeks or even months, during which time he would be free to stage nightmares for anyone he liked.

So they were going to break into Death, find Feodor, and pray that he could provide a solution. And was willing to tell them what it was.

"This is far enough," Josh said, and the bobbing flashlights formed a rough circle as the six teenagers came together in a small clearing. "Will, you and Whim mark the doorway. Deloise, can you hold flashlights for them? Mirren and Haley, start setting up the singing bowls."

From weighty duffel bags, Mirren and Haley unloaded eleven hand-hammered brass bowls. Each sang a different note when a wooden mallet was run around the lip of the bowls. The instructions for the ritual scientifically specified which notes the bowls should produce, and because a number of frequencies weren't part of the Western world's musical scale, Josh and Haley had meticulously hammered the bowls' bellies until they produced the desired, off-key notes.

Will marked out a rough doorway on the ground in salt, and then he dug a firebreak around it with a trowel while Whim filled the doorway with an even layer of gunpowder. Deloise placed extinguishers on each side of the doorway.

She and Whim were staying behind. They had decided this during what should have been a brief, logic-based discussion of who was needed on the trip and had instead turned into an emotionally draining scene complete with tears and threats. Mirren and Josh were going without question. Josh wanted Will to come because she didn't feel she could trust her own judgment; Mirren didn't know how much help Will would be when he couldn't stop trembling. Deloise broke down at the thought of Josh going, claiming that Josh had sworn never to do anything dangerous again after her first encounter with Feodor, and Will backed her up. Mirren still didn't trust Whim and didn't want him to come along, to which Whim had taken offense. He'd finally relented but made the mistake of trying to comfort Deloise, who threw a cup of fruit punch in his face when he put his arm around her.

In the end, Josh, Will, and Haley had agreed to go with Mirren.

Whim and Deloise were staying behind to make sure they didn't burn down the forest.

"What time is it?" Josh asked, wiping her hands on her jeans.

"Seven to midnight," Whim said.

Will pulled on a backpack he'd loaded with protein bars, water, and weapons. The ritual provided almost no information on what they'd encounter once they reached Death, only a few warnings.

"Remember," Mirren said, "don't eat or drink anything except what comes from Will's pack. Don't accept any gifts. Don't take off your shoes. And *don't* tell anyone your name."

Haley nodded. Mirren wasn't sure why he was putting on a violet-and-yellow cardigan, since the temperature hovered in the mid-eighties, but she still thought his sweaters were as much sources of comfort as of warmth.

"What do we do after you go?" Whim asked.

Josh glanced at Mirren, who shrugged. "Wait," Josh said.

"What if you don't come back?" Deloise asked, her voice still gritty from crying.

Josh bent over to check that her knife was secured in its shin strap, but Mirren thought she did it just to avoid meeting her little sister's eyes. "Keep waiting," Mirren told Deloise.

Mirren didn't doubt that Josh understood the danger of what they were about to do. Mythology was full of stories about heroes who descended to the underworld and never resurfaced. *Beware the tricks of the dead,* read the last line of the ritual. Will understood—he couldn't stop understanding long enough to pull himself together. And Haley was a born seer, who accepted the danger and the inevitability of these risks with his usual grace and gravitas.

The real reason Mirren hadn't wanted Whim to come along was that she wasn't sure he understood the danger. He was having too much fun.

"Let's get started," Josh said.

Ritual in hand, Mirren took her place at the bottom of the way. Gently, she struck the wooden mallet against the rim smallest singing bowl, and while it was still ringing out a clear, high A, she began running the mallet around the lip of the bowl. The note continued, coalescing into a golden ribbon of sound, bright and strong.

Three breaths, Mirren thought, counting as she inhaled and exhaled. After the third release of breath, she nodded to Deloise, who struck another singing bowl, this one an F just lower than the A, and added its voice. Every three breaths, another note joined the chorus, a D, then a G, then a slightly off-key B. Not only did the volume increase, but Mirren felt the vibration of the instruments moving through her body, creating a stir like currents in water. The sensation was not unpleasant, yet it raised an alarm in her, a primordial warning that she was playing with powerful forces.

Another F, a C, a note between D and E-flat. Each successive singing bowl was larger, its voice lower and deeper. When Josh struck the ninth note, the birds roosting in the trees around them took flight. When Will played the tenth note, the ground began to shake. Mirren struggled to keep her mallet in contact with her singing bowl. Almost reluctantly, afraid of what would happen, she nodded to Haley, who struck the last note from a bowl the size of a kitchen sink. It bellowed with the voice of an ancient leviathan, and Mirren felt her bones shake within her.

It's too much, she thought. *We have to stop—*

A sonic boom burst through the clearing. Mirren dropped her mallets and clapped her hands over her ears, and she saw everyone else do the same as a shock wave centered on the doorway sent them all tumbling onto their backs. The gunpowder—which they had assumed they would have to light—exploded into three-foot-high flames.

Holy shit, Mirren saw Josh mouth, but she didn't hear the words because her ears were stuffy and blocked.

What do we do? Deloise asked silently.

I can't hear you, Whim told her.

Josh helped Will up. *Come on!* she mouthed.

Even the orange flames couldn't give Will's face any color. He

let Josh take his hand, but he backed away from the burning doorway as she pulled him toward it.

Mirren clutched Haley with one hand and Josh with another,
and they descended on the doorway. Will was shaking his head
and trying to wrench his hand out of Josh's, and Haley was the one
who grabbed him, not by the hand but by the belt, and dragged
him forward.

The flames in the doorway vanished as suddenly as they had
appeared. Where the earth beneath them had been, now a black
hole stretched into the ground. Whim shone a flashlight into it, but
the space devoured the light, revealing nothing.

"Ready?" Josh cried, and Mirren could just make her voice out,
a buoy of sound in an ocean of white noise. "On three!"

Haley and Mirren counted with her. "One, two—"

Will shook his head desperately. "We can't!"

"Three!"

They jumped, pulling Will with them. Mirren felt herself
stretched and compressed at the same time, much as she imagined
going through a black hole would feel, a crushing sensation that
she escaped only through the distortion of her physical form, and
finally a *pop* that restored her to herself.

And then blackness, and the sound of lapping waves.

She didn't know how long she might have been sitting in the boat
before she came back to herself. Perhaps the shock of passage had
disoriented her. When she became aware of what was going on
again, she found that her companions were in a similar state.

She was sitting on a bench in a wooden rowboat beside Josh.
Haley and Will sat on a second bench, facing them. At the boat's
stern, an old man in gray robes stood beneath a lantern suspended
on a hook. He pushed the boat with a long wooden pole.

"Fair," he said to them.

Mirren blinked at him.

"You're fair," the old man said, but he sounded irritated.

"Uh," Josh said.

"The *fare*," Will told her. His lips were drawn tight and pale with anger, and only when he pulled off his backpack and began digging in one of the pockets did Mirren gather his meaning.

"He wants the boat fare," Mirren said. "For the passage."

"Oh." They all dug into their pockets and offered what they could find. The boat driver chose two nickels from Will's hand, a dime from Josh's, and Haley's quarter, and the forty-five cents must have satisfied him, because he planted his pole in the water and pushed the boat forward.

"Where are we?" Josh whispered, leaning forward. "This doesn't seem right."

"What, Feodor's education didn't include Greek mythology?" Will muttered. "We're on the river Styx."

Josh straightened up and looked around as if surprised—whether by the information or Will's tone, Mirren couldn't say.

Haley had his eyes pinched shut. Mirren took his ice-cold hand. "Are you all right?" she asked.

He opened his eyes and gave her a weak smile. "It's so quiet here."

It *was* quiet. The old man's pole hardly caused a ripple in the water, and not a breath of wind stirred the air. Mirren couldn't even tell where they were—everything beyond the water stretched into blackness, and they might have been crossing a starless ocean or traveling an underground tunnel.

"Excuse me, sir," Josh said to the old man. "Where are we going?"

The old man frowned at her. "Boat only goes one place," he mumbled.

They fell into silence. The darkness and the quiet seemed to encourage it, and Mirren listened to the lapping of the water against the boat, a sound as soft as kisses. She held Haley's hand until she felt his skin warm.

"Is that a light?" Josh asked. "Up ahead."

Mirren squinted into the abyss until she, too, could see a light, and as they drew closer the light expanded and took on a golden tone. Soon she made out a large templelike building set on a shore of yellow sand. The temple was round with a domed roof, surrounded by a circle of pillars. Though vaguely Greek, the dome was set with clear skylights, and colored stones created geometric patterns on the pillars.

The old man guided their boat up to the dock and tied it.

"Where are we?" Josh asked him.

"End of line," was all he said.

"You're telling me," Will muttered.

They climbed off the boat onto a dock made of white stone. The dock led directly into the temple, and sharp rocks covered the beach below. A wall on either side of the temple blocked Mirren's view of the rest of the land, but the intent was clear: anyone who arrived by boat would have to pass through the temple.

"Remember," Josh said as they walked up the dock, "don't eat anything, don't drink anything, accept—"

"Accept any gifts, walk barefoot, or tell our names," Will said. "We remember."

Josh shut her eyes briefly, as if to hold herself back, but she kept walking.

Mirren took Haley's hand again. He squeezed her fingers absently, staring down the coastline. The sand beyond the rocks wasn't just yellow, Mirren noticed as she followed his gaze. It shone, like gold.

They entered the temple through an empty double doorway. Inside, white marble reflected the sunlight that came in from skylights high above and bathed the chamber in warm light—or so Mirren thought initially. When her eyes adjusted, she realized that the yellow glow came not from the sun, but from three figures seated on heavy marble thrones.

"The living!" one of them cried in a voice that came from everywhere at once. "Who has brought the living among us?"

The figures were indistinct, three golden human forms swallowed up by their own luminescence. Mirren could make out the shadows of their eyes and mouths, but nothing else, no ears, no hair, no evidence of their sex. Their voices carried no gender markers, only an echo that clouded any accent they might have had. Mirren had heard them called many things: gods, judges, demons; now that she saw them for herself, the title that came to mind was the lords of Death.

"We came on our own," Josh said to the figures. Two of them rose from their thrones and walked toward their visitors, revealing astonishing height. As they came closer, Mirren found their luster painful to behold.

"Name yourself," commanded the figure that had remained seated, "you who have broken into Death."

"We aren't going to tell you our names," Josh said, and Mirren felt a flutter of panic inside, like the birds that had rushed from the trees.

She touched Josh's shoulder while stepping out in front of her friends. "Please forgive us," she said, and then stumbled for an instant while trying to decide what term of address would be appropriate. "Your Highnesses," she added, choosing the first nongendered term that came to mind. "We are four weary travelers who have come to beg your mercy. Our names are not fit for such glory as yours."

Then she curtsied. With her head down, she was able to glance behind her and see the others follow suit with awkward bows— even Josh.

Rising, she discovered that one of the figures was standing so close that she could feel its heat on her skin. She had to close her eyes as it brushed a hand along the side of her face, touching her hair.

"Nonsense," it said. "What are your names?"

"Begging your pardon," Mirren said, "we cannot say."

Now the other figure, which had been examining Haley with some interest, turned toward Mirren, and she felt its touch follow her spine from the back of her neck to the top of her hips, as if its radiant fingers could pass through her clothes.

"All beings have names," it whispered in a voice lower than that of the others. "Give us yours."

"I cann—"

"*Tell us!!!*" the figure bellowed, and it must have had breath, because it blew strands of hair across Mirren's face as she hid behind clamped eyelids.

In the quiet afterward, Josh said, "No." Her voice was calm but firm.

"Very well," the seated figure said, and Mirren felt the two beside her move away.

When she opened her eyes again, all three figures had returned to their thrones. Between Mirren and Josh, they had refused to give their names four times; maybe the lords of Death were allowed to ask only a certain number of times. The center figure, in a voice that betrayed none of its companion's rage, asked simply, "Why have you come, travelers?"

Mirren took a deep breath to steady herself before answering. "We have come to speak with a soul that resides here."

"And what is this soul's name?"

"Feodorik Kajażkołski."

The figure made a sound Mirren couldn't have reproduced or interpreted. "The *inumen*," it said. "Why do you wish to speak with him?"

She didn't know the term "*inumen*," but she could afford only an instant to wonder if it was part of the secret language of the dead.

Briefly, Mirren explained that someone in the World was going to use two devices Feodor had invented to upset the balance between the universes and that they needed to ask Feodor how to destroy the devices.

"The balance between the universes must be maintained," the figure on the right said, and the figure on the left—the one that had shouted at Mirren—abruptly rose and left the temple through an empty side door.

"You may wait," the center figure said. "We will bring the *inumen*."

"Thank you," Mirren said.

The figure that had walked outside walked back in just as abruptly, and Feodor Kajażkołski walked beside him. He arrived so quickly that Mirren found herself completely unprepared to face him.

She had seen him only in photographs, and she realized now that he photographed very poorly. Whereas his pictures always showed a simple man, someone who could be anyone, in person the intensity of his gaze and promising hint of a smile made him not just charismatic but hypnotic. He wore a white button-down shirt and gray slacks with a black belt and black shoes that looked somehow old-fashioned. He appeared perhaps twenty-eight; the edges of his thin lips still made a crisp line against his face, and a keen light burned in his gray eyes. Despite not being very tall, he filled the room.

Mirren heard Will's breathing speed up, and she saw Josh grab his hand. Josh didn't look too good herself.

"American children!" Feodor cried, a smile lighting up his face. "What a wonderful surprise! Always, you find me in the unlikeliest of places!"

Although he spoke with a Polish accent that softened the ends of his words, his tone was still somehow mocking.

"And you have brought me another friend," he added. "Please, an introduction."

"No," Josh said sharply, and this time Mirren didn't interrupt her. She'd thought that giving her name to the lords of Death would be bad; she sensed that telling Feodor would be far worse.

"Her name doesn't matter," Josh continued. "She's a friend of ours."

Feodor walked toward Mirren, a smile playing across his lips. "Perhaps you are correct." He tilted his head. "And yet, how familiar you look. . . ."

He can't recognize me, Mirren assured herself. She knew she resembled her grandmother, whom Feodor had known, but not to the degree that people could guess who she was. *He's just toying with us.*

"That red hair," he mused.

From the corner of her eye, Mirren saw Josh yank the knife from her shin sheath, but Feodor made no attempt to attack, only laughed.

"Get away from her," Haley said, stepping in front of Mirren.

"Oh," Feodor said. "Kapuścisko is in love!"

He pinched one of Haley's cheeks, then stepped away before Josh could attack him.

This is crazy, Mirren thought. Feodor had been in the room for only thirty seconds and he was already pulling their strings.

"Will, no!" Josh yelled as Will pulled a pistol from his backpack. Josh lunged toward him, but not in time to stop him from firing madly at Feodor.

The shots echoed in the cavernous temple, making it impossible for Mirren to count them. She and Haley grabbed each other at the same time, both of them trying to push the other out of harm's way, and they landed hard together on the floor. As Josh knocked him over, Will screamed and fired two or three more rounds, but when the noise of the gunshots and fracturing marble died down, the only sound left was Feodor laughing.

"The dead cannot be killed," he pointed out as Josh wrestled the gun from Will's hands. He held up his arm, which Will had shot a hole clear through, and Mirren watched the flesh close back up. Even the shirt healed.

"What is the meaning of this?" the golden figure on the left demanded, rising from its throne. "You have deceived us!"

"No," Mirren said, scrambling to her feet. "No, Your Highness. Please forgive my friend. He has been wronged by the *inumen*."

Feodor shrugged indulgently. "My queen speaks the truth. I forgive the boy."

He does recognize me! Mirren thought, and she felt cold inside and out.

Josh unloaded the gun, jammed it in her waistband, and pointed to one wall. "Go and sit," she ordered Will, and he reluctantly obeyed.

"Very well," the center figure said. "Ask your questions."

Josh, keeping one eye on Will, walked just close enough to Feodor to speak to him. "Peregrine Borgenicht has gotten hold of two devices you invented, a circlet and vambrace set that can control the Dream. We need to know how to destroy them."

Feodor tilted his head again. "I never built such devices."

"But you wrote the plans to build them."

"My plans were destroyed."

Mirren waited, uncertain as to how Josh would handle him or even if he could be handled.

"One copy wasn't destroyed. That's what Peregrine used."

Feodor studied her and then slowly shook his head. "Tell me the truth, and I will tell you how to destroy the devices."

Josh ran a frustrated hand through her hair. "All right. You recognized us—that must mean you remember what you did to me."

"Yes." If Feodor felt any guilt, it didn't show.

"When you sent your memories into my mind, you didn't just send the negative ones. You sent *all* of them, and since you died, your memories have been coming back to me. I remembered your plans for the devices, and I built them, and Peregrine stole them from me."

For the first time, Feodor appeared serious. "How unexpected," he said, and crossed his arms over his chest. "You remember *everything*? All my experiences, all my thoughts?"

"Not all of them. They're coming back to me slowly."

Feodor spoke to her in a language Mirren assumed was Polish, and Josh's face fell. *"Nie pamiętam,"* she said.

"Ciekawe," Feodor replied, and he wandered slowly away from them, thinking.

"This isn't good," Josh told Mirren.

Mirren agreed, but she waited without speaking until Feodor wandered back in their direction. "What do you think Peregrine will do with my devices?" he asked.

Josh explained their suspicions about the Karawar and the DNA database. "Clever," Feodor said. "How did you create an interface with the Dream?"

Josh told him about Bash and the towers and the risk of tearing the Veil. Feodor nodded and went back to wandering. He avoided going near Will, who sat against the wall with his arms crossed, glaring.

Finally Feodor spoke, but not to Josh or Mirren. Facing the three thrones, he said, "I ask that you forget my name and allow me to return to the World."

"No!" Will and Josh shouted at the same time. Will sprang to his feet.

Haley reached out and captured Mirren's hand. When she glanced at him, she saw something desperate in his face, not fear but dread.

"Your Highness," she began, but the center figure held up a hand as if to quiet her.

"Explain," it said to Feodor.

"Peregrine Borgenicht, the man who controls my devices," Feodor explained, "will use them to stage dreams and to wield power over the World. If he uses them long enough, they will destabilize the Dream on a large scale. These children will not stop him without my help."

"Then tell us what to do," Mirren said, "and we'll return and do it."

"The solution is not so simple. I must examine these towers the girl spoke of to know how to defeat him."

"No," Will said. "He's lying!"

"What assurance do you offer that you will return to Death?" the figure on the right asked.

Feodor smiled, just faintly, and Mirren feared the figures couldn't see it. "I will leave a hostage," he said.

"*What?!*" Josh asked. She actually outshouted Will. "No way! *Not* going to happen!"

Feodor shrugged innocently and said, "Then I wish you luck."

He began walking toward a side door.

"Wait," Haley said.

Feodor stopped walking and turned back to face them. Mirren's heart skipped a beat.

"I'll stay," Haley said.

Her knees dipped, and it was Haley who caught her and held her up.

"You can't," she whispered.

"You need him," Haley told her. "You won't defeat Peregrine without him."

"That's crazy," Will said, coming to stand at Haley's side. "We aren't leaving you here."

"No way," Josh repeated.

"You have to," Haley said. His face was calm, and Mirren couldn't understand why until she realized—

She gasped. "You *knew*! You knew that if we used the ritual, you would have to stay here. Oh, dear God, why didn't you tell me?"

He smiled sadly at her. "Because if I had, you might not have used it. And without Feodor, you don't have a chance of stopping Peregrine."

"This isn't happening," Will said. "J—don't let him do this."

"I'm not going to," Josh assured him. "It's not an option. We'll think of something else."

Mirren heard her, but she knew that Josh's protests were useless. She could see on Haley's face that he had already made up his mind, not just a moment ago or even a day ago, but long before that.

"I decided the night I met you," he told her.

Hot tears pooled in her eyes. "Will I ever see you again?" she asked.

He took off his cardigan and wrapped it around her shoulders. "I don't know," he admitted. "But I hope so."

"Kiss me."

He smiled and kissed her, and it was the kiss she had been waiting for since she'd met him. Knowing she might never get another made it all the more bittersweet, and when it was over she wiped the tears from his cheeks—his or hers, she didn't know.

"Stop," Josh said. "You can't do this."

"I love you," Mirren told Haley.

He smiled again. "I love you, too."

He kissed her again, briefly, before turning away. Will grabbed his arm, and Haley said to him gently, "You can't stop me. It's my choice."

"It's a crazy choice!" Josh said.

"It's still mine." He spoke to the lords of Death. "I will stay here as a hostage for Feodor."

"Very well," the center figure said.

"No!" Josh shouted. "No! We don't agree!"

"Take care of her," Haley told Josh.

Mirren saw Will grab at the gun in Josh's waistband, but she closed her eyes, knowing he was too late. They were all too late; they had been from the start.

"It is done," the figure said, and the air pressure in the temple changed.

Mirren was still crying when she opened her eyes and found herself sitting on a patch of charred earth.

Twenty-five

Chaos broke out in the forest.

"How could you let this happen?" Will shouted at Josh.

"*I* didn't!" she shouted back.

Josh could hardly believe her eyes—Feodor Kajażkołski, getting up from the forest floor and brushing the dirt from his gray pants, then tilting his head back to gaze at the starry sky above them.

"Where's Haley?" Whim asked. "Wait—is that—?"

"Who are you?" Deloise cried.

Feodor smiled at her, made a little bow, and then held out his hand.

"Feodor Kajażkołski," he said. "Delighted."

Deloise, who was too polite to do anything else, shook his hand, which caused Will to lunge forward while shouting, "Don't touch her!"

Deloise jerked her hand back as if from a hot teapot.

"Josh!" Will barked, as if there were something she was supposed to do.

Josh was at a loss. Feodor might steal Deloise's soul, but he wouldn't bite.

"What the hell is going on?" Whim asked. "Where's Haley?"

"He's gone," Mirren said, still sitting on the ground. The earth beneath her had been scorched by the door into Death, and soot covered her hands and skirt, but she didn't make any move to get up.

"Gone?" Whim repeated.

"Haley stayed behind," Josh said. "As a hostage. Until we return Feodor."

"They *kept* him?" Deloise asked.

"He said he wanted to stay—"

"You *let* him!" Will told her.

"I couldn't stop him!" Josh burst out, using a forceful voice as much to convince herself as Will. "You heard what he said—he knew he was going to have to stay! He decided weeks ago! I told the golden people or whatever not to let him. What else could I have done?"

"How are we going to get him back?" Deloise asked.

"He's not coming back," Mirren said in a soft, broken voice.

"He *is* coming back," Josh insisted. "He's just staying there as collateral to make sure we return Feodor when we're done with him."

"I thought you were just going to ask him what to do," Whim said.

Josh pushed her hands into her tangled hair. "Look, things didn't go as planned. Feodor said he needed to get back to the World to help us, and Haley offered to stay behind."

"How long can you leave Haley there?" Whim wanted to know. "Can he even survive there?"

"I don't know!" Josh shouted. "Stop yelling at me! I don't know! I'm doing the goddamn best I can!"

That shut everybody up. Will retreated to a fallen tree, and Josh was horrified to see tears on his cheeks. Deloise was crying, too. Will motioned her to sit on the tree beside him, and he wrapped his arm around her. Mirren, Haley's cardigan wrapped tightly around her, remained on the ground, rocking slowly back and forth.

"It seems I have arrived at an awkward moment," Feodor said.

Josh couldn't look at him. All her nightmares had come to life and were standing in front of her in the form of this small man, and he was giving her this polite little smile, this awkward, forgiving little smile.

When he'd walked into the temple, her first thought had been that she was so happy to see him. He'd been an old friend with whom she had waited years to reunite, and in that moment the years and miles between them had meant nothing, and just as she'd shifted her weight to run into his arms she'd remembered who she was and the impossible situation between them.

And now they'd lost Haley.

Josh pulled on fistfuls of her hair.

"Okay, okay," Whim said, seeing how she was yanking. "Stop before you end up bald. Come here."

He hugged her and she forced her hands to relax, but somehow neither Whim's bony chest nor his wiry arms were reassuring. The moon appeared from behind a cloud, bathing the clearing in an artificial silver dawn, and Josh remembered how the morning after the fire at her mother's cabin had been the first in an endless string of days without Ian. She feared this morning, feared it would be the dawn of days without Haley, and she wondered how she would tell his mother that Josh was responsible for the loss of both of her sons.

"We'll get him back," Whim assured her.

"I'm sorry," was all Josh could say.

When Whim released her, she saw Deloise and Will helping Mirren to her feet. Mirren had gotten soot on her face, which only added to her shell-shocked appearance.

"I'm sorry," Josh told her.

Mirren blinked at her and then said, "Why? If I couldn't convince him to stay, you couldn't have."

Somehow, knowing she was right hurt.

Mirren picked up one of the singing bowls and then placed it back in its suitcase, and her purposeful action seemed to wake everyone else.

Even Feodor tried to help, which resulted in Whim snatching a box of gunpowder out of his hands.

"No explosives for you," he said.

Feodor made a little smile. "Apologies, apologies. I only meant to assist."

Whim leaned close and said, "You sucked my little sister's soul out. She's lying in a hospital right now, wasting away, while her soul rots in a canister. When all this is over, I'll be the one sending you back to Death, and it won't be through any magic door in the forest."

Rather than appearing offended or upset, Feodor gave an acquiescing nod. "As you like."

He caught Josh's eye as they departed the clearing. Caught it, and held it, and all she could think as she stared into his gray eyes was, *He knows, he knows, he knows.*

What he knew, she couldn't have said, only that she felt he knew a truth about her that she would never have chosen to reveal, not to Feodor, not to Will, not to anyone, and she heard his voice as if he had whispered in her ear, *We are the same, you and I.*

She remembered how gently he had held her in her dreams, how tenderly, how sweetly he had kissed her.

She remembered the smug smile he'd worn when Haley said he would stay.

How he could be both of those people, she didn't know.

Josh turned her whole head away to break eye contact. "Go," she told him, but when she forced her feet onto the forest path, she caught sight of Will.

She didn't know what he'd seen or how much he knew—that her heart was a traitor, that she was powerless against Feodor, that everything was already lost—but she said quickly, to cover her tracks, "Keep your eye on him."

Will nodded and said nothing.

Though Josh felt that the trip to Death had taken at least an hour, Whim said that less than a minute had passed in the World. "Del didn't even have time to freak out," he said.

When they arrived back at their campsite before one in the morning, no one was tired, least of all Feodor, who kept gazing around in much the same way Mirren often did. He looked at his hands often, too, as if their solidity surprised him.

Whim was hungry, so he built up the fire and cooked a big pot of franks and beans. Initially, he dished out only five bowls, but Deloise pointedly passed hers to Feodor and he got the message. Feodor ate the beans slowly, with a peculiar look on his face, and he pushed the franks to the side.

"Let's get started," Josh said when he was finished, but Deloise said, "You barely ate, Josh."

"I'm fine."

"Nope," Whim said, and dumped another ladle of franks and beans in her bowl. "Now you get twice as much."

Josh gave him a look, but she ate. She'd gone through a thing after her mother died where she more or less stopped eating, and no one in her family had ever forgotten it. Tonight, though, it wasn't sorrow but impatience that made her reluctant; there were so many more important things than food right now.

So she ate, stealing glances at Feodor as she did. She wanted to be alone with him, where she could sort out the situation without Will watching her every second. Or she wanted to be alone with Feodor so she could confess everything to someone who wouldn't judge her.

He tortured you, she reminded herself. *He's not an old friend.*

But he *was.* He was the voice in her head, her inspiration, her terror. She had changed, she was not the girl who had nervously walked across the front lawn the night of her birthday, and he was the only one who could understand. He would forgive her bad judgment and her lust for power because they had come *from him.*

"May I ask where we are?" Feodor asked. "And also the date?"

Josh told him, despite the look Will gave her. What did it matter if Feodor knew when and where they were?

He made no visible response to the information.

"Please describe in detail the devices you built," he said to Josh.

She thought it was a strange request, but she outlined the circlet and vambrace, the configuration of wires, the placement of various crystals and magnets. Afterward he asked her to explain the towers Bash had built, and she did so as best she could, given that Bash had lied to her about how they worked.

Strangely, Feodor then returned to questions about the devices, particularly the vambrace. "And the polarization of the cephalic magnets?"

"South."

"How did you diminish the current sufficiently to avoid burning the skin?"

"I didn't, not completely. But I mitigated it by—" Josh stopped. "Why are you asking me this?"

Feodor lifted one pale eyebrow. "You brought me to the World to assist you. I am doing my best to comprehend the situation."

"But you designed the vambrace. Why are you asking me how it works?"

He begged her indulgence with a smile. "You must forgive me. Perhaps my recent resurrection has confused my memory, but I do not believe I created the devices you have described."

Nonplussed, Josh said, "What?"

"Of course you did," Will told him.

"What do you mean?" Josh asked.

"The headpiece you describe resembles an invention of mine, I believe, although mine was intended to produce a different effect. The armpiece—or vambrace, did you call it?—I do not recognize at all."

"Oh God," Whim said. "They sent him back stupid."

"But I drew it in my sleep," Josh argued.

Feodor made a little shrug. "Then I believe it would be most properly considered *your* invention."

She had wondered, while explaining the devices to Bash, how channeling Feodor's ideas through her mind might change them. Now she knew.

Josh saw herself then as she imagined Will had since he'd found out about her nightmares—as a stranger, a foreigner, even a monster. All those times she had criticized Feodor for the horrors he had created with his intellect; had she done any better when it was her turn to use his intelligence? Was her craving for control any less dangerous than his?

"Holey moley!" Whim said. "Josh, you're a genius now!"

Will got up from the table and walked away.

Feodor only stared at her queerly, waiting.

Josh remembered what Feodor had asked her when they were still in Death, what he had said in Polish so that the others wouldn't hear.

Why didn't I build the devices?

I don't remember, she'd told him.

And he'd said, *How interesting.*

But she remembered now. He had designed only the circlet, and it had been meant not to control the Dream, but to protect the wearer from dreaming.

And he hadn't built it because he'd believed it would drive the wearer mad.

"*Teraz sobie przypomniałam,*" she told him.

I remember now.

She was afraid to look at Will. Instead she looked down at her hands, which rested on her sketchbook, full of what she had believed were Feodor's ideas.

"What's going on?" Whim asked.

"So, if Josh designed the devices, can you still figure out how to destroy them?" Deloise asked.

Feodor brightened. "I believe so. I believe that if you built a second set of devices, replacing the southern magnet on the cephalic vein with a diamagnetic substance—perhaps antimony—and coating it with copper, you would, ah . . . *boost* the power of the devices to such a degree that Peregrine's devices would be no match for yours."

It could work, Josh thought. Using a diamagnetic substance had never occurred to her, but of course Feodor was exactly right.

"It might even diminish the current enough to keep my skin from burning," she said.

"Precisely! The devices, as you have designed them, will eventually break down the integrity of the subtle body, killing the operator, but this change will weaken the effect so that you will far outlast your enemy."

And the power would be immense. Josh wasn't even sure she'd have to think of something before it happened—the Dream would conform as fast as her impulses. Peregrine's brain wouldn't have time to register that she was there before she captured him, and then she would finally be able to bring peace to the Dream the way she'd dreamed of for so long—

"*Hell no,*" Will said.

Josh blinked at him. "What?"

He was standing at the far end of the campsite, next to Josh's car, as if he had been on the verge of driving away and stopped only when he realized what they were planning behind his back.

"You want *more* power?" he asked. "All along, you've been obsessed with controlling the Dream. You built two devices that could basically brainwash everyone in the World, and now your answer to dismantling them is to give yourself *more* power?"

Josh swallowed. *Yes,* she thought. *I just need a little more.*

"If that's what she needs to beat Peregrine," Whim said, "then that's what she needs."

"It would just be for a little while," Deloise began, and Will cut her off.

"Would it? Would it *just be for a little while,* Josh?" He began walking toward her, breaking a s'more stick into smaller and smaller pieces as he approached. "Would you stop Peregrine and then take the devices off forever? Would you throw them in the fire? Would you dismantle the towers? Or would you tell yourself that you know what's best for everyone and march into the Dream to fix everything the way you've been obsessing about ever since you found out—"

"Will!" Deloise cried, and only then did Josh realize that he was so far gone, he would have blurted out her secret to Feodor.

Will stopped and shook himself. "Find another way," he said curtly, and went back to breaking up the s'more stick.

Josh looked down at the sketch pad beneath her hands. She'd always felt it was full of dirty secrets. "He's right," she said. "I have to stop."

She rubbed at her tired eyes, longing to rub at her soul the same way, to shrug off this moral confusion. Did she want to build Feodor's better weapon because she wanted to protect the Dream or control it?

It didn't matter. She couldn't trust herself, not after all she'd done.

Yes, you can, a little voice inside her whispered.

She hadn't heard that voice in a long, long time, maybe not since the moment she'd rescued herself, Will, and Haley from death in the Dream so many months before.

Of course you could put the devices down afterward, the voice told her. *You would be disappointed, but you'd do it. Will is just afraid because Will is always afraid.*

She glanced at him, where he stood throwing bits of stick into the fire.

Maybe the voice was right. Maybe she would be able to use the devices one last time to defeat her grandfather and then let them go. But she knew one thing for certain: she would lose Will if she did.

"Think of something else," she told Feodor.

His earlier glee had cooled into something akin to distrust. "The best solutions are simple," he said. "I have given you a simple solution."

"It doesn't matter," Josh told him. "Building a bigger gun isn't the answer."

"You desire a moral weapon to point at an amoral enemy," Feodor warned. "Peregrine Borgenicht is not a stranger to me. You will not defeat him with your conscience."

"It's my choice," Josh said.

Feodor shook his head slowly. Josh recognized the emotion hidden deep in his expression—he didn't just think she was making a mistake, he was actually angered by her moral qualms. Feodor didn't believe in the limitations of conscience.

That Josh did reassured her.

"You can either come up with a different plan, or we can hike back into the forest and end your vacation right now," she told him.

He sighed. Then he smiled irritably and said, "Tell me again about the towers."

As Josh talked, Will came back to the picnic table and sat beside her.

By dawn, they had agreed on a new plan. It was a terrible plan, and Josh knew it. She suspected Will knew it, too, and Feodor actually laughed at them when they agreed to it, but it was the second-best plan they had, so they took it.

Afterward, they got ready for bed. "Ah," Feodor said, and then asked Josh, *"Gdzie tu jest toaleta?"*

She thought about telling him to piss in the woods and then shrugged. "I'll take you."

Whim refused to let them go alone, so the three of them walked the half mile down the road to the latrines. Whim went inside with Feodor, and Josh went to wash her hands at a nearby spigot, but when she straightened, Feodor was standing in front of her.

"This will not work," he said plainly.

Josh wiped her wet hands on her jeans, said nothing.

"I know you have not told me everything. I understand that you do not trust me, and that your friends would like to kill me, but if you wish to survive this encounter, you must confide in me."

The plan was not quite as bad as Feodor believed, but only because he didn't know that Josh was the True Dream Walker. And that was the last thing she would ever tell him.

She started to walk past him, but he touched her arm. He didn't grab her, he merely laid the cold tips of his fingers on her wrist.

"You said you have my memories. You must know something of who I am. I will stand beside you against Peregrine."

She didn't remember how Feodor knew Peregrine, if they had known each other. She did remember that he used to touch her like this in her nightmares, so lightly, such fleeting promises to draw her closer.

Right before he tore her to pieces.

Josh smiled at the sight of his skin against hers.

"I know exactly who you are," she told him, and she walked away.

After they had tied Feodor up and locked him in the trunk of Josh's car, and everyone else had gone to bed, Will found Josh sitting on the cooler beside the cooling fire.

He sat down beside her and took her hand.

"Promise me," she said, "that when this is all over, you'll still love me."

He kissed the side of her face, but she wouldn't look at him.

"I'll always love you," he said.

But she knew it wasn't true.

Twenty-six

Because they didn't know what they might encounter at the Weaver-Avish-Mckarr house—brainwashed parents, surveillance cameras, a torch-bearing mob—they decided to enter the Dream through the archway in the basement of Josh's mother's cabin.

Will hadn't been to the cabin since before their first encounter with Feodor; he didn't think any of them had. As they walked down the gravel drive toward the charred mess of rubble, Whim suddenly said, "Oh, my God! Is today the day?"

"No," Josh said tightly. "It's still two days away."

Will knew what she meant, but Mirren asked. "What's two days away?"

"One year since the cabin burned," Josh said.

"And Ian died," Deloise added, shooting Feodor an ugly look.

Will didn't think Feodor noticed. For the first time since his resurrection, he seemed confused, alarmed even. As they reached the remains of the cabin, he asked, "Where are we?"

"Just outside of Charle," Josh told him absently, her eyes searching for a way through the rubble.

But Will saw Feodor's face stiffen, not so much with anger as . . . fear?

"Whose home was this?" he all but whispered.

"What does it matter?" Whim asked, at the same time Josh said, "It was my mother's."

Will took a couple of steps toward them, uncomfortable with the direction of the conversation.

"You are Dustine Borgenicht's granddaughter," Feodor said. "I had forgotten."

He and Josh gazed at each other in a way that unnerved Will. Bad enough that they could communicate privately in Polish; could they read each other's thoughts now?

"Josh," Will said, but he had to shake her shoulder before she could look at him.

"What?" she asked.

"The plan?" Whim said. "Remember? Stopping your grandfather?"

"Right." This time she shook herself. "Right. Uh, I think we can use that beam to make a bridge to the basement stairs."

Ten minutes later, they were all jammed into one clear area on the basement floor. Will helped Whim push partially burned wood and the remnants of furniture and the scorched water heater out of the way while Josh located the archway to the Dream. Because this archway—which Josh's mother had died creating—had never been properly finished, no arch framed its edges and any bits of looking stone it had produced had long ago been swept away.

"Let's do a final equipment check," Josh said. They each had a roll of duct tape and a fanny pack stuffed with electronic signal transmitters.

Josh and Feodor had spent the day before building the transmitters. About the size of a sandwich cookie, each would emit a radio transmission when Josh pushed a separate activator. The idea was too far rooted in dream theory for Will to understand; all he knew was that once they had attached a transmitter to each tower—or as many as they could find—Josh would activate them and the entire network of towers would stop working without tearing the Veil. It had to do with signals—or waves, maybe?—and Dream particles and ionization.

Their first major hurdle turned out to have solved itself. When Josh shone reflected light onto the archway hanging in midair, the basketball court they had been so worried about locating appeared in front of them. But instead of the dozen basketball players who had been present when Josh first placed the towers, now several hundred people were crammed onto the court.

"This isn't right," Josh said. "This nightmare formed an hour and a half's drive from here."

"Maybe it shifted closer," Deloise said.

"If it had shifted," Josh pointed out, "it wouldn't still exist at all. Somehow the towers are preventing this part of the Dream from changing."

Feodor stepped closer to the archway. "I wonder if perhaps we are observing Kristiking's dreamspace."

"Which is what?" Will asked.

"Kristiking theorized that because the Dream does not occupy physical space, it is possible that all nightmares share space-time dimensions and occur simultaneously—"

"And I'm out," Whim declared. "Josh, give it to me straight."

"It means," Josh said, "that since the towers are preventing this part of the Dream from shifting, everyone who should be having their own nightmares in this area is having a big shared nightmare on the basketball court. It's not a good thing, but in this case it works in our favor, since we don't have to wander around in the Dream looking for the spot where Bash and I placed the towers."

"See how much simpler that was?" Whim asked Feodor.

Feodor eyed him dryly. "Kristiking would not think so."

Something was different about Feodor. Will had noticed it in the temple, and he noticed it again now. Although the man seemed just as dangerous as the first time they'd met, he struck Will as slightly less outright crazy. The manic glee in his eyes had dimmed, and . . . he was almost more attentive to the people around him, more aware of them as real people.

One by one, they jumped through the Veil; Will knew they each went for their own reasons. Deloise, because she wouldn't abandon her sister; Whim, because he wanted to kill Feodor at the earliest opportunity; Feodor, because this was the only way to extend his vacation; Mirren, because she was determined to save Haley; Josh, because this was her mess to clean; and Will, because he needed this to end. He needed all of it to end.

He just couldn't let Josh build even more powerful devices. The cycle would never end. More powerful devices would create more powerful enemies, which would require more powerful weapons, and so on, and so on. . . . No one solved problems by escalating the behavior that had created them. At least, not in psychology.

They landed in the center of the basketball court, where at least a hundred nightmares were occurring simultaneously. The court was jammed with people like right after a big tournament, and many of them were shouting at one another, some were tussling on the ground, one group was building a human pyramid.

"Try to stay together!" Josh called over the din. She led them along the edge of the court until they reached a corner, where she crouched down beside what appeared to be an aerosol can on the ground. "This is one of the towers."

"That?" Whim asked. "When you said towers, I thought you meant *towers,* not a can of hair spray."

"We called them towers because they work like cell phone towers," Josh told him. "Watch."

She pulled a transmitter out of her fanny pack and duct-taped it to the side of the tower. "Done."

"That's it?" Deloise asked.

"That's it."

Although Feodor claimed their plan was a terrible one, Will actually thought it was sort of clever. Once they had a dozen or so of the towers fitted with them, Josh would press that activator and send a signal that would deactivate not only the towers that were fitted with transmitters, but all of the towers.

Assuming, of course, that Peregrine and Bash hadn't increased the grid to include forty or more towers, in which case the signal would be too weak to destroy them all. And assuming Peregrine wasn't wearing the devices and didn't catch them installing the transmitters.

Will had been gung ho about the plan when they were back at the campsite. Now that they were in the Dream, he felt less certain. Especially because Josh knew the location of only the four towers that marked the corners of the basketball court, and the number of people around would make it difficult to find small cans.

As they crossed the basketball court, they discovered that the frozen area of the Dream extended into a formal garden. They began searching for more towers hidden beneath the ornamental shrubs and within flower beds. Unfortunately, the garden was as densely populated as the basketball court had been, and they struggled just to stay within sight of one another.

"I found one!" Deloise cried triumphantly.

We've been wandering around for at least twenty minutes, Will thought, *and we've only found five towers, and four of them were the ones Josh placed.*

Slowly, they made their way through the crowds. Will got jostled, elbowed, and even shoved, and more people stepped on his feet than he could count. The nightmares around him seemed to share a theme: interpersonal conflict. With the Dream unable to shift to accommodate the specifics of nightmares, everyone was just dreaming that they were in a mob full of strangers they didn't like.

Will estimated they'd been in the Dream for an hour by the time they found a sixth tower. Over the commotion of the dreamers, Josh called everyone to her. They huddled beside a fountain with a statue of an angry old man vomiting water into the pool.

"This isn't working," Josh said.

"Maybe we should split up," Deloise suggested. "We could cover more ground if we weren't trying to stay together."

"I'll stay with Feodor," Whim offered.

Will didn't like the idea of splitting up. He wanted to be able to keep an eye on everyone, to warn them if Bash or Peregrine showed up.

But it was already too late for that.

The first thing that caught his attention was the quieting of the mob. Rising on his toes, he saw that an entire section of the garden had not only fallen quiet, but gone motionless. The silence and stillness were moving toward him with the speed of an ocean wave, and he had just opened his mouth to warn the others when Josh screamed, "Abort!"

By then, the inertia was already overcoming them. Will watched in slow motion as Josh thrust her hand out, her movement growing slower the farther out she reached, and he waited for the archway to burst forth from her palm, and waited . . . and waited . . .

He felt himself still. He didn't so much go numb as terribly heavy, so heavy that he could no longer move, not even to breathe, and it was only by chance that his field of vision at that moment included Bash standing by the gazing pool.

"Look who I found," he said.

And then Will knew that this had been a very poor plan indeed.

Twenty-seven

Bash looked crazy.

From where Josh stood frozen, her arm thrust uselessly forward, she could see Bash almost directly ahead of her. He stood with his hands on his hips, wearing a button-down and khakis so wrinkled that he must have slept in them. He'd torn one sleeve off to make room for the vambrace, and above the circlet his black hair stuck up in greasy clumps.

What worried Josh most, though, was the crazy look in his eyes. They were bloodshot and overly wide, and they moved constantly, as if they were bouncing around in his head. Against Bash's pallor, his wet, red lips were parted as if with wonder.

Josh recalled Feodor saying that the devices would eventually kill the wearer. From the look of him, Bash had been wearing those devices since the moment he'd stolen them almost a week before.

"Josh," he said with a little giggle, and he stepped closer. He sniffed, then wiped his nose with the back of his hand, and Josh saw red smears on his skin. Now that he was only two feet away, she noticed blood crusted around the edges of the vambrace. "Wow, you brought the whole gang."

No one answered. They were all as frozen as Josh was, Will with his mouth half-open, Whim scratching the back of his neck, Deloise's mouth a perfect O.

Bash walked over to Whim and raised his fists. "She never loved you, you tool." He took a few quick steps on the balls of his feet before jabbing Whim in the face. Whim didn't move, didn't even rock back like a dummy would have. Bash might as well have been punching a marble statue.

"Ow!" he cried, and rubbed his knuckles. "Stupid, stupid."

As he flexed his fingers, he caught sight of Feodor, who had flung his arm protectively in front of Mirren. "Who is this?" Bash pondered. "A friend, or just a dreamer who wandered by? Tell me your name."

"Feodor Kajażkołski," Feodor said, only his mouth moving.

"What?" Bash cried. He released a hysterical laugh, high-pitched and wavering. "He's dead. Tell me your real name."

"Feodorik Jambulira Bronisławorin Kajażkołskiosci," Feodor repeated.

Bash stepped closer. "You do look just like him." He giggled, blinking his bloodshot eyes. "I guess I'll take you to Peregrine and let him sort it out."

Then he lifted his metal-clad arm and wafted his fingers through the air. An archway appeared a few feet before him, complete with a gray brick frame. Josh felt herself rise from the ground and shoot through the archway. As soon as she passed through the

Veil, her paralysis lifted, and she stumbled out of midair and into . . .

A very fancy living room.

Bash deposited the rest of her party around her, and their feet had hardly touched the marble floor before he was walking out of the room.

"Welcome home, Princess," he called over his shoulder with another quivering giggle.

"Where is my family?" Mirren asked.

He didn't answer, and as soon as he was out of sight, Josh turned to Mirren. "Where are we?"

Mirren swallowed. "This is the formal living room in my house."

"Why would he bring us to the Hidden Kingdom?" Josh asked.

"I don't know. He shouldn't even know this universe exists."

Before Josh could ask another question, Will grabbed her shoulder and spun her to face him. "Why didn't you open an archway?" he demanded.

She couldn't believe he was asking her such a stupid question, and her palms grew hot with anger. Shoving his hand off of her, she said, "Because I was frozen just like you were! This is why I told you this plan sucked. I warned you that this exact thing could happen!"

"We were all immobilized," Feodor pointed out. "She could not have opened an archway."

His head was tilted as if in confusion, which reminded Josh that he didn't know she was the True Dream Walker.

We aren't going to be able to hide that from him if we want to get out of here, she thought.

She dismissed the thought. What did it matter if Feodor knew her secret? Hopefully he'd be dead again in a couple of days. Assuming they could get out of here.

Even so, she waited until Feodor turned away to peer out the window before extending her arm and trying to open another archway. A handful of Veil dust glimmered in the air, then vanished.

"Bash must be stopping you," Mirren said quietly. "Maybe we can reach the archway to the World. It's in the stables."

"We should move now, before Bash comes back," Josh said. "Which way, Mirren?"

"Left at the door."

But the living room door was as far as they got. Josh tried to walk through and cracked her face so hard on an invisible barrier that she was knocked back. If Whim hadn't grabbed her shoulder, she would have fallen to the floor.

"Easy now," he said.

"There's something there," Josh told him.

They took turns banging on the invisible obstruction in the doorway. Their blows didn't even make a sound.

"Try another archway," Will said.

With no choice but to ignore Feodor's presence, Josh threw another archway. This time a shimmer like sunlit mist burst from her palm, but it faded away almost instantly.

"I am unclea—" Feodor began to say, but he was interrupted by Bayla's appearance at the doorway.

"That won't work," she said, and she giggled.

Bayla looked as bad as Bash, and all the worse because she normally appeared so put-together. Her designer jeans were stained with grease and soot, and she wore a dress on top of them, a color-block day dress that she'd zipped up only partway. Papery skin revealed bulging veins crisscrossing her face, and all her fingernails had turned purple. Her former beauty was almost unfathomable now.

"What happened to you?" Deloise asked, as though her shock had overcome her animosity.

"This is Peregrine's castle now," Bayla said. "He's going to make me a princess!"

Then she tried to do a little spin, but she lost her balance and careened into the hallway wall.

"What's wrong with her?" Mirren asked.

"I'm the star of the play!" Bayla told them. "I play Princess Mirren."

"She was fine last week," Whim said, swallowing.

"We traded, but not anymore. No more trades," Bayla said, frowning at him.

"Trades?" Whim sounded baffled.

"Secrets," she said, swaying from side to side like a little kid who couldn't stay still. "Secrets for kisses."

She made a loud smacking sound as she kissed the air.

"You were just using me to find out about Mirren?" Whim demanded. "You were spying on us for Peregrine?"

Bayla smiled as though he'd complimented her. "He wanted to know about Josh. But then I told him about Mirren and he got all . . . *excited*." She shivered at the word.

Josh cringed. Her grandfather had always wanted to know for certain that Josh was the True Dream Walker. He must have sent Bayla to seduce Whim, knowing that Whim was close to Josh and incapable of keeping a secret. But instead of dishing about Josh— or perhaps *in addition* to dishing about Josh—Whim had told Bayla everything about Mirren.

"But why are you helping Peregrine?" Whim asked. "It doesn't make sense!"

Bayla shrugged. "I had a dream. . . ." She picked at a scab on her arm. "I had so many dreams. . . ."

Will laughed queerly. "He staged nightmares for her."

"Who? Peregrine?" Deloise asked.

"Yes. He staged nightmares until he had control of her, and then he told her to seduce Whim and get him to talk about Josh."

Bayla stage-whispered, "He's my real father!"

"Your father!" Whim burst out. "He's not your father! I've met your father! He yelled at me for forty-five minutes once! You know who your father is, Bayla!"

"Shh," Deloise said, putting her hand on Whim's arm. "Calm down. She's not rational right now."

Deloise coaxed him to sit down on one of the white brocade

couches. He was trembling, and his face and neck had flushed the way they did when he was really upset. Josh could count on one hand the number of times she'd seen him flush like that.

"She was fine a week ago," he repeated.

"Staging would have allowed Peregrine to control her," Feodor said, "but it would not have led to this level of mental confusion. Obviously she has been wearing the devices."

Josh had already guessed as much. The burns down Bayla's forearm, the wounds that resembled leech bites, the black-and-red skin at her temples—they had all been inflicted by the devices. Josh touched one of her own burns in recognition.

"It's my turn next," Bayla said proudly. "After Bash."

"Those things are going to kill her," Whim said. "We have to do something."

"We'll be lucky to get out of here alive—" Will told him, and then broke off at the sound of footsteps in the hall.

Bash and Peregrine strode through the doorway as if the barrier didn't exist, and Bayla followed in her bare feet.

Peregrine smiled broadly at the sight of his guests. Although Josh had seen him only two weeks before, she was always startled anew by the painful imbalance of his features—the oversize lips and bulbous nose, the frighteningly large eyes. His face lit up when he saw Feodor.

"Kajażkołski!" he cried. "I didn't believe it when Bash said you were here!"

He offered his hand, but Feodor ignored it and opened his arms.

"It has been too long for a handshake, old friend," he said.

Josh watched in disbelief as they embraced.

"*What?*" Will burst out.

Feodor smiled coyly. "'Don't praise the day before sunset,'" he said, quoting an old Polish proverb.

"I knew we couldn't trust him!" Will cried.

He turned to Josh, his gaze blazing with fury, and she shook her head helplessly.

I thought I knew Feodor so well. I thought that since I had his memories, I had the upper hand.

But she hadn't remembered his friendship with Peregrine.

Greater than the shock she felt was the fear that she had once more incurred Will's wrath by making a bad decision. She had agreed to this plan for *him,* not for Feodor or for herself, but she knew that all Will would see was another example of her doing the wrong thing.

"How is this possible?" Peregrine asked Feodor.

"You may thank your granddaughters. They went so far as to fetch me from Death."

Peregrine released a laugh like the bark of a hyena. "My granddaughters," he repeated. "They're as impertinent and cocky as Dustine."

Feodor shrugged. He had an elegant shrug, as small and tidy as everything else about him, and Josh hated him for it. "How is Dustine?" he asked.

The question stunned Josh. She stepped backward again, bumping the backs of her knees on a coffee table, and she sat down on it.

Peregrine's spare eyebrows drew together. "You should know," he told Feodor. "Your man killed her, you bastard."

Feodor's smile faltered. "Pardon me?" he asked, his voice weakened.

"When your friends with the canisters attacked my family, the old bird's heart popped."

Josh watched the news register on Feodor's face. His breath quickened. "I am truly sorry, old friend."

She didn't know if she could trust his regret or not. Was every word he spoke, every flash of expression, every gesture, a lie?

Peregrine shrugged off the apology. "She had it coming."

"Don't talk about her like that!" Deloise shouted, at the same moment Josh sprang from the coffee table and rushed Peregrine. She didn't make it two steps before she hit another invisible barrier.

Her grandfather looked at her and laughed. "Haven't you figured it out yet? Bash controls everything here. And I control Bash."

"I hate you," Josh said.

Peregrine smiled. "I don't care."

But Josh watched as a fresh drop of blood appeared at Bash's temple and rolled down his cheek, leaving a wet, red trail. An idea began to form in her mind.

Peregrine clapped Feodor's shoulder. "This jewelry Bash is wearing—you built that, didn't you?"

Feodor responded with a modest nod, which only confused Josh more. *She'd* built the devices, not Feodor. If he and Peregrine were such great friends, why would he lie?

Whose side is he on? Josh wondered, but the answer came to her almost immediately. *His own. Always his own.*

"I knew it!" Peregrine cried. "The whole thing stinks of your piss."

"What is it you want, Peregrine?" Mirren asked, her voice as calm as ever.

Josh inched behind Will, whispering as she did, "Stay there."

Peregrine smiled at Mirren. Unlike Feodor, with his small, calculated amusements, Peregrine had a sloppy, slovenly grin. "I want your secrets."

Josh maneuvered herself far enough behind Will that her left arm was hidden from Peregrine's and Feodor's sight.

"What secrets?" Mirren asked.

"*All of them,*" Peregrine hissed, and his face darkened with long-held rage. "I want every secret your parents and your grandparents and your great-grandparents wouldn't give us because we weren't worthy, we weren't smart enough, or wise enough, or *good* enough."

Moving her arm as little as possible, Josh tried to open an archway. Nothing. She tried again. Nothing. But over Will's shoulder, she saw another drop of blood forming at Bash's temple.

"You think you're so goddamn special!" Peregrine ranted at Mirren, his crazed brown eyes swelling. "You could have changed the World a hundred times over, but all you did was sit on your secrets. You're a coward, just like your parents!"

Archway, archway, archway. The drop of blood rolled down the side of Bash's face, leaving a trail of pink on his ghostly skin.

"Do you truly think we should have molded the World to our liking?" Mirren asked. "What right did we have to make decisions for all of humanity?"

"What right did you have to deny them the choice? And you!" Peregrine snapped at Josh. "I know you're trying to open archways where you think I can't see. But it won't work. Bash!"

Josh went numb. She froze with her arm stretched out before her, a measly half breath left in her lungs.

Feodor leaned sideways, trying to see around Will. "How is she opening archways?"

Deloise, who must have caught on to Josh's plan, ran to the doorway and began kicking the invisible barrier. Bash froze her, too.

"Supposedly she's the True Dream Walker," Peregrine told Feodor.

Feodor looked back at Peregrine with an expression halfway between ridicule and wonder. "Is that so?" he mused.

Archway, archway . . . Josh closed her eyes and tried to open an archway with only her mind, but like in the Dream earlier, she was helpless as long as Bash had her immobilized.

"Didn't you Temper her?" she heard Peregrine ask. "She's alive, so she must have passed."

"Passing is not how I would describe it," Feodor said. "If she is the True Dream Walker, I would enjoy a demonstration."

Glass shattered. Out of the corner of her eye, Josh saw that Will had used a stone-topped end table to break one of the windows, forcing Bash to freeze him as well. Mirren rushed at Peregrine at the same moment, holding a peacock-colored vase over her head, and Whim tried to clobber Feodor with a porcelain ballerina.

Bash froze them all, and the room went still.

"Get Whim and Deloise out of here," Peregrine told Bayla. "Put them with the others."

Blood began to pool in Bash's eyes. Bayla picked up Whim's stiff form as if he weighed nothing and tossed him toward the hall. He bounced along the floor like a balloon filled with day-old helium, and Deloise followed.

"Leave the others," Peregrine ordered Bash. To Feodor, he said, "You want a demo? Let's give him a demo. Bash, unfreeze Josh. Come on, Josh, show us what you can do."

With air moving through her lungs again, Josh said, "I don't have to prove anything to you."

Peregrine smirked. "Don't you?" he asked. "Bash, why don't you provide a little incentive? I hear she's *very* fond of her apprentice."

Bash took in a deep breath, so deep that Josh expected him to shout or scream, but Will was the one who responded, releasing a choking sound and grabbing at his own neck.

"Will?" Josh asked.

He grabbed at his neck and shook his head.

He can't breathe, Josh realized.

"All right!" she said. "I'll do it. Watch."

"Bash, let her try."

She thrust her hand out again, this time in full view of her grandfather, and an archway exploded in front of her. Josh fought the temptation to go running through it. "Tell Bash to let Will go," she said.

Will's face reddened. Indents from invisible fingers marked his throat. But Bash closed the archway almost before Josh finished speaking.

Peregrine shifted from one foot to the other as if bored. "Do something else," he told Josh. "Alter the Dream."

Josh opened another archway, and then a third.

"Will, go through!" she shouted, but his knees buckled at the first step and he fell to the floor. His face had darkened to the color of a raspberry. Bash closed those archways, too.

"Something else!" Peregrine repeated.

"I can't!" Josh shouted, panic making her voice tight and high. "I can't do anything but open archways!"

"Bullshit!" her grandfather shouted back.

"Let him go, Bash!" Josh pleaded, and she heard the tears in her own voice.

But she also saw Bash put a hand on a china cabinet to steady himself. Blood ran from his ears. Every time he had to close an archway, the effort required chipped away at him.

"Come on!" Peregrine shouted at Josh. "Save your little boyfriend!"

Josh swung her hands out again, throwing archways like she was throwing punches, and Bash counterpunched by closing each one. She felt her energy begin to wane, her strength weakening. "I can't!" she repeated. "This is all I can do."

"Then you aren't the True Dream Walker, are you?"

"I don't know!" Josh admitted, as much to herself as to her grandfather. "I'm sorry. Maybe I'm not the True Dream Walker. I'll do whatever you want. Please let Will go."

She threw another archway even as she felt something within herself beginning to break down. Throughout the room, archways shimmered, the Veil revealing a dozen different nightmares. When Josh lifted her head, she saw that Bash's face was ghastly white, with stark red rivers of blood running down it.

He's going to die, she thought. *Maybe before Will dies.*

The realization of what she had to do hit her so hard that she stopped breathing.

I have to wear Bash out until he dies, and I have to do it before Will suffocates.

"What an interesting standoff," Feodor said conversationally, and Peregrine laughed.

Josh didn't know if killing Bash was fair or reasonable or moral, or even if Will still truly loved her, or if he would be able to love her once she became a murderer, and she didn't have time to find out. She just knew that she would never forgive herself if she didn't do everything in her power to save him.

Closing her hand around the plumeria pendant she wore, she said a silent prayer to the Dream. *I've tried so hard to be a good dream walker,* she thought. *Please don't fail me now.*

She was already exhausted—from opening archways, from the drama, from the guilt. She had very little energy left, but she gathered up what she could, a meager harvest of what was left of her. *Take everything I've got,* she told the Dream. *Just save him.*

She thrust her palms out to either side, releasing a cry as she did so, and dozens upon dozens of archways appeared throughout the room. They overlapped one another, stood within one another, crisscrossed the room like mirror images of one another in a fun house. Josh felt archways beyond archways open up—into the Dream, into the World, into the World beyond the Dream. Briefly, images of her basement archroom appeared, but they faded after an instant, and the arches collapsed, leaving behind a fine layer of fairy dust across the room.

Josh couldn't hold them open. She'd felt the power leave her, but something else as well, something important. Something vital. Something she shouldn't have given up. She fell to her knees, hollow and dizzy. As she did, she watched Bash mirror her fall on the other side of the room, heard his knees crack when they hit the floor. He reached out with his unencumbered arm toward the doorway, where Bayla stood watching with a confused smile on her face. For an instant he swayed as if praying, and then blood began to pour from his every orifice, and Josh knew he was dead before he landed on the marble because he made no attempt to soften his own fall.

Someone gasped, a sound like mud sucking at a boot, but Josh didn't know if it came from Will or Mirren.

Peregrine calmly removed a gun from the back of his waistband and pointed it at Mirren. Josh tried to stand, but she felt like she was trying to rise beneath a heavy blanket, and she didn't even have the strength to look behind her and see if Will was breathing.

"Bayla," Peregrine said, "it's your turn to wear the devices."

Bayla smiled brightly. She walked barefoot through the pool of her boyfriend's blood and wrestled his corpse for the vambrace and circlet. As she did so, she turned his head so that Josh could see his bloodstained teeth and slack jaw. All the capillaries in his eyes had burst, turning the whites of his eyes a solid, bright red.

Josh was too weak to gag.

Feodor walked past Josh so that he could check on Will. "Dead," he pronounced, and Josh felt useless tears gush from her eyes.

He can't be dead, he can't be, I'm so sorry, Will.

Bayla put on the circlet and vambrace, not even wincing when the wires bit into her skin, and presented herself proudly to Peregrine. He patted her on the head.

"Put Josh with the others," he said, and Josh felt herself lifted from the floor as if by magic. Desperately, she tried to turn her head so that she could see Will and prove Feodor wrong, but Bayla prevented her.

He can't be dead. As long as I don't see him, he's still alive.

As Josh floated out of the room, she heard Peregrine say to Mirren, "Now, about those secrets."

Bayla used the devices to fly Josh into a large bedroom, where five people were chained to a massive block of concrete.

"Josh!" Deloise cried. "Are you okay?"

Another set of manacles appeared and closed themselves around Josh's wrists and ankles, as if she could have tried to escape. Just breathing was difficult. Josh slumped to the floor between Deloise and Whim.

Nearby, a man, a woman, and a girl around Deloise's age sat on a couch. They all looked the worse for wear: the woman had clearly been beaten in the face.

"Who?" Josh managed to ask.

"This is Mirren's family," Deloise told her.

"Is Mirren all right?" the teenage girl asked.

Josh didn't even have the strength to nod.

"Where's Will?" Whim asked.

She closed her eyes. *He's not dead. He can't be dead. I killed for him, he can't be dead.*

Time might have passed; she wasn't sure. Her body was screaming at her, but she didn't know what it wanted or needed, only that she couldn't hold it up any longer.

Then suddenly someone was shaking her shoulders, and Feodor's face swam before her eyes.

"Open an archway," he ordered.

The mere thought caused a throb of pain between her temples. Josh's weakness pinned her to the ground.

"Give me the activator," Feodor said, but she looked at him skeptically. Her anger at his betrayal restored a measure of her strength.

"'Whom you befriend, you become,'" she told him, citing a Polish proverb, as he had done.

Feodor answered with another. "'Sometimes even innocence needs a mask.'"

Josh nearly responded in kind—she was favoring "'Your face and my ass are twins'"—when Whim said, "Speak English!"

"Who are you?" Mirren's aunt demanded.

In English, Feodor replied, "I am your only chance of escaping alive. Give me the activator, Josh."

"You betrayed us!" Whim said. He put his arm around Josh's shoulders. "We aren't giving you anything!"

Feodor's mouth tightened with irritation. "Stop being ridiculous. You claim to know me as well as I know myself—"

"No, I don't!" Josh hissed with the very last of her strength. "I don't even know who I'm talking to right now! Are you the Feodor who brushed his little sister's hair every night, or the Feodor who dumped his brothers in an orphanage? Are you the Feodor who invented modern methods of Veil repair, or the Feodor who created a drill powered by souls? Are you the Feodor who fought in the Battle of Warsaw, or the Feodor who helped the Nazis build—"

She ran out of breath, but it didn't matter anyway. What else could she say? She wanted Feodor to prove himself, even though she knew that was impossible, that there could be no redemption for the things he had done.

Bash's blood-filled eyes flashed in her mind. Perhaps there was no redemption for her, either.

Strangely, Feodor reached for her hand. His smile was small and sad. "I am all of those things," he said.

She wanted to turn away but couldn't, and even if she could have, there was no way to turn away from the truth. He had given her the answer to the paradox with which she had struggled for months: Was he a monster or a victim?

He was both.

Wasn't she the same? Hadn't she lied to her boyfriend and everyone else, and craved power, and built the devices when she knew how dangerous they were? And hadn't she done it all with the best of intentions?

"'Wherever you go, you can't get rid of yourself,'" Josh told Feodor, and she slipped the activator into his hand.

He smiled then, before turning away.

Twenty-eight

Will woke up in pain. His pulse rushed, a flash flood in his ears, making his eardrums throb, and every time he inhaled, he felt like he was breathing in crushed glass.

His eyes hurt, too, although he didn't know why. When he opened them, he saw Feodor crouching beside him with an impatient expression.

Then Will saw Bash.

He tried to sit up and had to settle for crawling away across the marble floor until he could prop himself up against the fancy curtains. Bash's back was arched, his burn-spotted arm stretched out as if he were reaching for help, for hope, for something that would have saved him from dying in agony.

The last Will remembered, he had been praying for the same thing.

"Don't be afraid; he is dead," Feodor said, as if that were some comfort. "Do you have a watch?"

Will stared at him.

"A timepiece?" Feodor asked urgently.

Will usually wore a watch, but he'd worn it into Iph Lake and it had stopped working.

"Do you have three brain cells left, or shall we use you as a coat-rack?" Feodor asked, losing patience.

"You're evil," Will managed to say.

"No one who knows me would disagree," Feodor said matter-of-factly. "Here." He removed his pocket watch and unhooked the chain from his belt loop. "I have modified this watch to keep time within the Dream, so you may rely upon its accuracy. I told Peregrine that I could alter these devices to keep them from killing him; however, I intend to fit them instead with two of the transmitters. Exactly fifteen minutes from now, I will ask him to test them. You have until then to find the towers Peregrine placed in this universe and fit them with the transmitters. At the fifteen-minute mark, I will activate the transmitters. Do you understand?"

Will heard about half of Feodor's second sentence before his brain lost track completely.

Seeing his blank stare, Feodor sighed angrily. "Perhaps Josh will take pity and keep you as a pet," he said, rising.

"Wait," Will said, the words scraping his throat as he spoke them. "Why should I trust you?"

Feodor rolled his gray eyes. "Your girlfriend wanted to know the same thing."

"I'm glad to hear that," Will replied, climbing to his feet. "You did try to kill us four months ago, after all."

"Four months?" Feodor asked, lifting his eyebrows. "I thought less time had passed."

Will didn't share Feodor's interest in time. "I should kill you right now," he said.

Coolly, Feodor said, "Try."

They both knew that Will was in no shape for hand-to-hand combat.

"You want me to believe that you've gone from wanting to kill us to wanting to save us?" Will asked.

Feodor smiled with just the corner of his mouth. "I never wanted to kill any of you. Your lives meant nothing to me. I wanted to escape that prison universe, and to do that, I had to kill you. Today, I want to escape *this* universe, but to do that, I need your help."

"Why? Peregrine would let you walk out of here if you asked him."

"No." Feodor shook his head. "We are playing a game, Peregrine and I, and we both know the other is playing. Eventually he will tire of testing how far I will go in order to keep playing." He straightened his shoulders as he prepared to leave. "If you do not wish to help me, I will do what I can on my own."

Will said, "Wait. How did you get the activator?"

"Josh gave it to me." Feodor produced it from his pocket.

Why did Josh give him the activator? Will thought. A bitter taste filled his mouth, ammonia and green onions.

She betrayed me. She betrayed all of us.

For him.

"I believe this plan is our best chance at survival," Feodor said.

Then I'm not going to let you be in charge of it, Will thought.

"I'll help you," he said, "but I want to be the one with the activator."

"If you aren't in the room with us, how will you know when Peregrine has put on the devices?"

"I'll go outside and put the transmitters on the towers, then come back inside and find you."

He held out his hand, but Feodor said, "You are being unreasonable. I will be in a better position to decide when to activate the transmitters."

"I don't care," Will said, his voice rising. "This is the only way I'm going to help you."

Feodor stared at him for a few seconds, his eyes as dark as thunderheads, and then smiled. He dropped the activator into Will's open hand.

"You'll find us in the file room," he said.

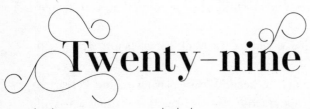

Twenty-nine

Mirren would have expected herself to be hysterical after watching Bash—and perhaps Will—die. Instead, she grew increasingly cold and matter-of-fact.

Life is a kamikaze mission, she reminded herself. *We're all going to die in the end, so we might as well do something important before we go.*

She stood in the file room, only ten feet from where Peregrine stood fiddling with the key chain he'd taken off the wall.

Three big steps, Mirren thought, *and I could grab him.*

Three steps was too far a distance; he'd shoot her by then. He had the gun tucked between his elbow and his side so he could examine the keys with both hands, and Mirren didn't doubt he was itching for a reason to shoot her.

She heard Bayla singing in the stairwell, but the person who floated into the file room wasn't Bayla.

It was Katia.

Mirren's cousin collapsed onto the floor as Bayla released her, and Mirren rushed to her side. "Are you hurt? Did she hurt you?"

Katia's silvery hair was in snarls and her clothes were stained, but otherwise she looked only a little the worse for wear. Her hug was reassuringly strong. "We thought you were dead," she admitted.

Mirren hugged her back tightly. "I'm okay. What about Fel and Collena?"

"They're all right. Peregrine's been holding us prisoner."

Reluctantly, Mirren released Katia and then rose. She could think of only one reason why Peregrine would have had Katia brought to the file room.

"I won't have her harmed," Mirren told Peregrine.

He smiled evilly. "Show me how to open the files, and I won't hurt her. You have my word."

Your word? Mirren thought. *And what is that worth?*

Before she could respond, Feodor entered the room carrying a chef's knife. "I'm afraid this was all I could find," he said.

Mirren had refused to tell him where her family's toolbox was. He'd told Peregrine that he could alter the devices so that they wouldn't kill the wearer, and Mirren hadn't wanted to assist him in any way. He had been gone a long time; she wondered how many rooms he had searched before giving up.

"Miss Bayla," Feodor said, "I will need to borrow the devices for a few minutes."

Petulantly, Bayla looked at Peregrine, who was holding the gun in his hand again. "But my turn just started!" she wailed.

"Don't be a brat," Peregrine said. "Take 'em off."

Bayla reluctantly removed the circlet and vambrace.

"Don't try anything," Peregrine told Mirren. To Feodor, he said, "How long will this take?"

"Ten, perhaps fifteen minutes," Feodor assured him. He set the devices down on top of one of the file cabinets.

"Make it ten," Peregrine said.

"Then can I put them back on?" Bayla asked.

"Stop whining." He made as if to hit her with the gun, and Bayla shrank back. "Now then, Princess, you were about to open the files."

Mirren glanced at Katia, even though she knew that the sight of her cousin would only make her feel worse. "Don't give him anything," Katia said.

She had always been the brave one: the one who talked back to her parents, climbed the castle walls, pulled out her own splinters. Mirren knew that Katia would endure whatever she could to protect the family secrets—and she didn't even know what those secrets were.

"I guess we'll have to do this the old-fashioned way," Peregrine said, striding over to Katia. He grabbed her by the hair.

"Don't kill her!" Mirren cried. "Please!"

"Oh, I'm not going to kill her. See, if I kill her, then I won't be able to torture her anymore." He grinned. "My father taught me that."

Katia's eyes were wide, but Mirren could see her trying not to show any fear. She allowed Peregrine to jerk her to her feet, one hand fisted in her hair, the other holding the gun to her face.

"You have to start small," he said. "I was going to start with ripping out her hair, but since I only have two hands—"

"I'll do it!" Bayla screamed.

Before Peregrine could even make a demand of Mirren, Bayla had sprung to Katia's side and wrestled a chunk of hair away from Peregrine's hold. She pulled, but all she managed was to yank Katia's head to the side. Katia winced but didn't make a sound.

"No, no, you're pulling too much," Peregrine told her. "Use half that much."

"Like, this much?" Bayla asked.

Mirren began to feel like she was floating. *This can't be happening,* she thought. *I can't—I don't know—how can I—*

Bayla, now clutching a smaller lock of hair, braced one foot against Katia's hip and yanked. Katia yelped as she swung her hips to the side, and Bayla came away with only a few strands.

Haley, Mirren thought desperately, *I wish you were here.*

"Let's brace her up against the file cabinets," Peregrine said.

Tears filled Katia's eyes as Peregrine forced her to stand next to one of the file cabinets. It came up to her chin. Bayla ran around the other side, so that she could brace herself against the cabinets when she pulled.

I'm such a coward, Mirren thought, but she closed her eyes. She couldn't watch.

She couldn't watch, and she couldn't stop them.

"Open your eyes!" Peregrine yelled at her. "This is the last time you'll see your cousin with a full head of hair! By the end of the night, she'll look like me!"

Katia gave Mirren a tiny, weak smile. Mirren tried to collect herself, to think, but she couldn't stop trembling. After all these weeks of threats and fears, and now seeing her cousin tormented, she was finally losing her composure.

Bayla yanked, and at the last second, Mirren shut her eyes. She heard Katia cry out through gritted teeth and something slam against the file cabinet, and when she looked, she saw Bayla holding a fistful of silver strands of hair.

"I thought her scalp would come off," Bayla said, examining the hairs.

"She's bleeding," Peregrine said. "That's enough."

Katia sneezed, then sneezed again. Blood oozed down the side of her face, the way it had Bash's.

He's going to kill her slowly, like he did Bash, Mirren thought, and then she heard Haley's voice.

Don't lose yourself, he whispered.

And for an instant, she felt him there with her, his hand squeezing hers.

She marched up to Peregrine, grabbed the hand with which he held the gun, and pointed the barrel at her cousin's temple. Peregrine realized what she was going to do just in time to jerk the gun to the side, and the shot Mirren fired went into the file cabinet next to Katia's head instead of into her skull.

Peregrine smiled, and Bayla began to giggle.

"Thought you were going to screw me out of my fun, didn't you?" Peregrine asked.

"I would rather see her dead than tortured," Mirren told him.

"We'd just start again with your aunt," he replied.

Then he shot Katia in the leg.

Katia screamed, not just out of pain, but from surprise, Mirren could tell.

"Missed the bone," Peregrine complained. "I'll get it with the next one. There's nothing quite like bone pain."

He glanced at Feodor as he spoke, and Feodor glanced back and shrugged coyly. Mirren didn't know what that meant, but she went to her knees beside Katia, who was trying to put pressure on her shin. The bullet had torn through her calf muscles, and she was bleeding from both entrance and exit wounds.

Mirren pulled her shirt over her head. With the long sleeves, she tied a tourniquet below Katia's knee and then used the rest of the material to put pressure on the wounds. "I'm sorry," she whispered. "I'm so sorry."

"Let me bleed out," Katia was whispering back, trying to remove the knot from the sleeves. "It'll be faster."

Peregrine laughed again, and Mirren didn't realize she was moving until her bloody fist connected with his face. She hit him hard enough that he fell backward onto his ass, and then Bayla tackled her, and they fell to the floor in a painful pile of elbows and knees.

Everything Mirren knew about fighting, she'd learned from Josh in a two-week period, and the knowledge wasn't enough to help her much. Bayla fought like a wild animal, with her nails and her teeth, growling and slobbering. Within no more than a minute, Mirren was bleeding from multiple bite wounds and her own patch of torn scalp, and one of her bra straps had been snapped.

"Stop it!" Peregrine shouted. "Stop it!"

He kicked Bayla, who reluctantly rolled off Mirren. Peregrine's eye was already beginning to swell, but he had no trouble aiming the gun at Mirren's face.

He trembled with rage. "I'll kill you!"

Mirren smiled a weak, bitter smile.

"Go ahead and shoot," she said. "I'm not afraid. I've got some-one waiting for me on the other side."

"You think I won't do it?" Peregrine screamed, pointing the gun at her again.

"I think you will," Mirren said. "I think you're depraved enough to kill me. But I've known that from the start, and I swore to my-self when I began this that I would do what my parents would want. You took their lives, and you might take mine and my family's, but that's all you're going to get from us."

The gun shook. "You stupid bitch," Peregrine swore.

Mirren's smile sweetened. "The file cabinets are reinforced tungsten steel, by the way. It'll take you years to cut them open."

Peregrine's whole body quivered. "You," he said, his voice trem-bling violently. "You . . . you . . ."

"Me, me, me," Mirren agreed.

Silence filled the room.

A martyr's death to seal her ruse, Mirren recalled, thinking of her scroll. From the way Peregrine held the gun, she could see straight into the barrel, and the dark void reminded her not of Death, but of deep space, and of gravity. *What's the ruse?* she wondered. *That I'm a martyr? That I'm a princess?*

Or is Death itself the ruse?

Katia grabbed Mirren's hand, and they waited.

"I believe the devices are ready," Feodor said calmly.

Peregrine's hand shook, and Mirren watched his finger tighten on the trigger.

"Of course," Feodor continued in the same casual tone, "you can shoot the girl before you test the devices. But I thought you might wish to use them to force her to unlock the cabinets. Or you might tear her body to pieces, rather than just shooting her."

The idea made Peregrine crack a smile. He was panting.

Slowly, he lowered the gun. Mirren released a breath she hadn't known she was holding.

"Fine," Peregrine said. "Give them to me."

When he looked away from Mirren, she felt as though she'd stepped out of a very hot spotlight.

I guess gravity isn't ready for me yet, she thought, and almost laughed. Instead, she hugged Katia. "Tighten the tourniquet," she whispered, and her cousin nodded.

Feodor carried the devices over to Peregrine, and as Mirren turned to watch him, she caught sight of a tiny movement in the file room doorway.

"Have you worn them before?" Feodor asked Peregrine.

"No."

Who is that? Mirren wondered. All she could see was a slice of blue fabric floating at the edge of the doorframe, perhaps a shirt. . . .

"Roll up your sleeve, please." Feodor turned Peregrine's arm in order to locate his veins.

Will ducked his head into the room for the briefest of instants.

He's alive! Mirren's heart jumped. She honestly hadn't been sure whether or not Peregrine and Bash had killed Will earlier—or Josh, for that matter—but when they'd left, he'd been lying motionless on the living room floor.

"Ow!"

Feodor had just clamped the vambrace shut around Peregrine's arm. "Apologies, apologies."

"Is it supposed to hurt like that?"

"I'm afraid so. The current requires access to the central nervous system in order to transmit electrical signals."

But something sour had entered Peregrine's expression, and he stopped Feodor from putting the circlet on his head.

Will peeked into the room again. He had something in his hand—the activator?

"Wait," Peregrine said. "Try them on her first."

He nodded toward Bayla.

"Yes, yes!" Bayla cried, rushing forward. "It's my turn!"

Feodor looked between them, and something in his face made Mirren think that this was not a good idea. "The devices have already damaged her system greatly. It will be impossible to prove that their new configuration won't hurt the wearer if we demonstrate it on someone already so injured."

He's up to something, Mirren realized as Will snuck another look at the room. *And Will—are they working together?*

Of everything that had happened to her in the last month, Will and Feodor working together seemed the most improbable.

"I want to wear them!" Bayla cried, and Feodor had to lift his arm to keep the circlet out of her hands.

"Then you test them," Peregrine told him.

This time when Will ducked around the door, he saw Mirren watching for him. He gave her the fleetest of smiles, and she felt a surge of hope.

But Feodor and Peregrine were staring at each other with such fire in their eyes that she was surprised the space between them didn't burst into flame.

"Do you think I'm stupid?" Peregrine hissed. With his unencumbered arm, he pushed the barrel of the gun into Feodor's gut. "Do you think I forgot what you did to me, *old friend*?"

"I think you've forgotten what I did *for* you," Feodor replied. He smiled, but his jaw tensed.

"I loved her—"

"Do not speak to me of love," Feodor snapped, and all the civil tidiness Mirren had admired before was gone from his expression. Now she saw the Feodor that Will was so afraid of, the man with the crazed rage in his eyes and the snarl that destroyed the crisp line of his lips.

Feodor lowered the arm with which he held the circlet, as if he had forgotten it. Bayla, who had been standing beside him, jumping up and down to reach it, grabbed the device out of the air.

"It's mine!" she cried, and jammed it onto her own head.

Feodor shouted, "Now, Will!"

For a heartbeat, nothing happened.

Then Peregrine's arm exploded.

Bayla's head blew apart like a dropped watermelon.

Peregrine, his face emptied by shock, stared at Feodor and then shot him in the gut before fainting.

The room shook, and Feodor fell to the floor beside Peregrine.

"Will!" Mirren screamed, throwing herself over her cousin.

Upstairs, something heavy crashed. Glass shattered, and the walls creaked. Plaster floated down like snow.

Mirren tried to put pressure on Katia's wound again, but Katia said, "I'm okay—help that guy!"

She meant Feodor. *She doesn't know who he is,* Mirren thought, and she didn't know if she should help him or not. If he died, would they still get Haley back? No one had told them.

Mirren didn't know what to do for Feodor except to put pressure on his wound, so she clapped her hands over the hole in his abdomen. Blood poured between her fingers, slick and hot.

Feodor groaned, his eyelids fluttering.

"What's happening?" Will shouted at him.

Mirren took off one of her shoes and used it to beat at the flames coming from Peregrine's arm. The vambrace had been blown to bits, and she couldn't bring herself to look at what was left of his arm for more than a second; the skin had blistered and burst like a microwaved hot dog, and his hand was gone entirely.

"We may have . . ." Feodor said, and his eyes fluttered again. "Activating the transmitters . . . destabilized this universe."

The floor began to vibrate, and the sound of crashing upstairs morphed into a crush of white noise.

"You must leave," Feodor told them. "Go."

"We can carry you," Mirren said.

"No! Save yourself, Your Majesty." His face had gone as white as the moon, his lips nearly colorless, but he smiled faintly.

Will grabbed one of Katia's arms and Mirren grabbed the other, but as they rose Mirren saw a crack in the ceiling running from both ends. It widened like a great maw diving down to devour them, and only when the ceiling collapsed did Mirren remember how much she had wanted to live.

Thirty

Josh was dying.

She could feel it in every bit of her body, a sense of shutting down, of one cell after another being turned off, of tiny fires burning out. The weakness that had suffused her limbs was fading to numbness, then to nothingness. Over the dragging of her own breath, she heard Deloise crying and begging her to wake up; she didn't even have the energy to squeeze her sister's hand.

But as the sensation of closure slowly shut her out of her body, she became aware of another place, somewhere deep inside her, that she could go, a place she remembered.

Death, she thought, and suddenly she wanted to go there, to escape the pressure of being forced from her own skin and instead run free on the golden shores of the river.

Something stopped her.

I'm not done, she thought.

I can't leave yet.

There's still so much I have to do.

She didn't think of her life or how she wanted to spend it. She didn't even think of the people she loved.

She thought of the Dream.

I was supposed to balance the universes.

She had failed. Why? Hadn't she had the power? She could feel it closer than ever before, but the tighter she held it, the farther away it moved.

You can't force it, Josh realized.

Somewhere, Deloise screamed. Furniture crashed, and a sound like a dozen trains approaching filled the air.

You can't force it, Josh thought again, remembering how hard she had tried to open an archway and save Will.

You have to follow it instead.

What did that mean? Now Whim was screaming, too, and other voices she didn't recognize.

You have to follow it—

Suddenly, she was surrounded by silence. She opened her eyes and found herself standing on a shapeless gray plain. Three strong lights shone away from her, illuminating three different paths.

On the left, she saw the gods of Death, radiating golden light, their arms outstretched for her.

In the center, she saw the Dream, the ocean of colored lights that were the souls of the dreamers.

On the right, she saw the World, all blue and green and bursting with energy.

But she didn't walk toward them.

You have to follow it, she thought, and she turned around to see where the lights originated.

Behind her, the gray brightened to white—white stone floor, white walls, an indistinct ceiling of white light. A few feet away, a rough-cut black pillar rose to waist height, water pouring down from it. Sitting atop the pillar was a pale stone shaped like an egg, small enough to fit in her hand, but just barely. The water burbled out from beneath the egg, and the reflection of the light on the moving water made the egg sparkle.

Follow it, she thought, and she put her hand on the egg. The shell was not completely smooth, but bumpy and a little rough, and it was warm, even though the water pouring down around it was chilly. Josh picked it up, liking the warmth in her hand.

And then she understood that some things were meant to be.

The knowledge hit her in a flash, a bright light turned on right before her eyes. *There is a plan for each of us,* she thought, and she saw the three universes as three stages where different parts of a single great play were being performed. They moved together like cogs in a clock, souls spilling from one to the next in a choreographed dance too complex for Josh to follow.

And her own part? She tried to focus on herself, on the line of light representing her path, but it was short and too bright. Her soul hadn't emerged from the Dream, as all the others had. Instead, hers simply appeared the moment she was born, an unexpected entrance in the play.

Because I'm the True Dream Walker? she wondered. *Is that why?*

She didn't even know if she was the True Dream Walker, but she followed the idea as it led her into memory. She remembered being in the Dream, watching Ian's body bleed out while she lay, helpless, on the floor. She remembered Will whispering to her, telling her that she had to admit she was the True Dream Walker and save them. She remembered giving her life up to whatever was meant to be, and how in that moment she had merged with the Dream so completely as to almost lose herself.

It's my ego, she realized. *I can't access the power with my ego in the way. I can't decide what should be.*

She was a servant to a greater power, and only when she was facilitating that power's intentions could she act as the True Dream Walker. It wasn't a god she served, or even a consciousness. It was the way of things, an inevitability, a current guiding souls.

Except mine, she thought. No path lay before her soul; she was forging it herself, every day, every moment.

She stared at the egg, feeling its heat in her palm, and within it she saw her own body, splayed on the floor with manacles attached to every limb. She saw Whim and Deloise cowering beside her with drawers over their heads to protect themselves from falling debris, and Mirren's aunt and uncle crouched beneath a mattress torn off the bed.

Stop, Josh thought, and the warmth within the egg increased. *Go back.*

She watched the bedroom walls straighten, the ceiling flatten itself out, and the plaster dust rise from the floor.

Get rid of those, she added, and the manacles vanished, along with the chains and the cement block to which they had been attached.

She felt the castle rise upright, like a pop-up tent opening. The Hidden Kingdom reordered itself neatly.

Josh's attention turned to the file room, floors below. Will, Mirren, and Katia lay curled in balls beside Feodor's bleeding body. Near the first row of files, Bayla's headless body was sprawled lifeless on the floor, and Josh passed her by without interest. There was nothing she could do for Bayla now.

Instead, she went to Feodor's limp form. He lay like a child, his small limbs heavy with the sleep of impending death. Josh touched him and waited, listening in a way she never had before.

Not yet, she thought. *Not yet.*

This wasn't Feodor's time. Not quite.

In his ear, she whispered, "All things grow toward the light. Even you."

His eyes flicked open, and he sucked in a great breath of air as the wound in his abdomen closed and blood rushed to his cheeks.

Josh ran her fingertips over Katia's leg, and those wounds, too, were healed.

There was one more person in the room, and even unconscious, pain and rage radiated from him. He'd lost his left hand, and the skin on his arm had burned away, leaving charred muscle visible, raw bones exposed to the air. But even more horrifying was the tangled mess of his mind. It was as twisted and thorny as an overgrown thicket from which no berries grew, and Josh knew she could heal him with a word.

Not yet, she thought again, this time with a different meaning. *He has to play out his purpose.*

But for the first time she felt something other than peaceful acceptance of the way things were meant to be. She didn't want to let Peregrine go on hurting people, and she struggled against the knowledge that she wasn't meant to change him. Maybe the wisdom was wrong—

In that instant, she lost the confidence and comfort that had come with holding the egg.

And she woke up standing in the bedroom.

Every cell in her body was alive, almost too alive, vibrating with energy.

"Josh?" Deloise asked. She was still crouched on the floor with a dresser drawer held over her head. "Wait—where are your chains?"

"Where are *all* the chains?" Whim asked. He gazed up at the perfect, smooth ceiling.

"What happened?" Mirren's aunt asked, peeking out from beneath the mattress.

Collena, Josh thought. She'd seen her in the vision and known her name. Also beneath the mattress was Mirren's uncle, Fel.

Josh didn't wonder how she knew these things or how the manacles had disappeared. When she had held the egg, all knowledge had been available.

"Peregrine's in the file room," she said. "We have to decide what to do with him."

She started for the door, ignoring Whim's and Deloise's protests of confusion. "Josh, what happened?" Deloise asked as she followed her sister down the hallway. "You were barely alive, and then the house started coming down."

"I'm alive now," was all Josh said.

How could she explain? For a brief moment, the way of all things had been clear to her, and she had been part of the stream of time, her own current helping to move it forward. But what could she tell Deloise except that she had left her body and held an egg? That she had somehow healed Feodor and Katia?

Except Josh was fairly certain she hadn't been the one to heal either of them. She had been the tool, but not the power.

She ran down the hallway and then down the stairs. She had

no trouble finding her way, despite having been to the Hidden Kingdom only once. The house's layout seemed to be part of the knowledge she now had.

"Josh," Will said when she burst into the file room, and the relief in his face was so real that Josh felt she could wrap it around her hand.

She threw herself into his arms, but he hugged her for only an instant before pushing her away by the shoulders.

"You gave Feodor the activator," he said.

Somehow she couldn't quite believe he was going to complain about that when Feodor's plan had likely saved both their lives. *I killed Bash for* you, Josh thought, but Will's expression contained no gratitude, only more accusations waiting to be voiced. There was no love in the look he gave her, and Josh wondered what direction their path took and whether they would walk it together or alone.

"I'm sorry," she said, and he shook his head, as if he couldn't believe how weak her answer was.

She turned away to escape his anger, and Mirren hugged her. Katia hugged her, too, even though they hadn't yet been introduced. Josh barely felt their embraces.

"Did you heal my leg?" Katia asked.

"Sort of," Josh admitted.

Feodor was standing with his blood-soaked shirt pulled up so he could examine his unblemished torso. Josh didn't hug him, of course, and he certainly made no move to hug her. In fact, he looked irritated.

"Thanks for your help," Josh told him. She knew exactly what he'd done.

"I demand an explanation," he said.

"Maybe later. Right now, we have to decide what to do with Peregrine before he wakes up."

Behind her, Whim was throwing up at the sight of Bayla's corpse. Feodor was pulling a bullet from his belly button, where his body had spit it out while healing. Mirren was examining her cousin's leg with gentle fingers, but she ran to her aunt and uncle when they entered the file room.

Josh ignored them all and sat down on the floor next to her unconscious grandfather. She had hoped that being near him would help her decide what to do, but if anything, it made the sense of peace she had brought back with her fade faster. Instead of seeing the path he was meant to take, all she could feel was her own fear that he would come after her again.

Will stood on Peregrine's other side. He used the toe of his shoe to nudge the gun across the floor and toward Josh. "Shoot him."

Deloise gasped.

Killing Peregrine was an option, Josh knew. Maybe the best option.

"He's insane," Will said. "If we don't kill him, he'll keep coming after us."

"I'm siding with this guy," Katia said. Will glanced at her and then did a double take, as if he hadn't realized she was in the room.

"You can't kill him!" Deloise cried.

Recalling the thicket that was Peregrine's mind, Josh said, "He's going to keep staging nightmares. We don't even know what World we're going back to, what he might have done to it. He could have turned Dad and Kerstel against us or convinced them to kill each other or to burn the house down."

Safety, that was all Josh had ever wanted. Safety for the dreamers, safety for her family. Safety for herself.

The same uncertainty that had snapped her out of her vision filled her now, and she wished she had been able to control her anger and fear long enough to see the path intended for Peregrine.

"So we'll put him in jail," Deloise said. "There are dream-walker jails!"

"Yeah, minimum security jails," Whim said, wiping his mouth with the back of his hand. "He'll break out the first day."

"Will is right," Feodor added. "This incident will only strengthen his ambitions."

"I agree," Mirren said, but then her eyes widened, and she grabbed the giant key ring off its hook and dashed into the maze of file cabinets. "Wait—maybe—"

"You can't kill him!" Deloise repeated, shouting it this time.

Josh tightened her hand around the gun, but she couldn't bring herself to point it at Peregrine. "He was going to kill us all, or turn us into slaves like Bash and Bayla."

"Josh, he's our grandfather," Deloise said, her eyes full of tears.

"I know," Josh said. She glanced at Mirren's aunt and uncle, who were standing near the doorway holding their daughter. "He hurt you, too. What do you think we should do?"

"Kill him," Katia said.

Fel and Collena exchanged a long look. Finally, Collena said, "The monarchy has never practiced capital punishment. Neither do we."

"Not even for him," Fel added, although the look on his face suggested he thought that maybe it was time to break with tradition.

They all want him dead, Josh thought. Carefully, she opened Peregrine's mouth and stuck the barrel of the gun between his teeth. The surest way to kill him was to shoot into the base of his brain. He was deep in shock, sweaty and pale. He'd never know what had happened; he'd never even wake up.

But the egg's wisdom tugged at her. *Not yet,* she kept thinking. *Not yet.*

"Josh!" Deloise shouted.

Will said, "Whim, take her upstairs so we can do this."

When Whim tried to grab Deloise, she hit him with a left punch so fast and sure that it would have made Muhammad Ali proud. Whim stumbled backward and careened into a row of file cabinets.

"Touch me again!" Deloise dared him. "Josh, don't do this!"

"I don't know what else to do," Josh told her sister. "How are we going to defend ourselves from him?"

She didn't know what else to do, but she didn't know if she

could do it, either. Why couldn't she have seen his path? The weight of the gun was making her hand tremble, and she was afraid she'd shoot by accident.

"Josh, you have to stop him while you have the chance," Will said, a frantic note entering his voice.

"Wait," Mirren said. She emerged from the stacks holding up a photocopy of a clay tablet with what appeared to be orderly chicken scratches on it. "We can banish him from the Dream forever."

"What?" Josh asked.

"How?" Deloise asked.

"This symbol. If you carve it into a person's skin, their soul can't enter the Dream."

Feodor took the photocopy and studied it.

"He won't be able to go into the Dream at all?" Josh asked. "Not even when he sleeps?"

"Neither body nor soul," Mirren said. "You understand . . . it's a forbidden act. To stop someone from entering the Dream . . . it's sacrilege."

"How will keeping him out of the Dream help?" Will demanded. "He'll just kill us when we're awake!"

"It'll keep him from staging," Deloise told Will. "Maybe if he can't enter the Dream, he'll lose interest in controlling Josh."

"Or maybe he'll sneak into the house and murder us while we sleep!"

Josh wondered if Will was right. Peregrine's interest had always been in determining the extent of Josh's powers as the True Dream Walker. He'd never borne her a particular enmity—although that would probably change after they turned his chest into scratch art.

"This appears to be from the Muzat School," Feodor said. "Impressive."

He held the page out to Josh, and she stared at the scratches. "We'd have to carve this into his skin? With a knife?"

"Josh!" Will protested in a near shout. His lips were pale with anger.

"Yes," Mirren said. "But . . . we wouldn't have to kill him."

Josh shook her head. "After what he did to us, I always thought it would be easy to kill him. But maybe it just isn't easy to kill someone."

"Maybe it shouldn't be," Deloise said.

"He's a murderer and a psychopath," Will said desperately.

Josh ran a hand through her hair. "I know," she assured Will. "I know exactly what he is."

Not yet, her mind said. *Not yet.*

She looked at her sister. "Can you live with using this symbol on him?"

"Being unable to dream could drive him mad," Mirren warned.

Deloise sighed. "He's already mad. At least this way he gets to live."

"Will," Josh said. "Can you live with it?"

She was almost afraid to ask, knowing how angry he was at her.

"I think we should shoot him in the head," Will said. "He *deserves* to die! How do you even know this symbol thing will work?"

"The Muzat School created a number of such symbols," Feodor told him. "The others have proven effective."

This information only enraged Will further. "I don't care!" he shouted. "He's criminally insane! Why can't we just kill him?"

"Because we aren't killers," Josh said.

Will gave her a look then that scared her. He wasn't the Will she knew, the one who had thought things through so carefully, who had been able to examine his own desires and emotions with such a rational eye.

"Josh, if you don't do this . . ."

He trailed off, and Josh didn't know if he couldn't think of a threat bad enough or just couldn't speak.

He's going to break up with me, she thought, *if I don't kill my grandfather.*

But she couldn't do it. Not even for Will. She had killed one person that night; she wasn't going to kill another.

She stood up and held the gun out to Will. "I can't kill him. If you can, that's your choice."

"Josh," Deloise said with alarm.

"Uh, is this a good idea?" Whim asked.

"It's a great idea," Will said, taking the gun from Josh. "I'll do it myself."

"Josh," Deloise said again. "Stop him!"

Josh shook her head. "It's Will's call."

Mirren put some distance between herself and Peregrine's body, and she drew Deloise away. When Whim started to step toward Will, Josh held out her hand to wave him off.

"What are you doing?" Whim asked.

Josh just held out her hand.

Will knelt at the top of Peregrine's head. He pressed the barrel of the gun to Peregrine's forehead, then changed his mind and put the gun in the old man's mouth.

Josh waited. Deloise watched through her fingers, and Whim jumped every time Will made any motion at all.

"Okay," Will muttered to himself. "Let's do this."

But he didn't do anything. Josh watched the gun tremble in his hand, the metal barrel clacking against Peregrine's teeth. From where she stood, Josh could see the lump beneath the back of Will's T-shirt—the scar from the skin graft he'd needed after their last encounter with Feodor. As much as Will blamed Feodor for his suffering, he and Josh both knew that Peregrine was equally to blame. He was the one who had manipulated them into entering Feodor's universe, knowing what they would face.

Still, the sight of the scar didn't make Josh willing to kill her grandfather. It just made her want to put her arms around Will and guide him away. It made her want to balance the universes once and for all.

Will repositioned himself, checking to make certain the barrel was pointed at the back of Peregrine's skull. He squared his shoulders and got a good grip on the handle. He took a deep breath.

He still didn't fire.

Josh had known he wouldn't. Well, almost known. She had been pretty sure. He'd shot at Feodor, but Feodor was already dead. For all Will had been traumatized, he was still a moral person underneath, and he couldn't shoot a living man in cold blood any more than Josh could. She felt an unexpected pride that he couldn't pull the trigger, not even against a man who had hurt him terribly.

"Oh, my God," Whim burst out. "Just shoot him already! The suspense is killing me!"

Will's head snapped up, and his face was filled with rage and, beneath that, humiliation. "Can you shut up for one minute, Whim?"

"It's been like ten minutes!" Whim protested.

Will sprang to his feet, yanking the gun from Peregrine's mouth. "You know what? This isn't my problem." He shoved the gun into Josh's arms, and for an instant she fumbled it dangerously. "All of this is *your* fault," Will told her. "So you take care of it. I'm done cleaning up your messes."

His words filled Josh with a familiar rush of guilt and shame. He was right that the situation they were in was her fault—not completely her fault, but enough.

He stormed out of the file room, and Josh ran after him, handing the gun to her sister as she passed. She heard a metallic sliding as Deloise removed the magazine.

"Will, wait!" she called, and she caught him on a landing between staircases. "Please, wait."

He had tears in his eyes. "I can't do this anymore," he said, all his anger burned away. "Josh, I can't do this. I don't want to do this anymore."

"I know, I know. You don't have to do anything else." She tried to take his hand, but he was moving too quickly. "We'll go home and you can rest."

"No, I don't want to go home! I don't want any of it!"

He means being a dream walker, Josh realized.

"I almost shot a man!" he wailed. "I can't—I can't be part of this! It's changing me. It's . . . destroying me."

"Will," Josh said, "this is the end of all the craziness. I promise. We'll go get Haley back and then it will all be over."

"Over? Are you kidding? You just assured that it *isn't* over by letting Peregrine live! And I can't—" He pushed the hair out of his eyes, taking dizzy, pacing steps on the landing. Josh tried to hug him and he pushed her away. "No! Don't touch me! I don't want any of it! I'm sorry. I'm sorry. I can't be with you. I can't be part of any of it."

Josh didn't know what to do, and her own panic was making her hands tremble. *He doesn't mean it,* she told herself. *He'll calm down and see reason.*

"Ask me for something," she begged. "Anything. I'll do whatever you want—go to therapy, or quit dream walking for a while, or go on vacation."

He shook his head, and the way he looked at Josh without seeing her, as if she no longer existed to him, made her realize that she had already lost him.

"I just want my mom," he said hollowly, and he wandered up the next flight of stairs, away from her and alone.

Later, after they'd found an emergency kit with a syringe of morphine to keep Peregrine sedated, and after Feodor had volunteered to do the cutting, and after Josh, Whim, and Mirren had spent an hour holding the old man down and putting pressure on his new wounds, her friends tried to convince Josh that Will would come around.

"He's all hyped up on adrenaline," Whim said. "He just needs a day or two to chill out."

"Once he gets some perspective, he'll be glad he didn't kill Peregrine," Mirren insisted.

They meant well, Josh knew. But they were wrong. Will wouldn't calm down and he wouldn't forgive her, because in the end, she had been the one who hurt him the worst.

Only Feodor failed to try to convince her that everything would be fine.

Feodor knew better.

Thirty-one

Two days later, Will sat alone on the couch in the guys' apartment and watched the Accordance Conclave coverage.

"Joining us now," said the reporter on the television screen, "is noted political analyst Jobe Calmikterie. Jobe, is there any doubt about the outcome here?"

"None," replied a middle-aged man in an ugly suit. "Now that Mirren Rousellario has been exposed as a traitor, the only votes she's going to get will come from fringe lunatics and hard-core anarchists."

"Like mother, like daughter, eh?"

"That's right, Myssa. I doubt we'll even see a statement from her regarding the Accordance Conclave. If she has any sense at all, she's left the country."

"I'd shoot her if I saw her," Myssa agreed.

Her words added another boulder to the mountain of despair Will already sagged beneath. He and the others had returned from the Hidden Kingdom to find that every dream walker they knew believed Mirren was evil—even Davita, who proudly announced that she had been the one to show Peregrine how to access the Hidden Kingdom.

Josh explained to them that they had been victims of staging, and even though they all believed her, they seemed unable to connect the staging with their certainty about Mirren. Right now, the adults of the household were in the living room, watching the election results and cheering for Peregrine. Kerstel was wearing a homemade T-shirt that read, "Babies for Borgenicht!"

Mirren herself was safely tucked away in the Hidden Kingdom (the entrance to which had been moved), but she had sworn to return to the World once everyone stopped wanting her dead. Will didn't know how long that might take, given how high anti-Mirren sentiment was running.

Myssa the reporter was standing in front of a projected map of North America, talking about which districts had turned in results already. The districts in which Peregrine had won were colored lime green, centered on Braxton. The districts in which Mirren had won were meant to be colored orange, but so far none were, not even far away where Peregrine hadn't been able to stage dreams.

"As goes Rome, so goes the empire," Feodor had said when he'd predicted this outcome the day before.

Feodor was in Whim's bedroom with Whim and Deloise, building some sort of cage that he said would help them restore Winsor's soul. "Assuming her brain isn't mush," he'd added when he finished explaining that he thought reunification would be possible. Will expected it was all just another trick, but he'd given up trying to warn anyone.

"Even with twelve more districts left to report in, this election has obviously been a landslide for Peregrine Borgenicht and the Lodestone Party," Jobe said. "It's a shame that he isn't well enough to publicly claim victory and truly enjoy this moment."

"Obviously we're all sending well wishes and congratulations to the hospital."

After Feodor had carved Peregrine like a roast, Deloise, Josh, and Whim had carried him out of the Hidden Kingdom and done a dump-and-run outside a Braxton ER. The Lodestone Party was saying he had pneumonia, but according to Whim's underground sources, he was really in a psych ward, babbling incoherently and missing a hand.

"Five more districts have just reported," Myssa said, and another burst of lime green appeared on the map. "Oh—and here's a surprise! Greenland has gone orange!"

Jobe laughed. "Do they not have Internet up there? How far behind on the news are they?"

"Of the fewer than five hundred dream walkers in Greenland, slightly over one hundred voted for Mirren Rousellario and eighty-nine for Peregrine Borgenicht." Sarcastically, she added, "Now we've got a real race on our hands."

Will groaned. Bad enough that Mirren was losing; did the reporters have to enjoy it so much?

The apartment door opened, and Josh appeared, carrying several poster-sized sheets of what appeared to be copper. She stopped short when she saw Will.

Deloise had told him that Josh had killed Bash to save him and nearly killed herself in the process. In fact, Del insisted that Josh had died for at least a minute. She had been performing mouth-to-mouth while Whim did CPR when Will hit the activator and nearly destroyed the Hidden Kingdom.

Will felt nothing but guilt about any of it. Josh had killed Bash, and Will had killed Bayla, and neither of them had been able to kill the only person who needed killing.

The sight of Josh standing in the doorway sent a throb of pain through his heart, both because the wound of losing her was so fresh and because he still loved her so damn much. He knew that demanding she kill her grandfather had been irrational, yet he still felt angry that she hadn't done it, which was supremely hypocritical since he hadn't been able to do it either. And he hated her for having shown him that.

The truth was, whether or not they'd killed Peregrine had been immaterial to the state of their relationship. Will would have broken up with her either way, he saw that now. Distancing himself from her and the constant danger she inspired was the only chance he had to regain some of his sanity. He needed space, and quiet, and peace. He needed to feel safe in the World again.

Besides, Josh was Feodor's in a way she had never been Will's, maybe not even in a romantic sense, but in some deeper, more thorough way. Feodor and his memories had changed who she was, and Will didn't know her anymore. He didn't trust her.

Will had overheard them talking in the office earlier. They'd been speaking Polish, and very quickly, as if they had so much to say to each other.

Will didn't have anything left to say to Josh. He didn't even know what he was doing in this house anymore, except that Whim and Deloise and his adopted parents had all insisted he stay, and since he wasn't eighteen yet, he didn't really have a choice.

Now, as Josh fumbled with her sheets of copper in the doorway, Will just stared at her and said nothing. He pinched his lips shut against the desire to say, *I'm sorry. I take it all back.*

"Sorry," she babbled. "I was just going to— I can come back later."

"It's fine," Will told her, his voice cracking. "Do what you need to do."

She set the sheets of copper against the wall and closed the apartment door behind her. Still not looking at him, she said, "About . . . I was . . . hoping, I guess . . ."

So we're back to this, Will thought, remembering how difficult she had found it to talk to him when they first met.

"I didn't mean to . . ."

Back then, he would have helped her, coaxed her into finding the words she needed, reassured her that whatever she felt was okay. The urge to do so was still strong in him, as was the desire to hold her close and reassure her without words.

He didn't have the strength to do either.

Finally, Josh just muttered, "Sorry," again, and fled to Whim's room with her copper.

As soon as she disappeared, another round of guilt hit him. He knew what it must have taken for her to even try to start a conversation about the way things had ended.

I should have helped her. She was trying so hard.

But he was afraid that one forgiveness would lead to another, and by tomorrow he'd be neck-deep in nightmares and danger and science he didn't understand. Being alone was so much easier and less frightening. He turned up the volume on the television.

"And it's official!" Myssa declared. "Peregrine Borgenicht and his Lodestone Party have been voted in as the permanent form of government for the dream walkers of North America!"

Lime-green confetti rained down on the stage, and the station cut to a shot of dream walkers celebrating at the Dashiel Winters Building in Braxton.

Will leaned back on the couch and closed his eyes, and the cheers filled his ears.

"Long live Peregrine Borgenicht!"

Thirty-two

Josh, Whim, and Feodor broke into the nursing home at two in the morning, crawling through a window in the accounting office and taking the equipment elevator up to the third floor, which was useful because they had a lot of equipment. Besides the copper cage, Feodor required various osmium plates, a wealth of crystals and magnets, a massive negative ion generator, a water pump with ten yards of tubing, and five gallons of seawater. Not to mention the canister containing Winsor's soul.

"If we get caught," Whim whispered to Josh as they rode the elevator up, "what do you imagine the nurses will think we're doing?"

She shushed him.

In the relative safety of Winsor's room, they got to work.

Despite the fact that they were—hopefully—about to restore her soul, Josh still felt sick when she looked at Winsor, and even sicker when she had to remove her friend's blankets and stretch her out, corpselike, on the bed. Feodor said to take off her pajamas, but Whim glared at him and he admitted that rolling up her sleeves and pajama pants would do.

Josh and Whim wrapped Winsor's body in plastic tubing and turned the pump on so that the seawater circulated around her. The thought had crossed Josh's mind that this might all be an elaborate ploy to kill Winsor, and she was sure Whim had thought the same thing, but to what end? Feodor had nothing to gain from her death and everything to gain from creating goodwill with his captors. So Josh didn't protest when Feodor put an oxygen mask on Winsor's face and connected it to the negative ion generator.

They spent the next hour attaching crystals and magnets to the cage, using a roll of copper wire.

"This is too weird," Whim said, his voice low. "Is this even going to work?"

"Feodor says it will," Josh told him.

"But don't you know? Don't you remember?"

There are so many things I don't remember.

The memory of how Will had stared at her that day in the living room came back full force, filling her with shame and sadness. The expression on his face had been so closed to her. She'd desperately wanted to remind him of his promise to love her no matter what she had to do, but his stillness and silence had made it more than clear that he no longer cared about keeping his promises to her.

"No," she told Whim. "I don't remember."

They went back to work.

But as Josh attached crystals to the cage, she kept recalling their first encounter with Feodor and how physically damaged they had been when it was over. This time, she and Will were physically whole, but she felt that they had lost even more.

Maybe if they saved Winsor and got Haley back, things would get better.

When the crystals and magnets were in place, Feodor said they had to wait half an hour.

"For what?" Whim demanded.

"To prepare her body. If she is not prepared to receive her soul, it will flee."

They waited a terse half hour. Whim played Yahtzee on his phone, but Josh just leaned against the wall with her arms crossed over her broken heart and waited.

"If I may ask," Feodor said softly to her as time dragged by, "have you attempted to open an archway since we returned from the Hidden Kingdom?"

"No." She hadn't even thought about it.

"A most interesting ability," he mused. "And one I have never seen before."

"Well, don't get too excited. It seems to be all I'm capable of."

She hadn't told him about the egg, or the visions, or the little voice inside her that had woken up and whispered, even now, *You have to follow it.* She hadn't told anyone except to say that in the moment she was near death, she had tapped into her True Dream Walker powers briefly and healed Feodor and Katia.

"Oh, but I am excited," Feodor said. "And I believe this ability might mean a great deal."

Josh looked at him. He sat in the rocking chair but didn't rock, and even in the meager light of the parking lot lamp beyond the window, she could see his bemused smile.

"Tell me," he said, "have you ever broken Stellanor's First Rule of dream walking?"

Josh shivered.

"How the hell did you figure that out?" Whim asked, getting up from the floor.

Feodor shrugged. "I read it in a very old prophecy regarding the True Dream Walker."

"I've never heard that," Josh said.

He smiled coyly. "I expect I know quite a bit that you do not."

That was true. But . . .

"If I'm the True Dream Walker, then why is opening archways the only thing I can do?"

"Just because you haven't been trained to use your abilities does not mean they don't exist."

Josh's heartbeat quickened in spite of her mind's warning not to trust him.

"And I suppose you could train me," she said.

"I could," Feodor agreed.

Her first thought was that Will would never forgive her, but Will would probably never forgive her anyway.

Her second thought was of Haley.

"Nothing is more important than getting Haley back," she said, which was almost true. It was true enough.

As Feodor opened his small mouth to respond, Winsor gasped.

Whim shot across the room, and Josh and Feodor followed him to the bedside. Beneath her eyelids, Winsor's eyes darted around. Her fingers twitched.

"Quickly," Feodor said. "Remove the oxygen mask tubing from the ion generator and connect it to the outgoing valve on the canister, but don't open it! Reconnect the ion generator to the ingoing valve."

Whim and Josh worked on the tubing, Whim's hands shaking with excitement.

"Josh, place the small osmium plate in her mouth."

"What if she chokes on it?" Whim asked.

"She won't choke. Turn off the water pump. Whim, open the ingoing valve."

"What about the outgoing valve?"

"Not yet. With alacrity, Josh!"

Whim leaned over the bed to turn off the pump while Josh secured the plate in Winsor's mouth.

"Open the outgoing valve!" Feodor cried. "Now, now!"

Whim spun the valve handle on the canister. "It's open!"

He stepped back from the bed, and they all stared silently at Winsor.

She began to cough.

Her jaws moved, slowly at first, then faster, trying to force the plate out. Josh reached in to help her, and she retrieved the plate just as the door blew open and a nurse came in. She flicked on the overhead light and everyone froze except Winsor, who continued to cough. "What's going on in—"

She stopped short when she saw Winsor in the cage. "Mary mother of Jesus!"

Winsor's eyes opened, and they were blue again, blue and clear and alive.

"Winsor?" Whim asked. He yanked the cage off the bed and clasped her face in his hands.

"She's awake," the nurse said with a gasp. "Dr. Guyer!"

She went running down the hallway, shouting for the doctor.

"You did it," Whim said to Feodor, his expression awed.

Feodor crossed his arms over his chest and smiled smugly. "I believe the appropriate expression is, I told you so."

She's back, Josh thought, and she felt a sweet, tiny glimmer of hope. *We saved her.*

"Winny?" Whim asked. "Can you hear me?"

Winsor coughed again, and she looked at Whim with terror in her blue eyes.

"Say something," Whim said.

Winsor opened her mouth, lips trembling, and screamed.

"SAAAAAM!"

Thirty-three

The second time they entered Death, Mirren brought three silver coins with which to pay the boatman.

He took them and grunted, as he had the first time, but Mirren thought his grunt sounded less cranky than before.

She sat beside Feodor in the boat, and Josh sat across from them. Mirren thought Josh's eyes were still pink rimmed from crying and she never seemed fully present, but she looked a little lighter since they'd restored the souls in the canister to their bodies.

Well, three of the four. One soul's body had already died, so they were bringing that soul with them to Death.

Josh said Winsor had woken up screaming for someone named Sam and that one of the souls in the canister had belonged to a young man named Sam. Even Feodor didn't seem sure what to make of that.

In gratitude to Feodor for restoring Winsor's soul, Whim agreed to break back into Death instead of shooting him in the face, and they'd all driven out to Iph National Forest to perform the singing bowl ritual again. Will had played his bowls but refused to enter Death, and Feodor had played Haley's part.

Mirren was jittery with the anticipation of seeing him. Yes, she'd lost the election; yes, she'd had to retreat to the Hidden Kingdom; but at least she could have Haley back.

The excitement made her talkative, and she asked Feodor something she had been wondering about since their first visit to the afterlife.

"Feodor," she said, "the gods of the underworld called you by a name, *inumen*. What does it mean?"

He smiled enigmatically. She didn't know if he found amusement in her question or in his answer.

"It means *clown*," he said.

For some reason, the answer made her nervous.

Inside the temple, the lords of Death shone brighter than ever. Haley wasn't there; Mirren had thought he would be, that he would anticipate their return.

"Your Highnesses," Mirren said, falling into a deep curtsy. "We have returned the *inumen* and wish to exchange him for the hostage."

One of the gods rose to circle Feodor, examining him.

"Tell us your name," it said, "and die."

Feodor, who had not bowed to the gods, said, "I propose a new arrangement."

"Arrangement?" asked one of the seated gods. "Do you treat Death so callously?"

"Wait," Josh said, her eyes flashing with alarm.

Feodor ignored her. "While I was in the World, not only did I help these children stop a powerful evil, but I restored three souls to the bodies from which I had taken them, and I have brought you a fourth."

"What are you doing?" Josh asked. "Feodor, stop."

Mirren's pulse began to pound.

"Before I died," Feodor continued, "I trapped more than sixty souls in a pocket universe. When my universe collapsed, those souls, rightfully dead, were lost in the Dream. If you allow me to remain alive, I will bring those souls to you."

"No," Josh said. "No."

"Where is Haley?" Mirren asked desperately. She felt dizzy and sick, and she grabbed hold of Feodor's arm, but she couldn't stop him from speaking.

"Without my help, those souls will remain trapped in the Dream forever," Feodor warned.

"His name is Feodor Kajażkołski!" Josh shouted, but to no effect.

The golden beings conferred. Josh grabbed Feodor and spun him to face her.

"What are you doing?" she demanded.

Feodor gave one of his light little shrugs, but then he fondly touched Josh's cheek. "Silly American child. Do you think the dead can be dropped off like a package on a doorstep?" He made a *tsk tsk* sound. "We are each on a journey."

Josh stared at him wordlessly.

We all started to trust him, Mirren realized. *With his soft accent and his good manners and the way he helped Winsor. We forgot who he is.*

"Please," she begged him as the tears ran down her face. "We need Haley back. Please don't do this."

"Ah, Kapuścisko. Such a sweet boy."

"He can't survive here!" Mirren cried.

"No one can," Feodor said shrewdly.

The lords of Death returned to their thrones.

"Every month, on the night of the new moon, you must return, bringing with you three souls," the central figure said. "If you fail to do so, we will come for you."

"What about our friend?" Josh asked. "The hostage?"

"He will remain a hostage, so that you might remember that the *inumen* is your charge to control."

Mirren couldn't repress a cry.

"Please," Josh begged. "Please. Return our friend. I'll stay in his place."

"The bargain is struck," the golden figure said.

For the second time, Mirren found herself sitting on the forest floor, crying.

That night she lay in Haley's bed, wrapped in the familiar sights of his things, unable to sleep. Wearing the sweater he had given her, she wandered aimlessly around the room for a while, looking through old photos, shamelessly going through his drawers. In the closet, she found a classical guitar, and she sat on the bed for a while, strumming it. But the guitar sounded like she felt, discordant and sad, as if they had both given up on Haley's return.

Finally, she put the guitar away and got back into bed, pulling the comforter around her. She pressed her face into his pillow and pretended it was his shoulder.

As her hand slid beneath the pillow, she touched something smooth and cool.

She pulled out a page torn from a steno pad and folded into quarters. With frantic fingers, she opened it.

Mirren,
Build the Royal Trimidion.

Epilogue

On the far side of the temple of the golden beings, Haley stood among the masses of the dead and trembled. He longed for a cardigan to wrap around himself, some small protection from the needy eyes of the souls that wandered to and fro, staring at him with a depth of hunger their physical bodies had never known.

He slid down against the side of the temple and stayed there, curled in a ball, for hours. Although they'd broken into Death in the middle of the night, the sun had been high in the sky here. Now it began to set, and Haley watched his last measure of comfort vanish beyond the horizon. His muscles ached from shaking. He felt as if his moment of bravery had emptied him of all courage, and as night crept over the land of the dead, he gave himself over to helplessness.

I'm never going home. I'll never see Mirren again. I'll never see Mom again, or Will, or Whim. I'm going to die here, alone.

Finally he began to cry, pressing his hot face against his knees, cursing himself and his gallant stupidity. Some of the dead paused to watch—their expressions confused, as if they were witnessing a ritual they only dimly remembered—but after a time, Haley became aware of a figure standing over him, waiting with his arms crossed and his foot tapping.

Haley raised his throbbing head. Against the blazing sunset, he could only make out dark hair and a familiar figure, and it wasn't until he caught sight of the stranger's aura—hot-rod red and cobalt blue—that he realized the stranger wasn't a stranger at all.

"Hello, little brother," Ian said, and he grinned.